HE NIGHTWARD

"*The Nightward* is a fascinating tale of royal politics, magic, and mayhem. R.S.A. Garcia expertly weaves a story that blends magic, technology, and mythology in the most riveting of ways. Set in a matriarchal society, *The Nightward* is a brilliant, timely read—I blew through it in one sitting!"

—N. E. DAVENPORT, AUTHOR OF *THE BLOOD TRIALS*

"No one builds worlds like R.S.A. Garcia—intricate, beautiful, and dangerous. A science fantasy epic with a rich foundation of Caribbean folklore, *The Nightward* expertly blends both genre and culture. Balancing grief and loss with her signature humor and heart, Garcia continues to prove that she is a master at her craft."

—KEMI ASHING-GIWA, AUTHOR OF *THE SPLINTER IN THE SKY*

"*The Nightward* takes off running and doesn't stop. Garcia has crafted a vibrant new science fantasy world filled to the brim with fabulous creatures, crackling action, and the persistent conviction that things are far stranger than they seem. Plus: war cats! Readers will be clamoring for the next volume in this exciting new duology from one of SFF's great talents."

—SAMANTHA MILLS, NEBULA, STURGEON, AND LOCUS AWARD–WINNING AUTHOR OF *THE WINGS UPON HER BACK*

"Epic along every axis, *The Nightward* is a complex tapestry of myth, loyalty, history, and power. I dare any author working in the fantasy space to create a land as rich and real, as inhabited with multilayered characters and deities, as Garcia's Gailand."

—PREMEE MOHAMED, NEBULA, WORLD FANTASY, AND AURORA AWARD–WINNING AUTHOR OF THE BENEATH THE RISING SERIES

"A compelling, complex, and absolutely captivating thrill ride! R.S.A. Garcia builds layer upon layer of emotion, intrigue, and adventure in a debut that will capture your heart." —SAMIT BASU, LOCUS AWARD FINALIST FOR *THE JINN-BOT OF SHANTIPORT*

"*The Nightward* is a genre-defying epic that features intricate world building, a fast-paced plot, and characters who will quickly capture your heart. The story explores the meaning of equity and the corrupting influences of power, in a fantasy setting that is original yet feels ancient. With its clean prose, limitless creativity, and unexpected twists, this novel delivers on everything I've come to expect from R.S.A. Garcia in the best possible way." —S. B. Divya, Nebula and Hugo award finalist and author of *Meru*

"A new queen must learn the extent of her powers, and her relationship with her protector, as both are thrust into a world of science, magic, and a realm descending into chaos in this wildly imaginative, new voice in fantasy. R.S.A. Garcia's new novel is an adventure and a half that never loses its touch with humanity."
—Tobias S. Buckell, *New York Times* bestselling author of the Halo and Xenowealth series

"Harkening back to the best of fantasy in worldbuilding and scope, Garcia writes a new page all her own that will be sure to keep readers turning. Fantasy at its most fantastical!"
—Ryan Van Loan, author of *The Sin in the Steel*

"Spellbinding from the first word to the last. R.S.A. Garcia's *The Nightward* is an expertly told genre-splicing story of a matriarchal society embroiled in political backstabbing, dark magic, and deception." —Veronica G. Henry, author of *The Canopy Keepers*

"In a word, brilliant! I love this story. In many more words, *The Nightward* is a breathless quest to save a young queen from the clutches of treacherous courtiers in the aftermath of a deadly coup. After all, nothing builds character like being hunted by powerful magical entities while your world falls apart. It grips you from the start and doesn't let go as you worry for the characters and all the directions in which the story can go. The subtle hints to another, ancient story in the world's past, and an intriguing cast of characters in a matriarchal society that is not without its problems, further serve to enrich the plot. I can't wait to see how this story concludes."
—Shari Paul, author of *Wild Meat* and *Bek, Ascendant*

THE
NIGHTWARD

BOOKS BY R.S.A. GARCIA

The Nightward

Lex Talionis

THE NIGHTWARD

BOOK ONE OF THE WATERS OF LETHE

R.S.A. GARCIA

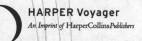

HARPER Voyager
An Imprint of HarperCollins Publishers

HarperCollins books may be purchased for educational, business, or sales promotional use. For information, please email the Special Markets Department at SPsales@harpercollins.com.

FIRST EDITION

Designed by Alison Bloomer

Map illustration © Mike Hall

Library of Congress Cataloging-in-Publication
Data has been applied for.

ISBN 978-0-06-334575-1

24 25 26 27 28 LBC 5 4 3 2 1

To Joan and Lyris, two queens who have gone before me.
Thank you for the Blessings you left me with.

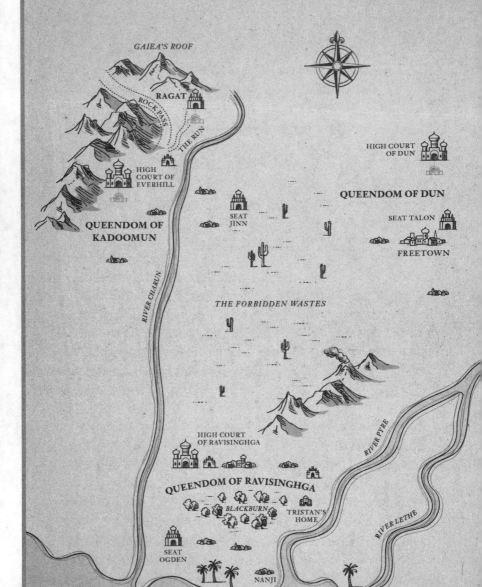

GAILAND

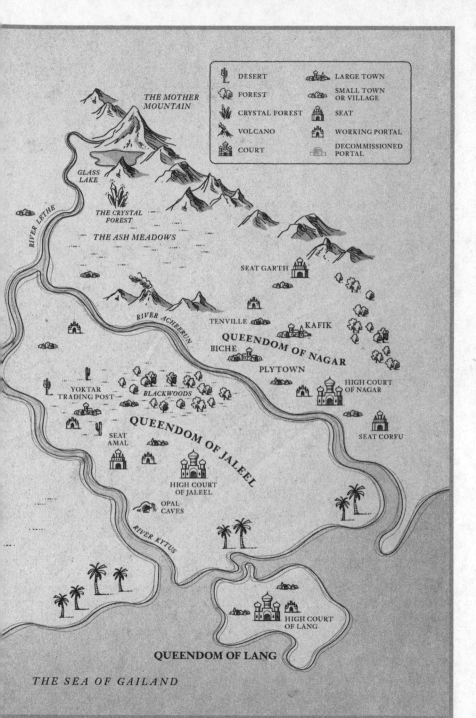

Then Gaiea took the Blessed from Chaos and brought them into Her bosom and henceforth it was no longer called the Place of the Testing, but instead the Place Where It Was Done. And the Masters wailed and tore their garments, for the firmaments of the heavens were closed to them, leaving only the Dark of Oblivion.

Then the Goddess said unto those who did not repent of their sins, "For your crimes against the Blessed and the very heavens themselves, you will be banished to the western mountains of Gailand, and you shall drink first and deepest of the Waters of Lethe." But there were some who refused to drink and who sought to deny their exile. They fought against the Goddess with the monsters of Chaos. In this, too, they failed, and Gaiea buried them in Her Desert and they were heard from no more.

—*The Blessed Scriptures of Gaiea*
The First Book of the Hand of Gaiea
Chapter 11: Verses 17–18

CHAPTER 1

SPIRIT

PRINCESS VIELLA OF THE COURT OF HAMBER, DIVINE SPIRIT OF THE SIX Queendoms, began her last day as the presumptive heir to the High Court of Dun by arguing with her exasperated bodyguard.

"But I don't want to go yet. I wish to see the klaxon," she said, taking another backward step up the crumbling spiral staircase to the tower. She held up the skirts of her white sari in one small brown hand so she wouldn't trip.

Luka Freehold clenched his fists and prayed to Gaiea for patience, aware that his desire to turn the princess over his knee and spank her as she deserved was treasonous at best. But she had almost given him a heart attack when he went to collect her from her rooms after breakfast and found her missing. It was pure chance he had guessed the reason for her questions the day before about the expected time of arrival for the Kadoomun emissary and thought to check the ancient tower, with its clear views of the courtyard.

Careful to keep his voice calm, he said, "Queen Elise has requested the princess attend the lady Sophia this morning for your final direction regarding the Ceremony this eventide."

Princess Viella looked up at the stone ceiling with a dramatic sigh. "I'm *busy*."

Luka gave her the full benefit of the withering stare he had inherited from his father, the captain of the Daguard. "The princess does not appear to be busy with much more than testing my fortitude."

She folded her arms, and jangling gold bracelets caught the sunlight slanting down from narrow slits in the exterior wall high above. She was a striking child, with thick, copper-tinted brown hair and eyes such a light brown, they were closer to amber. Unfortunately, she knew how to melt hearts with those eyes, and used her bright smile and precocious mind to wheedle whatever she wanted out of the entire royal household.

Except him. Out of necessity, he'd learned to steel himself against her infectious appeal, if only to ensure he carried out his orders—to protect her at all times. Even from herself.

"I have decided I do not like you. I will ask Captain Kemp to replace you with my old bodyguard immediately."

If only such wishes would make it so, he thought, chafing for what felt like the thousandth time at his role as a babysitter. He couldn't say that, though, and so Luka let a thin smile crease his face as he bowed his head and made fists of both hands against his shining breastplate. His ponytail tickled the back of his neck when he looked up again. "I'm heartbroken the princess has taken a dislike to me. However, it will be difficult to replace me, given your previous bodyguard is still visiting his family. Besides, I have it from him he would not return to this duty unless compelled by a threat of bodily harm, and even then, it would depend on the nature of the threat."

The princess made an irritated sound and stamped one tiny slipper on the uneven stair. Dust drifted down, and the gold anklets she wore added their music to her arm bands.

Seizing on her distraction, he reached for her arm, but quick as a dagen-cat, Viella turned and scampered up the steep, narrow stairs that twisted around a central column, disappearing around the bend. Cursing beneath his breath, he took the stairs two at a time, aware the music from her jewelry had abruptly fallen silent. When he reached the stone platform at the top of the stairs that ringed the tower's interior, allowing archers to fire down into the courtyard outside, he ran around it, searching, but finding no trace of her.

I'm playing hide-and-seek. Daguard and Dahomei ride to war on Kadoomun's borders, yet a Pride Leader must attend to the emergency of taking the princess to her lessons. He shook his head, annoyed. *No point in focusing on what cannot be changed. The sooner I have her in hand, the sooner I can prepare for the Ceremony.*

First, however, I must actually get her in hand.

There was one other place she could be. Returning to the closed door at the top of the stairs, he opened it onto a small balcony at the top of the tower. Green vines twisted and sprouted from the cracked stone banister and the floor beneath his feet.

Below him, two miles of waving grassland separated the High Court of the Queendom of Dun from the bustling capital of Freetown. Smoke from cooking fires twisted against the brightening pink-gold of the morning sky, and the rising sun gilded peaked roofs. From the court kitchen, the scent of curries and baking meats teased his nostrils. It was a glorious view, but Luka ignored the morning's beauty, searching the stone alcove on his right for the princess instead.

She must be on the other side. He marched to his left. Below, the carved wooden archway dominating the courtyard glowed. Its mellow wood accepted and threw back the rays of the morning sun as it hummed and vibrated. The Gate of Dun, first among the High Court's magical protections, was admitting new arrivals.

The tail end of a caravan passed beneath the archway. Twelve men, bare-chested and dressed in flowing white trousers, marched in lockstep beside a massive klaxon bird that had to bend its long-necked head to pass under the Gate. On its back, it carried one of the traveling houses of royalty; pale blue cloth embroidered with gold fluttered as it swayed.

The klaxon, prompted by a subtle tug on its gold-tasseled rein, threw back its crested head and sounded a loud note, sweet and pure as a harp. Turquoise feathers rustled before the trailing tail rose and fanned open behind the house, the pattern resembling dozens of eyes. Through the mind-touch, Luka felt his dagen-cat, Farain, awaken. The howl that followed—taken up briefly by other cats—was no surprise. Dagens were very jealous of their territory and had no love of birds.

He frowned at the visitors. The emissary from the Queen of Kadoomun was Queen Elise's final guest. *And if I don't find the princess soon, Lady Sophia will have my ears.*

He checked the rest of the balcony, but the princess was not there. *Where could she be?* In his mind's eye, for an endless, stomach-twisting second, he saw a tiny body falling off the balcony. He darted back to the stone ledge, gripping the cool, slick stems and furry leaves of the vines. But only the faded abstract pattern of the courtyard tiles looked up at him, red and yellow in the morning's fading shadows.

If she did not fall . . .

There was a soft clink behind him. He spun and held out his right palm to the doorway at the top of the stairs, circling it clockwise and muttering the counterspell Viella's former body-guard had taught him under his breath. A thin mist filled the opening, pearl and coral strands wrapping around themselves, coalescing into the tiptoeing form of the princess. Cold inside with frustration and relief, Luka grabbed her by the back of her vest.

"The princess will refrain from using her concealment spells in my vicinity from now on, or I will speak to the Dowager Mother about several unpleasant alternatives to her magic lessons."

Viella made a little squeal as he lifted her into his arms and started down the stairs. "I only wanted to see the caravan!"

"Be that as it may, you have inconvenienced the entire house-hold. Using magic to evade your responsibilities is not something the queen would look upon lightly. Also, if you wish to be put down, you'd better stop kicking my legs."

She stilled and he set her on her feet at the bottom of the stairs. She looked up at him, pouting. "I didn't mean any harm. It wasn't even True magic, just an Illusion."

"That may be so, but at your age, you should not use magic of any kind outside of your classroom."

Her eyes widened. "You won't tell Lady Sophia what I did, will you?"

That was exactly what he hoped she would think. Luka knew the princess held her teacher in high regard. *And an advantage in war should never be wasted.*

"I'll keep your activities to myself if you agree to put an end to your defiance and do as you are told."

She blinked, mouth open, dismayed. "But . . . that's not fair!"

"Perhaps. Do we have a pact?"

She made a face but held out her right hand. "Pact."

Luka laid her open palm against his chest and bowed his head over it before releasing it. "Now, let me accompany you to your classroom before Lady Sophia or the Dowager Mother comes looking for you."

※

"EXCELLENT, VIELLA. YOU'VE MEMORIZED YOUR RESPONSES TO THE Augur very well." Lady Sophia smiled at her, her eyes a dark gray, like storm clouds, in the sunshine that came through several long windows. Her smooth blond hair was a knot at the nape of her neck, and the dress she wore had long sleeves and a high collar, nothing like the saris they would wear later. Viella preferred the shalwar kameez she often wore to her cousin Sophia's skirts, but the Lady of Talon was lovely and elegant in them. Even more than her mother, who Viella thought was one of the most beautiful women in all of Gailand.

"We can move on. I'm proud of your diligence today, Viella."

Happiness burst inside her. Lady Sophia was not one to praise easily, so this meant her mother would get a good report. She needed that in case Luka told anyone about that morning.

Thinking about him made her eyes go to the Dahomei that stood watch at the door. The warrior-magician did not look at Viella, her gaze instead constantly roving the room, her hand on the hilt of the sword at her side. Her golden armor shone bright, and her matching helmet hid most of her face, except for stern lips and piercing brown eyes. As annoyed as she had been with him earlier, Viella missed Luka's familiar presence whenever she had classes with Lady Sophia. But the Lady of Talon went everywhere with the Dahomei her seat was responsible for training. It had been decided the Daguard would share the duties of the High Court's protection now, meaning Viella, her twin brother Valan, and her father, got their own Daguard bodyguards. But the ladies of Gailand did not have to adopt the court's nod to unity. They could do as they saw fit regarding their own security.

"Have you any questions for me about tonight?" Lady Sophia strode to her favorite window seat and settled herself and her skirts before beckoning Viella to join her. Delighted they would not be at the heavy desk that dominated the small room anymore, Viella scrambled up onto the pink, white, and gold cushions and pulled aside the sheer curtains to gaze down into the busy courtyard. Somewhere deeper in the court, music thrummed as the musicians practiced for the Ceremony of the Introduction to the Heir. It made her swing her feet in time to the beat.

"No, Princess, focus on me." Lady Sophia touched her wrist lightly.

Viella couldn't help whining a little. "It's so pretty outside today."

"There will be many pretty days, and many times you must ignore them. Today we've no time for distractions, Princess. This will be the second most important day of your life, and you would be best served by giving the preparations for the proceedings your full attention."

"But I haven't lived my full life yet. How do you know this

is the second most important day in it?" Viella frowned at Lady Sophia, who gave her one of her usual cool smiles.

"You are the heir to the throne of the High Queendom of Dun, Viella. The only day more important than today will be the day you are chosen by the Blessing to become the Hand of Gaiea, like your mother. On that day, you will receive the Boon, and become a vessel for all the knowledge and power of the Goddess Herself."

"If I'm not chosen, I want to become a dancer."

Lady Sophia made the little sigh that always meant she was about to chide Viella. "You are the Spirit of Gaiea until your mother passes, Viella, and no Spirit should make a life as anything less than a leader of her community. With no seat of your own to inherit, due to the Dowager Mother's . . . situation, you must either hope to become the Hand to all of Gailand or ensure you do well at your studies so that you can contribute as a valued Council member in Freetown."

"Would you let me be a Dahomei, if I got good enough at my magic?"

Lady Sophia gave a slight shake of her head, regret in her eyes. "Again, you are the Spirit. With time, you will far surpass any Dahomei at both the True Magic of the Sight and the Illusion of the Magic of the Word. But if you do not become the Hand, it would not do for a former Spirit to become a warrior-magician. Your job is to nurture peace and community. It is the queens and ladies of Talon who must protect, and fight for, the queendoms against the Ragat marauders."

Viella crossed her arms. "But all the Hand does is have meetings. It's so boring. I'd rather go to new places and not be told what to do all the time."

Lady Sophia glanced out the window into the courtyard, her hands folded in her lap. "One never knows what life will bring, cousin. You may yet get your wish. The Blessing does not always choose who we expect."

She leaned forward conspiratorially, a tiny smile on her lips. "Take me, for instance. When the last High Queen died without children, my family was among those the Blessing was expected to go to. Instead, it chose your mother, my much younger cousin by marriage, the only child of a wealthy tradeswoman who'd been a respected Elder.

"And soon after, I found myself entrusted with one of the most important positions in all of Gailand. Gaiea sends us where we will do the most good. She will do the same for you."

Viella thought about this for a while. "I guess you're right."

"I know I am." Lady Sophia squeezed her hand and gave her a wink. "I think we should move on to practicing your Sight now. Your Word is progressing well, Mordach is excellent at teaching Illusion, but True magic is the most important part of any queen's arsenal."

"I have a question first."

"Of course. Ask anything you'd like."

Viella hesitated then swallowed and asked, "Will the Scrying hurt? Valan said it hurts."

Lady Sophia chuckled. "And how would Valan know? He was a baby when he had his First Scrying, just like you."

"I guess someone told him." Viella shrugged. "I didn't really ask. He said he didn't want to do it because it hurts sometimes and then they take you away."

"Well . . ." Lady Sophia paused for a second. "I can guarantee it won't hurt either of you. The Augur will take a small box and place it against the back of your neck for a few seconds and then the box will tell the Augur whether the Blessing we all are born with will help you to be stronger in the magic of the Sight or the Word, or whether you're Unbound or Neutral. You both passed your First Scrying, so we know you're not Neutral. No one in Dun has been for many years now."

"So, they won't take us away after?"

The pleasant expression on Lady Sophia's face wavered ever

so slightly and Viella had a feeling that her cousin had decided not to say something very important. Without thinking, she reached out with the mind-touch and lost her breath as she was immediately, painfully ejected from Lady Sophia's mind.

"That was very rude, Viella," Lady Sophia said, and though her voice was polite, it was colder than before. "We do not touch minds without consent, and we ask permission before using the mind-speak. Only Daguard use this talent as you just did. And they use it to commune solely with dagens, with animals. Mind-speak is a rare gift amongst women and not to be abused. Especially as you are far too unskilled to it to be using it on others."

Tears sprang to Viella's eyes as she rubbed her aching head. "I'm sorry, Lady Sophia." And then softly, "It hurts."

"Let that be a reminder. Opening yourself up in that manner means others can hurt you. Never do it without a very good reason."

Viella lowered her head, sniffling. "I won't do it again," she said in a low voice.

Lady Sophia slid a finger under her chin and raised her head. A soft, perfumed kerchief wiped her face gently. "I'm sorry I hurt you. Will you accept my apology?" Relieved she heard no anger in Lady Sophia's voice and felt none in her manner, Viella nodded and gave her a timid smile.

"That's it, Princess." Lady Sophia smiled back. "This is no time for tears. Despite what Valan thinks, you have nothing to fear. The Scrying is not meant for one such as you. The people it searches for no longer exist in Dun, in the same way that there are no Neutrals here, only in Ragat. You will never have to leave your court."

And with that, Lady Sophia took Viella's hand and led her back to the desk and the scrolls scattered on it, the Dahomei's intense, protective gaze on them the entire time.

THE DOWAGER MOTHER FRANCES TWISTED ONE FINAL BRAID INTO A COIL on Viella's head and pinned it into place. "Finished. Stand that I may see you."

Viella slid off the plush, glimmering cushions at her grandmother's feet and stood, wincing at a jab from one of the many pearl-tipped pins in her hair. Through the narrow windows behind her grandmother, she saw that night had descended, and the glare of dozens of torches lit the courtyard outside. The lively beat of calypso seeped through the thick, wavy glass panes into the room.

Maroon and gold panels covered the walls of the dressing room. Matching drapes surrounded the bed next to her. Behind her was the ornate full-length mirror she had been studying the Dowager Mother's face in for the last hour, and a glossy wooden dresser with a matching chair, the back of which was carved into two dagen-cats facing each other on their hind legs.

The Dowager Mother, mother to Lord Consort Alain, grandmother to the twins, and head of the household of the High Court of Dun, studied Viella from head to toe with narrowed pale-green eyes that missed nothing. She smoothed strong, wrinkled palms over Viella's royal-blue silk skirts. "Hold out your hands," she directed.

Sighing with impatience, Viella extended arms draped to the wrists in transparent layers of gold-trimmed silk.

Her grandmother checked that the six bracelets, representing the six queendoms, adorned each hand and foot. Satisfied, she nodded; the tiny silver stud that pierced her left nostril winked at Viella.

"You are ready, and in good time, despite running Luka quite a chase this morn."

Viella felt her cheeks heat. *He said he wouldn't tell anyone! I should never have trusted him!*

A small smile creased the Dowager Mother's face and she winked. "The queen need not hear about the chasing though. It would only distract her on an important night."

Viella threw herself on her grandmother in a spontaneous hug. "Thank you, Grandmother. I won't misbehave again! I swear by . . . by Gaiea herself!"

The rich smell of sandalwood powder rose from her grandmother's sari as she hugged Viella and kissed her forehead.

"Better you only use the Blessed Gaiea's name for promises you can keep." She nudged Viella toward the door. "Go find your brother for me, then show yourself to the queen."

He's probably studying again, Viella thought. She waited until she was out the door and into the red-tiled hallways of the Hamber family's personal quarters, then she picked up her skirts and ran full-tilt down the corridors, her feet soundless in their soft-soled slippers. She passed one gold-armored Dahomei, who frowned at her headlong rush, but Viella ignored her.

She turned left at the next corridor. Here the tiles went from red to dark green and cream. The arches that marked the alcoves and passageways were a heavy wood, almost black. The carvings on them depicted scene after scene of the end of the Age of Chaos. Battlefields scattered with countless corpses of people. Dagen-cats fighting winged animals while the riders of both creatures pointed strange devices at each other that shot beams of light or tiny deadly stones. Huge arched gates from which armed warriors and streams of black wind seemed to flow toward the waiting armies of mostly women. After Viella passed under those painted arches, she reached a white fountain tinkling to itself at the end of the long corridor. The music in the Welcome Hall faded, becoming a harmonious murmur.

Surprised at how deserted the hallways were, she ran faster. The queen kept as few guards within the personal quarters as possible so that it felt more like a common home than a court, but it was odd she had not seen one Daguard since leaving the dressing room.

She rounded the corner—and a hand clamped down on her left shoulder, bringing her progress to a jarring halt. Her feet slipped out from under her, and she was lifted and set back on them. Breathless, she looked up into the face of the Royal Spellsayer, Mordach.

"Princesses should not run heedlessly," he said in his melodious voice. "Accidents do happen, after all."

Viella had once heard her mummy say he had a voice that could charm the clouds out of the sky, as befitted the first man ever appointed a Royal Spellsayer. All Viella knew was Mordach was fun and loved music as much as she did. Sometimes, when her lessons on Illusion ended, he would sing old songs to her, or tell her funny tales of his time training at the Court of Talon, mimicking servants and ladies alike until she cried with laughter. He would laugh with her, his chuckling low and mischievous.

Recently, though, he was quieter, distracted. He spent more time with her brother and less with her, and he hadn't told her a tale in several months. Normally that wouldn't have bothered her. Adults were always fretting over something or other. She'd not seen her mother for days because the courts were fighting each other over additions to the Code.

But there had been times Mordach's distraction felt . . . different. Times when he sat staring at her as she studied, and she felt the weight of his gaze and an emptiness in the room. As though she was alone and Mordach somewhere else.

No. Not alone. I wasn't alone.

Once, she had looked up from her book and stared back. It had been a mistake. His dark eyes unnerved her, made something tremble in the pit of her stomach and a small voice inside her murmur caution. They had sat that way for long minutes until he blinked, smiled, and told her the lesson for that day was done and she could leave. She had done so, relieved and confused.

The next time she saw him, it was as though she had imagined it. He put aside their books and instead took her kite-flying with her brother in the fields near the High Court. The afternoon had been warm, the winds high, and they shared one kite because

Valan lost his. They watched it float away as Mordach made a joke that had them laughing so hard and long, Luka raised his eyebrows at them from his position next to Valan's Daguard a discreet distance away.

Mordach released her shoulder and tilted his head toward her, waiting for her explanation.

"Grandmother asked me to find Valan," she said.

The Spellsayer's lips curved. He wore his night-black hair in a ponytail, like the annoying Luka, but strands escaped on either side of his angular face. This particular night, in honor of the Ceremony, he had dispensed with the black vest and trousers that were a symbol of his office. His full-length ivory robe was shot through with silver; the wide sleeves reached the back of his knuckles.

He moved to the side of the doorway behind him. "Consider him found."

She stepped into a room smaller than the dressing room, but with no windows. Instead, bookshelves lined all three walls from floor to ceiling, every one of them crammed full of manuscripts protected by leather or hard, shiny covers. Huge candle-holders and smokeless braziers made the room bright and hot. She smelled the heavy, oily scent of leafworm repellant, baking candlewax, and, beneath that, the mustiness of an airless, seldom-opened room.

Two desks faced each other before her, inkpots standing on the edge of their wooden, roll-back tops. Pens bristled from the pots, and thick white papers were scattered on both desks. Only one, however, seated her twin brother. He looked up at her as she entered, his amber eyes exactly like hers. He wore a vest embroidered in pink and white, with sheer white sleeves and matching trousers, an everyday outfit inappropriate for the Ceremony. As he moved something in front of him, his sleeve spread over the desk. An ink blot blossomed at the edges of the fabric, and he groaned and snatched his hand away, glancing at her and biting his lip the way he did whenever he'd been caught in mischief.

She had seen that look often of late, ever since Valan had started studying privately with Mordach after their regular lessons for the day were done. Valan had never kept secrets from her. They'd shared everything. But now she knew there was something between them, she just didn't know what. He acted like everything was the same, but it clearly wasn't.

Before she could speak, he said, "What is it?"

"Grandmother's waiting for you."

He glanced at Mordach, candlelight flickering along his short hair, the tips a lighter brown, like the streaks in hers. "I'm not sure I'm ready." His voice was uncertain.

Surprised, she took a second to find the words. "You have to be. It's almost time for the Ceremony."

"I'm not . . . feeling well," he said, his gaze on his ink-stained hands. She took hold of them impulsively, shocked when he squeezed them tight. Something was bothering him, and knowing he was sad made her heart hurt.

"Val, what do you mean? What's wrong?"

His lips parted, but Mordach's fingers brushed her shoulders. "The prince is tired after a long day of study, is all. But of course he will be at the Ceremony. You may leave. I'll see to it Valan gets to the Dowager Mother in time."

She frowned as Mordach smiled at her. It was the smile she knew. The one she trusted.

Valan slid his hands from hers and she saw the moment he changed his mind. "Nothing's wrong, Vee. Mordach's right. We'll talk after."

"Promise?"

"Promise."

She didn't want to leave, but if Valan said they would talk later, they would.

She looked back after she had passed into the hallway. Mordach was bent over Valan's right shoulder. The white pages had been shifted, and a huge old book that looked familiar lay beneath them. She saw the gold inscriptions floating above the page, changing shape too fast for her to read, bright against Mordach's shadow.

Mordach glanced up, shook his head at her reproachfully, and a moment later the door swung shut.

It was the least of a Spellsayer's abilities, little more than a trick, but it bothered her that he had shut the door on her. Shut her out. *It's always Valan now.* Hurt and not even sure why, she continued on to the one place she was always welcome.

❡❡❡❡❡❡❡❡

"IS IT TRUE THAT YOU FEEL UNWELL?"

Mordach's voice was a sympathetic murmur in Valan's ear, and his long fingers squeezed his shoulder in a light hug as he leaned over him.

Valan turned his head to look at Mordach, still biting at a corner of his lip.

"I . . . I don't know."

Mordach nodded, dark eyes full of concern as he crouched and turned the prince on his chair to face him fully.

"This is about tonight?"

Valan lowered his eyes, his hands picking at his trousers, his shoulders tense.

"What worries you the most?"

Valan hesitated, then whispered, "What if I do it wrong? What if I make a mistake?"

"Then I will be there to help you. We will all be there. Including your new friend. Don't you want to see him again? Didn't you have fun the last time?"

Valan looked up on an indrawn breath. "I guess so. Yes."

"And you learned a great deal as well, didn't you? Didn't that feel good? Using what you've learned?"

"It . . . it felt really good."

"As it should. You're doing wonderfully, Valan. After tonight, everyone will know how hard you've worked. How special you truly are."

Valan smiled. "And I can tell Vee and Mummy?"

Mordach stood, an answering smile stretching his face. "Of course. That's the whole point of this. For them to see how talented you truly are. But we need another session with your new friend, I think, so you will finish this lesson, then go to the Dowager Mother. In a few hours, I will come for you, and we will go down and practice together one more time. How does that sound?"

Valan's shoulders relaxed as he gazed up at his tutor. "It sounds good."

"Excellent, so we have a plan. First, we meet our new friends. Then we go to the Ceremony."

"And then I surprise Mummy and Vee, and the Augurs won't be able to hurt me or take me away." His voice warbled on this last, but he lifted his chin bravely.

Mordach squeezed Valan's arm lightly in agreement. "Be sure of this, Valan. I will never allow you to be hurt or taken away. I volunteered to be your tutor because I believe you are the future of Dun. Tonight, if all goes well, even the High Queen will have no choice but to agree."

<hr/>

VIELLA STOPPED OUTSIDE THE QUEEN'S DOOR, STARING UP THE ARCH for a moment. Gold leaf decorated the doorway—a replica of the Gate of Dun—and here the tiled floor and ceiling were white. The scene carved into the arch showed another battlefield with many dead and broken, unfamiliar shapes that Lady Sophia had explained were war machines. At the apex of the arch, a female figure floated above a crowd of women. A curling nimbus surrounded her like smoke but her back was to the kneeling women and her face could not be seen. Before her were the ruins of a vast structure, partially buried.

Viella bowed her head under the holy scene, as was proper. Then she fluffed her skirts and propped her hand against the smooth coolness of the door—only to feel it move inward under her touch.

Voices came from inside. *Daddy's here. He came back with the caravan from Kadoomun, just like he promised.* Joy swelled in her chest, and she started to enter, then hesitated. *They sound upset.*

". . . not convinced it's the right approach," her father was saying in a tone of voice she'd never heard him use before. "I did my best, but you know how she views me and my mother."

"It probably has more to do with the Ragat Army massing on her borders." Mummy sounded worried.

"You might be right. She's expressed gratitude for the Hands of Dahomei and Daguard you sent to defend her seat, but my stay was cut short to ensure I could return before any fighting broke out, and she refused to come back with me. Said it was no time to leave the court unguarded and she didn't want to be trapped outside her borders."

"I find no fault in that argument."

"Of course not. But I spent days with her. Her reluctance to vote in favor of the changes to the Code is not solely based on the trouble the men of Ragat are stirring up." Viella heard him make a tired sound. "I fear I was not the right ambassador to send."

Her mother sucked air through her teeth. "She's not bigoted, Alain, just—undiplomatic. She was not born to a seat, after all. The Blessing chose her over the other candidates at the Augur's Water Ceremony, just like every other sister queen."

"But we need her, Elise," her father hissed, frustrated. "Or we've wasted our time and Valan becomes a vulnerable pawn."

"That will never happen," her mother retorted, her voice sharp. "Viella loves her brother. She will protect him if need be, and she will continue my work and push for change. For unity.

The fact that we do not yet know his full talent is irrelevant. Sometimes children develop late. That's why there's a Second Scrying. You should have faith in Gaiea."

"Of course I have faith." Her father was angry now too. "Even if he isn't the Spirit, you know Mordach believes Valan has more promise than Sophia's ready to admit. And he's the Royal Spellsayer. Not so long ago, some would have said it was impossible for a man to achieve that position."

"Mordach is Unbound. Their magic is strong enough to challenge any woman's. But he longs for a successor, and you long for Valan to be strong enough to take his place one day. You might both be seeing what you wish for. If it takes a Second Scrying, he's probably strong in the Word, like most men, and that is no outcome to fear."

"If only it was just about that."

Silence fell, and Viella felt her heart pounding hard at the tension that filled it. Something was wrong between her parents. She could feel it. It hurt in her head in a way she'd never felt before. Desperation and frustration, love and anger warred in her, and she closed her eyes against it and tried to breathe as her heart pulsed.

"I know it wasn't easy going back. I appreciate that you took this on, given how hostile Everhill is to you," her mother said in what Viella thought of as her High Queen voice. When she used it, she was no longer her mother. She was Gaiea's Hand. "But you must trust that Gaiea has a plan. The Augurs will scry, and we will know his and Viella's strengths before the end of the Ceremony. She has done well at both the Sight and the Word, but even she only displayed her first skills last year. I have no doubt Valan will be talented too."

"But nothing like what you'd expect, given you are the Hand."

"Alain—"

"They will never doubt Viella, Elise, but my son . . . he will not live easy here. To survive the High Court, he must be exceptional."

"You know that—"

Her father spoke over her mother, raising the hairs on Viella's arms. "My time in Kadoomun made it very clear to me what they think of our marriage, Elise, even after more than a decade. They will use my bloodline against you, against him, even against Viella at every opportunity."

"Alain, you must calm yourself."

"And you must listen to me! If even Selene has doubts, I'm telling you the ladies are not ready. *Gailand* is not ready for what you want to do."

Her mother sighed, and Viella heard the rustling of skirts and the chiming of jewelry. "When are people ever ready for change? I will not be held hostage by the past. Despite resistance, have I not amended the Code so that Dun's highest positions and Elder Councils are now open to all? And as my lord consort, you have unprecedented freedoms."

Her father's voice dropped lower, and Viella strained to hear it. "But Valan . . ."

"Will be taken care of, always, under my rule and his sister's. Their love will not be divided by politics. The Code will change, and all of us—men, women, Unbound, Neutrals—we will come together and make Gailand strong under the Goddess. We will take Ragat from the marauders, and they will be the final queendom, as Gaiea intended."

"You know I support you in this. I believe in the Scripture." Her father's voice was low, sad. "But I wanted him to have a future, as I had in Kadoomun. Before."

"I know." Her mother's voice had dropped too. "You and Mordach will help Valan, teach him well, make him strong. I approve of the extra lessons to help him develop whatever True magic and Illusion magic he may possess. He will be safe. And I will not back down now. I will find a way to garner support from my sister queens."

Her father's laugh was bitter and tugged at her insides. "As always, you put your holy crusade before us."

"Alain, that's not fair. It is my reason for *being*."

"You think I don't know that? It's why you married me."

Viella frowned, her heart beating in her ears. There was something new here. Something very private.

"I married the man I loved." Her mother's voice was firm.

"You put aside the woman you adored to stabilize Kadoomun after the rebellion."

"And you have chosen me over the man you love. Alain, we both decided we would make this a real marriage. I've never wavered from that." After a long pause, her mother spoke again, very softly. "Where is this coming from? Is it the trip to Kadoomun? Has it stirred all this up? I ended it, you know that. I haven't seen her since you and I were promised to each other."

"Because she left Dun."

"Because I love *you*. I made my choice, and you gave me your heart and our precious children. I have no regrets."

"Is that true?"

More rustling. A soft sigh. "I've never lied to you, Alain. I put away the bracelet once I said my goodbyes. I didn't need it."

Quiet fell again, then came a whisper so soft, Viella had to lean into the door to hear.

"What if you're wrong? What if this is not what Gaiea wants?"

"I've read the Histories, Alain. All the Scriptures. Over and over again. But more than that, I'm the Hand. I *remember* it. It's time to put a stop to this. Gailand does not fear the things we should. There is so much more at stake than I can tell you."

"I am with you, my queen." A soft sigh that made Viella's heart ache. "But Mordach and I should take him. Tonight, Viella becomes yours. She becomes Dun's future. My son should have someone to support him, too, to prepare him for life at court when he is not the Heir."

"My love"—her mother's voice was low, anguished—"you know I cannot. Twins must face the Choosing together, it is the Code, even if we know the Boon will not go to a male. He must take the same path as Viella until he can no longer do so." And then, even lower: "But do not forget, the Boon is not promised. Perhaps our children will live the quiet lives we always wanted."

"The little hut?"

"A house or cabin, I think. They'll be too used to all this space by then."

Someone sighed. "By the river or the sea?"

"Any water will do, my love. The Waters gave us freedom. Water is the home of the Anchorite who helps Gaiea protect us. It will give them strength and peace. Connection to the ancestors. I won't be here by then, but perhaps you will be. I only ask that you . . ."

The voice became a murmur. Trying to hear better, Viella started to ease her way into the opening. The door creaked. She froze as it swung wide and then looked up, straight into her father's blue eyes. He dropped his arms from around her mother and turned to face her, surprised. He was wearing white, his high collar and sleeves embellished with pink gems and lavender embroidery. His trousers were longer than usual, brushing the tops of golden shoes studded with more gems.

"Viella? What are you doing?" He frowned, a line creasing his forehead beneath his neatly trimmed dark hair.

"I . . ." She saw the impatience in his eyes, so like Valan's sometimes, and for a moment his thoughts lay before her like an open book. *He loves Valan so much. He and Mordach are worried for him.*

She felt nothing in his thoughts about her. Tonight—*her* night—she wasn't on his mind at all. It hurt so much, her breath hitched.

"Gaiea's breath, what have I told you about eavesdropping?"

The book of his mind snapped closed. Her mouth tasted like she'd been sucking on a metal spoon, and her vision grew blurry. *He doesn't care about me.*

"Viella?" Queen Elise, Divine Hand of Gaiea, stepped around her husband. She took one look at Viella's trembling lower lip and scooped her into her arms. Viella buried her face in the coral-pink pallu draped over her mother's right shoulder and breathed deep of the comforting scent that was hers alone. "I'm sorry, Mummy," she whispered, "I'm sorry."

"Viella, darling, don't cry."

Her father made an exasperated sound behind her. "You think she heard?"

Viella felt her mother shake her head at her father. "You had better see to the guests, Alain." There was a moment of silence before the door closed, and then she was sitting on her mother's lap. For once, she didn't want to wander the room, touching the huge white-and-mother-of-pearl bed. Or lie on the pastel cushions her mother preferred to the stiff-backed chairs imported from Nagar, staring at the crystal candelabra hanging from the high, white ceiling. She simply held her mummy tight and tried to forget all she had heard.

The queen slid a finger under Viella's chin and smiled, exposing a slight gap between her two front teeth. Her long, dark hair was braided into a crown atop her head, studded with pink gems and golden pins. "What's all this about?"

She desperately wanted her mother to say her father loved her as much as he did Valan, opened her mouth to ask questions about what they'd said, but another thought, solid as a pebble, settled in her mind. *She won't tell me the truth anyway. I wasn't supposed to hear that. Any of it.*

Viella wiped a hand over her moist eyes. "Nothing. I fell down and hurt my knee."

Viella knew her mother would see through the lie. Queen Elise was the Hand of Gaiea, and Viella the Spirit of Gaiea. They could not be harmed by weapons or magic known to women, and they had never been sick once in their lives. Pain was a fleeting sensation; bruises barely formed on Viella before they faded. So it would be until she died and a new Hand was

Blessed to take her place. There was no way a bump on the knee would make her cry.

Viella expected her mother to chide her, then prod her until she told the truth, but the queen did neither. Instead, she bent to check Viella's knee, the light from the candles in her room sliding over the shining coils of her reddish-brown hair like a living thing. "It appears no damage has been done."

It came to Viella, in one of those bright moments of clarity rare in life, that perhaps her mother understood she could not say her real hurt without hurting more. That she knew Viella needed her mummy to hold her, whatever the excuse.

Queen Elise straightened, her arm still around Viella's shoulders. "You know, you could tell me anything you wanted, and I'd listen."

Listen, not help. Viella managed a smile. "I'm fine now, Mummy. And I'm sorry I cried. Grandmother says princesses aren't supposed to cry."

The queen hugged her again and whispered into her hair, "That's just a myth. Princesses cry all the time, when they think no one's looking."

"Do you cry?" She sniffed. Her mother passed her thumb under Viella's nose.

"What would a queen have to cry about when she has a daughter as beautiful as you?"

Warmth suffused Viella's body, and she laid her head against the queen's breast. "I love you, Mummy."

"Only half as much as I love you." She straightened a pin in Viella's hair and said, "I'm dying to show my beautiful twins to the Queens of Gailand. Are you ready to greet them with me?"

Viella nodded and slid off her mother's lap. The queen took her hand, and they left her beautiful white room together for the last time.

CHAPTER 2

SPEAR

"Y OU'RE LATE."

Luka looked up from belting his ceremonial sword around his waist. Captain Blane Kemp stood before him. The pounding rhythm of the tassa drums dropped in volume as the captain released the heavy drape behind him. The disapproving look in his father's dark eyes made Luka's blood heat. *Disappointed in me yet again. Gaiea grant that someday I manage to pour myself a glass of water without causing you offense.* Luka turned his attention back to the buckle.

"The princess took it into her head to spend time in the Old Tower."

"And how is it she managed to get that far before you missed her?"

"It was before breakfast. I was in the gayelle at sword practice. You know—that thing other soldiers do occasionally." He finished with the belt. His father took a step toward him, his own lacquered armor clanking softly. In the center of his breastplate was the symbol of the Daguard and the court of Dun; a dagen-cat poised on its powerful back legs, ready to attack. The captain's pointed helmet was entirely metal, unlike his armor, and sat easily on a head shorn of most of his hair.

"Watch your tongue, soldier, and remember who you address."

How can I ever forget? Luka clenched both hands into fists against the center of his breastplate and bowed. "Forgive me,

Captain. I will be sure to carry out the change of shift outside her room from now on, so that she does not slip her guard."

Blane sighed and raised his eyes to the ceiling. "What have I done to hurt your damned pride now?"

"Only taken me from my men and assigned me to kick my heels in the barracks of the most well-protected court in Gailand."

Blane rested a heavy hand on Luka's left shoulder. "It is well protected because of the women and men who protect it. The Dahomei have given us charge of members of the royal court for the first time. We cannot afford to be lax or negligent in our duty."

Nonsense. Everyone knew the Gate prevented anyone who intended harm to the Court of Hamber from entering. No weapon could pass under its arch without being detected. The armed Dahomei and Daguard on duty at the Gate this night were obliged to steer clear of the specially protected Grand Hall. Even now, he was forced to wear a ceramic sword—as was every other royal court's guard in attendance at the Ceremony—to prevent the court from alarming all night. In light of such powerful magic, where was the Court of Hamber's urgent need for his services?

Luka tried to hold his tongue but could not help himself. "I am a good soldier, Father. Did I not lead victoriously in battle against the Ragat scum for the last three winters? Did I not prove myself worthy of the Daguard?"

"You fight well, and you have the gift of the mind-touch. You would not be a Pride Leader otherwise," Blane replied.

"Then why do five Palms of the Dahomei and Daguard ride without me? Captain Natan chose me to join fifty of our best warriors, yet you refused his request. How have I so offended you that you would deny him the experience I could have provided? Why punish me by assigning me to the princess?"

"Punish you? By allowing you to serve at the most important Ceremony of our queen's rule?" Blane shook his head, a slow smile spreading across the hard angles of his broad ebony face. "Is it punishment to teach you the value of humility? Skilled soldier that you may be, you are but nineteen, and have much to learn. The time will come when you sicken of war."

"You always speak in this manner to avoid giving me the answers I need," Luka said through clenched teeth.

A fanfare cut the air like a clean knife, and cheering and applause rose in the hall beyond.

"Then think on these answers as you serve your *punishment*," Blane said, pulling him to the curtain. "Should I send every good Pride Leader to our farthest borders and leave our High Court guarded by common soldiers? What greater duty, what greater *reward* can there be for a soldier than to protect your sovereign?"

He pulled Luka close enough to whisper in his ear. "I am also trying to protect *you*, my son. Never forget, the life you have can be taken away if someone asks the wrong questions. And people do not ask questions of members of the royal court."

Captain Kemp thrust aside the curtain, and light and warmth poured through into the narrow alcove, though not enough to counter the cold that ran under Luka's skin after his father's words.

"We will speak later, where there is less chance of being overheard. For now—go to our princess. By keeping her safe, you ensure your own safety. Do you understand?"

Throat too tight to answer or ask the questions that swirled in his head, Luka nodded, then stepped from the shadows into the light.

※※※※※※

VIELLA WAS SO CAPTIVATED BY THE CHANGE IN THE SPACIOUS BUT usually empty Grand Hall, she almost missed the moment Luka appeared on her right, silent and wearing glimmering armor from head to foot. Captain Kemp followed, positioning himself between the queen's throne and Viella's. The soldier he replaced walked down the stairs to stand guard in an inconspicuous alcove.

A vein pulsed in Luka's jaw and his hand rested lightly on the hilt of his sword. The tapering point of his helmet made him look like the tip of a weapon, she thought.

Light blazed from torches and candelabras set in the walls and ceilings. The floor of the hall was tiled in red and yellow mosaics depicting tiny scenes of dancers and performers. Columns rose in two rows on either side of the room, forming small alcoves where miniature stages featured tassa players, limbo dancers, and Gatka—women stripped down to bands of cloth over their breasts and between their legs who weaved and bent, evading swift sticks and wooden shields as they performed their warrior dance. Their lean muscles glistened with gold-dusted oil as they moved.

Pierrot Grenades dressed in fluttering multicolored rags, faces painted beneath brightly colored hoods, displayed their knowledge with impudent rhymes and wordplay that made guests laugh and applaud loudly. Moko Jumbies dressed in a rainbow of tunics and pants that went down to the ground strode above the crowd on their stilts, some dancing on one leg while holding the other above them. Most of the jumbies were teenagers, trained at a special school and fearless in their youth. In the alcove nearest the stage, a band led by Freetown's best calypsonian played the most popular songs in Dun on steel drums and tamboo bamboo—which were bamboo stalks cut to different lengths and hit with sticks and pounded on the ground to make rhythmic beats.

Down the center of the hall, table after table made two parallel lines dressed in flowing red and gold linen and covered with curried meats; rotis and sada; peas and rice; roasts; stewed and geera pork; desserts like fried, crunchy kurma and milky sweet barfi; spiced prunes and candied coconut with hibiscus wine and bittersweet mauby.

The most important rulers in Gailand, dressed in their finest cloth and jewels, stood to applaud the High Queen as she entered. Pride made Viella feel twice as tall.

Queen Elise acknowledged their regard with a smile and a graceful bow of the head as her lord consort came to stand before his smaller throne trimmed in red velvet and gold. She sat and waved her arm for the gathering to do the same, the tinkling of her bracelets lost in the celebratory noise. Chairs creaked and cloth whispered like so many trees in a high wind, until only the Daguard, the servants, and the attendants of each court remained standing, dressed in their court colors like so many gaudy statues.

Viella was taking her seat at her mother's right hand when a horrible feeling swept over her. Her breath started to come fast, her heart thrummed faster and faster, and her vision blurred. But it had nothing to do with her. She was certain of that. Something had gone terribly wrong with Valan. She pressed her hand to her chest, trying to catch her breath as she scanned the area behind the throne, and the rest of the hall, looking for him.

"My Sister Queens," her mother began as Viella found a familiar face in the crowd. Lady Sophia sat at the table nearest the lord consort's throne, dressed in white and green that complemented her delicate complexion. Sitting beside her was the Augur, wearing the colorful embroidered silks of her office, intricate beaded jewelry hanging from her neck, hands peeking out from long, bell-shaped sleeves. Frowning, Viella thought about getting up to go look for Valan. *He's worried . . . and so scared. I have to go to him.*

Do not think it, a whisper intruded in her mind. *Remain exactly where you are until the queen says otherwise.*

Lady Sophia had gone against her own instructions and used first the mind-touch to read her, and then the mind-speak.

I thought you didn't want me using mind-speak yet!

If you insist on being mischievous, I will make an exception. You are not schooled enough in the consequences of your talents to practice them without permission. Now, pay attention to what the queen is saying.

Why were adults always telling you not to do what they were doing themselves? It was quite annoying.

Because we sometimes actually know better than you.

Viella wanted to respond, but she caught movement in the corner of her left eye and turned to see her brother standing next to his father, Mordach close behind him. Valan had changed into a tunic and trousers of royal blue and gold that matched her sari. A golden dagen-cat curled over his heart, and pearls and embroidery decorated his cuffs and high collar. He glanced across at Viella and gave her a small distracted smile before he sat in his chair, his gaze resolutely facing forward.

She breathed a sigh of relief. *He looks just like he always does.* She could still feel his emotions were high, but she understood then he must have been nervous about the Ceremony, only more than she'd realized. Something confused her, though.

That's not the entrance from the dressing room. Did he go back to Mordach's study? She shook her head, amazed at the idea of willingly spending that much time at lessons.

A burst of applause made her jump, and Viella realized her mother had reached the end of her speech. "And now to Gaiea's bountiful feast while we enjoy the entertainment sent to us in lieu of an appearance by my sister queen, Salene of Kadoomun, and graciously escorted here by the Lady Ashwin of Seat Jinn."

Her mother inclined her head in the direction of a frail-looking young woman seated at the same table as Lady Sophia. A tiara glittered in her light-brown hair, and diamonds glittered against her long neck and from her ears. Her yellow, silver-trimmed sari seemed to swallow her small body. Next to her was the tall, dark-haired Lord Consort of Jinn, dressed in black robes with a diamond-studded collar and cuffs.

A slender young man stepped into the open space between the stairs to the throne and the tables. His entire body glittered with silver dust, and he wore loose silver trousers that billowed around his ankles. The *tabla* drums began their sharp, hypnotic rhythm. The bare-backed, round-faced man sitting cross-legged as he beat one of them sang a song in one of the Old Languages in a high, piercing voice. The boy swayed, sinuous as grass in the wind.

Entranced, Viella leaned forward, aware that everyone in the court had grown silent, captivated by the dipping movements of the glittering arms, and the strength in the stomping, flashing ankles. More than once, she caught the eye of the dancer—*Did he smile at me?*—and sometimes she held her breath as he twirled like thistledown, or leaped high, like dagen-cats at play.

When the dance ended, the applause seemed to lift the roof to the heavens. Everyone stood, some calling down blessings on the anonymous boy. The Lord Consort of Jinn had a satisfied look on his face.

"Wonderful, simply wonderful," Viella heard her mother say, and there was a murmur of agreement from her father as they both rose from their thrones. Viella continued to applaud, ignoring the stinging of her hands. The boy bowed deeply to the throne, then his head raised and his gaze settled on Viella.

Come. The voice twisted around her mind, seeped into her muscles. *Come.* Viella gasped and trembled before the power of the plea; she tried to form a thought and failed.

Come.

Something clanged to her right. Viella sensed Luka turn his head toward the sound. She moved toward the stairs, still clapping.

"Viella?" Her mother's voice sounded far, far away, drowned out by the whispered plea. *Come to me.*

Something glimmered by the boy's right hand. *He's holding a candle? A torch?* It didn't matter. All that mattered was that she obey. She started to walk faster.

The boy raised his arm, still smiling, the glittering thing beginning to take shape now.

Viella!

The thought slammed into her, smashing the command in her mind like glass. *Luka?* A shout carried across the court. She groaned, holding her aching head, and tripped on the final stair, dropping to her knees. Something flew over her head, and she flinched instinctively, putting her hand down to steady herself. She twisted, blinking, and felt her mind clearing, sunlight breaking through mist. Luka stood on the stairs, his hand on his sword—but then Viella saw her mother and screamed.

Her mother was staring, bewildered, at the silver spear jutting out of her stomach. She touched her hand to it gently. Then, red blooming on her pink sari, Queen Elise crumpled to the floor.

⁙⁙⁙⁙⁙

LUKA HEARD SOMETHING CLANG BEHIND THE CURTAIN. HIS FATHER made a barely perceptible nod to him, *I will handle it*, and went toward the sound.

Luka turned back to the applauding court in time to see Viella reach the final stair—and to see a small flash of silver-red light coalesce near the dancing boy's hand. In the brief moment it took to understand what he saw, the boy raised his hand.

Viella!

The princess fell to her knees, the spear just missing her. He grabbed the hilt of his sword as the princess looked over her shoulder and screamed, her eyes wide and staring.

Then the queen collapsed, a small thud in the heavy silence, and gasps and screams broke over the assembled crowd. Luka raised his useless sword to throw a stunning blow at the boy, but another sword—one with a sharp metal blade—slammed into the boy's chest, tossing him back into the aisle between the tables.

Another weapon? Coldness filled the pit of his stomach as he realized that, however impossible it seemed, the Gate was not active.

He spun but could not find the source of the sword. Amid the screams and the crash of tumbling furniture and the breaking of glass, he heard a despairing cry. Lord Consort Alain had fallen to his knees beside the queen. His face twisted with a grief that made him ugly as he pulled her to him, and tried to tug the spear from her body.

"Elise," he said. "Elise . . . Elise!"

Behind him stood Prince Valan, his eyes wide with shock, his chest heaving with quick, shallow breaths.

As he lowered his arm, Luka heard noises outside, coming closer. Sounds he had not heard since his return from the fields of Kadoomun a month before. The clash of swords, the cry of voices, the pounding of feet.

Gaiea preserve us.

Battle.

A horn blew, loud and long and deep. It shivered along his nerves until his hands and feet tingled. He gripped his worthless sword in a reflex action. *The Ceremony. Everyone in this hall was unarmed for the Ceremony.* He took a step down the stairs, looked around, and realized that was not true.

The air wavered around him; power thrummed along the hairs on his body, made them stand erect. The queens and ladies of the court had begun to erect defenses—because some of the servants among them were attacking, using whatever knives and sharp objects were at hand.

Even as he watched, a richly dressed courtier buried a knife in the back of Lady Sophia, then cut the throat of the Augur sitting next to her. The lady fell across her table, green-and-white skirts going limp. The courtier dropped to his knees a second later, mouth agape in a soundless shout as a shimmering *force* slammed into him from the outstretched, upright palm of the pale-faced Lady Ashwin of Seat Jinn. A Moko Jumbie collapsed, stilts over-turning tables as it went down.

A scream drilled into his ears. Viella had risen to her feet and stood, arms outstretched toward the throne, tears flooding her cheeks. She was alone in the center of the stage, death in front of her . . . and behind her.

Idiot! he yelled at himself. *Move!*

Two steps and he scooped her up with his left arm. With his right, he launched his sword into the air, gripped the blade as it came down, and drove the hilt into the face of the manservant who had come up behind the princess. The man fell backward, and Luka, tossing aside the sword, relieved him of the large carving knife he held before he could hit the ground.

On his arm, the princess continued to scream, but she did not resist as he took the stairs again. To his left, the curtain in the side entrance came down with a ripping sound, and his father fell through, a black-clad bundle on top of him. As the figure straightened above the Daguard captain, Luka recognized what he was looking at.

Ragat marauders—this far east? How? But there was no time to think on that. He reversed the knife he held and threw it. Despite the lack of balance he'd felt in the weapon, the marauder was so close, he did not miss. The blade buried itself to the hilt in the black bundle.

His father flung off his attacker, straight into two other black-clad assassins who came screaming through the ruined side entrance. They went down in a heap, tripping up more men behind them. Blane leaped to his feet, grabbing the sword the dead marauder had dropped, and in a split second Luka saw his gaze go from the murdered queen to her weeping husband and her paralyzed son. His father pointed to an alcove on Luka's left. "Through there!" he shouted.

Luka glanced at the alcove, where a dead maid rested half on and half off the stage, then turned to see his father pulling the lord consort away from the queen. Lord Alain struggled, so Blane threw him over his shoulder. Another Daguard grabbed the prince. More Ragat fought through the side entrance and the

Daguard holding the prince kicked down the thrones, collapsing them like dominoes onto the newcomers.

They need help. Luka took a step toward them.

"No! Get the queen out of here!" His father turned his back on him and cut down the curtain hanging at the side entrance behind the prince. He ran his sword through the marauder standing there and plunged through the opening.

The queen's dead—

But then he understood. *Queen. Viella's queen now.*

His heart pounding, Luka went to the alcove, tossing the dead maid aside with a disrespect he had no time to ask Gaiea's forgiveness for. Leaping onto the stage, he pressed his hand against a brick low in the right-hand corner, a brick marked with the small, barely visible carving of the head of a dagen. With a soft grating sound, the stone wall before him swung open. He ducked through and the door closed him into the musty darkness beyond. He guided himself with a hand on the cold, dry wall, Viella's hitching breath loud in his ears.

When he emerged from the long, winding tunnel, he stood under the Old Tower's balcony. The wall scraped closed behind him, crumbling stone leaving no trace of the doorway. There were no torches here, as the visitors were not supposed to see the older part of the court.

Outside? He sent me outside, and not to the quarters where we can defend them together?

He set the queen down in front of him and peered around the corner of the wall. Beyond, harshly lit by flickering torches, men struggled against one another with swords and bare hands. He recognized too many fallen bodies by their shining armor. *And Gaiea help us, the gold of the Dahomei armor lies among them.* Charged with guarding the court grounds, the Ragat could not have entered the hall without first removing the Dahomei. What weaponry could so easily overrun the warrior-magicians?

Servants and performers ran screaming, only to fall under

swords or arrows before they reached the darkened Gate. It stood black under the star-drenched night, its magic mute. The sight only confirmed Luka's worst fears. Threw his mind back to what he had glimpsed while looking at the dancing boy. *Only powerful magic could undo the Gate—and Ragat has none. The marauders have been aided by this court. By* him.

He looked down at the now-silent queen. She stood limp under his grip, exhausted from the silent weeping that had dampened his shoulder as he'd felt his way along the tunnel. Most of the pins in her hair had come loose, and feathery strands hung down. For a moment he wavered. *I cannot save her alone. Not against all this.* But then he remembered the look in his father's eyes as he pointed to the alcove. *He would do whatever it took. He trusts you to do the same.*

Taking a deep breath, Luka concentrated and sent an urgent summons outward from his body. A screech answered him, one that thickened into a spine-stiffening growl. Then another and another. He heard the Ragat scum chirping to one another in sharp tones. The klaxon bird, trapped in its nest, sounded a honking note of terror.

Viella looked up at him, the same fear trembling along her body. "What is that?"

"The cats," he said. "I've commanded them to come to the aid of the Daguard."

Viella's eyes grew wide. "You're using the mind-speak?"

"It's not exactly the same. I use the mind-touch because dagens don't talk." He knelt in front of her and turned her to face him. "It is very important you listen to me now, Your Majesty. Do you understand?"

She nodded, her honey-colored eyes just visible in the shadows.

"Whatever happens, do what I say, when I say it. Stay with me, no matter what anyone else says or does. You must trust me now. Both our lives depend on it."

"I trust you," she said in a small voice.

"Good." He stood and sent out one more thought. Yowls filled the courtyard, punctuated by screams. Seconds later, his cat, Farain, appeared, his tail lashing the ground, his golden beard dripping blood on the stones. Almost as tall as a horse, his body red as the blood on his teeth, Farain threw his head back and roared at the night sky, the sound alone enough to unhinge a woman's courage. Luka felt the scream building in Viella, and he clamped a merciless hand over her mouth.

"Silence," he hissed.

Tears slicked his fingers, but she shuddered and then went still. He removed his hand and called the cat closer. With one more twist of its red tail, the cat obliged, thinking vague bloody thoughts in its indistinct but unique mind. Farain had no saddle right now, but Luka had done without on many occasions.

Gripping a handful of the long, coarse fur that ridged the cat's spine, he swung himself up onto the sinewy back, tufts prickling him between the joints of his armor. He bent down and swept the gasping princess—*no, queen*—onto Farain, settling her between his arms.

"Grip with your legs—tight. Good. Hold the fur with both hands. Don't let go."

She followed his instructions without a word.

"Now," he said, half his mind engaged in soothing the cat into accepting this extra and unaccustomed burden, "this would be a good time to use that incantation you're so fond of."

"I can't," she whispered back, fear making her voice tremble. "I only know how to hide myself for a few minutes."

He sighed. "Then hold on and pray that Ragat arrows find their target with more difficulty when a dagen's speed accompanies it."

He spun the cat around and dug his heels in.

///////////

MUMMY!

The thought went round and round in her head as Luka carried her through the dark. *I have to go back! I want my mummy!*

But she didn't say the words out loud, couldn't force them past her closed throat. Her head was empty and swollen at the same time, her cry for her mother rushing around inside it in an endless circle. When they reached the outdoors, Luka put her down, his hand heavy on her shoulder. Part of her was comforted by his grip—it was something solid and real in an unreal world. The other part wanted to shake it off, wanted to run back screaming into the tunnel, but when she looked over her shoulder, all she saw was a wall.

She stood, numb inside, barely hearing the questions Luka put to her until he gripped her mouth with firm fingers and she heard him, really heard him, for the first time.

"Silence."

She's dead. Mummy's dead.

She sobbed behind his fingers, tears spilling over even though she tried to hold them in.

She's dead. But you're not. And you mustn't cry. Not now.

She focused on trying to gulp air, on trying to breathe and think. Then she realized he meant for her to climb onto the back of the huge, slobbering cat. Her knees went weak and for a terrible second, she thought she would scream again.

You can't scream. You'll shame Grandmother and Mummy. Princesses shouldn't cry when others can see them.

So she scrambled up the back of the animal, nose wrinkling at the musty cat smell, and tried to grip the broad back with legs that felt spread to their limit.

"Where are we going?" she asked, holding tight as the cat moved beneath her like a boat rocking on water.

"To another hidden entrance, near the kitchens. We have to rejoin your father and find somewhere we can defend you and the prince."

Beneath them, the cat leaped forward, the force of his speed pushing Viella into Luka's torso. The wind tore away her yelp of surprise. In a flash they were galloping toward a knot of fighting men, Farain's screech vibrating at the core of her.

But something else vibrated too. Something wrenched at the heart of her, twisting her insides. She gasped, eyes watering, and yelled: "Stop! Luka, the Gate! The Gate!"

"What?"

An arrow slashed past her nose on a murderous slant. Still, she barely noticed it, seeing only the change in the Gate.

Slowly, ever so slowly, a pale glow had begun at the top of the arch. Like night edged with moonlight, the hovering ambience was growing, spreading beyond the apex.

"What is that?" Luka's murmur vibrated against her back.

Something bad . . . very bad. Viella opened her mouth, but what came out was "We have to go through it! Now!"

His strong arms tightened around her, and he bent forward, the engraving of the cat on his chest pressing cold into her. Shouts surrounded them, and more arrows pierced the air in whistling arcs.

"Viella, we can't . . ."

But the rising sense of urgency in her, the pain that twisted her stomach made her scream, "*No!* We have to go now! It will be too late if we don't. Please, Luka!"

The silvery light extended tentacles down the side of the arch and the walls; wriggling, twisting things that made bitter saliva rise in her mouth. Her mind started to whirl. *If I stay, I'll die, if I stay, I'll die, if I stay . . .*

The voice buried inside her became a roar, forcing its way up from her stomach to her throat with the strength of its truth.

"*Luka!*"

The cat changed direction suddenly. She started to slide off, but an arm was there, pulling her back against a hard, armored chest, and then they were at the Gate—*through* the Gate, the silvery glow intensifying with her pain for a horrible second—before she was free, the pain gone as suddenly as it had begun.

She twisted, the cat jolting her up and down. Behind them, silver tentacles touched the ground on either side of the Gate and the walls around it. Sparks rose. The sky above the court wavered before every light went out and she couldn't see the tops of the watchtowers. Or anything else, for that matter.

Valan and Daddy and Grandmother are still in there.

For the first time, it hit her that she was alone now. Alone except for Luka. *Mummy's dead.* The sorrow gripped her by the throat, made her eyes blur. She faced forward, seeing nothing before them but dark grassland and star-studded sky.

They rode for a long time, the cat moving so fast she felt slightly sick. Wind whipped her hair loose from its pins and flapped silk against her ankles. Her legs were sore, and Luka's harsh, irregular breath heated her neck. Once, the cat missed a step, and Luka grunted as though pained, but they kept going.

She was surprised when the cat began to slow, gamboling from left to right as it went. She held on as best she could, the tall grass scratching bare legs exposed by her wind-tossed skirts.

"Luka," she asked hesitantly, "could you make—Farain walk straight? I can't hang on right."

Silence. The wind rustled the grasses. In front of them, between the pricked-up ears of the beast, she saw the faint glow of Freetown in the distance.

"Luka?" She twisted to look up at him, frowning.

Farain came to a complete stop and bent his head, snuffing at the grass. The arms around Viella dropped away.

Without a sound, Luka slid off the back of the cat. Armor clanked as he hit the ground, starlight gilding the dark-slicked arrow that had gone straight through his right shoulder.

CHAPTER 3

TALON

MORDACH STEPPED OVER PRONE BODIES AND RED, STICKY POOLS of blood without looking down, his gaze focused on what was ahead of him. A distant din surrounded him: the clash of weapons, shouts and screams, the crash of falling furniture. A serving boy, clothes torn in patches, ran past him, eyes wild in his young face. Mordach spared him not a glance. He held a twisting quasiflame before him. The blue, yellow, and green smokelight wavered and leapt in an unceasing dance that exposed all that lay before him, even what was hidden behind solid stone.

It was the quasiflame that showed him the Ragat marauder before he stepped out from his hiding place in a shadowed corner outside the Royal Suite. Mordach stopped, glancing at the blood-edged sword in the man's hand as he pointed it at him. "Have you no sense? How many men do you think can summon a quasiflame?"

The marauder paused. The black cloth he wore covered every part of his body, except the blue eyes that studied the Spellsayer above the strip of cloth over his mouth. He stood just three-quarters the Spellsayer's height but carried himself straight as a pillar.

Mordach made an imperceptible but patient nod toward the dancing image in the palm of his hand—and the large ruby ring he wore on his third finger. The symbol of his office. Quick as a zandoli ground lizard, the marauder dropped down and touched his forehead to one knee, turning his sword so that it lay on the ground with its hilt toward Mordach.

"Forgive my mistake, Spellsayer," he said in a halting version of the speech of the grasslands. "Daguard fought hard for lord consort and prince. I am careful."

Mordach motioned the man to his feet. "You are what they call the Ambush, the leader of this force?"

The man bowed in answer.

"And have you captured the lord consort and Prince Valan?"

"Many lives were lost. But they are captured."

Mordach closed his hand, extinguishing the quasiflame. "Then your mistake is forgiven, Ambush. Take me to them."

Ambush opened the door of the queen's bedroom on a group of black-clad men that stood in a semi-circle before the lord consort and the prince. Their swords pointed toward where the prisoners sat on the floor, but neither prisoner looked up. The prince stared vacantly to his left, and the lord consort sat with his head bowed between his hands, rocking back and forth. Behind them, the bodies of several Daguard lay heaped in front of the bed and the spreading pool of blood and red-lined footprints on the once-clean floor made the air heavy with the smell of iron and offal.

Ambush made a chirping sound, and two of the guards slipped aside so that Mordach could step between them. One left the room, leaving the door open. Mordach looked at the lord consort, but Alain did not raise his head, so he knelt in front of the prince.

"Valan?" he murmured. The prince did not respond. Mordach raised his hand . . . then stood and spun, grabbing at what seemed to be empty air behind him. At his feet, Alain's body faded to nothing. Beneath his fingers, a solid arm appeared, rising to meet the shoulders, neck, and head of the lord consort. Eyes wild and furious beneath his disheveled hair, the lord consort brought a hand up, but the Spellsayer said two words and Alain was pulled backward, as though by an invisible rope, slamming into the wall across from the bed with a force that made the window frame shudder.

As Lord Alain moaned in pain, Mordach stared at him, disappointment plain on his face.

"Surely you did not think your talent at Illusion, skilled as you are, would be enough to blind me. These Ragat, perhaps, but not the Royal Spellsayer, Alain." He paused, and then said in a soft voice, "Not one who knows you as well as I."

Fury colored Alain's voice as he strained to say, "I no longer believe I ever knew you, nor you me."

"Nevertheless," Mordach replied, "though you may be able to use the power of the Word in this room, once you stepped into that doorway, the wards I've created would have prevented you from leaving without me."

Alain's chest heaved as he fought to catch his breath. "You want to be able to use magic in this room. Why?"

Instead of answering, Mordach touched three fingers to Valan's head. "Sleep," he said, the timbre of his voice making a nearby candle flicker. The boy slid bonelessly forward into his arms, and Mordach took him to the bed and laid him on the pillows.

"What have you done to him?" Lord Alain gasped. Veins stood out on his neck as though he struggled to move, but not one of his fingers so much as twitched.

"He's in shock, Alain. He requires rest. I want to make sure he gets it."

Lord Alain's laugh turned into a shout. "Rest! Rest you say, and his mother murdered in front of him. Will he wake rested enough to forget that, I wonder?"

Mordach froze. "What do you mean, his mother? What of Viella?"

Alain rolled his head back to look at Mordach, his teeth bared. "You bastard. You did this, didn't you? You brought them here."

"What of Viella?"

Alain's chest lifted and fell. "She lives."

Mordach grew still. Then he turned to the Ragat warriors

and pointed a finger at them, muttering one line in the Command tongue. They snapped to a rigid immobility.

"What are you doing?" Alain gasped.

"The princess must not leave the court."

Mordach raised his arms, palms up, as if in supplication, and all the candles in the room flickered. He closed his eyes and whispered in a swift tongue that sounded like the wind in the leaves of a tree. Then the wind *did* begin to blow, softly so that it blended with Mordach's words at first, but building until Mordach's whispering drowned beneath the roar of air that held the lord consort stiff against the window-frame.

The candlelight in the room flickered and danced, danced and flickered, and at the height of the din, every flame grew impossibly tall. Mordach shouted a word and darkness fell, harsh, smothering and silent as a choked-off scream.

⸻

PAIN SLICED THROUGH LUKA, AND HE BLINKED, DISORIENTED. *WHAT HAS happened? Where am I?* The sharp edges of his armor dug into him, but his right shoulder hurt the worst. It burned, the flame becoming hotter with each passing second. Somewhere, a child sobbed, but all he saw before him was darkness. With a grunt, he levered himself up with his left arm. An unspeakable grinding agony went through him.

"Luka!"

He turned his head and was almost knocked over by the princess. Her arms could not make it around his torso, but she squeezed tight anyway. He gasped. Looking down, he saw the tip of an arrow protruding from the gap between his arm and his breastplate. *Gaiea take them to Her Desert, it hurts.*

Viella was babbling something, and he cleared his throat to answer her. "What did you say?"

She looked up at him, and now that he was no longer lying

down, starlight made it easier for him to see the tears that had swollen her eyes and silvered her cheeks.

"I thought you were dead. I thought I was alone."

He forced a smile so that she would feel better. "It will take more than a Ragat arrow in the shoulder for you to be rid of me."

Her answering smile wavered, but he was glad to see it nevertheless. Farain's instinctual thoughts touched his mind, curiosity tinged with a desire to run. *We go nowhere until I get this thing out of me.*

"I need your help, Viella."

She nodded, still holding him tight. He gestured for her to stand, and when she did, he twisted until she could see the ties that held his armor together. Before he could say anything, she knelt and started working at the tight knots with small fingers. It took forever, it seemed, but finally the last tie fell loose, and she stood and helped him pull the breastplate free. He gasped when the edge of it touched the arrowhead protruding from the front of his shoulder, and dropped the treated wood to the hard ground with a crash as soon as it cleared his head.

"I must ask you . . . to do something . . . very hard." His breath came short with the pain that extended its reach as far as his head and as low as his groin.

"What?" Her soft question was almost lost beneath a rising gust of wind.

Luka raised his hand, grasped the arrow shaft, and before he could think about it, broke the head off with one snap. He dropped the deadly point, feeling fresh blood seeping down his arm.

"Get behind me . . . and pull the shaft out."

"Luka." Viella's eyes filled with tears. "I don't want to hurt you."

"It will hurt more if it stays in." He gritted his teeth, shivering as the wind swept through the sleeveless vest, cooling the sweat on his skin. "You can do it. Just . . . pull with all your strength. Don't stop. Until it's out."

Although he knew she must have been terrified, she didn't refuse him. He felt her gentle hand on his back and then a full minute of agony followed as she tugged and he leaned until the shaft came free. He rocked forward, blood flowing freely down his back and chest, and heard her hit the ground with a thump.

"Viella?"

"I'm all right." She knelt in front of him, her forehead creased with worry. "You're bleeding. Do you want a bandage?"

He raised his eyebrows. "You know how?"

"Dowager Mother does it for Valan all the time. Sometimes I help her." She extended her arms, the silk of her vest fluttering in the wind. "Tear it and I'll tie it on."

They managed it working together, with Viella pulling against him as he tugged at it, one-handed, until it ripped. She wrapped the silk around his shoulder, then helped him tie the end in a firm knot.

By the time he got to his feet, a strong wind had kicked up. Farain came closer, nuzzling his good arm, and Luka sensed his growing hunger. *This wound must be seen to, and we need assistance, shelter.*

He looked behind him toward the court—and froze. Beside him, Viella took his hand in her little fingers.

"In Gaiea's name," he gasped, staring at the absolute darkness where the High Court of Dun should have been. "What has happened?"

"I don't know. But it's getting bigger."

She spoke truth, he realized. From that distance, he saw the irregular edges of it, spreading like a slow-moving ink spill and swallowing the stars before it. A wind as cold as ice blew his hair back from his face and fluttered Viella's dress. Guiding Farain through the Gate instead of turning back to the court had not been a mistake. The part of him that had responded to the absolute terror and certainty in Viella's voice had made the right decision.

"Luka." He glanced down at her as she bit her lip nervously. "I think . . . I feel like it wants me, somehow."

He stared at the abomination, his jaw tight. "I have no doubt it does. It's that damn Spellsayer."

"Mordach?" Viella's eyes opened wide. "But he would never do something like that."

"I would not swear for him, if I were you, Prin—Your Majesty." Luka bent and picked her up one-handed. He ignored the pain in his shoulder and his own light-headedness as he settled her on the war cat. *How fast it is moving?*

Viella shook her head as he prepared to mount. "Mordach is our cousin. He loves us. He would never hurt us."

Luka swung himself up onto Farain and sent the cat a picture of their destination. He pulled Viella against him as the cat took off, then bent down to whisper into her ear so that the wind could not take his words away. "He is responsible for your mother's death, my queen. I saw it with my own eyes."

She said nothing, but he felt the tremble in her body and held her closer. "You have my word as a Daguard that you will come to no harm at his hands ever again. He will pay for your mother's murder."

She did not answer him, and they rode in silence. At some point, he felt her relax against him, and realized with astonishment that she slept. *She is a child, after all, and pushed to her limits this night. I must get her safe to someone who can hold against the Spellsayer and whatever he has conjured. Then I can return to the fight.*

Cradling her against him, Luka dug his heels into Farain and uttered a harsh cry. The cat leaped ahead, howling its freedom. Together, they raced away from the hungry, spreading darkness toward the comfort of Freetown's lamps, burning bright in unsuspecting homes.

VOICES WOKE VIELLA FROM HER SLEEP. SHE YAWNED, FEELING CHILLED, and tried to stretch, only to find her movements restricted by the iron band around her shoulders.

". . . comes to Seat of Talon this night?"

The voice was loud, and it came from high above her.

Viella blinked and craned her head backward to find the speaker, but all she saw was a massive sand-colored wall capped with large torches at regular intervals along its height. The flames wavered in the strong wind, sending the cloying smell of oil and smoke her way.

"A Pride Leader of the Daguard, and an emissary of Her Majesty, the queen, has urgent news for your lady."

A seat. We're at a seat. A mixture of relief and anxiety woke Viella fully. The certainty in Luka's voice vibrated through her body, and she waited in the silence that followed, afraid to breathe in case she disturbed the tug-of-war going on above her head. The cat shifted restlessly under her, pads silent on the cobblestone street, impatient to be moving. *They'll help. They have to.* Viella bit her lip and blinked to fight back tears that pricked behind her eyes. *I don't want to stay out here in the cold. Please.*

Without warning, the wall in front of them shimmered and fell away like a severed curtain, revealing closed bronze gates. They swung open with barely a creak, and Luka clicked his tongue at Farain. Moving with sinuous caution, the cat padded forward into the courtyard beyond.

Viella had a brief impression of fountains and many trees and shrubs, some flowering and filling the night air with their heavy perfume. The light from the torches did not penetrate the overhanging trees well, and she strained to see the three figures in the bright archway ahead. As the cat made its way down the stone path, the three figures solidified into the gold armor of two Dahomei standing on either side of a small woman wrapped in a pale-blue floor-length robe. These Dahomei wore skirts that ended just above their knees, like the court Dahomei did. Their helmets glistened like mellow suns.

It was the woman in the robe who spoke first, her voice as light and clear as struck crystal in the silent garden. "This is the emissary, Eleanor?"

"My Lady," the Dahomei on her right answered.

Farain whuffed and bared his teeth. Luka clicked his tongue at him and made a guttural sound. The woman stepped onto the path and waved a graceful arm. Viella saw her long blond hair curled against her breast and knew her instantly. Relief flooded her, and for the first time she felt safe.

"Come forward, boy; you have nothing to fear if you are who you claim to be."

"You are the daughter of Lady Sophia?" Luka asked as the cat started forward again.

"You may address me as Lady Gretchen. You bring a message from Lady Sophia, I assume, as she's at the High Court . . ." She stopped as the cat entered fully into the light and she saw Viella. She took a sharp breath, a line forming between her clear gray eyes.

"Princess." She bowed and made the sign of respect, fists clenched and pressed to her chest; the Dahomei followed her lead. When she straightened up, she spoke quickly. "My apologies, Your Highness, but I fear I must dispense with protocol. Daguard, speak your piece."

"I am Luka Freehold, Pride Leader of the Daguard, and personal bodyguard of the Princess Viella. We are in need of shelter and aid. The High Court has been attacked by Ragat marauders and Queen Elise has been murdered."

"What did you say?" The Dahomei glanced at each other, and Viella saw the lady grasp the folds of her skirts tightly. "The Queen is dead? There are Ragat in Dun? How? How did they get here?"

"I do not know, but I believe they had help within the court," Luka replied, his voice grim.

Lady Gretchen gestured to one of the Dahomei. "Take the cat

to the stables, Annan. Tell the captains to meet me in my quarters for instructions. When you are finished, join me there as well. Princess, Daguard,"—she gestured to Luka—"come with me."

⁄⁄⁄⁄⁄⁄⁄⁄⁄⁄⁄⁄

LUKA FLINCHED AS LADY GRETCHEN PRESSED A PALM TO HIS SHOULDER. She looked at him, eyes narrowing. "I hurt you?"

"My Lady, perhaps it would be better if your healer saw to me later." *There's no time to waste on me.* When he had first reached Freetown, a look over his shoulder showed the darkness had not moved much. The winding streets and houses had hidden the court from view since then. But all his instincts told him the darkness would continue to disperse.

To come for them. For *her.*

"My healer tends to another this night. Your wound cannot wait." She sat next to him on the small yellow sofa, her knee touching his for a second.

Luka fought the urge to pull away as she tugged at the make-shift silk bandage. He had not thought the lady herself would try to tend to him. It made him uncomfortable. "My *news* cannot wait."

"You may speak as I examine you."

Don't be fool enough to refuse a lady's generosity. He averted his eyes and began speaking, looking everywhere but at Lady Gretchen. The room they had retired to was small and sparsely furnished. The cream floor was painted with tiny white flowers and a fluted pillar stood in the middle.

Two mounds of tasseled green cushions decorated with yellow and silver flowers were placed invitingly on the floor on either side of him. Viella had chosen the pile to his left to rest on. It was not far from a small glass door.

Lady Gretchen had stopped touching him, but now she chanted soft words, a frown on her face as she concentrated, and the air around her fingers wavered a little, like a heatwave above the grasslands on a hot day. His shoulder felt numb for a moment, then the pain returned, like teeth digging into his flesh. His voice faltered then, but he recovered and continued.

Across from him, the Dahomei called Annan appeared in the doorway. Behind her was the one called Eleanor, clearly the Lance to Lady Sophia, or the captain of the Seat's Guard. She took up a position near a wooden desk to the right of the doors. The only things on it were a feathered pen and a glinting black rectangle the size of his hand. It looked ancient but well cared for despite its tarnish. Probably an ocular, he realized, one of the magical relics that could send messages over long distances. Every seat and court had at least one.

Luka finished his story. Lady Gretchen made a sound in her throat, her lips tight with anger.

"The invaders cast a glamour over the court to confound rescuers." With a sigh, she lifted her hand. "The arrow that caused this wound was darkened. Its filth blocks my magic."

"My injury can wait," he insisted once more.

"Not for long." She gestured to Eleanor without looking. "Bring my unguents."

"My Lady." The Dahomei strode out and Luka caught a glimpse of shorn red hair under the back of her gold helmet. Annan took up Eleanor's vacated position.

Lady Gretchen leaned back against the arm of the sofa, her gray eyes direct and unwavering. "You say you saw my mother fall?"

"I cannot be certain of her fate, but she was attacked."

"All of them," she whispered, fingers twisting in the sash of her silk robe. "All of them trapped in the High Court."

All Luka could think was his prince, his father, his Daguards, even the Dowager Mother were trapped in the court while he sat safe elsewhere. He gripped the arm of the sofa. *How could this have happened? How could Mordach have betrayed the queen?* "My Lady, you are certain you did not hear the Horn?"

"Certain." She shook her head. "There was no call to arms. Nothing strange occurred in Freetown before your arrival. That must have been the purpose of the glamour."

"But you understand our situation?"

Lady Gretchen's face, already unusually pale for one with royal blood, looked almost bloodless, her cheeks stretched tight over high cheekbones. "The princess is now the queen, the High Court is overrun with Ragat marauders, and my mother likely sups with Queen Elise in Gaiea's Garden this night. I comprehend the situation all too well, Daguard."

Luka nodded, impatient. "My Lady, the Royal Spellsayer is to blame for this treachery."

The lady raised her eyebrows. "You are fearless to accuse Mordach so, to a lady who knows him well, no less."

"I speak only of what I have seen." Luka lowered his voice. Few realized it, but Viella had very good hearing and he did not want her to revisit the worst of that night's terrors. "The boy that compelled the prin—queen—he had no weapon when he began his dance. Yet moments before the spear was thrown, I saw a shimmer behind him, the mark of a glamour lifted for a moment. A hand appeared and handed him that spear. I recognized the ring on its third finger—it was the Spellsayer's ruby, his mark of office."

Lady Gretchen did not explode into anger at his accusation, as he had expected. She rose from the sofa in a swirl of sky-colored silk and strode to the stained-glass window behind the sofa. Luka turned to follow her progress, pain lancing along his arm from his shoulder.

"My Lady, the Gate was constructed to keep out those with the intent to harm. Only members of the High Court should have been able to enter with weapons. How else could anyone have evaded it?"

She stood with her back to the room, hands clasped behind her. "You make a convincing witness, Daguard. Even if superior magic was used against the court, he could have used his ocular to summon help."

The bastard wished no help. "Ragat has no magic. Who knew the defenses of the court well enough to smuggle in at least five Palms of Ragat warriors? Who could have darkened the weapons the Ragat used so that they killed Dahomei so easily?"

"Who could have darkened a spear enough to kill the Divine Hand of Gaiea?" Gretchen murmured.

"My Lady?"

She turned to face him, her pale face as smooth and expressionless as marble.

"As Gaiea's divine Hand, Queen Elise carried Gaiea's Blessing and protection, but her magics were vulnerable to dark materials. The silver that abounds in the earth of Kadoomun. The opals from the caves of Jaleel. The spells of the *Nightward*." She closed her gray eyes and shook her head as she whispered in a fierce voice, "We were all fools. We knew he was ambitious, but Elise trusted him—my mother trusted him."

Luka frowned, feeling fresh blood beginning to seep from beneath his bandage and drip down his arm. He wiped at it, cleaning his hands on his undershirt.

Lady Gretchen opened her eyes. "The queen cannot be hurt with weapons forged by the hands of women. But a man—a special man with the magic of the Sight, smelting dark materials and speaking the *Nightward* over them—that's another thing entirely."

"*Nightward*! That's the name of the book."

Luka swung around. Viella sat up straight on the cushions, her brow furrowed as though she fought to remember something.

Lady Gretchen spoke in a gentle voice. "To what book do you refer, Your Majesty?"

"The one Valan was reading." Viella spoke quickly, as though she did not enjoy being the sudden focus of attention. "He's always reading this big book in Mordach's study. I saw the name on it today. It's called *Nightward*."

The doors creaked open to admit Eleanor, a red silk purse in her hands. Several other women, some still pulling on their flashing armor, followed her in. Swiftly, Lady Gretchen gave them instructions to prepare to ride to the High Court, a fact Luka was only dimly aware of as he reached for his shoulder to try to stop a fresh trickle of blood. The moment his fingers touched his flesh, the pain that gripped him made him drop his hands. When he looked up, the women had all departed again, except for Eleanor and Annan.

"Gaiea's breath," Lady Gretchen said to herself. "This is far worse than I thought if he's opened it."

"I don't understand," Luka said.

"Lady Gretchen believes you," Viella said softly, wiping at her eyes. "She thinks Mordach . . . hurt Mummy."

"I'm afraid so, Your Majesty. The Introduction of the Heir is the most important event to occur around the future queen's tenth birthday. But an even more important event occurs before that."

Striding forward, Lady Gretchen took the purse from Eleanor. "The Handing-Over is carried out a year before the Ceremony. Only the queen, three trusted ladies, and the Royal Spellsayer will be witness to it."

She sat next to Luka. "At the Handing-Over, the Royal Spellsayer receives the final implements of her office, the queen blesses her ring, and she is given the *Nightward* to hold against the darkening of Gaiea's light. After that, it is official."

"What is?" Luka asked.

A pungent smell of sweetgrass filled the air as Lady Gretchen opened the purse and removed a pair of scissors and a small tin. She bent and snipped away all of the drenched silk of Luka's dressing, revealing a ragged hole in his shoulder. He watched in dismay as the bloody rags fell on the clean sofa. Hot lines traced themselves down his arm and up his neck, but he did not move.

"The line of succession. If the queen should die before the heir is of age, then the Royal Spellsayer acts as regent." She opened the tin and removed a greenish paste. Luka looked away rather than watch the application.

"The Spellsayer has to be of royal lineage, with mastery of both Sight and Word. She is the perfect regent to avoid bickering amongst the sister queens and ladies, the most trusted official in the court—and the most powerful besides the queen and the future heir. My mother was expected to be Spellsayer, but Queen Elise appointed Mordach, no doubt in part to further her ideas about unity."

There was no mistaking the underlying bitterness to Lady Gretchen's words. Luka drew in a pained breath as her fingers dabbed. Resentment flooded him, the same resentment that had fueled his choice to live the life of a soldier instead of finding a wife to settle down with. *Ladies such as her think us out of our depth in important positions. As if we attain them so easily, and without competence.*

Still, he did not serve her. He served the memory of his dead Queen—and her living daughter. Nothing mattered except getting the queen safe and returning to the court with enough help to purge the Ragat and the cursed Spellsayer.

"Lift your arm for me."

Luka gasped as she started to wind a tight bandage around his shoulder.

"Valan was the last piece of the puzzle," she continued, twisting cloth with salve-shined fingers. "Mordach is an Unbound, with great power. He could exploit the connection between the twins to compel Viella to go to the dancing boy. Nothing else could enspell a High Queen. He would be rid of both his most formidable barriers in one treacherous move." She tied the bandage with a hard tug and rocked back on her knees to study her handiwork.

"The salve will take a few hours to cleanse the darkening. Once the sweetgrass has done its work, I'll try the healing again."

Luka rose to his feet and pressed his aching arm to his chest before bowing. "I'm in your debt, Lady."

Rising to her feet, Lady Gretchen handed Eleanor the purse. "It is the Queendom of Dun that stands in your debt, Pride

Leader Freehold. As it is, the events of tonight can only lead to open war, with the Ragat and with others."

"Others?" Luka moved his arm experimentally. He had freedom of movement, despite the pain that made him clench his teeth.

Lady Gretchen's words were sharp. "The Ragat attacked the court. Mordach has clearly conspired with other men, and those in Ragat, to kill our High Queen and advance the cause of the barbarous marauders. All those involved must be punished."

Her eyes bright with emotion, Lady Gretchen all but ground the last words between her teeth. Luka forced himself to stay silent, aware it was not his place to speak. Her logic was undeniable. Still, he could not imagine it was more than a few traitors and Ragat marauders who had planned and executed the attack with the help of the Spellsayer.

Queen Elise had been beloved by all; it was one of the reasons she'd been able to advance the most progressive Civil Codes anyone had ever seen. Viella was the darling of the courts of Gailand. There would be war, yes, but surely only with the Ragat and the Spellsayer until the High Court could be retaken. *Just let me ride with the Dahomei, and I'll be glad to rid the court of every traitor I can find.*

"The ladies of the courts of Gailand will not stand for this, regardless of the fates of their queens. Many will die if the Spellsayer wields the *Nightward* against us, but we have no choice. He cannot be allowed to seize the throne. Gailand must not return to the Chaos of old."

Chaos of old? Luka frowned, but before he could ask a question, the lady drew in a breath. "Of course . . . I have been a fool." Her gaze focused on him. "You say the High Court was covered by blackness as you made your escape?"

"It was as though it had been swallowed by a starless night."

"Swallowed." Lady Gretchen's eyes narrowed. "I fear you may be more right than you know, Daguard. I must see this glamour for myself."

VIELLA CLIMBED THE NARROW STAIRS TO THE BATTLEMENTS WITH LUKA in front of her and one of the Dahomei behind her. She knew Lady Gretchen was somewhere ahead with the other Dahomei, but she could not see around Luka's armor-clad thighs.

The rough stone hurt her feet through the thin slippers she wore, and sometimes a chill draft went through her robe, forcing her to hold it closer to her body. After a few minutes, an open archway appeared above her with the night sky sparkling beyond. She stepped out onto a narrow walk that ran all the way around the top of the seat's wall.

Lady Gretchen stood a few feet from a pillar that held a massive bowl as tall as Viella herself. Fire crackled and roared in it. Viella joined Lady Gretchen with Luka on her right and the guard on her left. None of them made a sound as they stared into the distance, and Viella had an idea what they were looking at. Steeling herself against the sight she had already witnessed, she stepped to the wall and stood on tiptoe. She still could not manage to smother the gasp that immediately rose to her lips.

What had only been an inkblot before had grown into a massive, solid nothingness. Not only had the High Court disappeared, but most of the grassland between it and Freetown as well. The horizon before them was completely dark. Tentacles so black they made the blackness of the night seem pale by comparison snaked along the sky and crawled across the land. Heart beating hard, Viella grabbed Luka's arm, causing him to glance down at her.

"Viella?"

Behind her, she heard a low voice she recognized as Eleanor's. "This changes things greatly, My Lady."

"Indeed, it does." Lady Gretchen made no attempt to hide her grim tone.

Viella could not speak. At that moment, one of the ropy lengths of darkness lifted away from the ground and swung a bulbous head in her direction. Her throat dried, and a cold, silvery feeling flowed through her veins. A nameless compulsion made her want to throw herself, screaming, against the wall. Instead, she hid her face against Luka's arm, the smell of blood and sweetgrass somehow keeping her anchored. *But it saw me, and it will eat me. I know it will.*

Luka shook his arm slightly. "Are you all right?"

"I don't want to see any more," she answered, still not looking up. The cold feeling was beginning to fill her stomach now, and she felt ill. She sensed someone kneel next to her.

"Your Majesty, you must be brave."

She twisted her head. Lady Gretchen's clear-eyed gaze met hers. "It's hurting me."

For the first time, the lady touched her, smoothing her hair from her forehead. Then she let her hand rest on Viella's brow. A smell like the land on a summer's day surrounded her, and her eyes slid closed.

Inside Viella, the cold melted. Warmth pushed it away like the sun's rays on a chilly morning. With it came a memory of her mother's smile, the smell of her perfume as she hugged Viella. *I want Mummy.* She felt tears start to trail down her cheeks.

"It is the *Nightward*." The hand lifted away from Viella's forehead, and a sudden draft cooled the skin there. "And it comes for her."

"Comes for her?" Luka repeated.

Viella opened her eyes as Lady Gretchen rose to her feet, the wind snapping blue silk around her ankles. *She knows. She knows it saw me.*

"Daguard, the queen must not stay here. The darkness will soon reach Freetown. Once it arrives, it will seek out the queen— and we will not be able to stop it."

Viella saw a pulse ticking in the side of Luka's jaw. "But My Lady, I brought her here because she would be safe with you."

"And she should have been. Every Dahomei learns their

trade at Seat Talon. We have magic far beyond all but the Augurs and Seers. That is why I can tell you, she is not safe here, so close to a danger we have not seen in many ages. The queen must leave Freetown immediately."

Go out there again? But it's dark, and I . . . I . . . Viella wiped her tears and clung even tighter to Luka's hand. "I don't want to go. I want to stay here."

Lady Gretchen sighed. Her gaze sought out the space beyond Viella's head, but Viella did not turn, unwilling to face that sight again. *It might hurt me worse this time.*

"I would keep you here if I could, but we can no longer afford the comfort of what we want. You must go with our Lance, Eleanor Delacourt. Only the Dahomei have magic that can help protect the queen against this." The Dahomei appeared at the lady's right hand as if called. "Eleanor, take a Palm of Dahomei and ride with the queen to the Seat of Garth. You must cross the River Lethe before the darkness arrives."

Ride with me where? A suspicion started to form in Viella's mind as Luka tugged his arm from Viella's grasp, lowered his head, and crossed his arms. "My Lady, if you would allow it, I would join your forces here and help keep this creature at bay until the queen has passed out of its grasp."

"Your request does you great honor, Daguard. We need every Dahomei and soldier we can get. Eleanor will assign you to a post before her departure."

Lady Gretchen started toward the stairs with Luka in tow. That was when suspicion became a certainty in Viella's mind.

"Wait!"

All heads turned toward her. The lady had a patient expression on her face that reminded Viella of how Lady Sophia looked every time she fussed during her lessons.

"I'm sorry, Your Majesty, but there is no time to waste. You must leave—"

"Not without Luka."

"What?" He took a step toward her, his lips a thin line in the flickering light. "Your Majesty, I'm needed here."

She shook her head, stricken. "*I* need you. I want to stay with you."

"You can't," Luka whispered. "You must go with the Dahomei or risk dying."

Viella could feel everyone's disapproval, and the tears wanted to start again, but then she remembered who she was, and what was coming, and the certainty deep inside her raised its voice.

"You must come."

"That would not be best."

"Why?" Viella looked directly at Lady Gretchen. "He's my bodyguard."

"You'll have the Dahomei and my Lance, my right hand, with you. They'll know how to keep you safe."

The lady's voice had a coaxing quality to it Viella didn't like. She folded her arms. "Luka keeps me safe."

"Your Majesty, he's a Daguard. His skills are no match for the magic that hunts you."

"He's *my* bodyguard and he saved me." She looked at Luka, pleading with her eyes. "If you hadn't called me from the dancing boy, I would have died. I know it."

"Your Majesty?" Luka looked confused and exasperated. "I don't understand. I never called you."

Viella frowned but didn't allow his denial to distract her from her goal. "I don't know any of your Dahomei. I'm not going without Luka."

Luka's gaze darted from Lady Gretchen to her, and she could sense his dismay. "Your Majesty, you promised to do what I say tonight."

"You said you wouldn't let Mordach hurt me again. How can you do that if you're far away?" Viella lifted her chin and tried to look like she wasn't shaking inside.

"She has a point," Lady Gretchen said.

Luka shook his head. "My Lady, I can do more here."

"She is your queen." Lady Gretchen's gaze slid over Viella. "And her request is not unreasonable. If your presence will make her more comfortable on her journey, then it is best you go."

Luka flicked his arm toward the wall. "And the High Court? What of them?"

"We will free the court with or without you—but not before the queen is safely away. Our mission to retake the High Court cannot succeed so long as the queen is in danger."

"She has seen much this night. She asks for this because she is afraid, not because it is what's best."

Lady Gretchen shrugged. "Whatever eases her mind is what's best for our queen. You are young. Perhaps you do not yet understand that you serve her, not yourself."

Without another word, Lady Gretchen went down the stairs, the Dahomei trailing behind her. Luka stood looking after her, his hands stiff at his sides.

He's angry. Part of Viella was sorry, but the other part was just glad she had got her way. She couldn't be separated from Luka just now, that she knew for sure.

〽〽〽〽

LADY GRETCHEN'S WORDS BURNED IN LUKA'S MIND AS HE TOOK THE stairs as quickly as he could with the queen in tow. *My father and comrades trapped in that—Dark, dying to save our queen, and I must leave the fight to others.*

He asked Gaiea for the strength to hold his tongue. He had an idea Lady Gretchen suspected some of the thoughts that had raced through his mind in the moments after her pronouncement.

You should never have let Viella come to the wall with Lady Gretchen. It had scared her. Perhaps that was why she had lied. *Called her indeed. I had no time to speak.* He could barely remember his own thoughts, it had been so chaotic. But he remembered the violence and the blood and the screams and the clash of arms. No doubt Viella did as well.

He strode across the pink-tiled lobby that led back to the main hallways and the lady's receiving room. Behind him, he felt Viella stumble and tug on his arm. The movement made pain lance through his right shoulder.

"Luka, wait, I—"

He stopped and looked down at her.

Viella's eyes brimmed with tears. "I can't walk so fast."

"We must hurry, so unfortunately, you'll have to try."

But he took her hand and slowed his steps a little.

The receiving room was empty when he entered, the small glass door at the back of the room open on the garden beyond. He caught a glimpse of a moving shape and went to the doorway.

Lady Gretchen stood next to a small white fountain shaped like the clamshells Luka saw on his visits to the coast. In her hand was the metal rectangle he'd seen on the desk. A billowing image rose from it now, forming a turquoise-edged oval that floated above the ocular's blue-lit surface.

A face shimmered within the oval's brilliance. But before he could see its features, the lady passed a hand over the image and the face collapsed. The ocular glowed blue a moment longer before the light died and the lady lowered her arm.

She walked across the grass toward them, her skin almost translucent in the light from the doorway. "I have spoken to the Spellsayer of Garth. That seat has the largest contingent of Dahomei after my own, and their Spellsayer is powerful. They can protect the queen. Lady Mai will expect you tomorrow evening. Eleanor has already gone to rouse a Palm, and Annan will see to your provisions. I will leave you now. I must visit our library and prepare spells we can use against the Dark."

"My Lady, I appreciate all you have done for us, but I would make a suggestion, if you would hear it."

She studied him for a moment. "Speak."

"We do not require a Palm of Dahomei."

Lady Gretchen shook her head. "The queen must have the best protection I can give."

"But she requires speed most of all. The portal to the seat of Garth is less than a day's ride. A Palm will be too slow to leave. If the mission is to get her to Garth as soon as possible, the fewer riders we have, the more speed we can muster. If you fear your Dahomei cannot stand against what approaches, what value is there to adding numbers that would only slow us down?"

Lady Gretchen studied him, her lips a thin line. Then she stepped past him and headed to the table. "What do you suggest, Daguard?"

"Let the queen go with me and one of your Dahomei, someone who knows Seat Garth well. We should not have to stop along the way, but if we do, a mother and father traveling with their child will bring less attention than a Palm traveling with their queen. Once we reach the Portal, pursuit will not be possible without the proper *geis*."

Lady Gretchen placed the ocular on the table. "You speak sense," she said, her tone polite—and grudging. "I must make a request of the queen." She turned and focused her attention on Viella. "Your Majesty, you must leave your bracelets behind."

Viella gasped. "But I'm not supposed to take them off."

"I know what you've been taught, Your Majesty, and there's no time to make matters clearer." Lady Gretchen sighed. "If things had run their normal course, Queen Elise would have explained all to you. But we have little time now. And it is essential that your bracelets do not cross the River Lethe with you. A Spellsayer would be able to track you easily through them, as their magic is unique and powerful."

Luka frowned. "But they are the mark of her office . . ."

"Be assured, Daguard," Gretchen said firmly, "this is not a

matter for *your* concern." She turned her attention back to the queen. "Please, your Majesty."

Viella hesitated, looking from Lady Gretchen to Luka. Then, she slowly nodded.

Well, at least we won't have to explain them to anyone we encounter. He took a deep breath, aware that what he was about to say would not be entertained easily. "I have another request."

"So many," Lady Gretchen said with a sardonic raise of her eyebrows. "Go on."

"I want it understood that I will lead this mission and the queen will remain with me. If I am to be her bodyguard, so be it. The queendom is in turmoil. She cannot be entrusted to anyone outside of this seat."

Lady Gretchen studied him, her gray eyes glinting like metal. "My Dahomei outrank you, Daguard. You ask too hard a thing."

"No." Viella drew closer to Luka's side, her cold fingers squeezing his. "I want him. Nobody else."

Lady Gretchen gave her an impatient look. "Your Majesty, he's but a Daguard and a soldier. No man may be solely responsible for your safety, particularly not now the court is under attack."

Viella raised her chin. "I trust him."

"My Queen—"

"You said I could have whatever made me feel comfortable."

Lady Gretchen's expression smoothed subtly as she pressed her lips together.

It's not so easy when you're the one being commanded, is it? Luka thought with a certain vicious satisfaction.

Lady Gretchen sighed and folded her arms. "Very well. The Queen will be your responsibility. You will have sole charge of her. However, my Dahomei will decide all other matters."

Reined in like an ordinary soldier. Luka covered his dislike of the new arrangement with the appropriate bow. "Of course, My Lady."

A knock on the door interrupted them.

"Enter," Lady Gretchen called.

A young boy, clad only in trousers and a blue skullcap, with a tousled, sleepy look about him, entered and bowed.

"My Lady, we are ready."

"Good." She waved a hand at the child. "Go with the boy. I've made arrangements to have the queen outfitted with warmer attire."

"Perhaps your boy can direct me to where I might find something to replace my own clothing?" Luka suggested.

"Ulen, see to the Daguard's needs, then take him to the stables. The others will wait for him there."

Viella held out her hands. "Will you take my bracelets now?"

Lady Gretchen shook her head. "Your Majesty, the bracelets are a symbol of your position. Only the Spirit wears them. Only the Spirit can remove them."

Viella studied the golden gleam of the plain circlets. Without another word, she tugged them down over her wrists. Handing them to Lady Gretchen, she balanced herself with a hand on Luka's leg and pulled at the gold on her ankles. They slid off with surprising ease, Luka thought. In the Lady's hands, the twenty-four bracelets and anklets seemed much smaller. *Made for a child. And a child she was—until tonight.*

In a small voice, Viella said, "Thank you for your help, Lady Gretchen."

"It is my duty, Your Majesty." Lady Gretchen inclined her head to the queen. "You don't need to thank me. I will keep these safe until you are ready to claim them, and your throne, again. I pray to Gaiea it will be but a short while, but as long as the women of Talon hold this seat, you will have a friend in Free-town."

CHAPTER 4

MAIDENS

WHEN VIELLA ESCAPED THE SUFFOCATING CONFINES OF THE dressing room, she was wearing soft burskin trousers and a matching wrap over her vest. She followed one of the servants through hallways much narrower than the High Court's. Her hands and ankles felt oddly light without her bracelets. She wondered where everything she wore had come from. *I haven't seen any other girls.*

She wouldn't have minded talking to someone her own age. All the adults around her kept arguing over who got to tell her what to do. It was tiring.

The blue-capped boy in front of her pushed at a tall golden door and, face scrunched with the effort, held it open while Viella passed through. Outside, the courtyard blazed with light as Dahomei and servants rushed past, stopping only to bow hurriedly as she drew near. The servant threaded his way through them, looking back often to make sure Viella did not stray.

The night air felt colder on Viella's face, even though her new clothes kept her warm. A stiff wind blew now, wrapping trousers and cloaks around the legs of hurrying servants and Dahomei. Ahead of her, the horses in their stables were stamping, snorting, and kicking up a fuss like cats did when they sensed one of the grassland storms approaching.

A black-and-white horse stuck a long head over its gate and whinnied at her. She rarely got to enjoy horses—except for Town Days, when the royal family went to Freetown for some event or another and there were parades in their honor. Her mother had explained to her once that horses and war cats didn't like each other, and so it wasn't fair to the horses to be around cats. It made them very upset. The cats at the High Court were therefore kept far from the stables, and most of the Dahomei's horses were kept at Seat Talon.

Forgetting the servant, Viella walked up to the horse and stood looking into its soft brown eyes. "Hello," she said. "You're pretty. Do you have a name?"

"Your Majesty." A frown creased the servant's forehead as he spoke. "Please. She's waiting, and she doesn't like to wait."

Who? Viella wanted to ask, but she had an idea questions would not get her very far, so she patted the horse on the nose and continued down the faded brown stone path that fronted the stables. The path ended in a much smaller courtyard, laid with a mosaic of colorful stones in a circular pattern. Small wooden buildings stood on either side of the yard; the double doors were open on the one to her right. Three horses waited as several stable hands scurried about, loading provisions and carrying tackle to and fro.

A tall woman with orange-red hair cut close to her skull shouted orders in a tone and volume that made Viella want to put her hand over her ears. The woman wore riding clothes, dark brown in color. Her vest left her muscled arms bare in the twisting glow of torches. She turned as the servant boy stopped behind her, and even from a distance Viella felt the intensity of the woman's hazel gaze. It was the Dahomei Eleanor, Lady Gretchen's Lance.

"You're late," she said.

The servant bowed. "My apologies, but the queen had to be fed, and bathed, and—"

Eleanor waved an impatient hand. "No matter. You've done your duty. Leave us."

Viella thought she sensed the servant's relief as he rushed past her. In fact, she almost wished she could go with him. She stood, uncertain what to do next. Eleanor looked her over and Viella had time to notice the freckles that dusted the pale-brown skin of her broad nose and high cheekbones. Eleanor brought her fists up to her chest and bowed.

"Your Majesty." She lifted her head, her gaze watchful.

Viella tried to think of something to say, but could only come up with "You're coming with us?"

Without looking away, Eleanor reached out and grabbed a boy rushing past behind her by the collar of his shirt. "That's the wrong bit for Flor. The third one from the door, on the right."

"Yes, ma'am." The boy tried to bow. Eleanor released him and he went back the way he had come.

"Yes, your Majesty," she continued. "I will be your guide. Have you ever ridden a horse before?"

Viella nodded. "When we went to visit Queen Salene last summer. She has great black horses they let me ride every day."

"Good."

The Dahomei turned back to the horses and started to inspect them, one by one. Viella stood, biting her lip. *What do I do now?*

When Eleanor reached the second horse, a small brown one with a white stripe down his nose, she muttered. "This isn't tight enough."

"What are you doing?"

Viella spun. Luka stood behind her, a cloth bag flung over his shoulder. He wore a white shirt with a dark blue rough-cloth coat and trousers. The kind of ordinary attire she'd seen servants dress in when they were sent on errands.

Eleanor straightened and gave him the benefit of her un-smiling gaze. "I'm checking the queen's horse."

"The queen doesn't have a horse." Luka took Viella by the hand and led her forward. Instantly, Viella felt safe again. "She rides with me."

"Protocol dictates—"

"Protocol has no place here," Luka interrupted. Viella looked from one to the other, sensing a confusing tension. "We are a family, remember?"

The Dahomei said nothing for a moment, then called, "Oliver!"

"Ma'am?"

"Take Peace back to the stables."

"Yes, ma'am."

Eleanor turned and vaulted onto the back of a midnight-black mare with an ease that left Viella breathless. *I want to do that!* A stable hand ran up and fastened a bag to the saddle.

"He's yours." Eleanor nodded at a dark-brown gelding that pawed the courtyard with impatient hooves. "His name's Roland. Try not to upset him. Horses don't take to cat-lovers too kindly."

"And what of my cat? Farain?" Luka's voice was sharp.

"On the other side of the court, of course, where we have a separate stable. He'll be well taken care of until you return for him." She raised an eyebrow at him. "Surely you didn't expect otherwise? Only Daguard ride such beasts, and we are but a simple farming family." With a soft word to Flor, she moved off.

Luka watched her go, silent.

"I don't think she likes you," Viella said.

Luka didn't answer. Instead, he guided her over to the gelding and fastened his bag to the saddle. Roland brought his head around and snorted at her. Before she could touch his nose, Luka's strong hands had lifted her onto the saddle, then settled himself behind her.

Roland set off across the courtyard and Viella held tight to the pommel, leaning back against Luka's chest and into the circle of warmth his arms created.

Eleanor waited for them at the closed main gates. With her was Lady Gretchen, dressed in the armor of a Dahomei. Her hair had been twisted into a thick braid that circled her head, and she carried a helmet under one arm. Viella thought she looked small standing next to the horse. She had the kind of look on her face that Luka wore every time Viella secretly watched him in the gayelle, at combat practice.

As they drew level with Eleanor, Lady Gretchen walked over and held Roland's reins. She lowered her voice, but Viella heard what she said anyway.

"My guardswomen tell me the darkness has reached the outskirts of town. It will be at the seat shortly."

The hairs on Viella's arms rose.

"Eleanor will take the fastest route across town. Do not stop before you cross the river. Gaiea's Blessing is upon it. The darkness cannot follow you over it. That should give you time. Put as much distance as you can between the High Court and yourselves. The greater the distance, the harder it will be for Mordach to track you."

Lady Gretchen turned and signaled to the wall. Once again, Viella watched as solid stone faded away. Wind blasted through the aperture, making her squint against its force. *It's cold. So cold.*

Lady Gretchen stepped back, a few loose strands of hair blowing across her face. "Ride, Queen." She raised her voice over the howling of the wind. "Be safe."

"Gaiea be with you, My Lady," Luka said, his chest vibrating against her back.

Beside them, Eleanor said, "Hold the seat, My Lady. We will return with help."

Lady Gretchen stared at Viella but spoke to her guardians. "Think only of the queen. If the Seat of Talon falls, I free you of your allegiance, Eleanor. You may give your loyalty to another seat and fight in the coming war."

Viella's mouth fell open, but Eleanor said nothing, only nodded once. Luka sounded shocked. "My Lady, the seat cannot fall. We will come back—"

Eleanor's mount shot through the gates, turning left, its hooves clattering on the cobblestones.

Lady Gretchen slapped Roland's flank. Viella was pushed back into Luka's chest as Roland took off, his breath misting the air in front of him. The wind pushed all the warmth out of the circle she sat in.

"Why is it so cold?" she cried.

Luka guided the horse around the smooth curve of the court's wall. He bent down to whisper, his breath warming her chilled ear. "The *Nightward* must cause it. I have never felt the night be this cold."

"But why?"

Luka's voice was stern and matter of fact. "Such things are not taught to Daguard. I think, Your Majesty, the lady might know, but she has more pressing things on her mind."

Houses rushed past Viella on both sides of the street. Tall and short, broad and narrow, their domed roofs stood out against the star-strewn night sky. Lamps shone out of most front windows, a welcome light to lost or traveling strangers. To Viella, it was as though an eye peeked out from every home, watching her speed past.

A stiff breeze tore at her wrap, curled chill fingers over the hands that gripped the pommel. Viella squinted, doing her best to avoid Roland's wind-whipped mane. Ahead, Eleanor rode low over her horse's neck. Flor's tail streamed out behind her like a banner. The sharp sound of the hooves drumming on the cobblestones bounced off Viella's ears.

The streets curved through Freetown, sometimes sharply, sometimes with a gentle bend. Several times, Viella saw more lights flare to life in houses as they went past. Once, a silhouette appeared in a doorway. *We're waking up the town.* She wondered if they would talk in the morning about what they'd heard and seen. If they would find out at that same moment what had happened that night.

You can't think about that now. She swallowed, trying not to dwell on how tired she felt, how hungry she still was, and how her legs ached from being spread wide.

Roland made a sharp right turn, and the houses were not

jammed so close together anymore. They had little paddocks, pens and even a barn between them.

"How much longer?" she shouted.

Luka spoke into her ear. "Not long."

Sighing, Viella hung on.

⁂

LADY GRETCHEN WATCHED FROM THE WALL AS DARKNESS ATE THE TOWN. Slipping, twisting, crawling, the tentacles pulled themselves along rooftops, encircled houses, and snaked up walls. In the sky above, the entity waved like so many slow-moving pennants. Streams of it flowed down onto the streets and homes like oil, swallowing whatever it touched with a speed and focus it had not shown crossing the grassland.

"My Lady," Annan said, "what will happen to the townspeople?"

"They will sleep," she replied. "In this form, the Dark only searches. What it wants, it will take. The rest, it leaves behind. It will not harm those who do not oppose it."

"In this form?" A Dahomei on Lady Gretchen's right frowned.

"If it fails to find Viella before she crosses the river, it will be forced to retreat. But it cannot rest until its mission is fulfilled. Something else will take its place."

"What?" Annan drew her sword as the Dark flowed to within a few streets of the seat.

"Only the one who controls it knows that." Lady Gretchen drew her sword as well.

"Did you find any books about how to defeat it?" Annan asked.

Lady Gretchen spared her a glance. "The histories only say the magic of the Dahomei and the High Queen weakened it enough for Gaiea to trap it within the *Nightward*. We must put our trust in Her now. She alone can save us from what comes."

Around them, the wind stopped as suddenly as it had begun.

For the first time, a gentle sound became apparent. A rhythmic hissing, like waves on sand just before it ebbs. As they watched, the Dark covered every part of the city before them. One by one, the lights in the houses went out.

The first questing tentacles reached the wall below the southeast corner. They touched it and snapped back from the red sparks released by the energy that surrounded the seat. The Dahomei and their lady watched as a swarm of tentacles swept toward the wall like grass snakes, setting off a shower of sparks. The sound grew louder, sandpaper on sandpaper. A smell of burning filled the air.

Darkness gathered at the base of the wall, pooling there and setting off bright-red flashes.

"Ready yourselves, Dahomei!" Annan called. The archers moved to the front of the walls and nocked their arrows. Wraithlight on their swords glowed fire against the Dark that pressed down from above, making the sky glow red above them. The steady hissing was painful to the ears. Minutes stretched into months in the crimson night.

Light flared and flashed. Dahomei raised their hands to their eyes. There was a muffled boom and air rushed past them. Silence followed, like that found in the Dead Woods in the Queendom of Jaleel. The women blinked and scrubbed at their eyes.

The hissing began again. Soft and satisfied.

"Archers! Fire!" Annan cried.

Shafts of flame whistled downward. The Dark rose up, wave climbing upon wave to meet them.

<hr />

A LOW FENCE, WHITE AND GLIMMERING LIKE A RIVER MAID, LOOMED OUT of the night. Before Viella could make a sound, Roland had leaped it. Luka's arm tightened around her waist. Effortless flight was replaced by a jarring landing that made her teeth draw blood from her tongue. Blinking back tears, Viella tried to catch sight of Flor again. Only a blurred smudge spoke of their position. Something scratchy slapped repeatedly against her bare ankles as they raced across an open space.

To her right, she saw the friendly yellow eyes of the houses. They seemed to be drawing away from her even as the stars in front of her drew no closer. Roland's breathing sounded labored. A white cloud blew back from his nostrils to mingle with the one from her own nose.

A meadow, or a field. She didn't care one way or another. She just wanted to stop riding for a moment. Her entire body hurt.

Then a cold touch along her spine made her neck snap back so that she bumped the top of her head on Luka's jaw. He grunted.

"Have a care, Your Majesty."

The same *compulsion* she'd felt earlier gripped her body. "It's here!" she shrieked, breathless.

Luka's breath blasted the side of her face. "What's here?"

She struggled to turn and look back but couldn't see past his bulk. "I can feel it! Back there! Hurry, Luka!"

She felt him twist in the saddle. "There's nothing behind us, Viella."

Yes, there is. Certainty wound through her, taking fear with it. "You're wrong. It's behind us."

For an answer, Luka bent even lower and urged the horse to go faster. Deep within her though, Viella knew it was all for naught.

They see me. We aren't fast enough. We won't make it.

Cold tears blew back from her cheeks as the wind grew stronger.

⫻⫻⫻⫻⫻⫻

IT OVERWHELMED THEM WITH STUNNING SPEED. THE DARK PRESSED INTO every corner, every edifice, forcing the Dahomei off the walls, snuffing out all the torches, sinking the seat into a blackness pierced only by the drawn sword or the occasional arrow.

But even that light grew dimmer every moment, and the Dahomei had no choice but to retreat, barricading the doors behind them.

Still, it came. Seeping through window cracks like oil, spreading under doors like spilled puddles. The sound of breaking glass echoed all over the seat as those apertures that did not swing open gave way under the pressure.

As the swords and arrows died, pitch-black tentacles pulled gold-clad Dahomei toward the Dark, the armor first going a dull bronze, then fading altogether as the warriors were swallowed whole.

Lady Gretchen stood at the entrance to the library, where many of her family's treasures were hidden—and along with them the queen's bracelets of office—cutting and slashing at the bulbous heads that rose like hydras from the Dark.

"Will it never stop coming?" Annan, captain of her guard, shouted.

Lady Gretchen swung her sword from left to right, then up overhead. Pieces of the Dark fell to the floor, sizzling, smelling of dankness and smoke before wisping into nothingness. "It has grown too large, too powerful."

She pierced a blob that launched itself at her, ripping downward. Globules scattered, disappearing as soon as they hit the ground. More blobs slipped and slithered away into cracks and holes.

"What's it doing?" a Dahomei asked.

"Only a small part of it deals with us, while the rest searches for the queen. Once it realizes she isn't here, the entire thing will move on."

"Your orders?" Annan swung her sword in a blinding arc, and Dark rained on the floor like water.

"Take what Dahomei you can find and go to the cellars. Protect the servants. If your weapons die, throw them away. Survive. The fight does not end here." Lady Gretchen kicked backward with one foot and the door swung open. She backed into the library. "Use the passageway in the wall behind me."

Annan moved with her, still wielding her sword, her helmet long gone and her black braid swinging free down the middle of her back.

"I cannot leave you, My Lady."

"I order you to do so. Make haste, Dahomei."

Annan turned and ran. Lady Gretchen did not watch her captain go. Instead, she charged the Dark, cutting and piercing with a speed and fury that spoke of desperation.

The Dark poured through the door, spread over the walls, and consumed the ceiling above her. Then it stilled, pulsing like a heart, tentacles waving like beckoning fingers.

Lady Gretchen paused, chest heaving, sweat plastering the strands of hair that had escaped her braid to her cheeks. She held her sword before her, ready.

The wall of darkness in the doorway slit open down the center. A tall silhouette that moved on two legs stepped though, her reflection swirling within it like an oil slick atop water. It started to narrow, forming shoulders and a head, even as it advanced toward her. With a loud cry, Lady Gretchen charged the creature and brought her sword down through the top of its featureless skull.

Instantly, the blade's light died. The sword flew from her grasp, crashing into a desk. A tentacle whipped out of the torso of the creature and wrapped around her neck, lifting her.

Choking, scratching at the slick, cold band around her throat, Lady Gretchen saw the gap she had made in the creature's head close, and a maw open below it.

The girl is not here.

The voice was deeper than a well, a vibrating monstrosity that filled her head and brought tears to her eyes. A smell like many small dead things filled her nostrils and made her gag, made her mouth taste of dirt.

"You're . . . too late," she managed to whisper.

More tentacles sprouted from the thing's torso, some of them tangling around one another in their eagerness.

Yes. But we see her. She is not far.

The form dissolved, leaving only tentacles that shot toward Lady Gretchen, grasping legs, arms, head, torso. Her armor dulled as she went limp. Hissing to itself, the Dark pulled her in.

///////////

MIST COILED ACROSS THE LAND, WEAVING BETWEEN ROLAND'S THUDDING hooves. Luka squinted, trying to keep Eleanor's horse in sight. The sound of the hooves ahead of him faded, and there was a strange smell of burning in the air.

He blinked moisture out of his eyes—and realized he could no longer see or hear anything but Roland's hooves and his own heavy breathing. *Gaiea's breath. Where is the Dahomei?* All he saw was a wall of white, shifting as if driven by a nonexistent wind. The silence dampened his ears like a wet blanket.

Beneath him, sensing Luka's confusion, the horse slowed and then stopped, snorting.

Viella gripped his arm in a painful vise. "What are you *doing*? Don't stop!"

"Viella," he said, knowing his voice was sharp yet unable to help himself, "I can't see in this, and neither can Roland. We must stop and listen for the other horse. We can't afford to lose track of the Dahomei."

"But they're right behind us!"

The horse spun under them, pawing and twisting as if sensing something in the fog. Luka's wounded right shoulder burned with the pain of keeping Roland in check. Nothing moved except the mist; it seemed to mock him. *You've lost her. How could you do that? How could you let this happen?*

He strained his ears but heard only his heart beating. "Do you hear them?"

"No." Viella almost sobbed. "Can we *please* go?"

The burnt smell grew stronger. *Is that . . . whispering?* He looked up. The sky above seemed darker than usual, but here and there a star peeped out. *There should be more. We're away from the town.* Coldness settled in his stomach as he realized what that expanse of unlit darkness meant.

"Luka," Viella whispered, "if I make it light, will it help?"

"You can do that?" *Gaiea's Desert, I could use a light right now.*

"I think I can. I used a Word to create light when I was playing hide-and-seek once."

"Do it," he said.

Viella stretched out one small hand over Roland's head, which was now barely visible as the mist pressed in.

"*Surya,*" she cried, her voice flat and unnatural in the stifling fog. A thin, wavering light lined her fingertips, as though she held her hand over the glass of a lamp. She moaned in frustration. "It didn't work."

"Try again," he suggested.

"It . . . hurts."

Luka racked his brain for what the Dahomei had taught him about using magic. There'd been nothing about pain.

Perhaps the magic is not the cause of the pain. "Try to ignore the pain. Think about what you're saying. The word of power can be anything—any word that's special to you—so long as it's the same as your intention."

"Intention?"

"What you want to happen. Whether you use the magic of the Sight to see beyond this world to what you wish to bring into it, or the Word to speak Illusion, you use words of power to focus your desire."

"Focus." She nodded. "Lady Sophia tells me that all the time."

"Yes. Try to do that." It was hard to see her expression, but he thought she looked determined as she faced forward again.

"*Surya!*"

The light pulsed, brightening before it sank back down to a glow.

That is *hissing.* Luka looked around them now, searching for the source of the sound. The horse whinnied and side-stepped. He squeezed with his heels, tightened the reins, but still Roland danced. Luka looked up—and saw not one star.

"Viella," he whispered urgently. "Concentrate. Put all your strength, all your Blessing, into it. *Now.*" Something in his voice must have said it all. She rose up in the saddle and leaned forward over the pommel.

"SURYA!"

Light blazed forth, so bright Luka covered his eyes against it. He heard the hissing fade, and a sizzling noise took its place. The ashy taste of smoke lined his mouth and throat. The horse neighed—

—and from somewhere to their right, another horse answered. Hoofbeats, flat and strange, echoed through the white.

Thank Gaiea.

Viella sank down and Luka felt weakness in her body.

"You did well," he said to her.

She bit her lip and turned her face up to his. "Dowager Mother taught me that Word. Do you think she's okay, Luka? Do you think Valan and Daddy are with her?"

Not sure what to say, Luka settled on nodding. *Gaiea forgive me for lying, but later will be soon enough for her to face the loss of her family.*

Flor burst through the dissipating fog. Eleanor did not waste time with questions. "Stay close!" She spun Flor around and dashed along the path the light had cleared.

Holding tight to the queen and swallowing against the taste in his throat, Luka spurred Roland on. As the fog swirled away from him, he smelled water and damp silt. A faint murmur started on the edge of his hearing. *The river. How could we have been so close and not known?*

Because something had not wanted them to know. That had to be the reason for the fog. Luka's lips pressed into a thin line. *If it had not been for Viella . . .*

The ground changed under them, the soil feeling less and less compact. Ahead, he made out a faint glimmer. Without warning, both horses burst free of the remains of the suffocating mist. The heavy scent of wet soil hung in the air, and he heard the river babbling to itself. He looked over his shoulder.

The fog had disappeared. There was nothing behind them but a solid wall of darkness. His heart leaped when he realized how close it was—and how quickly it must have moved to catch up with them. *We have minutes before it is on us.*

Viella groaned in his arms. He looked down at the inclined top of her head, worried, but he could not stop to check on her.

The horses picked their way down the sloping bank of the River Lethe. Eleanor looked back to make sure they were following, and once she reached the shore, she urged Flor to the side to wait while Roland came down.

Without warning, Viella started to twist in the saddle, her hands working at the arm Luka held over her waist. Frowning, he glanced down at her.

"What is it?"

She did not answer. Instead, she fought harder, her short nails scratching at his skin, her body bucking against him. His shoulder went numb, then a tearing pain lanced through it. *Gaiea's breath, what was wrong now?*

"Stop that," he said, his voice sharp. A snarl was her response. The sound made the hairs on his neck stand up. It didn't sound like a noise a little girl would make. *The Dark. It's too close. It's affecting her.*

As if to confirm his fears, Viella leaned forward and sank her teeth into his arm at the same moment Roland stepped onto the shore.

Eleanor's voice cut across the silence. "Daguard, what is it? What's happening?"

Luka had no time to answer. He grabbed a length of Viella's hair that had come loose during her struggle and pulled on it until her head bent back at an angle. Her blank eyes frightened him more than the snarl. And still she fought, her hands pushing at his arm. He had no choice.

Dropping the reins, he dragged her around until she almost faced him and shook her hard. "Viella! Stop!" *Wake, My Queen! Free yourself from whatever has you in its grip.*

"Daguard! What are you *doing*?"

Viella spat at him, and her hands scratched at his face. Eleanor pulled alongside and leaned over, but Viella's outflung arm caught her on the nose and she drew back. Luka seized the arm just as Eleanor leaned across and grabbed her shoulder. Viella's eyelids fluttered, her head fell forward, and she went limp in his arms.

"Damn you to the Desert, Daguard," Eleanor growled. "You can't put hands on the queen. A sleep spell was all you needed."

Typical Dahomei. I only have the mind-touch and a few spells. "I don't know any," he shot back, adjusting his hold on Viella. He pulled her close with one arm and collected the reins with the other. "Where's the ferry?"

"Further upriver." Eleanor's terse voice said everything. She spoke to Flor in a low tone, and the horse stepped forward until the water lapped at her hooves. Luka urged Roland to follow, wondering how he could speed across a river without dropping Viella. *Without drowning, for that matter,* he thought as he surveyed the broad expanse that stretched too far for him to see the other side.

"Then how do we cross?"

Eleanor rose in her saddle and extended her hands toward the lapping water.

"Maiden, I beg an urgent audience!"

The waves ebbed once—and stopped. Water pooled around

Roland's hooves, motionless. The river grew smooth as glass. Two heartbeats later, a ripple formed in the center of the river, opposite them. The ripple expanded until it touched the horses' hooves and dissipated.

Behind them, Luka heard a faint hissing.

A slender, pale figure rose from the water, the movement as smooth as a blade. The river maiden moved toward them, gliding without disturbing the river's surface. Its inner light lit the night like a single candle flame.

The maiden's long black hair hung to her waist, straight and shiny. The delicate features of her face were outdone only by the beauty of her silver eyes. The globes of her breasts had no nipples; her body had no sex or navel. She was a thing created, not born. Maidens were immortal—and shy. This one, though, extended slim arms that glittered with fine scales toward Eleanor. Her smile revealed many white, pointed teeth.

"Sister, I answer your call."

Sister? he wondered. But then Viella twitched in Luka's arms, her voice a soft moan. He rubbed a comforting hand between her shoulder blades, burskin scratching his palms, and his gaze went from the maiden to Eleanor and back again. *I can hear the maiden. She is strong in the mind-speak.*

"We are attacked. Queen Elise lies murdered. The *Nightward* has been opened. We are charged with taking the new queen to safety, but the Dark follows us. I beg safe passage across your domain."

The hissing grew louder as the maiden's gaze drifted over them. Luka refused to look behind him and fear trailed fingers across the back of his neck.

The maiden twisted, stretching out her hand over the river. Ripples spread outward from her, separating into parallel lines that cut a path through the river. Water ebbed away from the path until the level of the river dropped so low, Luka could see small rocks rising from the bottom.

"*You may pass, Sister. The way is clear to the other side. I will hold against what follows you.*" The maiden's silver eyes glanced back at them. "*May Gaiea go with you.*"

Eleanor inclined her head. "I am forever in your debt."

The maiden shook her head, strands of hair twisting slowly in the air as she did so. "*No, Dahomei, it's we who are in yours. The* Nightward *is open. We must remember the lessons of the past and work together.*"

At that moment, a thin tendril of black curled itself around Luka's wrist. Cold sank into him, so deep and so shocking he could not move.

Before he could cry out, or even fight it, light flared around his hand, golden and warm. The blackness sizzled away into nothingness with the sharp scent and putrid taste of burning skin, but when he reflexively checked his arm, he was unhurt, the sudden pain already gone. He raised his eyes to meet the maiden's gaze. She lowered her hand, light still leaking from it.

"*Hurry now.*" She gestured to the waiting path. Luka needed no second invitation. Roland responded to the pressure of his legs, trotting into the shallow water. Cold droplets flew back into Luka's face as the horse splashed its way around the exposed rocks. Behind him, Flor's hooves clicked on the pebbles that littered the bottom of the river.

Then total darkness fell, and he could not see a thing.

"Keep moving!" Eleanor's voice cut across the silence.

Obviously. He didn't say what was in his mind, though, but rather concentrated on holding on to Viella, ignoring the pain in his shoulder and giving the horse its head. Roland kept going, undisturbed by the path ahead in a way in which he hadn't been in the fog.

The trek seemed to go on forever while the river lapped around them and the hissing returned. Luka's lips moved unconsciously in seldom-spoken prayer.

Without warning, light blossomed about them, swirling and

softly white. Through its pearlescent glow, Luka made out the low, black rise of the opposite bank.

Thank Gaiea.

The light had faded by the time Roland clambered up the slippery soil, blowing heavily. Flor joined them at the top with a stern-faced Eleanor.

"Keep going. Don't look back." Eleanor rode off, galloping through the copse of trees that edged the river. Luka rode after Flor, trusting Roland to pick his way between the trees.

When they emerged from cover, open land lay before them, the short grass ruffled by the cool wind that came off the river.

I can see the grass.

Luka looked up. Above him, a multitude of stars shone down from a clear sky. In the west, the sky had begun to fade to gray as night gave way to morning.

He bent low over Roland's neck, his hand around Viella's chest. She did not stir. Her body slumped against his with all the grace of a sack of potatoes.

Sunrise will find her in a lot of pain. Luka did his best to keep her in some sort of position as they galloped across the grasslands. But there was no help for it. The ride ahead would be long and tedious. The new queen's pain, he was sure, was only just beginning.

⁄⁄⁄⁄⁄⁄⁄⁄⁄⁄

THE SOUND OF HORSES' HOOVES SPLASHING THROUGH THE RIVER STILL reverberated through the fog when the Dark coalesced on the shore, questing tentacles retreating into its solid void. The River Maiden faced the pulsing entity, scorn twisting her features into something less beautiful.

"Minion, you will sully my banks no further."

A ripple went through the Dark, and a bulge detached itself, forming into a silhouette. One red eye burned at the top of it, pulsing and expanding at will.

Maiden. It spat the word like a curse. **You risk much for nothing. The girl will die. Your kind cannot stop us.**

"*You speak lies and you over-reach yourself. Leave my waters or know the pain I brought you before a thousand times better.*"

She raised her arm, golden light limning it like a sun's corona. The Dark made a sharp hissing sound. **Insolent! Fear you not what was born of a god?**

"*I bear no allegiance to your God, underling.*"

The silhouette drew closer, its feet making no sound on the grass. **You waste my time. Grant us passage, half-breed.**

The maiden's laugh burbled like water over stones. "*Even if I wished to do such a foolish thing, how will you cross a river Blessed by Gaiea Herself?*"

The Dark hissed, undulating.

Blessed? What is it to us but pain? We were born of pain. We live in it. We will find a way, however long it takes. The Dark seemed to breathe into itself. **And when we do, we will take you into ourselves. An eternity in the Chaos—with us—is that your wish?**

The maiden threw her head back, mouth wide in a soundless expression of mirth. "*You think yourself still in the First Age. Your time is gone. I am strong now that She rules.*"

The Dark's hissing almost became a roar. **A river maiden? Construct born of another construct? A darkling could finish your impertinence.**

The maiden spat upon the waters. The saliva floated for a second, like a droplet of moonlight, before sinking below the surface and drifting away from her, still shining. She smiled, her teeth gleaming.

"*Well then, brave one. Come take me into your Dark.*"

The silhouette's burning eye swallowed its head, and tentacles detached themselves from its torso, questing with their bulbous tips.

Behind the maiden, the waters swelled, sending wave after

wave toward shore. The creature paused, head lifted as if scenting the air.

Treacherous bitch!

Water parted as maiden after maiden rose from the river, each as bright as a flame. The brilliance of their combined presences blazed across the night, drowning out the light of the droplet of saliva that had called them all. Opalescent light swirled in the depths of their illumination. Like a physical force, the light pushed at the darkness. The void bent away from it, hissing in pain and fury.

The creature's tentacles whipped out at the light, breaking into ash at the point of contact. A maw opened beneath the eye and an inhuman roar issued from it. Even that could not break the barrier, the sound dying against the growing, dancing radiance.

As countless forms gathered around her, the river maiden raised her hands before her, palms upright. *"Come, underling, show me your bravery. Since you value pain so, why not take us all?"*

As one, the other maidens raised their arms toward the creature. Light poured forth, funneled through the first maiden in a vicious beam that seared right through the creature's eye and into the void. The Dark fell away from it, collapsing into ash that dissolved into nothingness. The light spread like a grassland fire, eating up the void until nothing stood in its place but the open land and clear, star-filled sky.

The maidens lowered their hands, their glow dimming to reveal that they all shared the same silver-scaled skin and dark hair. The Guardian of the River Lethe spoke without looking at them.

"Sisters, our work is not done. Take the news to other lands. The Nightward has been opened. War has come to us again. We must prepare. I myself will go to the First."

Without a word, the maidens slid back into the water, silver scaled tails churning the water around them. In seconds, the river stood empty under the silent night.

The creatures of Gailand share no Blessing with this Abomination. That which flows through all She holds dear has been corrupted within the Dark. It is a being of Chaos, which lives in the space between the stars.

It is a thing out of balance. Made of endless hunger and servant to that which offends Gaiea. It is death, Oblivion's harbinger, and all that look upon it will not see the face of the one true Goddess should the Day of Her Return come.

Gaiea's Blessing, bestowed on those worthy to be Queen, the seal of the *Nightward*, the Boon of her Hand, these things guard against the Dark and keep it buried in Her Desert, where it must remain. For the Dark is the first and the last, the one who opens the way. Those who pray for its return pray for Gailand's end.

—*The Divine Histories of Gailand*
An Account of the Weapons of Chaos
Dyane, Hand of Gaiea, Fifth Queen of Dun

CHAPTER 5

FLAME

N A ROOM LIT ONLY BY STARLIGHT, MORDACH FELL TO HIS KNEES, trembling. Motionless bodies surrounded him as breath rasped from his throat. A shapeless form detached itself from the blackest corner of the room and moved toward the Spellsayer.

"We have failed you."

Mordach cursed under his breath and raised his head to stare at the floating, ever-changing shape. "How?"

"We are weak yet. The maidens held the river against us. It will take time to go around it. The Blessing is strong within it."

"Because Gaiea intended it so. To keep you trapped here." Mordach pulled himself up from his knees, stumbling a little as he did so. "Perhaps we can try something else."

The Dark waited.

"You can—divide yourself, can you not?"

The form hissed and drifted into a vague man shape. **"Yes."**

"Then let us use that to our advantage, as it would be impossible for me to command you once you cross the river. Spread yourselves out. Search every corner of the queendom. You can be in many places at once. When one of you finds the princess, the others will come to your aid."

The Dark swirled. **"To do that we need vessels. Humans we can manipulate."**

Mordach ran a trembling hand over his hair, smoothing it into place. "There are many bodies in the court. Take a few that have not been too badly damaged. Deliver your prisoners to the storm cellars first. They've been made ready."

The Dark hissed.

"The princess most likely travels with a Daguard. Pick bodies that held authority in this life. Bodies that might have been a comrade to him."

"A trap." The Dark swirled and absorbed its man shape. "We find this . . . agreeable."

"Work quickly." Mordach warned. "The princess must be secured before the final ritual begins." Mordach snapped his fingers, muttering under his breath. The candles flared into life, casting light everywhere.

"It has been too long. My power wanes. I must replenish myself regularly or I will weaken."

"Then go now. Meet me in my quarters when you're ready. Become Sycrens. Use the bodies as riders."

"Yes, Spellsayer." The Dark flowed out the door, an undulating banner. The moment it left, Mordach leaned on a candle stand for support. He passed a trembling hand over his sweating face as he stared at Alain's motionless body. When his gaze fell on Valan, he took a deep breath and closed his eyes for a moment. Then he pushed away from the stand and went to the Ambush's prone body. One pass of his hand above the Ragat's face and the blue eyes opened.

"Command your men, Ambush. I require their assistance."

By the time the Ragat leader had risen to his feet, the other Ragat warriors had been awakened. The Ambush looked back at the still-unconscious forms of the prince and the lord consort.

"What of them?"

Mordach's gaze lingered on Alain, but he replied without hesitation: "They will sleep for the moment. You will move them later. We must concern ourselves with the Grand Hall.

Follow me." He swept out of the room and the Ragat shadowed him, their feet silent on the blood-stained tile.

///////////

BIRDSONG AWAKENED VIELLA—A PERSISTENT TWITTERING THAT DRIFTED down from above. She opened her eyes, blinking away the sleep. Sunlight dazzled her, making her head ache.

Why did Grandmother let me sleep so late? A soft wind kissed her cheek. The sunlight shifted out of her eyes, and she saw leafy branches and a bird's nest high above her, straw hanging like a beard from the bottom. Two brilliant yellow birds with black wings balanced on the edge of the nest. One chirped and jumped down into the nest, disappearing from view. The other remained on the edge, fluffing its feathers and cocking its head so that one black eye peered down at her.

How did I get outside . . . ? She raised her hand to rub her eyes—and saw her bare wrists. Memory rushed back. Her mother falling. Valan's wide eyes. Lady Gretchen stroking her face. Luka shouting at her to make the light. A coldness filling her head with whispers in a voice she knew . . . then darkness.

Luka! She started to sit up, then fell back, her legs and torso sore and tender. Her mouth tasted musty.

"You should wake her." The voice was flat and pointed. *The Dahomei.* She turned her head.

A few feet away, Eleanor stood with her back to Viella, hands on her hips. Luka squatted in front of her, stuffing something into his dingy canvas bag.

"She's tired."

"We have to keep moving."

"I know."

Uh-oh. Luka was not pleased. And Eleanor sounded like her mother when she had a disagreement with Lady Sophia.

She would never raise her voice, but Lady Sophia backed down without a word when her mother used that tone.

"You know. Is that all you have to say?"

"Yes." Luka fussed with the drawstring on his bag, still not looking at the Dahomei.

Eleanor's shoulders lifted and fell as though she were taking a deep breath. "You forget yourself, Pride Leader."

"Do I?" Luka slipped the bag over his shoulder and rose to his feet, his gaze finally meeting hers. "You speak to a Daguard, not Ground-Troop. I may not have the magic of a warrior-magician, but I ride into battle before you do, so you can cast spells in safety."

Eleanor's voice hissed across his. "You think yourself better than me?"

"I merely state the fact that Daguard do more than carry ceremonial swords at the High Court. What woman can seat a war-cat for more than a few minutes?"

"War-cats." She spat the word. "Those beasts are barely more intelligent than their riders."

Luka's body went very still. "I'd like to see you talk to your horse the same way."

"You impudent—"

"She is my queen too," Luka continued, as though she had not spoken. "I have been charged with her well-being. And I say we can wait until she wakes."

Eleanor took a step closer to him. "You do not wish to clash swords with me, Pride Leader. Not when Queen Elise lies dead because we Dahomei entrusted the Daguard with the High Court's protection for the first time." The disgust in her voice was unmistakable. "If you think I will leave her solely to your incompetence—"

"Incompetence!" Luka growled through clenched teeth, and Viella knew he spoke softly only to keep from waking her.

"More Daguard blood was spilled last night than Dahomei—and in a court that should have been amply protected by your magic. You dare to call us—*my father*—incompetent?"

His anger made Viella physically ill. *They can't fight. Not now.* Because if they fought, who would protect her from the Dark?

She sat up, grimacing at the pain. "Please stop." She flung off the saddle blanket that covered her as Luka's gaze shifted, and Eleanor spun around.

"I'm awake, see? We can leave as soon as you want to, Eleanor." She tugged her soft brown wrap more securely about herself.

The Dahomei's eyes widened, then she inclined her head. "Your Majesty, I apologize if I gave offense. You were not meant to hear our conversation."

"You should have something to eat." Luka brushed past Eleanor, ignoring the narrowed gaze she sent his way. He knelt in front of Viella.

"How do you feel?"

"I'm fi—" Viella started automatically. Luka shook his head ever so slightly.

She lowered her eyes. "I'm . . . sore. And hungry."

"Then we eat," he said, a certain triumph in his voice.

Eleanor turned away. "I have a salve that may help with the soreness." She strode through ankle-high grass to where the two horses stood, reins draped around the tree's lower branches.

"Here." Luka offered her a small bundle of white cloth. Viella unwrapped it to reveal the perfect brown circle of a wheat-bake. Her mouth sprang water at the dusky flour smell.

"It's cheese."

She took it gratefully. As she sank her teeth into the soft bake and felt crumbs tumble down her chin, Luka pulled a flask from his pack.

"Respectfully, Your Majesty, listening to private conversations is considered rude," he told her beneath his breath.

Behind him, Eleanor was coming back and the metal tin in her hand flashed sunlight at Viella's eyes.

"Sometimes we have to do it. Mummy said a good queen knows what's going on around her." She took another bite and continued through a full mouth, "Will you stop arguing now? I don't like it when you're angry."

Luka held out the flask to her as Eleanor came to a stop behind him. "Have some water."

A whisper of sound came to Viella, borne on a light wind.

"Your Majesty, when you're ready—" Eleanor began.

"What's that?" The sound was louder now, rhythmic.

"I hear it too."

Luka turned on his heels, scanning the waving grass that reached calf-high beyond the wide clearing under their tree. Eleanor did the same.

"There." Eleanor pointed. "Southwest. Do you see them?"

"Two, three Palms, do you think?"

"Three." She nodded. "Could be a patrol returning, or scouts."

Luka stood. "We weren't expecting any. Was Talon?"

"No." Eleanor glanced at Viella, who started to eat faster, aware they might have to leave.

"Shouldn't we hide the queen?"

"What queen?" Luka kept his voice casual as Viella finally spotted the bouncing shapes of the approaching group. "Our daughter, remember? We're on our way to visit your mother, just outside Seat Garth."

His voice was calm, and Eleanor said nothing in reply, but Viella's stomach filled with dread as the group drew closer, sunlight glittering off it.

"I'm not hungry anymore," she said in a small voice to no one in particular.

Tense seconds passed before Eleanor shaded her eyes with the hand not holding the tin and let out an incredulous "Huh!"

Luka stared at her. "What is it?"

"Hiding is definitely not necessary." The relief in her voice made Viella relax a little.

Luka shaded his eyes as well. He whistled softly. "Gold armor."

"Dahomei." Eleanor took a few steps forward.

"But whose?"

Viella put down her bake carefully. *He's still worried.*

"It matters not. They'll know me, and I'll know them. The Seat of Talon is the Dahomei training ground. No Dahomei achieves the gold without first coming under our command."

Viella clambered to her feet, brushing crumbs off her trousers and passing a hand over her mouth. Mummy had said many times it didn't look well for a princess to be careless of her appearance; now that she was queen it might be even more important. She took a step toward her guardians, but Luka turned, as if sensing her movements.

"Stay back, Viella."

"But Eleanor knows them . . ."

"That may or may not be true." He glanced at the Dahomei. "I'm sure she won't begrudge me my caution."

"Do as you please, Daguard," Eleanor replied, her back still to Viella.

Luka gave Viella a pointed look and, sighing, she stepped back into the shadows under the tree's low-hanging branches.

The wait took forever. The shiny blobs turned into torsos and sun-struck helmets that trailed purple pennants. Viella stopped looking directly at them, her eyes dazzled by the morning light. When the Palms surrounded them, it was with a suddenness she didn't expect. Horses swarmed into the clearing, snuffling and pawing while armor creaked and clashed in close quarters. The sharp, tangy sweat of horses filled the air.

Eleanor lowered her hand from her eyes. "You're far from home, Margot."

A bay danced forward, his rider a small woman with dark freckles dusted across her tanned face.

"As are you, Eleanor. I wish I could say we're well met, but nothing good can come of a day like today." Margot's words were grim, but her large black eyes held glimmers of friendliness, and Viella liked her at once. The other women she rode with were silent on their horses, their gaze watchful, their faces impatient.

"What has Lady Mai told you?" Eleanor asked.

Margot snorted, a frown between her eyes. "What do ladies ever say? As little as possible. I know Queen Elise has ascended to the Garden, and that Seat Talon has sent the new queen to Seat Garth for safety. Lady Mai instructed us to ride to Lady Gretchen's assistance." She looked directly at Viella. "This is our queen?"

Eleanor looked back at Viella and gave her a small nod. She came out from under the overhang, careful to hold her head high and wishing desperately she didn't feel so small in the presence of so many horses and armored women.

All the Dahomei bowed low over their horses' necks.

"Your Majesty," Margot said, her voice low, her gaze hard. "I'm Captain Margot Greensleeves of Garth. There are no words for our sorrow at your loss. Know that all Gailand grieves with you. That no Dahomei will rest until we've cleansed the High Court of the Ragat scum and returned you to your throne. Go with Gaiea. Lady Mai will protect you until this matter is at an end."

Viella gave her a small smile as hope and warmth flowered within her. "Thank you, Captain."

"The *Nightward* has been opened," Eleanor told Margot.

A ripple of shock ran through the group. Margot's eyes widened. "How is that possible?"

"Mordach must have betrayed us. The court has been glamoured and the rest of the royal family is still trapped inside. Lady Gretchen had no chance to go to their aid. We left her preparing for an attack from a force of some kind—the Dark. It followed us until we reached the river. A river maiden stopped it, but it may not be gone. We don't know if it bypassed the court, or if Lady Gretchen was defeated. You'll need to be cautious."

"The warning is appreciated." Leaning forward in her saddle, Margot took a good look at Luka before she asked Eleanor casually, "Who's your young friend?"

"This is Pride Leader Luka Freehold, the queen's personal guard."

Luka inclined his head.

"Doesn't he speak?" Margot asked with raised eyebrows and a slight smile that revealed a missing tooth on the upper-left side of her mouth.

"Too often," Eleanor said. Luka stiffened at her words but didn't reply.

Margot glanced at Viella again. "Your Majesty, you don't look anything like yourself. A disguise?"

"Precisely," Luka replied.

"Ah." The bay shifted and the Dahomei tightened her grip on the reins. "So, he does speak."

"When I have something useful to say."

"Useful. That's a new one." Viella was sure no one else heard Eleanor's muttered comment, as the expressions on the faces of the women before her didn't change.

"I'm not sure you brought enough Dahomei with you," Luka said. "Lady Gretchen believed whatever approached would be difficult to overcome."

"We have no time to wait for more reinforcements," Eleanor shot back at him. "Would you risk losing the seat to whatever followed you from the High Court?" Viella saw her fingers squeeze the tin in her hand until the blood left them.

"I would risk a moment to consider what we face. The *Nightward* is open. Losing several Palms to forces we know little about is hardly a better solution," Luka pointed out.

"You like running too much for my taste," Eleanor replied, turning her gaze away.

"I *like* very little of what has happened this past night. But we must give care, and due thought, to every action we take."

"Then we'll take care, Pride Leader." Margot sounded more amused than anything else, and Viella was grateful she didn't join in the argument. *I hope they don't do this all the way to Garth.* Above her, one of the birds let out a chirp, as though agreeing.

"Do as you think best, Margot. I trust your judgment," Eleanor replied. Viella wasn't sure she spoke the truth. Eleanor's back was as stiff as her voice.

"Your Daguard speaks sense, Eleanor. No harm can come of heeding him." The bay tossed his head, and Margot ran a soothing hand through his mane. She tilted a glance Luka's way. "She can be a bit of a pain. Loves being contrary, if memory serves. Be sure not to let her under your skin, or it could get bloody. That's how I lost this tooth." She smiled so he could see it.

"Margot," Eleanor said, voice flat, and folded her arms across her chest.

"But I promise, once you get to know her"—she straightened up in her saddle—"she'll annoy you even more."

"*Margot.*"

The Dahomei captain grinned. "We'll leave you now. Would you like a few of my women to go with you as escort?"

"Thank you, we'll manage," Eleanor said.

"It's best we attract as little attention as possible," Luka explained.

"I don't know, Eleanor." Margot shook her head. "Doesn't seem like he speaks too often to me."

She whistled out of the side of her mouth, and the Dahomei around her spurred their horses. With a thudding of hooves, the clang of armor and the moist smell of upturned earth and horse dung, they rode off.

"Margot!" Viella called impulsively. The captain hung back.

"Could you—would you please find my brother? Make sure he's safe. Daddy and Dowager Mother too?"

Margot's gaze softened. "Your Majesty, I vow I'll do all I can to find them. Once I do, they'll be under my personal protection until you're reunited."

Margot glanced at Eleanor and Luka. "Try not to kill each other before you get to Garth. If nothing else, think of your charge." Then she rode off behind the others, her chuckle trailing behind her like her helmet's colors.

"Interesting woman," Luka said.

Eleanor looked down at the tin in her hand. Viella saw the fading imprint of her fingers on the silver lid. "She's a pain in the ass and always has been." She looked at Viella, her gaze carefully blank. "I'm sorry, Your Majesty, but we've wasted enough time and must be going."

As she went for the horses, Viella saw a tiny smile kink the corner of Luka's mouth.

⁂

BLOOD SPREAD IN ACCUSING PUDDLES BETWEEN THE TABLES OF THE Grand Hall. A spoiled smell curdled the air as unattended food soured. Banners and colors trailed to the floor, sad reminders of the festivities that had barely begun before they ended.

And everywhere there were bodies. Some bore gaping wounds and were sprawled in their own blood, but others appeared to be unharmed. Slumped in chairs, prone on the floor, stretched across tables—they lay unmoving, without the need to take a breath, so powerful was the Hinder spell that held them in its grasp.

"Your magic is strong." The Ambush stood next to Mordach on the dais and surveyed the hall with subtle turns of his head.

Mordach ignored the statement. "I can only hold them until

sunset. Remove the dead bodies. The survivors are to be divided and placed in the storm cellars. Ladies and lord consorts to the group cells and the queens must be separated into isolated chambers."

"Which be which?" The Ambush's very blue eyes held a quizzical look.

"Obviously, the queens will be wearing their bracelets."

"Not queens." The Ragat warrior frowned as he struggled to find the words. "Ladies and . . . others."

"Ah." Mordach rubbed a weary hand against his temple. "You have a point." And he did; some of the servants were almost as well dressed as the ladies and lord consorts. "Such finery must be confusing to one unfamiliar with it. Very well. Bring the bodies past the dais and I'll identify them."

"And the servants?" The warrior gestured at the corridors behind them. "Fighters?"

"The courtyard for the bodies and most of the servants." Mordach glanced around the Hall. "Leave a few alive to tend to the prisoners and the court."

The Ambush bowed, then trilled a short series of sounds to his men. Some disappeared behind the curtained recess that led to the corridors behind them while others ran down the steps into the hall. With no hesitation, they grabbed bodies that seemed too heavy given their short statures and tossed them over their shoulders with ease. Their feet light and careful, they worked in silence.

Mordach knelt next to the body of the dead queen. Her head lay tilted to the side, eyes closed, and mouth open as though she slept. He slid a hand under her cheek, turning her face toward him. A trickle of blood marked a path from the corner of her mouth to her ear. He wiped at it, then bowed his head.

"Forgive me," he whispered, too low for anyone else to hear.

"This one I will take?" The Ambush knelt opposite him and held out his arms.

Mordach closed his hands over the silver spear and pulled it from Queen Elise's body with a jerk. The stain on the pink sari spread a little then stopped.

Several Ragat approached with bodies for the Spellsayer to identify. He did not seem to notice. Spear in hand, he continued to stare at the dead body in front him.

"Spellsayer?" the Ambush asked again.

Mordach glanced around. "Those are all for the courtyard."

The Ragat trotted off with their burdens while the Ambush repeated, "I take the queen?"

Mordach nodded. "There's a study just off my quarters."

The Ambush bent immediately to hoist her onto his shoulders. Behind him, more Ragat approached.

"Wait, Ambush."

Mordach strode down to one of the warriors and lifted the chin of the woman he carried. He scrutinized a face as pale as milk as the Ragat struggled to gather his burden of green-and-white skirts. "Take this one as well. Leave her in my quarters."

"Yes, Spellsayer."

HEAT SPIRALED UP FROM BENEATH ROLAND'S HOOVES AS THE HORSE trotted through the savannah. Luka wished for a cooling breeze, but the air had grown still as midday approached. Now and then it puffed, hot and unpleasant and smelling of crushed grass and dust. Sweat prickled on his forehead, tickling its way down the sides of his face and nose. A half mile ahead, a stand of trees beckoned, offering shade and a place to rest.

Viella pushed at the arm Luka had around her waist. "Ugh. You're sweaty and you're making me wet."

"Heat has been known to cause sweat, Your Majesty," he replied. Eleanor rode just ahead of them and he was glad of it. He'd had enough of her stony stares for one day.

"You don't have to hold me. I can hold the pommel. See?" She demonstrated and turned a hopeful gaze up at him.

"You're in my care until we arrive at Garth. I'd rather not stop to pick you up if you fall."

She scowled. "Who says I'll fall?"

"Who says you'll stay on?"

Viella faced forward, mumbling something under her breath.

"I'm sorry, Your Majesty. What was that?"

"Nothing."

Luka let it go. He had too much to consider. Like what would be the best way to return to the High Court, fast. It heartened him that Palms of Dahomei rode to help Lady Gretchen. If they were in time, he had no doubt they would take the fight to the court. He wanted to be with them then, wanted to find his father and comrades and help them himself, but in the end, it did not matter who did it as long as it was done.

And Margot seemed quite capable of getting the job done.

Margot. A smile tugged at his mouth. A cool breeze on a hot afternoon, she had come and gone too soon. There was something about her that had caught his attention.

A Dahomei who says what she thinks, even if it is in front of the men. And it didn't hurt that she drove Eleanor to a cliff's edge either.

To say Lady Gretchen's Lance annoyed him was only half the truth. He felt her opinion of him every time she looked at him or spoke to him. No, it was more than annoyance. She was *insulted* that a Daguard had been given authority over her, however small that authority might be.

Of course, it would never occur to her that he was as uncomfortable as she was. A rough soldier asked to protect the High Queen during a time of crisis—he did not feel in any way prepared for what was asked of him.

Margot would understand. A Dahomei who didn't speak in cryptic, stilted sentences. Half of him wished she were accompanying them to Garth instead.

The other half once more hoped he would be riding back to the High Court before the evening ended. The prospect of being able to go into battle again was a relief of sorts. The queen needed those around her to be suited to their roles. If he was irritated by one Dahomei, he would not do well in a new court, filled with strangers. He was a better soldier than bodyguard, where the only life he need fear for was his own. Viella would be well rid of him in Garth.

I will not remain there long. A court of strangers, without my father, is no place for me. Fear prickled him at that thought, but he forced himself not to go down that path. His father would not be easy to kill. Luka had to believe he was still alive. In the meantime, though, he had given Luka his orders. He would focus on keeping the queen safe and worry about how he would continue to keep himself safe later.

"I'm hungry," Viella said.

"We'll stop for lunch in the trees," Eleanor said over her shoulder.

"Can we go faster?"

"It's really up to your . . . bodyguard to set the pace."

Then why do you insist on riding up front? Gaiea's breath . . .

"I have no objection if the queen is willing to bear her bumps and bruises."

"I'll bear them, I promise." Viella twisted in the saddle, her voice eager, her amber eyes pleading.

"There's the weather to consider." Eleanor shifted the reins in her hands, her body swaying in time to Flor's movements.

"Weather?"

"Look behind you."

Luka twisted in the saddle. In the distance, to the northwest, dark clouds gathered in an otherwise blue sky.

A grassland squall, most likely. Short, intense rainstorms blew up without warning every now and then, often playing themselves out within the hour.

"We should have time to make the trees." He faced forward again.

"Can we race?" Viella asked.

"No." Eleanor and Luka answered at the same time.

Still, Luka urged Roland on as Flor picked up the pace. The cantering hurt his shoulder, sending spider-legs of pain along his arm and back. *Maybe I shouldn't have been so hasty. Too late now. The Dahomei will seize on any complaint as a sign of weakness.*

They traveled the rest of the way in silence, heat making every moment drag. Even the grass nodded in slow motion as they passed, despite their increased speed. By the time they made the edge of the trees, Luka was grateful for the shade and the soft winds that shook the leaves above them.

They walked the horses a short distance before Eleanor brought Flor to a stop and dismounted. She nodded at the base of a huge tree, its roots gnarled like benches. "The queen can rest there."

She walked over to Roland and helped Viella down. Luka said nothing, but part of him was grateful he wouldn't have to strain his shoulder. He swung himself down, his feet sinking into the carpet of fresh-fallen leaves that covered the sweet rot of old and dying vegetation.

Viella sat on the knobby roots, stretching her legs out with a dramatic sigh. She lifted the edge of her pants and examined several tiny scratches. "Luka, the grasses cut me."

"It happens." He removed the canvas bag from the saddle. "The hurt can't be much."

He watched over Roland's back as Eleanor led her horse to a tree and looped the reins over a branch. She pulled out a water-skin from her saddlebag, poured water into a calabash bowl, and allowed Flor to drink.

"It's not," Viella said behind him. "They're fading already."

Eleanor glanced across at them, but Luka turned away and joined Viella at the base of the tree.

"I think this is a grannynut tree," she told him as he undid the bag's drawstring.

"Is that so," he replied. "You've seen a lot of grannynut trees?" Out of the corner of his eye, he saw Eleanor lead Roland away and give him water as well. That surprised him. He hadn't thought of her as the type to worry about anyone's horse but her own.

"There was one behind the stables. It had the same big shiny leaves and the funny nuts that look like a wrinkled face. But I don't think it was this big."

"I know the one you mean." He pulled two linen-wrapped parcels from his bag. "Cheese or . . . cheese?"

Viella wiped beads of sweat from her nose and gave him a wavering smile. Her heart wasn't really in it, but she was trying. *Poor, brave, girl.*

"Cheese."

"Excellent choice." He handed her a sandwich and his waterskin. Once Viella had begun to eat, he went over to where Eleanor stood with Flor. She watched him approach, her hand stroking Flor's neck.

"My thanks for watering Roland." The words came out easier than he'd thought they would.

Eleanor's brow furrowed for a moment, then she said, "Not necessary. You should continue to save your water for the queen. I'll see to the horses." She turned her back on him.

He did not know what else to say, so he went back to Viella's side and hunkered down.

"Don't worry," she said, wiping crumbs from her lips. "She'll like you once she gets to know you."

Luka shrugged, pretending nonchalance. "Your Majesty, that matters not to me. I thanked her for her kindness."

"Oh." She thought for a second, dusting her hands off against her trousers. "That's good then. Can I pee now?"

Gaiea's breath. He hadn't thought of that. He glanced over his shoulder, then smiled a slow smile at Viella. "I believe, Your Majesty, that it would probably be best if Eleanor assisted you with that."

//////////////

MORDACH PAUSED INSIDE THE DOORWAY TO QUEEN ELISE'S BEDROOM. Alain glanced up at him, his lips pulling tight before he turned his attention back to settling Valan under the sheets of the big bed. Mordach made a signal to the Ragat standing guard, and they slid past him, out of the room, closing the door behind them.

"What do you want?" Alain said. The ice in his tone could have chilled the room.

Mordach joined him at the side of the bed and stretched thin fingers toward Valan. Alain grabbed his hand in a tight grip.

"What do you *want*?" he asked again through gritted teeth.

"Alain, believe me. I am sorry for your pain." And even though his hand was caught by Alain's, he reversed the hold, entwining his fingers with the lord consort's. Alain pulled his hand away with a curse, rubbing it against his leg.

"Don't you use your honeyed tongue on me, Mordach," he said, his voice shaking. "Not after what you've done."

"What I've done?" Mordach's voice was soft. "Did I do it alone, Alain?" He placed a hand on Valan's head, tender fingers stroking the burnished brown of his hair. "Was I the only one who cared for him, after all?"

"Gaiea damn you to Her Desert," Alain spat, furious.

"Already done," Mordach whispered without looking at him.

"He's my son. *My son.* You had no right to commit this . . . this evil in his name. You bear the burden of your own actions, Mordach." His voice broke and he wiped tears from his eyes with the heel of his hand. "Why? *Why* did you kill Elise? She was doing everything she could to make Gailand better. Your mother was her father's only sister. She didn't deserve this. *We* didn't deserve this."

Alain stared at Mordach and his breathing hitched. "Gaiea's breath, why did you spend all that time with Valan if you were going to kill his mother? This was never about helping him develop his magic, was it?"

"His magic," Mordach said softly, "was not the only reason the throne wouldn't be his."

"Where is my daughter? Have you—" Alain's voice broke and he sat abruptly, burying his head in his hands. When he spoke again, his voice was barely more than a weary, heartbroken whisper. "Tell me what you did to her. Tell me why I'm here, alive? You must know I won't help you."

Alain never saw the brief emotion that twisted Mordach's face before he turned his back to the lord consort. He heard only the Spellsayer's calm reply.

"I did not intend for things to happen in this manner. But this may be for the best."

Alain rose to his feet with a cry, backing away from the bed. "What is wrong with you? Have you gone mad? Why do you speak to me like this?"

Mordach spun, his hands grasping the lord consort's shoulders in an unforgiving grip. "Do you remember your father? Do you remember what he lost because of Elise? I'm trying to save Valan from his fate. I'm trying to change things so I can give him the one thing we have been denied—the power to live as we choose."

Alain flung his hands up, breaking Mordach's grip. The Spellsayer took a step back, his palms raised. Alain, breath heaving in his chest, stared at him without speaking, studying Mordach's face with narrowed eyes.

"Gaiea save us," Alain whispered. "Those are my father's words. He believed as Ragat believes. What have you *done*?"

The Spellsayer lowered his hands. "Alain . . ."

The lord consort grabbed Mordach by the throat, but before he could squeeze, the Spellsayer touched his fingers to Alain's forehead, caught his suddenly limp body, and sat him in the chair. He kneeled before him, stroked the dark hair back from Alain's slack face and kissed his eyelids. He leaned his forehead against Alain's, his hands squeezing the motionless fingers in Alain's lap.

Then the Spellsayer got to his feet and left the room. When he locked the door, he stood with his back against it, his head bowed, and his eyes closed as breath escaped between bared teeth. He slammed his fist against the wall before he turned and started down the long corridor.

When the hallway sank into a darkness too deep to be natural, he stopped and spoke into the inky depths. "You are ready." It was not a question.

"Yes."

"Is it safe to look upon you?"

A purring sound filled the air. "It is better if you do not. We are . . . Sycrens, and riders. Newly made. Hungry."

A low screech cracked a tile on the floor next to Mordach.

"Hurry. You know where they're headed. If they reach the Portal before you, they'll close it. You must capture the princess before she receives her Boon. It may be a matter of days—a week at the most."

The laugh that filled the corridor would have made a grown man cry out with fear. Tiles crackled underfoot as something heavy shifted its weight.

"When we return?" The question was heavy with malice.

"By the time you return," he answered, "you will see your Masters again. And we will all be free."

"Ah." The sound was satisfied, gleeful. "Then we shall see who is weak. We shall *all* see, Spellsayer."

And with a rush of wind that pushed Mordach against the wall, the Dark left him.

//////////////

AS THEY GALLOPED INTO FREETOWN, THE CLOPPING OF THEIR HORSES' hooves echoed up and down the deserted street, following Margot and her troops like a specter.

"The Welcome Elder should have greeted us at the edge of town," one of the Dahomei remarked.

"Who knows what happened here last night? We must be cautious and get to the seat as quickly as possible," Margot replied.

They passed houses that remained tightly shut, even in the bright light of midmorning, and paddocks where cows and horses stood silent, watching them go by with large, unblinking eyes. In one house, there was a glimpse of a nightshirt-clad body lying just beyond the open doorway. By the time they reached the seat, the silence had taken on an unnerving quality; even the insects and birds made no sound.

Black streaks of smoke or dirt smudged the walls of the seat. They were worst along the edges of the gaping entrance, no longer hidden by its enchantments. Above the walls, the empty guard posts looked charred as if by flames.

"Gaiea's breath," Margot said, and raised her hand to her heart in a respectful gesture to the Goddess as they rode into the courtyard and halted their sweaty horses.

The garden had been destroyed, the earth scorched, the trees and shrubs blasted into firewood. Even the tiles in the courtyard had lost their color. Ahead of them, the windows of the seat stared like blind eyes. What was left of the doors hung from their hinges, and glass sprinkled the ground under the windows like diamonds.

The ground crunched beneath Margot's feet. She drew her sword from its scabbard and the clean blade gleamed in the sunlight. "Rachel, Genevieve, Suzanne—search the courtyard. Be sure to check the stables. The rest of you, come with me." She strode between the broken doors, into the blackened seat.

Light struggled to penetrate the corridors. Despite the bright day behind them, the sun did not move past the entryway. With a snap of her fingers, Margot called a quasiflame to guide her way, the twisting yellow strands casting an unusually weak light. She picked her way amongst the debris, her sword at the ready.

The seat was almost unrecognizable from what it had been during her time as a trainee. Works of art lay broken on the floor, furniture destroyed, beautiful rugs shredded, doors shattered. The ceiling above them sent down drifting flakes of soot that felt like oil. Every few feet, she passed a dull sword or an empty boot or glove.

They descended to the cellars, where the cool earthen corridors closed in on the search party. The quasiflame glowed stronger, as if the taint of the upper rooms had not managed to penetrate the lower levels. The rooms were filled with neatly stacked barrels and reed baskets, covered calabash bowls and woven sacks. The torch braces were empty of their usual burden.

At the end of a long corridor was the only door in the cellars. A heavy metal thing, constructed to protect the room behind it from the power of the great storms that sometimes roared ashore from the coast, hundreds of miles away. In the Storm Room, the town's inhabitants could wait out the weather if their homes were not strong enough to withstand it. The seat's lady, as the military guardian of the community, would often join them.

Margot paused outside, gesturing to those who followed her to be still. She raised her sword, the Dahomei behind her mirroring her action.

"I'm Margot of Garth," she called. "The Lady Mai sent me to help. If you can hear me, it's safe to come out."

There was a pause, then the clanging of locks being released filled the narrow corridor. Eventually, the door swung open, and the light from many torches blazed out at them as a large woman appeared in the doorway.

"Praise be to Gaiea," Annan said, her voice weary.

Margot's gaze swept the room. "Is there anyone else in the seat?"

"We're the only people left. If you made it here, the cursed Dark must be gone." Annan's voice was grim, her black hair untidy about her smudged face.

Margot sheathed her sword.

"Margot Greensleeves, captain of Lady Mai's court."

"Annan Rosewater, captain of this seat."

Margot cast a glance over the people thronged together in the cellar. "Common folk?"

"Servants," Annan replied. "The Lady Gretchen sent them to safety and commanded me to protect them."

"Alone?" Margot studied the space more closely as she entered the chamber. An earthen ceiling curved above her, and the silent occupants regarded her from the floor, or from makeshift seats atop barrels and crates.

"The Dark took my companions."

Margot placed her hand over her heart again, murmuring a short prayer to the Goddess. "I met your Lance on the way. She spoke of this Dark but understood little of it. Do you know what it is?"

Annan shook her head. "I . . . it's hard to describe. It was unstoppable. Our swords hardly slowed it. The lady said it was released by the *Nightward*. That it searched for the queen."

Margot frowned. "I'll need to speak to your lady. She might be able to tell me more." She spun, searching the group of silent servants. "Where is she?"

"Margot . . ."

She glanced back at Annan. What she saw on the Dahomei's face made her draw in her breath. "No—"

"The Dark . . . consumed her." Annan's shoulders fell, as if the burden of her news weighed her down. "As it did all the other Dahomei."

"Your Seer?"

"Gone."

"Seat Talon was protected by the best Dahomei outside of the court of Dun." Margot's eyes were wide with shock.

Annan nodded, tired. "The Dark took them all."

Around them, the flames in the torches flickered as one. Then, without warning, they grew tall in their brackets, blazing like pyres. Gasps and cries of shock filled the air as everyone rushed for the center of the room.

There was a booming sound above them, then another, and another, like impossibly large footsteps, coming closer.

"*Gaiea, protect us as you did from the Chaos.*" Margot whispered the old prayer, hand pressed between her breasts. Then she drew her sword along with her Dahomei. All eyes turned to the doorway. Silence pushed into the space around them like a swelling bubble.

Somewhere, a sound between a screech and a moan began. It grew closer and closer until it was a rumble they felt through the floor beneath their feet.

"Close the door!" Margot shouted.

The Dahomei nearest the door moved to obey, but a rush of air screamed down the empty corridor and into the cellar. Everyone was thrown to the floor, or against the wall. Some people knocked over bowls and barrels as they went down. Shrieks and shouts of surprise were almost lost beneath the roar of the wind and the crash of tumbling, rolling items as the wind blew the torches out and slammed the iron door shut.

THE HORSES SENSED IT FIRST. ELEANOR WAS HELPING VIELLA STRAIGHTEN her clothes when Flor tossed her head and danced, snorting. The Dahomei frowned at her, trying to calm her down. Luka glanced at them as he tied his bag shut.

Roland whinnied and backed up, tugging hard on the reins looped around a low tree branch. Luka took a step toward him, then realized the light was beginning to fade. He looked around, but all he saw were swaying treetops as the wind blew harder. He stepped onto the path and stared back the way they had come.

The very air vibrated against his skin as a low rumbling began. It made him think of Dun's infrequent landshifts, but the ground was steady beneath his feet. He squinted down the darkening path. Black clouds boiled together in the tiny patch of sky he could see, and grass gusted this way and that. He turned to Eleanor, but she was already dragging Viella behind the shelter of a tree as the horses pawed the air beside her, their neighs lost in the wind.

"The tree!" she yelled at him, pointing at the grannynut with his bag at its base. "Hide!"

Stunned, he started to speak—and staggered back as air blasted down the path at him, shoving him backwards. Viella's mouth opened on a scream he could not hear as she held out her arms to him.

It comes. He didn't know what *it* was, but icy fingers touched his neck, made his hairs stand on end and his shoulder ache like a rotted tooth. There was no time to think. No time to hide. *And it doesn't matter. It will see us anyway.*

He fought his way to the grannynut and slid around the trunk with his back to the path. Somehow, he knew he could not afford to lay eyes on whatever approached.

Sound boomed its way toward him, forcing him to cover his ears as it drew closer. It was the end of the world. Fear blocked the breath in his throat. His blood shivered in his veins as he sank to his knees.

Behind him, a roar louder than a dagen, harsher than any human cry, lashed at the woods. Things hit his body as they fell from the trees. Above the roar, a dreadful cracking began, and the ground beneath his feet vibrated with sound and impact. In the middle of it all, he heard the sound of wings flapping, like bedsheets on a clothesline, and a shout of laughter that was terrifyingly inhuman.

Gaiea protect me. Gaiea save me. Gaiea bring me to your Garden and spare me the Terrors of Chaos and the Oblivion at the end of all things.

He clenched his ears tight in his hands, his head ringing so loud, it seemed like forever before he realized the wind no longer pushed at him, trying to topple him over. He opened his eyes.

Light rimmed his knees, his arms, his feet. Soft as the glow of a candle and the deep red-gold of a setting sun, it rippled along his fingers as he held them out, astonished.

I burn, he thought, panicked. But as he stared, the light flashed, like the sun's final moment before dipping beneath the line between sky and sea. And then it was gone. He breathed hard, his stunned mind trying to make sense of it. *What was that?*

He did not know. He could not be sure. Nothing like that had ever happened to him before. But part of him went cold at the thought that all those years, he had hated his father for leaving him on his own for so long. Hated him for making him lie about who he was. But now . . . his father might have been right. Right to hide him. Right to keep Luka away until he was old enough to protect his own secrets.

Right to be afraid.

"*Luka!*"

Viella's screech pierced through his bewilderment and dread. The horses neighed and he could hear them pawing the ground.

He crawled around the base of the tree. Across the path, Viella stood in the circle of Eleanor's restraining arms, her light-brown eyes wide. Luka pushed himself to his feet, trying hard to ignore his aching shoulder.

In one movement, Viella pulled free of Eleanor and threw herself at him. He stumbled back under her weight, his gaze lifting to meet Eleanor's. They stared at each other for just a moment—

Surprised? Why is she surprised? Did she see?

—before she turned to the still-frantic horses and started speaking to them in a low, calming tone. Luka's heart lurched in his chest as he stared at Eleanor, willing her to look at him again. If she had seen, what could he say to excuse what had happened? What explanation could he give that would not make a Dahomei suspicious?

None. Because you don't know what happened either. And not knowing is just as dangerous.

"I thought you were hurt, or that it took you, and Eleanor wouldn't let me go, and she said she couldn't protect you without giving us away, and . . ."

"You speak too fast for me to follow." Viella was trembling, he realized, and he held her away from him so he could look down at her. Her tear-streaked face made his chest tight. He summoned a smile for her benefit.

"You should not worry for me, Your Majesty. I'm not the one that matters." He stroked her thick hair back from her face and wiped her tears with his fingertips. "Were you harmed?"

She shook her head, biting her lip. "But Eleanor said . . ."

"She said what?"

Luka shot at glance at Eleanor. She stood with the horses—calmer now, but still snorting and shying a bit—and she would not meet his gaze. *Better to face her head-on.* Taking a deep breath, he strode across the path with Viella, her hand in his.

Eleanor handed him Roland's reins without looking at him. "We make for the Portal, now."

"What did you say to her?"

Eleanor swung herself into the saddle in one sharp movement. "Later," she said, gathering her reins.

"Why is she upset?" Luka persisted, settling Viella onto the horse.

"Must I speak twice?" Eleanor's harsh tone seared Luka's ears as he mounted Roland. "*We have no time.*" And she took off, Flor's hooves pounding into the earth.

Always orders. Never answers. Luka swallowed his anger, determined not to let Viella see him unsettled. *But perhaps she saw nothing after all.* He brought the horse around, hoping that was the case, praying to Gaiea that Eleanor would have no questions for him when next they stopped.

"Brace yourself," he told Viella before digging his heels in and sending Roland after Eleanor.

CHAPTER 6

JENNYTEC

MARGOT CLIMBED TO HER FEET, ARMOR CREAKING. "ANNAN?"
Around her, she heard people pulling themselves off the floor, some groaning, but she couldn't see anything.

"I'm all right," Annan replied. The door was wrenched open, letting faint light back into the room.

"What in Gaiea's name was that?" someone asked.

"Something I'm glad we didn't face in the open," Margot said. "Annan, we must get these people out of here."

Once two of the Dahomei had gone ahead and returned with the news that the way was clear, the Dahomei started ushering the servants outside. Margot waited until they had all entered the corridor before she drew closer to Annan.

"Do you think as I do?" She kept her voice low so that none of the common folk would overhear them.

Annan looked her in the eyes, her lips a straight line. "That whatever passed over us came from the court?"

Margot nodded. "Could it have been part of what attacked the seat earlier?"

Annan shook her head as they started walking. "Hard to say. The noise—it was not like that last night."

Margot tapped her lips thoughtfully with one finger. "Something else then." She was silent for a moment. "I would see the court. I understand it is glamoured."

Annan nodded. "Hidden from sight and time. I wouldn't have believed it myself had I not seen it from the battlements.

It's as if the night itself came down and cloaked the court and then crossed the fields to Freetown."

"It's as the queen said. This is old magic, loose in Freetown once again."

They had arrived at the main level of the seat, and there were sounds of a commotion filtering through the devastated doors. Tension tightening her muscles, Margot quickened her pace as they approached the servants milling around in the area just inside the door, obviously nervous. The Dahomei leading them were outside, staring off to their right.

"What is this?" Margot strode through the crowd as they parted for her. "Why do you all stand—?"

She stepped into the courtyard and a deafening roar filled the air. She spun in time to see a huge red body turn the corner, bounding straight at her. Gasps and screams rose behind her, but before she could move, something knocked her to the ground. The war-cat pounded across the yard and, without pausing, leaped over her.

Breathless, she rolled onto her side after it passed and saw it dash through the open gate, tail held high.

A hand reached down to her, and she took it, hauling herself to her feet. Annan looked her over, worried.

"Did I hurt you?"

"Only my pride aches, having taken a fall twice today." Margot grasped Annan's arms in thanks. "You may have saved my life."

A Dahomei skidded around the corner, pausing to bend over, hands on her knees as she struggled for breath. Fresh blood welled from claw marks across her forearm. "Has it escaped? Did it hurt anyone?"

"Apparently, just you." Margot raised an eyebrow at the warrior. "You are one of Lady Gretchen's detail. Perhaps you know—what was a dagen-cat doing here, with horses around?"

"It came with the Daguard that brought the queen." The

Dahomei straightened, her breathing slowing. "We kept it from the horses, but after the wind and the noise . . ." She shrugged. "A couple of us tried to calm it, but it broke the stall and side-swiped me."

"It was certainly in a hurry." Margot turned to look at the open gates. "And frankly, I pity those at its destination."

"Should we not chase it? Bring it back before it does harm to someone?" Annan asked.

Margot smiled, a wry twist of her lips. "I doubt we have a horse that fast." She glanced up at the battlements and reddening sky. "And freeing the High Court must come first. We must break through the glamour as soon as possible."

⁄⁄⁄⁄⁄⁄⁄⁄⁄⁄⁄

BY THE TIME MORDACH RETURNED TO HIS QUARTERS, THE SURVIVING servants had lit torches in the main corridors, but true to his orders, they left the hallways to his rooms dark.

Mordach used his quasiflame to find his way, and once inside his rooms, blew a spell toward the braziers. They came alive with billowing green smoke, which settled into the familiar yellow glow of flames.

Books lined shelf upon shelf, towering to the ceiling. Piles of the more recent and less fragile additions were on the floor, neatly stacked against the walls. The few surviving ancient tomes, encased in their thin metal sleeves, were enclosed in a spelled, locked glass case that could not be opened by anyone but the Spellsayer. It hung at eye level opposite the door and was the first thing one saw upon entering the room.

Mordach's anteroom was large, circular, and had just one slit of a window next to his writing desk, which was directly below the glass case. The tiled walls and floors were a deep turquoise with scattered white leaf patterns. Thick beams of wood met in the center of the high ceiling above him.

On the floor, next to the desk, her skirts spread around her like petals, lay Lady Sophia. Her cheeks were pale, and blood stained the soft green layers of her bodice. A dirty handprint made a black smudge on the bare forearm draped across her stomach.

To Mordach's left, a wooden door led to his private rooms. Set flush in the walls, it bore no handle or hinges. Mordach drew his fingertips lightly against the upper right-hand corner of a panel of wood. A silver moon glowed into view before fading away, and the door swung open.

The Spellsayer strode to the unconscious Lady Sophia, lifted her with an ease that belied his thin frame, and carried her past the waiting door. The moment he entered, it shut behind him.

Mordach's private quarters were smaller than the anteroom. A bed faced a fireplace, where steady purple flames gave off an even heat. The walls of the room glittered like a star-seeded night sky, and the high ceiling disappeared into shadow. A table near the fireplace took up most of the space; it was covered in bottle after bottle of strange, shifting ingredients, sheets of scribbled parchment, and even a quivering red flame here and there that burned over small, flat glass dishes. One metal tome was open, the words it contained floating like golden smoke above it, the letters flickering slightly every minute or so.

Mordach laid Lady Sophia on the plain, rumpled sheets of his bed. Crossing to the table, he selected a tiny vial filled with fine powder. Taking it to the lady, he poured shining dust over her parted lips. Then he placed a hand on her forehead and spoke softly.

Lady Sophia opened her eyes on an indrawn breath. She blinked as Mordach placed a finger to her lips.

"Do not move," he said.

He ripped the delicate material of her bodice, exposing a ragged stab wound. Drawing a finger along it, he whispered sharp words that made the air around his hand turn gray and wisp away. When he removed his finger, smooth skin had taken the place of the wound. Mordach kneeled, wiping a trickle of sweat from the lady's forehead.

Lady Sophia used careful hands to feel the skin peeking through the gap in her bodice.

"Ah," she said to herself when she encountered nothing but drying blood.

"The healing is permanent," Mordach said. "There will be no scar."

She nodded, her gray eyes, light as silver, studying him. "I'm in your quarters."

"Yes."

"The Ragat attacked?"

"Yes."

She paused. "The queen . . ."

"Is dead." Mordach shifted on his knees but did not look away. "Viella escaped with the new bodyguard, Kemp's son."

Lady Sophia raised herself onto her elbows, wincing a little. "You're sure the queen is dead?"

"Her body lies in my study."

She inhaled deeply. "And the lord consort?"

"He and the prince are enspelled in the queen's quarters."

Lady Sophia considered this for a moment, then a small smile tilted her perfect lips.

"You've done well."

"Viella survived the dancer's call . . ."

Lady Sophia slipped her legs over the side of the bed.

"She won't get far. Not with the *Nightward* open. And we have Valan and the others, don't we?"

"Yes."

"The court is still glamoured?"

He nodded. "Yes."

"Yet you worry." She leaned forward. "Tell me."

"It was supposed to be Viella."

"Luck is with the little one . . . for the moment. But the Boon is still ours. Elise's Blessing is still here. With the others, we should have more than we need for the next stage." Sophia sighed, a satisfied sound. "Either way, the Court of Hamber will soon be at an end, and a new era will begin. Oh, how I would love to see the look on Jenista's face when word reaches her on the border." She smiled, the faintest touch of color smudging her cheeks.

Mordach frowned and she touched his shoulders.

"There is more. Unburden yourself."

Mordach took a great breath and sat back on his heels. He clenched his fists in his lap. "It is nothing."

"It is Alain," she guessed. He flinched slightly and she sighed. "You have regrets."

Mordach met her gaze, his face like stone. "Regret means nothing now. I believe this is the only way to truly, permanently change things."

"And that change has already begun. The Dark is awakened. And now, all the knowledge of the Designers and Masters awaits us, along with their greatest weapon."

Mordach opened his eyes. She moved to brush his hair from his eyes, concern etched into her expression. He caught her hand in his. "He will understand, will he not?" he whispered, as if to himself. "I've done this to make a world where he and Valan will have the power to end the Ragat and stand shoulder to shoulder with the ladies of Dun. I've sacrificed everything for Valan. If the Augurs had scried him, they would know what he was. He would have been lost to us. They will both understand. Won't they?"

"Of course, they will. *He* will. You care so much for Valan, and you saved their lives. The Augurs would have never let the boy go free. Alain only frets because of his wife's death. But it simplifies things. It was always going to be risky, imprisoning the Hand herself, even if we already knew we could capture the other queens."

Mordach looked up, his gaze blank. "You think my mistake a benefit?"

"It's a complication, of course. The idea was to keep the Boon from ever going to Viella." Sophia tilted her head at him. "But the *Nightward* is unclear, and there's little chance Elise would have survived what's next anyway. We can proceed, and once we capture Viella and take her Boon, we can forge a new, better Gailand."

"I don't know what happened. Viella moved at the last second . . . I couldn't adjust the boy's throw."

Sophia waved her hand. "I care only for results. The past is most happily dead." She stroked Mordach's hair gently. "And you must stay strong for the boy. Without Valan, we have no access to the Masters, no link to Viella, no claim to the throne. You must ensure he does his part."

Mordach nodded, even as his hands flexed at his sides. "We must finish what we've begun."

"That's all that matters now," Sophia agreed. "We made a decision, didn't we? To do what had to be done."

He met her gaze with his own. "And it will be as we wish."

THEY RODE HARD TO THE PORTAL, THE SECONDS PUNCTUATED BY THE dull pain that stabbed Luka's shoulder with every movement of the galloping horse below him. Viella held on, not saying a word, loose strands of her hair whipping his face. Before them, Eleanor found her way between the trees with unnatural speed. With the pain in his shoulder, and Viella's safety to see to, he had difficulty following her. So, it was no surprise that she broke into the Portal's field first, slowing her horse to a prancing halt. Her cry of rage reached him just before he, too, broke from the trees.

To the east, a dirt-packed road led away from the Portal and disappeared out of sight, around the wood. The road led to the ferry landing on the River Lethe, and was the usual route to Freetown, though too long and winding for their mission. Before him, dominating one side of the field and reaching just below the treetops, was a broad arch, much like the one that guarded the High Court.

Carvings covered its surface, and it was broad enough to admit six horses side by side. The etchings were in a language no one could read anymore, and the angular shapes sometimes softened into curves and tiny script—magic so old and powerful, it was said it was from the time of Gaiea's Descent to Gailand. The arch was not gilded gold, like the High Court's, but a silvery metal that neither rusted nor faded. Bright as a full moon, it was harder than any substance on Gailand. Weapons did not scratch it and magic had no effect.

On the right side of the arch, embedded in its surface, was a square of transparent glass. When the hand of the speaker was placed on the glass and the *geis* was spoken, it would glow a bright green, the field behind the arch would disappear, and the Portal's opening would fill with whisper-thin strands of twisting red light, like crimson rain. The rest of the time it stood a silent, shining guardian before the vast savannahs and their seats, which separated Dun from the Queendom of Jaleel in the south.

But today it was not silent. Today, the silver arch snapped and sparked like a fire, violent red lines running along its curved length as smoke bled from the ruined *geis* panel. Grooves raked it, as if the indestructible metal had been clawed by an angry animal. Worse, the Portal's crimson rain showered down, sometimes lashing the grass in spurts, the ground red as if with blood in the late-afternoon sun.

"Gaiea's Desert," Eleanor said through her teeth. "They forced the Portal open. How? What could do such damage?"

"That matters less than the real question." Luka warily studied the sparks that twisted along the arch. Viella's little fingers squeezed his arm, but she said nothing to betray the fear that made her cling to him.

"What question?"

"Is it safe to go through?" Luka glanced at Eleanor. "Do they wait for us on the other side?"

Eleanor's eyebrows drew together. "It passed over us before, thanks to my veil."

"Can we pass through a Portal while hidden?"

Eleanor made a small sigh. "Others may be able to, but it is not possible for me."

"Luka." Viella twisted to look up at him. "What does it mean?"

"What does what mean?" He glanced at her upturned face. *She looks tired, but there's something else too . . . Something different.*

She pointed to the Portal. "The writing. Who is Jennytec?"

Luka frowned. "What do you speak of? Do you see someone?"

Viella looked surprised. "Of *course* not. There's no one there. But can't you read it?"

"Your Majesty," Eleanor interrupted, her voice tense as her shoulders, "no one can read the writing of the Masters."

"Well, how is it I can?" Viella asked, annoyed.

⁄⁄⁄⁄⁄⁄⁄⁄⁄⁄⁄⁄

IT WAS ALWAYS THE SAME. THEY MADE THE DECISIONS OVER HER HEAD, as if she wasn't there, and became annoyed when she spoke up. Well, this time they were being untruthful and she would not stand for it. She was queen and she knew what she saw.

Without warning, her pointing hand began to tremble. Viella watched it, surprised, before lowering it. *They won't listen if they see me shaking.*

She had been careful not to say anything. Careful not to give in to the terror that filled her when Eleanor grabbed her earlier in the woods. The noise, the flying things, the darkness . . . it had come down on her like something demented, but her screams were lost in the gale.

"*I'll protect us!*" Eleanor's voice in her ear had pushed out the chaos. "*Stay close to me, Your Majesty.*"

She'd twisted in Eleanor's tight grip, yelling back, "*What is this?*"

"*I can't be sure. We must pray it passes quickly. My veil can only hide us for so long.*"

But Viella had seen Luka, trapped across the path, unprotected. She'd struggled in Eleanor's grasp. "*Luka!*"

"*Your Majesty, please!*" The Dahomei's hold had remained firm. "*There is nothing I can do. I can't split the veil, or create another, without weakening ours.*"

"*No!*" Viella had stretched out her arms, but Eleanor had turned her away and crushed her to her chest.

"*My Queen, only True magic can blind this thing, and the Daguard has none. You must be brave now.*"

The words had sent a hot pain through her heart. Her skin grew cold, and her body tingled as if her arms and legs had gone to sleep all over. She'd tried to tell Eleanor, and found her mouth was not her own. It had remained stubbornly closed.

Then she'd heard it. The laugh that was a scream. It was as if someone doused her in ice water. All the warmth left her body. All thoughts left her mind. Her sight darkened, as if she had closed her eyes. Terror made her mouth taste like copper spoons. Her body had drifted away from her and she rose, rose through the air in the darkness. It was a long time before she was still, trapped in a void where nothing could reach her but fear. Cold, twisting fear that wrapped around her ankles, wrists, throat, like ropes.

She'd spent an eternity floating, paralyzed and dumb, manacled by slithering things. And it dawned on her there was someone else with her. She could see nothing, touch nothing, and the bonds around her grew tighter and tighter, but with every second the feeling became more certain. Someone was there. Someone she knew.

Then the darkness broke, and she was breathing hard in Eleanor's arms as evening sunlight filtered through the leaves above her and the Dahomei said words of concern.

When she'd seen Luka, unharmed, she'd run to him, glad Eleanor had been wrong. But even having him back hadn't made her feel better. She'd tried to forget the void as they rode, but the coldness within her chest and limbs was stubborn and slow to release her.

Now they were in front of the Portal, which she had only seen a few times in her life from the curtained confines of a traveling house. For the first time, she could clearly see the etchings on the massive frame; the thousands of tiny symbols that danced in the jerky scarlet light. But what drew her eyes was the large block writing curved along the very top of the arch. The first part she did not understand.

TRANSLOCATION PORTAL BATCH C429AX711TEST

The second part, written below the first in slightly smaller print, she understood immediately.

PROPERTY OF GENETECH ENTERPRISES, GANYMEDE

So, when Eleanor told her she could not read it, it frustrated her. She knew it said something very important—that was clear—and now it seemed the grown-ups in her life knew less than she did.

"You can read the Portal's writings? You're sure?" Luka asked.

"Yes. Can't you?"

"Your Majesty, you must forgive us, but we cannot see what you see." Eleanor glanced from her to the Portal. "What do the writings say?"

"That the Portal belongs to someone called Jennytec. I don't think I can say the rest right."

"But Gaiea brought the Portals to Gailand," Luka said, looking at Eleanor.

The Dahomei nodded. "I learned the same histories you did, Daguard. The queen may not be reading it correctly."

Viella folded her arms. "I'm not lying!"

"I would never accuse you of that," Eleanor said. "What I mean is, you may not understand fully what you see."

"You just don't want to listen to me." Viella could feel frustration tightening her throat. The sensation panicked her, reminding her of the void. "I want to go. I'm tired of being here."

"It may not be safe," Luka said to her in a soothing voice that made her want to hit him. "The—thing that passed over us in the woods may be on the other side."

Viella rolled her eyes. "Don't be silly. The Dark is gone."

"What do you mean it's gone?" Eleanor's voice was sharp, her gaze no less.

"I mean it's gone." Viella cocked her head at them. *Do they know* anything? "Don't you feel it? If it was still here, I'd know."

Luka and Eleanor looked at each other.

"Back at the riverbank . . ." Eleanor started.

Luka nodded. "She felt something then—was in the grip of something. She might be able to sense it." He turned back to her. "Can you feel it even through the Portal?"

Viella turned her gaze back to the crimson Portal. The last evening rays of the sun illuminated its base. The truth of her words made her shudder inside. "If it was on the other side, I would know." *Just like I always know where Valan is.*

Until now, a small voice said within.

The realization hurt, but she pushed it away and glanced up at her frowning Daguard. "You can trust me, Luka."

"We may have no choice." Eleanor shook her head, biting her lip. "We can't go back. It waits for us there too."

"Then there is no point in staying here." Luka's arms flexed around her as he shook the reins. Viella grabbed the pommel, her heart pounding in her throat. *It's not there . . . but I hope we don't meet it again. I really don't want to meet it ever again.*

"We must be ready for anything, Daguard," Eleanor said.

"Don't worry about me, Dahomei. I can take care of myself. And the queen."

Then they were moving, and the Portal was coming closer, a ruby mouth waiting to swallow. Viella's last thought was to hope she wouldn't be far away from Valan for much longer, then the hooves beneath her skipped a beat and the world, coated in blood, swirled away from her.

ALAIN LOOKED UP AS THE DOOR TO THE QUEEN'S QUARTERS OPENED. "Sophia?"

Lady Sophia swept across the floor toward him. She had changed from her torn dress into silken yellow trousers and a white bodice with long, gold-embroidered sleeves. The collar rose high around her neck, and her hair had been swept up onto her head. She looked regal—as if the room had been built for her.

Alain got off the bed where Valan lay, still as death. His jaw flexed as he looked from her to Mordach and back again. His eyes narrowed. "You're unharmed. Of course. He couldn't have done this alone."

"Oh, I was harmed. Stabbed, actually."

Behind her, Mordach made a subtle movement of his head toward the door, and the Ragat guarding the lord consort filed out.

"Praise be to Gaiea," Lady Sophia said, coming to stand in front of Alain, "Mordach was able to revive me."

"You speak the Goddess's name after killing her Hand?" Alain's spat at her feet. "There are no words for your sins. Gaiea's Desert is too good for you."

Lady Sophia eyed the floor. "Nasty habit. But to be expected of a backwater savage from Kadoomun."

Alain took a step toward her, and raised his fist.

"Alain. No." Mordach moved in front of Sophia. "Don't."

"Oh, let him try, if it makes him feel better. He has reason to be angry." Sophia flicked an unconcerned hand as she walked past them to the bed.

Alain spun. "The both of you will answer for your crimes. I will fight to my last breath to make sure that happens."

"It is not news to me, Alain, that you don't know what's best for you." Sophia glanced at him with pity in her eyes. "We spoke about Valan's future, about the need for change. I tried to gauge your reception to our plans. But you aren't half the man your father was. You weren't ready to do whatever was necessary to put an end to a system that limits everyone's potential. Mordach is."

"If I'd had any idea this was what you meant . . ." He took a harsh breath, and his voice broke over his next words. "I thought you meant the Code. You supported the changes. Elise thought you were on our side."

Lady Sophia sat next to Valan and smoothed the sheets drawn over his sleeping body. "I still am." She met his angry dark gaze with her icy gray one. "But I am not Elise, and the sooner you understand that, the better. Mordach."

The Spellsayer raised a hand toward Alain. The lord consort gasped, his face contorting with pain, but he was preternaturally still. "*Mordach* . . ."

"He tried to talk to you before, Alain, and you wouldn't listen." Lady Sophia laid a gentle hand against Valan's cheek. He nuzzled into it, murmuring. "So, you'll listen to me now. And I will speak plainly, so you can fully understand the position you find yourself in."

She turned toward him as Mordach's fingers flexed and he groaned horribly. "You will keep the boy in line. It is your only value to me. Mordach, of course, would rather not lose you. But we are a united front in all things. I do not suggest you test our resolve."

Mordach flicked his fingers at Alain. The lord consort stumbled backward, trying to catch his breath, his furious gaze focused on the Spellsayer. "What in Gaiea's name do you want with my son?" His voice was hoarse. "He's just a boy!"

"Oh no." Lady Sophia shook her head, the faintest smile on her face. "He's so much more than that, Alain. In fact, none of this would have been possible without Valan. I'm quite fond of him really. It would be a shame to distress him more than we already have."

Mordach lowered his hand and Alain's chest heaved as though he'd run a mile. "I'm sorry, Alain. But in the end, you will understand it had to be this way."

Lady Sophia's sharp voice made Alain turn toward her. "Your son lives in a world where he'll always be second. A second-place heir. A second-place citizen. Surely you remember your child-hood, Alain?"

She grasped the boy's limp fingers. "Your father was raised in Everhill, but he never told anyone his true roots. He never forgot them either. When his wife became queen, she allowed him so much leeway, he took the throne from her with a Ragat insurrection.

"Elise and her Dahomei drove the Ragat back across their borders and gave the Queendom of Kadoomun to a blacksmith's daughter instead. Your father was talented enough to be able to study the Histories and find a way to take a queendom from a warrior-queen, yet all he accomplished in the end was a hole in the ground with his name above it. A name no one dares speak to this day."

Alain clenched his fists, a shiver coursing through his body. His dark eyes held a grief terrible to see. "I lived that story. I don't need your history lessons."

"I don't say this to mock you or cause you pain. I say this to remind you how easy it is to erase those who try to rise above their place. Elise made promises, but she would never have kept them."

Lady Sophia's gray eyes locked with Alain's. "We can all be on the same side, Alain. If you want."

"And my *daughter*, my mother—what of them?" Alain sneered. "Everything you say is more lies to twist those around you. So many people are dead because of the two of you."

Mordach turned away and went to one of the narrow windows. Sophia shrugged. "You're not. Valan's not."

"So only my daughter needed to die. How lucky for me," Alain said, his voice shaking.

Lady Sophia sighed, turning her head to stare at Mordach's back. "Elise wouldn't do what was necessary to keep Gailand strong. Someone had to admit that"—she glanced at Alain— "and *do* something about it."

"What do you want, Sophia? What do you *want*?"

She smiled the small smile of a woman with a secret. "Only what was taken from me."

Alain frowned as she rose to her feet and shook out her trousers.

"Time is of the essence." She spoke to Mordach's back. "Did you ready the dungeons?"

Mordach replied without looking around. "They were warded against the prisoners. They will not be able to create so much as a quasiflame down there. Our magic will not be affected."

She bent to touch her lips to Valan's head. "I will return for him. Until then, Alain, you have a choice to make, and whatever it is, your son will pay the price."

She strode to the door, her silks whispering like cronies with a secret. "Come, Mordach. We must see to the queen now."

Mordach turned, and for a moment, his eyes met Alain's. The two men stared, not moving, tension spinning tightening threads in the air between them. Lady Sophia, holding open the door, repeated, "Come."

Without another word, the Spellsayer followed her out.

//////////.

MARGOT SAT ON HER HORSE, THE WIND IN HER FACE, STARING ACROSS the waving grasslands. Like a section cut out of a vivid painting, the black hole that had replaced the High Court beckoned to her. Bulbous heads and thin wisps of Dark jostled for space on the edges of the glamour, twisting in on themselves as blobs of darkness ran across the green fields, turning it yellow wherever it touched.

She'd watched as her Dahomei tried unsuccessfully to carve a path through it. The glamour expanded in any direction they tried, blocking their path and consuming any weapon used against it. She'd summoned all the Dahomei together and they'd blasted the glamour with their magic. But it only grew, moving farther outward as if feeding off their efforts, and consuming a horse its rider barely had time to leap from. After hours of failure, she'd had no choice but to signal retreat.

"Gaiea's breath," Margot whispered, her hands tight on her reins as they rode back to the seat. "We've only made things worse. The Daguard was right. We need more help."

Next to her, Annan nodded. "Lady Gretchen knew it would be difficult to overcome. But we had to fight it. We had no choice. The queen couldn't risk staying."

"Yes, but when she and Lady Mai spoke, she didn't convey the—sheer size of it. She didn't have time."

"No time? What do you mean?"

"There was a problem with the oculars. Lady Mai tried to contact your lady after the initial arrangements, to find out more about what she needed, what she'd learned. But she never answered. Lady Mai hoped I would find out why, as well as aid Lady Gretchen. She never imagined it might already be too late."

When they arrived back at Talon, Annan followed Margot into the seat. Glass crunched under Margot's feet as she walked across the tiles, swerving to avoid Dahomei and servants busy lighting torches and righting furniture. She paused in the middle of a dimly lit corridor. "Where are your lady's rooms? Where she keeps her ocular?"

Annan pointed to the doors, the battle scars on her hand visible as a nearby servant lit a torch. Its light revealed the capsized furniture and torn cushions within. A cool evening breeze came in through the broken doors that led out into the gardens, spreading the scent of jasmine and ashes.

Annan picked up the black rectangle from the debris on the floor in the room. "Here. Lady Gretchen's ocular."

Margot took it and pressed her thumb to it. For a few seconds, nothing happened, then the ocular lit up and blue light began to race around the edges of the small device in faster and faster increments. Its flat surface displayed a circle broken at the top by a short, vertical line. The symbol blinked green before fading. Then, above the ocular, a blue oval unfolded, glowing moon-bright.

Margot opened her mouth to speak—and froze. The oval had become black as night, fading into the evening shadows that crowded the room. She dropped the ocular, holding her wrist and backing away as it hit the floor with a clatter.

Annan went to her immediately. "What is it? What happened?" She grabbed Margot's hand and caught her breath at the angry white marks on her palm.

"I don't know." Margot frowned as Annan touched the marks with careful fingers. "They don't hurt. My hand is just—numb."

Margot picked up the ocular. Multiple cracks had formed on its surface like spider webs, its shine dulled. Try as she might, she could not coax light from it again. Margot's lips formed a thin line. "It no longer works. And there is no fixing a broken ocular."

Annan took the relic from her, turning it in her fingers as she shook her head in disbelief. "The lady Sophia has had this forever. It was a gift from her grandfather. She left it with Lady Gretchen when she went to the High Court. How do we contact the other seats if this cannot be fixed?" She handed the device back to Margot.

"I fear that is the least of our problems." Shadows crowded in around them as Margot turned to Annan. "I believe something is wrong in Garth."

"But there was nothing wrong when you left."

"Yes. But if something has happened in Garth . . ." Margot gripped the metal ocular tightly. "If something has happened, Annan, my lady is in danger. And the queen and her escort are riding right into it, with no way for us to warn them."

"Chaos take it," Annan said, horrified.

Margot threw the now-dead ocular violently into a corner, the clatter reverberating through the room as she dragged a hand through her hair. "I made the queen a promise. I intend to keep it. I'll ride to a Guild and summon help to break the glamour. You gather all our Dahomei and find the queen before they get to Garth. Once you have her, ride to the nearest Guild and send word to me. By then, reinforcements will be here, and I'll have made new arrangements for the queen's safety. I only pray we're in time to catch them."

CHAPTER 7

SYCREN

FIRST, THERE WAS A VOID. THEN, VIELLA SMELLED GRASS AFTER A light rain on a hot day. A horrible jarring feeling ran through her body. She clenched her hands instinctively, clutching roughness. She could hear again. The wind in trees. Insects chirping. Horses snorting. Her own breathing, light and fast, filled her ears above the throbbing of her heartbeat.

Are we there? Shapes swam out of a red mist. She raised one hand to rub her eyes as the world beneath her stopped moving. The mist faded and she blinked away blurriness.

She was in a clearing. The last rays of the sun waned in the sky above her, leaving darkness pressing in from all sides on the wide path before her. Trees stood thick about the clearing and path. Stars pricked the velvet sky, and light clouds floated by in the strong breeze. Her fingers clutched Luka's arm, and she felt his chest rising and falling against her back, fast as the throbbing in her head.

"Viella?" Luka's voice was a concerned murmur.

"I'm okay," she replied, knowing instinctively what he wanted to hear. Next to them, Eleanor rubbed her forehead and grimaced.

No one said anything for long seconds. Then Luka spoke. "There's no one here."

"The navigator would have left already." Eleanor held out her hand, and a purple quasiflame bloomed above it. She held her hand out toward the trees, making a circle on her horse before confirming, "We're alone."

"I told you," Viella said. It was good to see the empty clearing and feel Luka's solid presence relax slightly against her. Despite knowing the Dark was not at the Portal, there had been a tiny part of her that saw the approaching red maw of the Portal and screamed for her to go back, go back, or she would never go home again.

You're not safe here.

The voice whispering to her made her skin bump. It was too soft to identify, but she knew it wasn't hers, so she ignored it. It had been wrong before.

"Garth?" Luka asked tersely.

"It's less than an hour from here," Eleanor replied. "If we ride hard—"

"Lead the way." Luka gathered his reins.

Viella's heart pounded so hard in her chest, she felt the rhythm of it in her throat. Her guardians did not talk, and the wind squealed low in her ears. When they broke from the trees, the hulking shape of a mountain range rose to their left, blocking the night sky with its obsidian peaks. At its feet winked the lamps of a town almost as large as Freetown. A road wound through the town and up the lower tiers of the mountain. Torches picked out its length at irregular intervals. It ended at a large fortress, ablaze with light that bounced off many domes and peaked roofs.

Nightfall reduced everything around Viella to shades of black and gray, but she saw when Eleanor waved a hand and slowed her mount so that Luka came alongside. The Dahomei turned in the saddle, her face indistinct in the gloom. "Stay close to me. There's a path through the mountainside to the seat. I suggest we take it. It avoids the town."

Luka gave a curt nod. "I agree. The fewer people who know we're here, the better."

They rode toward the mountain, Eleanor a gray blur low over Flor's neck. Viella clenched her legs tighter as they sped up, nerves making her stomach queasy. Once they reached Garth everything would be all right. They would get help, and they would go back and rescue Valan and Daddy and Grandmother. She was desperate to go back to her family and have all of it be over.

When they reached the beginning of the wooded mountainside, Eleanor pulled ahead of them and turned her horse to the left. She rode straight toward two entwined trees. Above Viella, Luka uttered a curse and started to pull at his reins. "Eleanor!" he called out.

But the Dahomei did not slow. Instead, she called over her shoulder, "Stay with me! Do as I do!"

The trees were huge in the dimness. A voice whispered urgently deep inside Viella, but she ignored it, knowing she had to control her fear. Eleanor charged at the trees, low branches reaching down as if to grasp her head.

Then the trees were gone and a narrow path, glowing a faint silver in the gloom of the forest, unfurled before them like a ghostly carpet. The horses' hooves made no sound as they left the undergrowth and rode the path's twisting, steep length at a breakneck pace. Viella looked back and saw only black behind them. The road disappeared as soon as they passed, trees and brush closing in as if they had never been disturbed.

Ahead, the trees thinned out and the path faded away beneath their feet like moonlight in the wake of a sunrise. Viella squinted at the wavering torchlight that shone down from the seat ahead of them, illuminating the clearing in front of the trees as Eleanor and Luka both brought their horses to a halt near its edge. The wind had quietened, and Viella could hear the horses breathing and feel Luka's heart thumping faintly against her back as he held her closer.

"We are here, Your Majesty." It was the first time Viella saw Eleanor smile, and it transformed her serious face, scrunching the freckles on her nose.

Viella returned the smile, but a knot in the bottom of her stomach pulled tight. "I'm hungry."

Eleanor's laugh was low. "We could all do with a meal and a bath. Garth is very close to several mountain springs that . . ."

"Eleanor," Luka said quietly. "Listen."

She glanced at him. "Daguard?"

"Listen."

Eleanor was silent. "I hear nothing."

"Exactly," Luka said, his voice grim. "Garth knows we come. She glows like a beacon. Yet I heard nothing on our way up. Nothing in the undergrowth. Not even an insect."

Eleanor's smile waned. "You're right. I've never heard a seat so quiet." She walked Flor to the edge of the trees and Luka followed.

In front of them, a green lawn ended at the base of a huge stone wall. Viella craned her neck to see the top, where torches blazed from pillars at regular intervals. People moved along the edges of the wall, the light catching on their armor, but she heard nothing.

"I don't understand," she said, looking up at Luka. "Is everything okay? Are we going in?"

"I'm not . . ." he began, but then Eleanor's sharply indrawn breath made Viella's gaze go to her. The Dahomei had a hand over her mouth, and her wide eyes were focused on the wall above.

A creature had alighted near one of the pillars, turning its huge head to and fro, as if searching for something. A massive black body, darker than the darkest night, rippled in the light from the torch. The two legs Viella could see ended in huge glimmering claws that crushed the stone beneath them, sending shards and dust cascading down the wall. High above its misshapen head with its wide snout, something red as blood protruded from its back. Its eyes shone blue as lightning during a summer storm, lit as if from within, like demons of old. But the creature shocked her less than who jumped off to stand beside it, his hand stroking the flickering hide of the monster, his gaze searching the forest below him.

Viella would know Blane Kemp, Captain of the Daguard and Luka's father, anywhere.

⚊⚊⚊⚊⚊

LUKA'S CHEST CONSTRICTED, THE BREATH CAUGHT IN HIS LUNGS, unable to escape into the still night air. Blood beat in his ears like tassa drums, drowning out all awareness and thought for painful seconds. It took a tug on his hand for him to realize someone was speaking in a low voice.

". . . I think it is?" Eleanor's hazel eyes were as wide as a child's. "They're extinct, right?"

In the midst of his confusion and pain, Luka's brain struggled to make sense of what she said.

"The creature, you mean."

"Yes. The . . . ?" She looked at him for help.

"Sycren."

"A Sycren." She breathed the word, tasting it. "But that's not possible."

"No," he agreed, his mind still reeling. *How could this have happened? My father . . . The prince and the lord consort . . .* His mind shied away from the thought. Instead, he said, "They died out during the Age of Chaos." Mercifully so, he thought. As a Daguard, he knew the histories of Sycrens. They were the ancestors of the much tamer dagen-cats, and their loss had not been lamented. During the age of war and pestilence, their appetite for destruction had laid waste to many towns, given rise to horrible myths and tales. Few witnessed their power and lived. But the coming of Gaiea had rid the land of them.

Or so they had thought.

"Who is that with it?" Eleanor frowned. "The rider. He looks familiar . . ."

Her question slashed at Luka's heart in a way she could not understand. Before he could reply, Viella answered, excited. "It's Captain Kemp. It's Luka's father—"

"That is *not* my father," Luka growled, the words bitter agony on his tongue, but true all the same. Both Eleanor and Viella fell silent, shock written on their faces.

Above them, the thing that looked like Blane Kemp said something to the creature and it tossed its head back, spread leathery, crimson wings, and with one downstroke, rose into the night. It disappeared from view in seconds. Its rider cast one more gaze over the surrounding forest, making Luka's skin prickle with awareness, before turning away from the wall.

"That is not my father," he repeated, and faced Eleanor so he could not see the wall. He did not need to be close to be sure. The thing on the wall did not move like his father, a man whose every movement he knew by heart after years training together in the gayelle.

And his father did not ride Sycrens.

It is a glamour. A cruel trick. Curse them to Her Desert for what they've done.

"My father . . . is dead." He ignored Viella's gasp—unwilling to think of how he would have to explain eventually that her brother, father, and grandmother might also be—

(I should have been there with him. At the end. The last words we had were angry ones. Goddess forgive me.)

—gone, and turned Roland around, his hands and heart cold and shaking slightly. He had one mission now. His father's final order.

"You're sure?" Eleanor asked, and something in her voice made sorrow sweep through him so hard, he closed his eyes for a moment. *No time for that now. No time for grief.*

He opened his eyes. "I'm sure. That's not him. It's a trap. We must get away from here as fast as possible."

"You are right," Eleanor said, her voice grim. "The queen is in danger here. Sycrens cannot be hurt by the magic of the Sight or the Word. We cannot fight one and win by ourselves. Garth is no longer safe for us."

Luka nodded. For once, they were in agreement. His mind barely made sense of what had happened, at how swiftly things had changed, but he knew what he felt. When he looked at the wall, even at that distance, he saw his father's face and body—and sensed something twisted and greedy. It was as if an aura surrounded his father now—a dark, pulsing nimbus that only he could see, not with his physical eyes but with his whole body and mind. They cringed away from that far-off figure.

They're gone. Dead. I left them behind, alone. To face—whatever that is.

Luka took a deep, steadying breath, tried to breathe past the squeezing tightness in his chest. Digging his heels into the horse's side, he followed Eleanor back down the path.

It was chilly amongst the silent trees. The path glimmered beneath the horse's hooves—crushed stars. Luka tried to keep his mind blank, but fear, anger, and heartache flooded him. He barely noticed when they emerged from the trees onto the plain. He reined Roland in when Eleanor stopped.

"What now?" she asked, her voice low as she cast a worried gaze back the way they'd come. "We made contact only with Garth. The next seat is several Portals away, and those Portals stand in the middle of big townships like Plytown, Biche, and Kafik."

Luka shook his head, forcing his mind back to the problem at hand with effort. "If they are here, we must assume they wait for us ahead. They know we will try for the seats. They may have sentries in all of them."

"Where will we go?"

"It is less important where we head than making sure we find cover before sunrise."

"We need a destination, Daguard." Eleanor did not try to hide her exasperation.

"We need a *plan*, and that requires time for thought," he shot back. "There are long-dead ancient creatures searching for us. We should stay off the roads."

"Obviously." She let out an exasperated breath between her teeth. It made his blood flow hot.

"You have better ideas?" he challenged, expecting a harsh reply. But Eleanor surprised him by remaining silent. She clucked to her horse, and Luka followed her lead as she set off parallel to the mountain range, deep in the grass, where the town's lights could not reach them. Ahead, low hills rose like jagged teeth.

The night air chilled Luka through his broadcloth vest. His body hurt in new places, unaccustomed as he was to riding in a horse's saddle. And his shoulder—broken slivers of pain splintered down his arm, neck, and back with every jarring movement. A gap opened up between him and Eleanor as he tried to concentrate on holding the reins, on keeping Viella tucked within the warmth of his body, on following the horse in front of him.

So, when a hulking shape dropped down in front of them, it was all he could do to stop Roland before the horse crashed into it. He gritted his teeth as he squeezed his legs and held the reins tight; the horse reared, neighing as it pawed the air. Beyond the kicking hooves, Luka spotted Eleanor's horse turning. Then Roland's feet came down and pain exploded through Luka's body.

Blood-red wings thumped the ground, and piercing blue eyes lit the grass with a frosty glow. Viella's scream was lost in the screech that blasted Roland's mane into Luka's face. It was the cry of a dying woman being ripped limb from limb. His arms wrenched cruelly as the horse turned, galloping back the way they had come in a mad frenzy.

Luka gripped Roland's heaving sides with his legs as best he could. Fear made a cold stone in the pit of his stomach.

You panic like a common coward.

But he had seen the blue glare of the Sycren's eyes when it

lifted its head. The coiling shapes that passed through that light. Obscene shapes he could not quite recognize; twisting nightmares that triggered his most primal urge to flee. He knew with complete certainty that if he paused, if he waited for one moment, the Sycren would cut him down like a scythe to wheat.

I cannot look in its eyes again. Whatever lives in it will . . . touch me.

Thudding hooves and harsh breath filled his senses until some instinct made him duck low over his saddle, Viella curved against him. Air lifted the edges of his hair, and then the Sycren was hovering before them, hissing, wings spread to block their way. Luka tugged on the reins, the horse tried to turn, and before he knew it, a tremendous jolt flung him from the saddle. He rolled when he landed, coming up in a crouch.

Viella lay an arm's length from him, a small heap midway between himself and the horse kneeling in front of the Sycren. The beast had dropped to all fours; even so, it dwarfed the fallen horse.

Luka threw himself to land at Viella's side, uncaring that he came down on his abused arm. She turned over as he did so, eyes wide, and he pulled her into his arms, fingers running over her little body, searching for breaks or bumps.

"Are you hurt?" he whispered.

He felt her head twist from side to side against his chest. He looked up in time to see the Sycren dart its black head at the horse that had gone to its knees before it. Roland screamed and thrashed, lashing out with his hooves. The head darted again, and blue light spilled around the horse's body, limning it like hoarfrost. The light pulsed as the horse made strange whistling and huffing sounds. Luka inched backward with Viella, trying to keep as close to the ground as possible. He knew Eleanor had to be close by, but he dared not take his eyes off the Sycren.

He saw the moment the blue light around Roland stopped pulsing, dimmed, and caved in on itself. Without sound or warning, the horse deflated, a pricked balloon.

Luka's heart tripped in his chest. His short sword had been in the pack on Roland's saddle. He had nothing to fight back with. *Gaiea save us. Descend once more to your people and protect us from the Oblivion of Chaos.* Behind him, he could hear faint rhythmic thudding as Eleanor rode back for them. He dug his heels in, trying to push himself away faster.

The Sycren's head swung in his direction, black snout scenting the air. It breathed in, rib cage swelling before his eyes. A screeching laugh rode the wind. And Luka knew he was out of time.

In one movement he rose to his feet, spun, and ran as fast as he could toward the approaching horse. The top of Viella's head whacked his chin once, numbing his jaw, but she made no sound. *Please Gaiea, do not let me fail her.*

Flor was so close, he could see her sides heaving as she halted. But when he raised his gaze to the saddle, Eleanor screamed something at him. Instinct made him drop to his knees and roll to his left. Light flashed in the corner of his vision and the smell of rotting carrion slicked his nostrils, made bile rise in his throat.

He came to rest with his body curved over Viella's. She was breathing as hard as he, her eyes huge with fear. He looked up and saw the Sycren claw at Eleanor. Somehow, the Dahomei managed to dance Flor out of the way. Terrified now, Flor snorted and dashed. Eleanor was struggling to keep her under control when the Sycren lost interest and started toward Luka again.

You have no choice. The queen cannot die here. The Daguard must not fail again. Luka got to his feet and put Viella behind him.

"Listen," he said without looking at her, "you must wait until I charge, then run toward Eleanor."

"You want me to run away?" Her small voice trembled a little.

"Yes. I will distract it. Do not look back and do not worry for me. I will follow." He spoke the lie with conviction, knowing that Viella would obey faster if she thought he was behind her.

The Sycren slinked across the grass, wings spread like a

canopy. The soft sound of an almost human chuckle reached him. Its black hide glimmered and rippled—water under a night sky. Behind it, Eleanor finally succeeded in wheeling her horse around.

"When I tell you to, run as quickly as you can."

The Sycren growled, its head dipping low as it prepared to leap.

At that moment, Luka's perception canted, as though the world tilted slightly off its axis. A red mist unfurled in his mind and his mouth tasted of copper. *Bloodlust . . . Farain!* He twisted and grabbed Viella, crouching over her protectively as the Sycren leapt toward them—

—and a shadow passed over him, slamming into the creature, knocking it backward and rolling with it in a tangle of wings and paws.

Relief pounded through Luka with the fierce thumps of his heart. *Praise be to Gaiea!* He got to his feet as the Sycren leaped away from Farain, spitting like a cat tossed into water. The dagen-cat roared, baring sharp teeth as it stalked the monster in a circle. Luka had no idea how Farain had found his way to them, but he had no time to ponder.

"Run," he urged Viella. "Run!"

They dashed for Eleanor as the Sycren swiped at the cat. Farain was half the size of the monster, but more nimble than a horse. It ducked, then clawed at the creature's black snout. Enraged, the Sycren screamed, lofted itself, then dived at its opponent.

They bit and snapped at each other, moving so quickly it was hard to see. It was all Luka could do to stay focused and ignore the tumult of Farain's battle frenzy in his head. The cat had never been so angry, so antagonized. But he would need every bit of his resistance, Luka thought, remembering Roland's death. He sent it bloody thoughts, added his anger to its ferocity, even though he knew it was already a lost cause. Farain would not, could not survive long. *But the queen can get away. That is all that matters.* He handed Viella up to Eleanor, who sat her across the front of her saddle. The Dahomei looked down at him.

"Go. I will do my best to hold it," he told her.

"No! Luka!" Viella screamed, reaching her little hands toward him, but Eleanor wasted no time. Flor took off, tail streaming behind her, and within seconds they were swallowed by the gloom, leaving nothing but the sound of thundering hooves. Luka wondered for a moment if Eleanor had, once again, chosen to shield them with magic. *I hope so. I hope it never finds them again.*

A roar rent the air, bloodcurdling in its intensity. Midnight blue clouded Luka's mind, and his blood became cold water flowing sluggishly through his veins.

Farain!

He put his hand to his head as he shook it. His feet tangled with each other as he tried to go to the dagen. It was too late. The cat lay on the ground as the Sycren struck again and again. Icy light sparked off red and gold, illuminating the slavering, sharp, black-tipped teeth of the Sycren. The cat yowled and Luka felt its strength, and his, draining away like water from a broken cup. He dropped to his knees, weakness swamping his body.

Without warning, as he watched, the Sycren backed away from the cat, shaking its head as if something had caught in its jaw. Luka blinked blurry eyes and saw a thin thread of red hanging from the creature's snout, like bloodied spider's silk. He frowned. *What is that?*

The monster flapped its wings, agitated, lifting off and settling down again, just a few feet from the war cat. He could see ragged holes where Farain had torn the delicate membranes between hollow bones. The dagen-cat growled at the Sycren, its head dropping back to the ground. Dizzy, Luka tilted forward, stopping himself with outstretched arms. *What is this? What is happening to me?*

The thread of red lined the creature's mouth now, and tiny branches extended up the sides of its jaw. The Sycren was distressed, whimpering and clawing at its face. Farain lashed the ground with his tail and Luka realized the blue light that had covered the cat was fading, overcome by a reddish glow that began where the Sycren had bitten. Luka slid down onto the ground, his arms boneless, his skin hot as flame. In his mind, blue was shifting to red, an animal satisfaction edging his thoughts. Thoughts that were becoming hard to hold on to. Thoughts that melded with hunger, and triumph and reveled in blood and—

(*termination*)

—death.

The Sycren slipped and went down on its back legs. Red covered it like a hood. It threw its head back and screeched. The sound shivered through the earth, but it reached Luka as a muffled vibration as the world started to spin away from him.

Gaiea, help me. I can't. I . . .

The last thing he saw was the Sycren tumbling over into a red-gold heap, like the embers of a dying fire. Then a numbing blackness claimed him.

<hr />

MILES AWAY, IN THE DESTROYED SEAT THAT WAS ONCE GARTH, THE THING that wore Blane Kemp's skin stopped in midstride as it paced the battlements. Around it, all the other soldiers stopped moving as well. As one, they lifted their heads and scented the air.

An inhuman sound of anger rumbled from Blane's throat. In that moment, it experienced something it had not felt in an age. Not since its last lifetime. Loss. A severing. Pain. "Something—"

"Has hurt me," the soldiers on the rooftop finished together with one voice. One by one, they gathered around Blane in a circle. Their bloodied swords caught the light of still-burning fires. Their boots crushed bone and tissue beneath them as they moved. The rooftop was an abattoir, covered in bodies and splashed with blood till there was no surface left untouched. The scent of copper and excrement hung in the air, and below it all, the rotting stench of carrion.

Blane swung toward the wall, where the mountain sloped away below them in a well-lit path. "Part of me has been . . . eliminated."

Growls of agreement met its words.

"The Sycren failed to stop them. They will not come here. But I will follow."

"Follow." The bodies around it, some of them bearing gaping mortal wounds, echoed its words back to it.

"I will kill the thing that has hurt me."

"Kill the thing!"

"And I will feed." Blane smiled, revealing rotting teeth and a black, pointed tongue. "On everything."

"Feed." Voices filled with glee whispered like leaves. "Everything. Everything—"

"Will die." Blane finished, and its pointed tongue licked cracked lips.

The dozen or so men that surrounded it ran to the battlements and, without pausing, leaped into the night air. Swirling clouds of darkness materialized into a Sycren beneath them, red wings spread high. The corpses landed on their backs, two or three to a creature. With a cacophony of screams and laughter, the four Sycrens banked as one, then curved away from one another, flying in different directions.

The Blane creature stared out into night, sensing life riding toward it, far below. A group that smelled of the same power that accompanied the one it sought. They were armed and searching. Not that weapons would save them. It needed to eat in order to split itself again. The life-force it sensed below was more than enough.

Chuckling, Blane dropped onto all fours and bounded down the stairs from the ramparts, into the shadows.

IIIIIIIIIIII.

LUKA AWAKENED TO A WET ROUGHNESS ON HIS CHEEK. *WHAT . . . Where . . . ?*

He did not move at first, far too tired to try and hurting everywhere. When the sensation came again, he opened his eyes and blinked away the blurriness.

Stars spun above him. And Farain crouched beside him, licking his face with a huge tongue. The cat was confused and suspicious of Luka's stillness. But he sensed its pleasure when he raised a hand to stroke its nose. He thought good things at Farain, raw steak and endless ear-scratches, his way of thanking the cat. Farain purred, nudging his hand for more strokes.

What happened to me? Why did I faint? Luka was convinced it had something to do with his link to Farain, but he had never heard of a rider so close to their cat that they experienced the same physical response at a point in time.

How did he find us after I left him? Did they send him? Did he break free? Or has something happened at Seat Talon? There was no way to know. Until they found safety at another seat, they would know nothing of the High Court. It was a sobering realization.

Luka sat up, one hand on his throbbing shoulder. It hurt more now than it had all night. He needed to dress it again. To his right, behind Farain, a hulking shape rested, wings trailing like broken sails. He knew without having to approach it that it was dead.

Frowning, Luka looked down at the cat curled beside him, blood seeping from several tears in its side. "How did you do that? How did you kill it?" *How did you not die? How did I not die?*

He tried asking Farain in his mind, but the cat seemed

uninterested, showing him only a red mist that flickered like the Sycren's hide as it licked its outstretched paws. Luka ran his hands over Farain's injured side, wincing when his fingers touched slickness and torn flesh.

It's too dark to treat him properly. I'll have to wash him. Make a poultice . . .

Farain snapped at Luka's fingers as he touched a sore spot. He shushed him with a few whispered words and got to his feet gingerly. Taking a deep breath, he walked over to the Sycren. He stood next to it for a moment, frowning at the motionless body. Even lying on its side, the creature came up to his shoulders. A stink of death rose from it. The wings were such a dull red, they were almost black, and its furred hide had lost its mesmerizing shine. Its huge head was flung back at an odd angle, teeth bared in a rictus of pain. Deep grooves marked its face like scars. Its glowing eyes were darkened orbs.

He touched a finger to the huge torso. The flesh felt rock hard, petrified as an ancient fallen tree. Something about it sent uncomfortable shivers—

(don't touch it—it will enter you)

—down his spine, and Luka pulled his finger away quickly.

He inspected poor Roland. Or rather, what was left of him: a depression in the grass marked by wind-scattered dust. Luka rubbed the silky remains between his fingers and sent up a prayer to Gaiea for Roland's brave sacrifice. He did not know what kind of magic the Sycren wielded, but he knew now why historic texts had called the dagen's long-extinct ancestor a terror.

What magic could reduce a horse to dust in seconds?

Whatever it was, Farain was clearly the source. He went back to Farain, sending a testing thought to see if the cat would be capable of carrying on. For an answer, Farain climbed to his feet, stretching first his front and then his back legs. Yawning, he waited for his master. Luka grinned, shaking his head as he gathered fur in his hands. "Thank you, my friend. You saved me. Now, let us find Eleanor before her trail disappears."

He swung himself up, feeling the comforting heat of muscle and bone between his legs. The instant he was settled, Farain took off on silent paws, the Sycren's body diminishing in the distance, a grave marker beneath cold skies.

///////////

LADY SOPHIA PUSHED OPEN THE DOOR TO MORDACH'S STUDY AND A torch sprang to life as though it had been expecting her. Light spilled over the gleaming wooden floor and illuminated the ceiling-high rows of books. The circular room closed in on them, wooden beams as thick as a man's leg arching down from a central point in the ceiling. There were no windows here, and mustiness warred with the scent of leaf-worm repellant. Two broad desks were shoved together in the center of the room, and two chairs were pushed out of sight into the shadows of the far wall. The desk was surrounded by standing braziers, and with a word, Mordach lit them all. Smokeless yellow-and-green flames flickered as Mordach closed the door behind them.

A body lay atop the desks, one bejeweled arm dangling over the edge. Queen Elise's hair dragged on the floor, and the hem of her sari was torn and dirtied. The hole in her chest, with its dark-red edges, teemed with a life of its own. A black substance swirled within it, swelling and deflating like a living heart.

Lady Sophia walked around the desk, never taking her eyes off the corpse. The queen's lashes feathered her cheeks, her lips parted as though she still breathed.

Lady Sophia shook her head in disbelief. "Death has made her lovelier than she was in life."

Mordach remained behind the braziers like a supplicant at an altar, a huge book held against his chest. "It is the Boon."

Lady Sophia nodded. "It keeps the Spirit within her. She is not truly dead until it has passed from her to her heir."

"I intended only to sully Viella's body and prevent the Boon from entering. But the spear's dark magic has also kept the Hand from ascending."

"For a time, yes." The long sleeves of Lady Sophia's gold-and-white bodice fell back from her slender fingers as she held a hand over the pulsing hole. "It fights to escape even as we speak. I must applaud you, Mordach. This is most powerful magic. You've once again proved that you're worthy of the post of Royal Spellsayer."

"Soon," Mordach replied, his voice hard, "that post will be irrelevant."

Sophia made a soft hum in agreement. "We still have need of it for now, so let's make sure this magic will hold until we find the new queen."

Mordach's ivory-and-silver robe whispered along the floor as he went to the desk. A few words were etched in the Old Language along the spine of the book he held. He carried it to where Lady Sophia stood and opened it in front of Queen Elise's body. Inside the book, a metal rim encased shimmering pages that were not solid. He held a hand over them, gold inscriptions and diagrams flicking past in the air as he did so.

He and Lady Sophia read aloud as the pages flipped and scrolled, repeating the words in tandem until they were in harmony and bouncing off the walls, a stir of echoes. Lady Sophia held out her hands over the queen's head and chest while Mordach held his own hands out toward the lower half of Elise's body.

The substance in the center of the queen's chest started to swirl counterclockwise. Faster and faster it went, pulsing in a regular rhythm that matched the words echoing through the room. Without warning, it spilled over onto the queen's chest. It trickled across her body in all directions, shiny midnight streams that stretched downward, like a soucouyant's knobby fingers. The fingers met, twined together, branched out again until Queen Elise's body had disappeared beneath the black pulsating mass, thin tendrils waving in the air, seeking like an insect's feelers.

Mordach dropped his hands and fell to his knees, breath harsh in his throat. Beside him, Lady Sophia held on to the edge of the desk, her shoulders bowed as she breathed through an open mouth. She tossed her head back and laughed, a surprised sound.

"Mordach! Have you ever felt . . . so . . ."

"Alive." He shook his head, his eyes closed, mouth open as he breathed deep.

"I felt this once before, you know," Lady Sophia said, her expression dreamy. "I was at Elise's home the night after Queen Leena died. A companion to my cousin in the difficult weeks after her own mother's passing. I felt it when the Boon came. There was this—glow that filled my bedchamber. So much—power."

Something shifted in her face and her smile faded. She let go of the desk and straightened her shoulders. "Then Elise walked through my door and it left me and went to *her*." Lady Sophia looked down at the mummified body. "It hesitated. I *know* it hesitated. But she came in and took it. A power she has never fully wielded as Gaiea intended her to."

There was a hard look in Lady Sophia's eyes when she met his gaze. "That is at an end. If we succeed, even Her Boon won't be enough to reverse it."

"Viella is a child, and without the Boon." Mordach rose to his feet, his chest heaving from the exertion of the spellcasting. "It will take weeks for this spell to weaken. She cannot stop us."

"By then, the Boon will no longer be the greatest power in Gailand," Lady Sophia agreed, wiping sweaty palms on her silken trousers and tucking stray strands of hair behind her ear. Mordach watched her preparations.

"You are ready?"

"I am. This was always going to be most difficult part for me."
She sighed and shook her head. "But there's no avoiding it."

"To the storm cellar, then?" Mordach asked.

Lady Sophia met his eyes. "To the cellar."

VIELLA WOKE WITH A START. HER DREAMS HAD BEEN FILLED WITH RED
and blue, and things that hissed around her while she stood in
the dark, unable to scream or move. She opened her eyes to the
graying light of dawn. The fine shale under her whispered as
she sat up and pulled her blanket tight around her shoulders.
She could not stop trembling.

It wasn't a dream. It was real.

Tears dampened her cheeks, and she rubbed them with
gritty hands.

"Your Majesty?"

Eleanor sat with her back against the curving wall of the cave
and her feet stretched out beside the dying embers of a smokeless fire. Flor stood on the other side of the fire, munching on
something.

"May I . . . I mean, is there something . . ." Eleanor's voice
trailed off as Viella shook her head. She knew what Eleanor
wanted to ask, and she didn't want to hear it. She didn't want the
Dahomei's concern. She never knew if Eleanor meant it, or if she
was just doing her duty. She missed her mother and father and
grandmother, but most of all she missed her brother. The other
part of her. Her constant companion. The connection they had,
one that had simply been there her whole life, was gone as if it
had never been. She couldn't feel him anymore, and after her
dreams, it alarmed and terrified her.

She was tired, so tired, of having everyone she loved taken
away.

And now Luka's . . . Her mind shied away from the word, afraid to even think it. Viella stared at the rapidly lightening opening to the cave, hugging herself under the blanket.

"He was a brave soldier. A good Daguard," Eleanor said. "He did what he had to do."

Viella's throat grew tight, and she blinked moisture out of her eyes. "He could have come with us."

"Flor could not carry us all, and I'm better with horses than he is."

"I don't care!" She glared at Eleanor. "And you only care that you didn't have to stay and face that . . . that . . . You're just a coward who didn't want to die!"

Flor snorted, looking at her with reproachful liquid-brown eyes. Viella burst into tears.

The Dahomei didn't move, which was fine, as the last thing Viella wanted was to have her near. She wanted Luka. Wanted his familiarity and annoying orders and cheese jokes. Anything to hold against the memory of the monster that had almost killed her. A monster whose very presence had sent her mind into a tailspin of strange feelings and familiar terror.

What do I do? She doesn't understand, and I can't tell her because she doesn't care about me. I'm all alone and I want Mummy.

The thought of her mother made her heart hurt. It was easier to not think about the night of the Ceremony with Luka around. She could almost pretend things would be normal again soon, as long as he continued to be with her, just like he was at court. But with him gone, she felt the hurt inside her open as wide as the valley they had passed through to get to the caves.

"Your Majesty." Eleanor's voice was soft. Viella dashed tears from her eyes, yet refused to look at the Dahomei. Instead, she stood and went to the opening of the cave, which was partially obscured by the branches and brush Eleanor had used to cover their tracks. She looked out at the hilly landscape, at the road that wound through the tree line several feet below. Dawn cast a soft, gold light over everything, but she could still see her breath hanging in the air as she exhaled.

"Your Majesty, I understand that you are in great pain right now. I cannot imagine the horrors you've seen. But you wound me deeply when you call me a coward."

"Why do you care? You didn't even want to come with us because you don't like Luka."

"Not so." Viella heard little rocks shifting and rolling as Eleanor came over to the opening and stood behind her. "I was . . . bothered by the idea that you preferred the Daguard to protect you. It is the sole desire of every Dahomei to serve the Divine Spirit and the ladies of Gailand until their last breath. When I heard what had happened, I wanted nothing more than to ensure the safety of my queen. When you chose the Daguard over me it was . . . difficult to accept."

Viella faced her, arms folded. "I'm the queen. I can choose who I want."

Eleanor nodded gravely, her hair sandy in the strengthening sunlight, her light eyes kind. "But I am Dahomei. I pledged to serve you in all things. I want nothing more than to do that, Your Majesty. And now that we must journey on together, will you let me? Or will you dishonor a brave Daguard's sacrifice?"

Viella shook her head, unable to answer, unwilling to acknowledge that Luka was indeed gone.

"I will never leave you, Your Majesty." Gentle hands grasped her shoulders. Viella looked into Eleanor's eyes and saw the truth of the Dahomei's words. "I will allow nothing to hurt you. I will take you to safety and I will stand at your side as long as you let me."

A bird called somewhere outside. Within seconds, another had answered it.

"You promise?" Viella cocked her head to one side, wiping at her eyes.

"I swear, Your Majesty, by all that is holy. By Gaiea Herself."

It was a serious oath, then. A pledge witnessed by the Goddess. The Dahomei was telling the truth. Viella slid her hands
tentatively around Eleanor's waist and laid her head against her
stomach. A heartbeat passed before the warrior knelt and pulled
her into a tight hug.

Viella closed her eyes, letting herself take strength from her
new protector even as her mind whispered that she was betraying
Luka. *You don't know her. She could be saying what you want to hear.*
A shiver of doubt went through her. The voice had been right,
after all, about Garth not being safe. Suppose it was right once
again?

It doesn't matter. She's all I've got. What choice do I have?

The voice had no answer to that.

Eleanor stiffened under her hands. A sharply indrawn breath
made her look up.

"What is it?" Viella asked, the image of red wings swept
across her mind for a frightening moment. Eleanor was staring
past her at something, her brows drawn together. She shook her
head, as if in disbelief. Then a slow smile spread across her face.
She rose to her feet, turning Viella around as she did so. Viella
stared out of the cave's entrance. There was movement beyond
the tree line on the road below. A flash of blue cloth and golden
fur, and Viella's heart leaped like a dancer.

She was out of the cave before she knew it, running and
sliding down the hillside toward the dirt road. Hands had pulled
at her blanket, and Eleanor had said her name in a low, urgent
voice, but Viella twisted out of her grasp and kept going. There
was wetness on her cheeks, but her gaze never left the road below.
Stones slid around her and branches broke off shrubs; one even
hit her in the face. She didn't care. She couldn't find the voice to
call out. Instead, she ran full-tilt into the road, right in front of
the cat and its rider.

Luka pulled on Farain's fur with a soft curse, and the cat
halted. Viella ran around to the side, Luka reached down, and

then she was in his lap and crying like the baby she wasn't anymore. Eleanor skidded to a stop next to them and Farain turned his head to look over his shoulder.

It was a while before Luka's words reached her. "I'm all right," he was saying. "It didn't hurt me. I'm all right, Your Majesty."

She leaned back so she could see his dirt-streaked face, smearing her tears with her forearm. "Is it dead? Did you kill it?"

"It's dead," he said, his voice gentle.

"Good," she said, and hit him on the chest. Once, twice, three times. The blows weren't very hard, she wasn't strong enough to hurt him, but with his wound, it was enough to make him suck in air.

"Never again," Viella said, clenching her fists, and the voice that came out of her was stern and so unlike herself she felt almost detached from it. "I chose you, Luka, and you will stay with me. You can't leave me behind. Okay?"

Luka's brow furrowed as if he was trying to make sense of her. Viella didn't care. She knew instinctively this was necessary. If she didn't say something now, it would keep happening.

"Do you understand?" she asked again.

Another moment passed before Luka nodded slowly. "Yes, Your Majesty. I understand."

That voice still thrumming inside her, she turned to Eleanor. "I appreciate everything you said in the cave. But Luka is my bodyguard. You came with us. Not the other way around."

Eleanor inclined her head and brought both hands against her chest. "Of course, My Queen. I have made my pledge, though, and I stand by it. I will keep my word and ride at your side as long as you wish me to."

"Okay." Viella sighed. Tension—and the voice that was hers but not—left her. Suddenly, she was soft and weak with gratitude.

And hunger.

"Can we eat breakfast now?"

Water is Gaiea's Blessing. It is the giver of life, the protector of all things, the repository of Her Glory.

It was Gaiea that freed us from the Masters and Designers. It is Her Blessing that seals Oblivion and its Dark within the Halls of Creation, protecting Gailand from the horrors of the Age of Chaos.

The River Lethe contains that which curses the forces of Chaos and grants the people of Gailand peace from their past, and serenity in their future. The Great River flows from the Mother Mountain itself, throughout this continent, its tributaries touching all shores, on the way to the Sea that surrounds Lang. From its waters came the First to defy the Masters.

This, then, is the greatest responsibility of the queens of Gailand, and the High Queen herself, she alone whom Gaiea has entrusted to Hand Her Histories to. The queens must protect Gailand against the powers still at work here, and against anything that may arise to force us back to the mistakes of the past.

Because I know our Histories, because I am Her Hand, I cannot simply allow what is happening to continue. With each cruel decision to divide our people from their families, from their children, from each other, Neutral or Adept, we slip closer to what Gaiea saved us from. I must find a way to unite us, to bring all the Forts back under the control of Dun, or we will be no better than our former Masters.

As we are now, we risk a new Troubles, one that will lead to the Summoning.

—Diary of the Hand
Daily Reflections for the Spirit, The Duty of the Hand
Elise, Hand of Gaiea, Tenth High Queen of Dun

CHAPTER 8

DOUEN

JENISTA STAR, LANCE TO THE HAND OF GAIEA AND COMMANDER OF the Palms of the High Court of Dun, was standing over her maps when the tent flap in front of her was pulled open. Daylight, watery but indisputable, entered the room with a blast of freezing air. She looked up as the tent flap fell back into place, her long, blond ponytail brushing the parchment in front of her on the foldable table.

"Agnes. Raven." The warriors who had entered inclined their heads as Jenista straightened, folding her hands into the furred sleeves of her winter coat for warmth. "You have news of the front?"

Raven shook snow from her regulation white fur cloak and glanced at Agnes, as if looking for permission from Jenista's guard to speak. Agnes stared ahead, her back ramrod straight under her own cloak as she placed her fighting staff against the ground at her feet. Their gold helmets gleamed in the steady light of flames that rose from several metal basins scattered around the tent. Jenista frowned at them as the silence stretched. "Speak."

"Yes, we bring news," Raven said in her lilting voice. She had been born in the Queendom of Kadoomun, and their accents flowed like the many rivers that crisscrossed their land. "But not only of the front, sister." Her dark eyes were troubled, and she gripped her own fighting staff with gloved fingers. "The new Seer has asked that you come to her tent. Immediately."

Jenista rounded the hardwood table without hesitation, picking up her sword from its resting place against a chair. She belted it around her waist and was outside before Agnes and Raven caught up, their breath steaming in the frigid air.

"Sister, there is more," Raven said as Jenista pulled on gloves covered with white fur on the backs of the hand for camouflage. "The sun rises this morning on an empty battlefield."

Jenista missed a step, stopped, and turned, her blue eyes crinkling at their corners. "What madness do you speak?"

"Not madness. Truth. The Ragat withdrew. All of them."

Jenista scrutinized her, one hand on her sword's hilt, the other on her hip. "How could one hundred Palms of fighters disappear overnight? The Ragat have no magic. They would have had to move tents, animals, weapons . . ."

"And yet they are not there. The blizzard must have hidden their movements."

It had snowed viciously for the past two days, making it near impossible for a Dahomei to see past the tip of her nose. Many of Jenista's forces were from the warm land of Dun, with little experience of Kadoomun's cold season. Despite being outfitted with everything necessary to survive the chill, Jenista knew her people were miserable, though too well trained to complain. She had been relieved when instead of having to deploy her forces to push back against the Ragat incursion, the enemy had remained well behind the huge stone piles that marked the border at half-mile intervals, allowing the Dahomei to hunker down during the frigid blast.

Jenista curled her fingers around her sword. "Something is wrong here. Why mass so many men on the border, then retreat?"

"That is the question." Agnes's dark brows drew together. "I fear we will not like the answer."

Jenista turned on her heel and continued walking on the hard, uneven ground, dodging horses and women, Daguard and tents with the practiced ease of experience. Snow fell lightly, coating her eyebrows, lashes, and nose, and filled the air with the sharp scent of frost. "I feel threads, sisters. Threads connecting these events. Threads that dance me like a puppet."

Her expression was so grim, those she approached scuttled out of her way, saluting her with lowered heads. Jenista returned every gesture without stopping. When she reached the brown hide tent farthest from the battlefront, sandwiched between an officer's mess tent and common sleeping quarters, Agnes and Raven took up guard outside, and Jenista entered without waiting for a summons.

Inside, a mix of brown and black furs covered a small cot at the back. At the foot of the bed, a round metal warmer stood on squat legs. The pipe that jutted from its top vented smoke out of a hole cut in the roof. The Seer preferred not to waste magic on personal comforts, conserving her energy instead for one of the most important and difficult jobs in the army.

Seers were specially trained Augurs who possessed such strong magic of the Sight they could discern changes in Gaiea's Design, the life-force of Gailand. They could use this power to perceive the future and guide an army's battle plan, or a seat's investments, with the knowledge they had gained. Once, Seers had even been powerful enough to control forces like the weather. But fewer and fewer were born every year now, and it was hard to find Augurs, far less anyone gifted enough to perform the feats of the Age of Chaos.

In the center of the brushed dirt floor was a small circular wooden table. A scuffed shiny black rectangle rested on it. Rose-pink tendrils of light bloomed from its surface, rising in a slim column from the ocular and twisting around the edges of an image.

The Seer stood behind the table, her hands clasped in front of her gray skirts. She was a small woman who barely reached Jenista's shoulders, with silver hair braided into a circle around her head. Her eyes had a slight lift to the outer corners and were a warm chocolate brown, but the spirit that looked out of them was an old one, much older than her unlined face and pale-brown complexion.

Jenista inclined her head to the Seer, who had given up all personal belongings, including her name, when she gained her office. "You summoned me. You have news of the shift you sensed days ago?"

"Indeed." Her voice was a soft, soothing contralto. But her gaze was sharp and direct, and a smile did not touch her wide, pink lips. "I could not reach the Seers at Talon or Garth, but earlier today, I sensed another, much smaller change in Gaiea's Design. Soon after, an ocular reached out to us. One of your sisters needs to speak with you. I am boosting our ocular with my own Blessing, as the ocular on her end is very weak. I have almost lost her several times."

Jenista frowned, her golden brows almost touching. "A Dahomei?"

The Seer gave a single firm nod. "Margot of Garth has news for you." She waved her hand at the image before her and stepped back to make room for Jenista. The commander rounded the table. A dark-haired woman, freckles scattered across her upturned nose, stood in an old library. Books spilled from crammed wooden shelves onto more jumbled book piles on the floor, and dust motes danced in early morning sunlight that streamed in through high, square windows.

"Margot." Jenista did not try to hide her surprise. "You're at Garth?"

"No, sister." Margot's voice sounded far off, but clear as a bell. "Lady Mai sent me to Seat Talon. I'm using the ocular at Freetown's Augurs' Guild. Thank Gaiea I've reached you."

"Our Seer sensed a great change in the Design. You know what she saw?"

"I do." Margot took a deep breath, then recounted the ambush of the High Court, the death of the queen—which brought a cry from the Seer and an indrawn breath from Jenista—and the escape of Viella and her protectors. By the end of her tale, Jenista's eyes were bright with unshed tears. She slammed her fist on the table, and a ripple distorted Margot's image.

"That's why the Ragat abandoned the battlefield."

Margot frowned. "They've left Kadoomun's borders?"

"Sometime in the past two nights, they crept away. They did their job, after all. They forced us to leave the High Court in the care of Daguard—men who could not possibly repel a magical attack of that scale. We have been pawns in someone else's game, Margot."

Margot ran her hand through her hair, sweeping aside messy strands. "My home may be gone, Jenista, my lady dead. The *Nightward* has been opened, and I need many more Dahomei if I'm to free the High Court. As we speak, I've sent all the women I had to find and protect the queen on the road." Determination and anger tightened her features. "I need reinforcements."

"Have you spoken to Kadoomun? Any other queens?"

"I haven't been able to reach them. Something frequently disrupts the oculars. You're the first I've been able to reach."

Jenista straightened in thought, folding her arms across her breasts. "I will leave a small force here and send the rest to you immediately. I'll start back for the High Court as soon as I've informed the court of Kadoomun of this tragedy. We'll spread the word, gather our forces, but we must be careful whom we trust. The new queen must be safe, and the High Court retaken before the seats panic."

"Dahomei." The Seer sat on her makeshift bed, small fingers gripping her knees, exhaustion writ in every line of her body. "I am sorry, but I cannot hold the ocular open for much longer. I must rest."

"No apology necessary, Seer," Margot replied with a respectful nod.

"Please, take your rest," Jenista added. She turned back to Margot. "Keep your ocular near. I would speak with you again soon."

"By then I will have reached the sister courts, or their seats. Let's hope their cooperation is forthcoming."

"We can't afford to *hope* for anything. If the queens have not survived, and the seats become consumed with their power games before we regain the High Court, all of Gailand will suffer."

With that, Jenista stood back from the ocular, and the Seer came forward to take it into her hands. Margot's image wavered and collapsed downward into the ocular. The device shone pink around its edges before fading back to dull black. The Seer laid the ocular on the table with fingers that trembled with fatigue. Behind her, Jenista sank down onto the bed and covered her face with her hands. The Seer waited, giving the commander a few quiet moments. Finally, she said in a soft voice, "Our Hand is with Gaiea now."

Jenista wiped her cheeks and raised her head, her face twisted with grief. "This will be the last time I fail my queen. Blood will flow, Seer—here, in Ragat, wherever I find those who gave birth to this scheme."

The Seer dipped her silver head. "What has happened is not of Gaiea's will." She met Jenista's gaze with her own. "You may count on my assistance in whatever way you most require."

"Thank you. Rest now. I will take the news to my captains and officers and prepare them for our new mission."

※※※※※

"HOW DID YOU GET AWAY?" ELEANOR KEPT HER VOICE LOW.

Viella sat by the fire, munching on bread and talking to Flor. Luka had rewrapped his shoulder, and Farain had allowed his wounds to be cleaned. The dagen-cat was already healing, as was normal for his kind. He waited at a discreet distance from the cave to avoid spooking the mare.

Luka and Eleanor were by the cave entrance, sharing a sandwich between them. Luka pulled the bread apart with his fingers, relishing it despite its stale dryness, grateful to be alive and hungry and able to feed that hunger.

"I'm not sure," he admitted. "It was Farain. He withstood the attack and somehow—reversed it."

"Reversed it? In what way?" Eleanor's hazel eyes caught the sunlight, and he saw rich flecks of brown and green in them. His heart sped up for some reason and he looked away, focusing on her question.

How do I explain it? How do I say that we linked in a way we never have before? That something came out of him I've never seen?

"I'm not sure. Something went wrong with it," he said finally. "Farain—poisoned it."

"How does a dagen poison a Sycren?"

"Apparently by allowing it to bite him."

Eleanor looked out onto the bright morning, her brows drawn together. "Is that all that happened?"

Luka stopped in the act of putting another morsel in his mouth, frowning. "Should there be more?"

"I don't know. You answer questions with questions, Daguard." Eleanor looked directly at him, her lips a thin line. "There are things about you that do not make sense."

Luka slipped a morsel into his mouth, savoring the hard, crusty bread and sharp cheese. "It's you who are making very little sense."

"In the forest, before the Portal, I think it was the Sycren that passed over us."

Sudden tension made his muscles tighten, but he kept chewing, trying to keep it from showing. "A good guess." The conversation needed to end, he realized. She was starting to edge into dangerous territory. And Dahomei expected answers when they had questions.

"So how did you survive, Luka? Yesterday and last night you should have been dead. Yet you are here before me. Will you not tell me how?"

Luka froze. *I have asked myself since the woods.* For a moment his thoughts went to his parents and all they had defied to be together. All they'd risked bringing him into the world. The rules they'd broken. *Could it be . . .*

No. What had happened with the Sycren could have nothing to do with who he was. It would have been obvious long before now if he had that kind of talent. He had the mind-touch and some skill at the Word, but that was it. His magic was not strong enough to protect him from such a storied beast. No, his survival had to be linked to Farain. Perhaps he had been close enough when they had been in the woods. He was lucky the dagen-cat had followed him.

He finished his sandwich and dusted crumbs from his leg. "Perhaps it was Farain. We are lucky he was nearby."

Behind them, Flor nickered as Viella giggled. Eleanor studied him, her forearms braced on her knees, the sandwich forgotten. "Luck such as you have had is not luck."

"What do you mean by that?" he asked, meeting her direct gaze.

"Who was your mother, Luka?"

His heart thumped hard in his chest. There it was. The question he and his father had feared his entire life. "What?"

"Your mother." Eleanor's gaze was unwavering. "Your name is Freehold, but that is a common name among orphans, and you are no orphan. Did you know your mother? Was she from Freetown?"

"She was not from Freetown." He rose to his feet, panic in his throat, fingers digging into his palms. He refused to let himself think on her. For all he knew, the Dahomei had magic that could divine his thoughts. "And you have no right to ask that."

"Luka." Eleanor stood to meet his gaze head on. "The queen

has made her choice. But I am Dahomei. I have *every* right to ask your mother's name anytime I choose."

Every time. It comes back to that every time. Rage made him tremble. "If you think to belittle me, you waste your words. I am Daguard. *You* do not command *me*. All that is required of me is that I do my duty. You do not need my mother's name for me to do so."

He turned away from her and went to Viella, shale slipping under his feet in angry whispers. Viella looked up at his approach, her smile relaxed, a brown smudge on her tan cheek, her eyes a dim gold in the weak light at the back of the cave.

"If you are agreeable to it, I propose we leave now," he said to Viella. He could feel Eleanor's approach as palpable pressure on his back. He let righteous fury swallow his panic. *She can go to the Desert with her questions.*

"I'm agreeable," Viella replied. She stood and dusted off her pants. "Do we ride the cat from now on?"

"It's probably best if we don't ride together. Farain would draw too much attention if we encounter someone."

"But we only have one horse and I want to ride with you."

"I've been thinking about that, Your Majesty," Eleanor said as she halted at Luka's side. He stared straight ahead, refusing to acknowledge her presence.

"If we travel off the main roads, Luka can ride Farain. There's a village, Tenville, a few miles from here, between Plytown and Biche. We should be able to procure a horse there. Once we've done that, you can ride with Luka again. Perhaps, at that point, we should send Farain home."

"He hasn't got a home at the moment," Luka pointed out, glaring at her. "He's quite capable of following at a distance to avoid spooking Flor. Since he's the only thing we have that can stop a Sycren, I think sending him back might leave us at a small disadvantage."

Her unsmiling face and icy gaze said she was as angry as he was. "You would risk revealing us to outsiders?"

"No. But if we're revealed, I'd like to have something to fight with besides a short sword. And given what happened at Garth, we must be on guard for anything."

He knew he had won when she didn't say another word and instead went to prepare Flor, her shoulders tense. He relaxed slightly, relieved he'd distracted her from the only question he could never answer without risking his life.

Viella watched Eleanor go and sighed. "I don't like it when you fight."

Guilt pricked him, but he hid it with nonchalance. "Why do you think we were fighting?"

"When you get all private like that, it's usually because you don't want me to hear, and that's when you fight." She turned back to him and folded her arms. "You have to stop that, you know."

"It would be easier if Eleanor didn't use every opportunity to provoke me." As soon as the words were out, he regretted them. It was injudicious of him to criticize a Dahomei, particularly in front of the queen. But Viella surprised him by shrugging.

"You provoke her too."

"Me?" He was shocked. "I've done nothing to her."

Viella rolled her eyes. "That's what *you* say. Dowager Mother says it takes two to start a fight and one to end it."

"Not in every case," he muttered.

She scrunched her face, thinking hard. "Maybe. But you should think about what you did to make her angry and not do it anymore."

"Your Majesty, when it comes to Eleanor, I try not to think of her at all." With that, he went to see to Farain.

LADY GRETCHEN STARTED AWAKE, HER HAND SPASMING, CLUTCHING
for a sword it no longer held. Breath rushed from her throat in
uneven gushes. When she sat up, it was with one hand to her
head. She brushed at a tacky black substance on her broadcloth
vest and trousers and tried to rub her smudged hands clean;
the armor she had worn was gone. She stood, her feet bare and
covered with dark splotches.

The stone floor had dirt and mold grimed into the cracks.
There were no windows, and the walls were gray-black rock. On
her right was a small wooden bed with an uncovered mattress.
On her left was a shining metal bucket. In front of her, narrow
bars formed a locked entrance, a single slender chain hanging
from it. The torch on the wall outside her cell made the bars and
chain glisten; like the bucket, they looked brand-new.

Lady Gretchen raised her palm. She gazed at it for a few
seconds before closing her hand into a fist with an exasperated
explosion of breath.

"The magic of the Sight won't work here."

She looked up, startled. Lady Sophia stood in the corridor
beyond the bars, her yellow silks like sunshine in the flickering
dimness.

"Mother!" Lady Gretchen closed the distance between her
and the gate in a heartbeat, reaching through the bars to grasp
her mother's hands. Lady Sophia smiled as she squeezed her
daughter's fingers in return.

"I thought you murdered." The words came out in a shaky
rush. "Oh, praise be to Gaiea, I thought you lost to me forever."

"I am much harder to kill than that." Lady Sophia touched
her smudged face, flicking pale fingers at the black grime that
clung to her. "You are in such a state. I must get you out of here
and into a bath." She drew closer to the bars as she smoothed
Lady Gretchen's tangled braid. "You are safe now. I'm so glad
we're together again."

Lady Gretchen's smile slowly faded. "I don't understand. Where are we? What happened to you? A Daguard brought me word of an attack on the court and then . . . then the Dark came to Talon."

Lady Sophia turned to the shadows that stretched back the way she'd come. "See how you terrified her?"

Mordach came forward; his pale robes seemed to float around him in the darkness. "The fastest way to retrieve her and the princess was the Dark."

With a cry, Lady Gretchen wrenched away from her mother. "What is this? Why is *he* here?"

"Gretchen." Her mother's tones were soothing. "You must calm down. There is much you do not know."

"I know that his hand is at work here." Lady Gretchen pointed a trembling finger. "You destroyed my seat and killed my women. You opened the *Nightward* and loosed a demon from Gaiea's Desert into this world. Your very words give you away."

She turned to her mother. "I don't know what lies he's told you, but the Spellsayer's tongue may as well be forked. You cannot trust him."

Lady Sophia sighed and closed her eyes. "Mordach. Leave us."

"She is not amenable." Mordach took a step forward, his face hard. "You must realize that."

"She is *my* daughter." The sharp retort halted his steps. "Now would be a good time to check on the Portal. Let me handle the affairs of my seat."

The Spellsayer bowed and disappeared into the shadows.

Lady Sophia approached the gate and waved a hand over the chain. It slipped free and she swung the gate open on silent hinges, casting a distasteful gaze around her as she halted in front of Lady Gretchen.

"He could have cleaned it before he brought you here."

"It's a storm cellar, and he's made it into a prison," Lady Gretchen pointed out. "It's not meant for comfort."

"You are a lady of Gailand. He should show more respect."

"Why would he? He is a liar, a traitor, and a murderer."

Lady Sophia strolled past her, leaving the door open. She sat gingerly on the bed and picked at the worn mattress. "Tell me about this Daguard. He had Viella with him? You helped them escape?"

"Mother." Lady Gretchen faced her, her face flushed, her eyes narrowed. "What is this?"

Lady Sophia raised her head, her lips set in a thin line, her eyes as clear as her daughter's. "Something that should have happened a long time ago."

Lady Gretchen gasped. "Betrayal? Murder? War?"

"If necessary." The Lady of Talon studied the woman who stood in front of her. "Although this can't be betrayal if it is done in Gaiea's name. I raised you to think for yourself. You know my feelings on Elise's plans for progress. You disagreed with them as well."

Lady Gretchen frowned, folding her arms across her chest. "I thought the changes she wanted were—extreme. There are certain positions that should be kept for the ladies of Gailand, who better understand the needs of the many must outweigh the needs of a few. Her changes to the Civil Code would disrupt our system of governance."

"Exactly. I suppose it is a happy coincidence that with Elise gone, her dangerous ideas will find fewer champions."

Gretchen stared. "But I thought . . . isn't that what you and Mordach want? Equality within the Code?"

"Oh no. We are well past that now." Lady Sophia shook her head, her expression unreadable. "Mordach and I have been close since he returned from his time with the Augurs. He has never forgotten that had he not been forced to stay at the Guild for years of instruction, he could have seen his parents before they died. He spoke with me often about his feelings of anger and oppression. His ambitions, not only for himself, but for all men. However, to realize those, he needed more power.

"The only way to get that was the *Nightward*. It's full of instructions, histories, and spells powerful beyond imagining, whether you're an Adept at the Sight or the Word. When Elise passed me over, she had no idea we'd planned for Mordach's selection for years. It's the main reason I championed the changes to the Civil Code." She smiled a fond smile. "He thinks of me as he did his dead mother. She was a smart, gifted woman." She sighed. "There are so few of those left now."

Lady Gretchen's eyes were wide with shock. "You *planned* this? *With* Mordach?"

Lady Sophia stood, and her voice was gentle when she spoke. "Have you not listened? I was saving us, Gretchen. All of us. The Age of Chaos was so long ago, we have forgotten its cause. But I have not. I read the Forbidden Histories as a girl. The *Nightward* only confirmed what I discovered. Elise wanted to renounce the lessons we learned. Destroy what we worked so hard to create." Her voice grew harsh. "Her plans would have us ignore the power we already hold."

"But Elise was the Divine Hand of Gaiea! You forsook our Goddess with your actions, Mother!"

Lady Sophia snorted. "Gaiea. You've read the Histories, and yet you don't see it. *She doesn't care.* She destroyed our world once, just to remake it in Her own image. They say She ascended, but what does that mean? Even the *Nightward* doesn't say.

"If we believe the High Queens and the Scriptures, the best interpretation is that She gave us over to Her custodian, Her Hand, and never looked back. But what if that was a fantasy, Gretchen? What if it was a lie told to control a new world?" She took a step toward her daughter. "What if we're alone, Gretchen, and the only real authority in this world is in the line of the Hand and the *Nightward*? Shouldn't that lie with those who will use it as it was meant to be used?"

Lady Gretchen took a step back, staring at her mother as if seeing her for the first time. "Is that why you let me read the Forbidden Histories? Is that why you taught me so much of the past and of the line of the Hand?"

"*Yes*." Lady Sophia stepped forward, grasped her daughter's shoulders. "Do you see? I hoped to be the Spellsayer someday. So many families ascended to the line of the Hand by attaining the dominance of Sight and Word. But I couldn't master the Word. I hoped for a son, whose residual Blessing might Unbind me, or a gifted daughter, but you took after me too much. I had to find a different way.

"So, I waited, studied, planned, and then Mordach came to me about his fears for Valan. By that time, he was in love with the lord consort, and they'd shared many things with each other, including exactly how his father was able to take Kadoomun from Frances.

"It would seem that on rare occasions, Neutrals who are exiled to Ragat turn out not to be Neutrals. That they are simply late to their talent. We've comforted ourselves with the belief that Ragat has no magic, but like so much else I've discovered since opening the *Nightward*, that's not true. They have the Unbound, and more. They just didn't have the numbers to be effective. To truly strike a killing blow, especially after losing so many in the failed Kadoomun Rebellion.

"Mordach and I had the access to make small numbers irrelevant, and they had what we needed to carry out our plans. After that, it was easy to convince key servants in Dun, and a few other courts, to join with us for their own betterment."

"You helped that man betray us all to the Ragat, and for what? The ladies of Gailand will never follow either of you after this, and the Ragat cannot hope to hold the High Court against them." Lady Gretchen's voice was steel as she pulled away from her mother's embrace. Lady Sophia heaved an irritated breath.

"You are thinking too small. Focused on the wrong things. I understand. For a long time, I was focused on the power of the Hand too. But that was before we knew about the Ragat and Valan. Before we opened the *Nightward*."

"Another blasphemy!"

"My daughter." Lady Sophia's tone carried only a hint of the frustration her expression refused to betray. "I'm telling you Gaiea, the High Queens, the Code—none of it *matters*. What I know now, what I've found, is the true power of the *Nightward* and the High Court. Once we have it, nothing can stand against us. Not Ragat, and maybe not even Gaiea, if She was who the Scriptures say She was."

Silence fell between them, and echoes from other parts of the court filtered down into the cell. Lady Gretchen brushed past her mother to sit on the bed, her head lowered, her hands braced beside her on the mattress. Lady Sophia studied her, her face and shoulders tense.

"Gretchen. Do you hear what I'm saying?"

"How could I not? You're a monster." Lady Gretchen's voice was low but still audible.

Lady Sophia took a step forward. "You're surprised—"

"Surprised." Lady Gretchen raised her head, tears glistening in her eyes. "You never knew me, Mother. You never *bothered* to know me. I lived my life to please you, and you never once spared a thought for who I was."

Lady Sophia's eyes narrowed and she batted the air with her hand, as if knocking something away. "Don't be ridiculous. I raised you, gave you the very best in training and education. You are the finest lady in the land, and everything I have done, *everything*, is to ensure that we both have the life we deserve."

"How you justify things in your own twisted mind," Lady

Gretchen spat. "What you did was plan the murder of your cousins and your queen. You have manipulated and lied to those who trusted you. You are mad with the lust for power and you blaspheme against the Goddess. At least Mordach did this for love. For those who are our fathers, brothers, sons—"

"Is *that* what you fret over? You think those who helped us are innocent victims? You see your father in them perhaps?" The scorn in Lady Sophia's voice was unmistakable. Lady Gretchen rose to her feet, her skin pallid except for the bright-red spots high on each cheek.

"What if I do?"

Lady Sophia laughed, one hand over her stomach as if trying to hold in her mirth. "Oh, Gretchen. Your father was the third son of a merchant with enough money to buy his way into a re-spectable place in Dun's society. Nothing more, nothing less."

"He was my father!" Lady Gretchen's voice bounced off the walls, echoed down the corridors. "Whatever he was, he loved me until the day he died. I don't know what you are, but you don't love anyone but yourself. I refuse to call you my mother. You are a traitor to my queen, and I will not be part of your schemes!" Without warning, she darted toward the open cell door.

Lady Sophia sighed, raised one hand and said, "*Rester.*" Gretchen rose into the air, her back bent like a bow as she gasped with pain.

"When you think on this later, remember, I came to you openly. I shared my hopes and dreams for us. *And you refused me.*"

Lady Sophia swung her hand toward the bed. Lady Gretchen crashed into the stone wall, bounced off it, and landed awkwardly on the bed. She moaned as she lay there, unmoving.

Lady Sophia stood over her, looking down with a face twisted by disappointment and anger. "Everything I do, I do for you, for Dun, for Gailand. I cannot express how upsetting it is to realize that I have not raised a daughter worthy of the line of Talon."

"Then . . . kill me. I would . . . rather die than . . . live up to your . . . expectations." Lady Gretchen's chest heaved as she tried to speak and draw breath at the same time. Lady Sophia pointed her index finger downward and spun it in a half circle. Gretchen's body twisted till her feet lay on the bed. The Dahomei gasped in pain. Her mother's eyes narrowed.

"You are my only daughter. Soon you will realize that I have risked it all for the truth. To put an end to the limits we chafe under. Perhaps you will come to your senses then. But if you do not, I have a better plan for one so . . . devoted to her child queen."

Still pointing at the paralyzed Dahomei, Lady Sophia whispered a single phrase over and over again. A sibilant sound that tickled the ear like a light finger. Lady Gretchen grimaced, her head tossing from side to side.

A thin, black line spun itself out of Lady Sophia's pointing finger—silk from a spider's spinneret. Wrapping around itself faster and faster, it made a line to Gretchen's ear. When it touched her, the Dahomei froze, her eyes wide open and staring at the ceiling. She tilted her head toward the line, as if listening to a very faint sound.

Lady Sophia stopped speaking. Lady Gretchen's eyes closed and her breathing grew even. The thin line slid into Gretchen's ear until it disappeared altogether. Lady Sophia brushed her hands together, as if dislodging dirt, then bent her head and whispered into her daughter's ear, "When the time comes, remember this. There is no place you can hide from me. My blood runs in your veins. I will always be with you."

With that, she turned and left, locking the cell behind her with a gesture.

Mordach was waiting for her at the top of the stairs. He leaned away from the wall as she closed the storm cellar door. "Did you convince her to join us?"

Lady Sophia shook her head as she slid the bolt home. "My daughter shares my strong will." She faced him, her gray eyes glinting like steel in the light of the torches. "But she will come around. I have a surprise for her when she wakes."

Mordach tucked his arms inside his voluminous sleeves, his gaze cautious. "A surprise?"

"Yes. Is there anyone you trust to send down to her? She'll need assistance when she wakes, but it must be someone of good standing. I won't have my daughter in the hands of a common servant."

"We both know who could do the job. However, her allegiance cannot be assumed."

Sophia raised a delicate eyebrow. "Excellent idea. We will need her later, but this might be enough to distract her until then."

/////////////

FRANCES ATUNA, DOWAGER MOTHER OF THE HIGH COURT OF DUN, former Sister Queen of Kadoomun, was pacing her tiny, spare bedroom when the sound of the bolt being released made her spin to face the door. She clasped her hands behind the pink skirts of her sari. When Mordach entered the room, closing the door firmly behind him, she exhaled in a rush of air.

"So, it's you then."

Mordach held her gaze with his. "Yes."

Frances nodded, her expression thoughtful. "I wondered who would come. What of Alain and my grandchildren?"

"Alain and Valan are fine. Resting at the moment."

"Resting?" Frances's lip curled with contempt. "Do not think me a fool, Mordach. I have lived this story. You have brought this upon us and there could be only one reason. Speak truth now. Is my family still alive?"

"I cannot speak for Viella. Otherwise, I have not lied." Mordach swept his robes around him and sat on the overstuffed chair beside the small bed with its clawed wooden feet.

Frances inhaled before nodding, as if agreeing with some unspoken thought. "So, Viella has escaped. Praise be to Gaiea. I was on my way to the Ceremony when I saw a band of Ragat leaving the lower levels of the court. They dragged me in here before I could raise the alarm. I said to myself, Why don't they just kill this old woman? And then I knew." She stood in front of him and raised his chin with a light hand. "You told them they could not, didn't you?"

Mordach's fingers trembled a little as he held her wrist, but his voice was calm. "I had no desire to harm you, Frances. You have been good to me."

"And you're in love with Alain. He wouldn't look kindly on you killing his mother." Frances pulled her hand away. "The servant who brought me dinner told me Elise is dead. He said blood flows in the courtyard under black skies with no stars. What magic have you released, Mordach? How is it the Ragat walk these halls?"

"I cannot speak of it now."

"Cannot," Frances said, "or will not?"

Mordach did not look away. "It is not why I'm here."

She absorbed this for a moment, then turned away to study the tapestry that decorated the wall above her desk. "You have come to ask me something. What is it?"

"I have an offer and the lady Sophia has a request."

Nut-brown shoulders went rigid under pink silk. "The lady Sophia? She is part of this?"

"Yes."

"Then I must ask: Why are you doing this?"

"All will be revealed soon."

Frances scoffed. "She planned this?"

A long pause before a quiet "We planned it together."

"So, I assume this . . . carnage is not the end of it?"

Mordach did not reply.

"Elise did not deserve what you did to her." Frances's voice had no inflection.

"None of that matters anymore." And in a low voice, "But we can make her death the cost of something greater."

"You've come to ask me to join you then." She faced him. "Why would I do that?"

"Because you wish to see your son and grandchildren again."

Frances sighed. "I am old enough that I've made my peace with death, Mordach."

"I don't threaten you with death. You can remain here, locked away, or you can be free to move about the court. Free to see them again, spend time with them. It is your choice. But I make this offer only once."

Frances gave a dry chuckle. "Gaiea damn you both to the Desert." She met his gaze. "Tell me what you want of me."

'//////////

HEAT ROSE FROM THE HARD-PACKED DIRT OF THE ROAD AND TRAVELED up the loose burskin legs of Viella's trousers. Her throat was grainy with the dry, dusty air, and no wind moved the trees on either side of the narrow road. Viella opened the neck of her wrap and fanned herself with one hand, trying to cool the sweat that caused tendrils of her hair to stick to her neck.

"How much further, Eleanor?"

"Not much."

"You've been saying that all morning and we had lunch already."

"I beg your patience a little while longer, Your Majesty."

Viella rolled her eyes. *The cat would have been more fun. At least Luka makes conversation.* "I'm tired of riding Flor. I want to join Luka."

"Luka is providing protection for us, Your Majesty. He can

ill afford to have his attention divided. We agreed I would purchase the horse. They won't sell to a man they don't know in these small villages."

Viella sighed and settled back against Eleanor, accepting her fate. She amused herself by searching either side of the road for any sign of Luka and Farain, but she saw nothing but trees and shrubs, still as statues in the afternoon heat.

They came to where a few goats grazed in a clearing, tethered on long ropes to some sturdy stakes in the ground. To the left of the road, a small white hut faced them, a multicolored fall of beads drawn across its entrance. A woman sat on a mat in front of the hut, legs folded beneath the striped cotton of her skirts. She watched the goats while chewing on a stick.

"You must remain silent in the presence of the Welcome Elder, Your Majesty," Eleanor warned in a low voice. "Children of your age should not speak unless they are spoken to."

Viella huffed, irritated, but did not argue. At least she was going to be meeting new people, something she loved. When they weren't being attacked, Luka and Eleanor had said little to each other over the past three days and the quiet always made her mind go to how much she desperately missed her family and her home.

When they pulled up in front of the old woman, she took the stick out of her mouth. Eleanor dismounted and helped Viella down. Together, they approached the woman and Eleanor bowed from the waist, tugging Viella's hand discreetly so she would know to follow suit.

Viella bowed, her skin prickling under the woman's open regard. The Elder had blue eyes and skin the color of caramel. Her white hair was streaked with black and braided in neat rows. Wrinkles mapped her age on her face, but her legs were folded beneath her with the ease of youth. Viella recognized the stick in her hand as chotlu, an herb the people of the grasslands chewed to keep their teeth strong and their breath clean.

"I bring greetings from the open road, and from my family of Freetown," Eleanor said, her voice as warm as her smile.

The Elder inclined her head. "The family of Tenville accepts your greetings and welcomes you to our homes." Her voice was scratchy but pleasant. She waved a hand in front of her, and Eleanor joined her on the mat, tucking her legs underneath her.

Viella sat behind Eleanor. Only an adult could sit beside Eleanor. As queen, Viella was one of the people entitled to have a village Elder greet her first. An Elder would have seated her inside the hut if she knew who she really was. But Viella put that aside. It was a game, she told herself; a game in which she got to pretend to be a different person. That was more fun than being fussed over any day.

"What news from Freetown? Has the Ceremony ended? Will there be a procession?" The Elder slid the stick into her mouth and bit down on one end.

"I left Freetown before the arrival of the sister queens," Eleanor said with a regretful smile. "I have no doubt they'll have a procession, but I won't see it. I have urgent business in Plytown. My daughter's horse fell ill after visiting my mother in Garth. I thought to buy a horse here."

The Elder looked disappointed, but she nodded, the stick in her mouth moving as she spoke. "If there is one, it might pass through in a few days. I saw the last one when Queen Leena was Introduced. I was hoping to see another before I went to Gaiea's Garden. I hear the princess is a delicate thing, prettier than her mother even."

The bleakness that swamped Viella at the mention of her mother made tears prick at her eyes, and she must have made some sound because the Elder swung her gaze toward her. She looked away from the old woman's kind but curious stare, twisting her fists in her trousers as she studied the brilliant green of the treetops.

Eleanor said briskly, "I've been lucky enough to see them once myself, Gaiea bless them. But on the matter of the horses . . ."

The Elder removed the stick and gestured behind her with it, down the dusty road that twisted out of sight. "We've two horse breeders—the Singhs and the Edmudsuns. You'll find an animal easy."

"And the town factor?"

"Fourth house on the left as you enter. Blue stonework. Not likely you'll miss it. He's at home and will be happy to have a sale to arrange on a quiet day like today."

Eleanor inclined her head toward the Elder. "Gaiea bless you and yours, today and always."

The Elder returned the nod. "Perhaps you'll stay on a day or so before leaving? Give us a chance to exchange names?"

Eleanor rose to her feet and Viella stood with her, eyes downcast and relieved to be going. "The urgency of my business will not allow us to visit properly. But I shall spread word of Tenville's hospitality to all those I meet on my journey."

The Elder smiled and returned the chotlu to her lips. She was absorbed in watching the goats by the time they rode off.

Five minutes later, the road went from dirt to cobblestones, and they found themselves passing paddocks where cows and horses grazed, watching them ride by as they chewed. Small huts stood near the fences. A woman dressed in a loose black broadcloth dress hung out washing beside one of them. Eleanor waved and the woman waved back before turning her attention to clipping sheets to a rope strung between two trees.

A bare-chested boy ran past in the opposite direction as they entered town, his coarse orange trousers flapping in the breeze. He paid no attention to them, dark eyes focused on the triangular kite he was trying to launch, long blond hair whipping over his shoulder. They stopped in front of a low blue stone wall that bordered a whitewashed house, and Eleanor dismounted.

"You'll have to wait here," she said, and Viella nodded, relieved to be left outside. Talk of her mother had taken all the fun out of pretending. Eleanor rang a bell that hung from the eaves over the door. A voice called out from behind the house, and though she could tell it was a man, Viella could not make out the words.

Eleanor glanced over her shoulder. "I won't be long. I'll get us invited inside so you won't be in this heat. Luka is near too. Shout if you need either of us."

"I know." She hadn't seen him, but she'd felt Luka's eyes on her all day. "I won't go anywhere."

She watched Eleanor disappear behind the house then turned her attention to her surroundings. Dust whirlwinds spun across the brown and gray-blue cobblestones. Houses lined the street, some with their doors open, but no one was about during the intense afternoon heat. At court, the Dowager Mother would have made her take a nap on a day like this.

The boy with the kite went by again with a shout of triumph, the twine high and taut over his shoulder. Viella watched him go, her heart contracting. She remembered her brother running across the court grass, laughing at her over his shoulder, hair just like hers tossing in the wind. She didn't want to think about Valan, or her mother, or anyone. But the Elder's words and the sight of the boy made her blink back burning dampness. She missed her family and her home with a pain that went to the core of her.

Please Gaiea, let them be all right. Don't let Daddy or Valan or Grandmother be hurt.

A feeling came over her—slow and heavy, like someone wrapping her in wet cloth. It started in her head and moved downward until her entire body felt numb and distant. The world receded, a candle being carried down a tunnel until a sudden draft blew it out and left her in the black.

She was alone. There was nothing here, not even light, and the only sound was her quick, frantic breaths. She remembered this place. She had been here before, when Eleanor held her in the forest and protected her from the passage of the Dark. She'd been chained then, paralyzed. The memory made her heart miss a beat.

She tried to reach out, tried to find something to hold on to. But there was nothing.

"Hello?" She had not moved her lips, but the word echoed around her, building in intensity until she covered her ears with her hands to block out the hammering vibration of it.

Cold hands slid over hers.

She screamed, tried to shake them off.

"Viella?"

Confusion tumbled through her. "Valan? Val, is that you?"

The hands touching hers burned the way ice did when she held it too long. "Vee? Where are we? What's happening?"

Viella turned her palms over and closed tight fingers on his despite the pain. She could feel him as if they shared the same head. Weariness swamped her, uncertainty clouded her mind. It was as if someone had awakened her early from a deep sleep.

"I don't know. I don't even know how I got here. But I'm so glad it happened—I miss you so much, Val. Are Daddy and Grandmother with you? Are you still home?"

"I don't—I'm not sure. I'm tired, Vee. Really tired."

"No!" She tugged at his hands as she felt him slipping. "You can't sleep, Val. Talk to me. Where are you? What's happening in the court?"

His hands tightened on hers. "I think we're still home. I don't remember much. Just . . . being in Mordach's room and . . . and . . ."

His hands clenched, the burning so bad she thought her skin would come off. She whimpered and tried to pull free.

"Vee . . . I remember. Mummy—Mummy's gone, isn't she?"

She wanted to cry, but tears would not come in that place. "Yes. But Val—"

The hands clamped down again, harder this time. Viella squealed in pain. "Val, you're holding me too tight."

"What are you talking about?" Valan sounded bewildered. "I'm not touching you."

Dread flowered within her. "Then . . . who's touching me? Who's in here with—"

The hands pulled hard, dragging her forward. She screamed, tried to keep her balance, and failed. Down and down she went until—

she hit the ground hard with a grunt of pain. She landed at full stretch, her arms in front of her, and the breath left her body. She tried to get to her knees but an iron grasp on her wrists forced her to stay on her stomach.

"LÂCHER!" she cried. Lady Sophia had taught her that spell for breaking unwanted holds, but the grip on her wrists tightened. Frowning, she lifted her head to see who held her.

Shock made her immobile for a second as every hair on her body stood up. Then she screamed.

〰〰〰

LUKA HELD FARAIN'S FUR LOOSELY IN HIS HANDS, HIS THOUGHTS STILL on the fight he'd had with Eleanor as he followed her to the village. The cat did not need help picking its way between the trees; it was better to give him his head.

He had almost betrayed himself with his reaction to Eleanor's perceptive question. *She knew what she asked. I am Daguard. My mother's name is irrelevant. To ask is to insult me.* Family names were exchanged between those who wished to be friends, or when there was a desire to establish bloodlines for future interactions. Why would she care about his bloodlines?

Unless, of course, she had guessed the truth of his birth. A chill ran over his skin. *Impossible. Mother is gone. No one knows who she was. Father hid that well, for both our sakes.*

Yet, for years after his birth, his father had feared Luka would be taken away, perhaps even put to death. He'd left him with his aunt, who agreed to raise him. By the time he joined his father at the High Court, his mother had been dead for years, and he was simply the new Daguard captain's son. Blane Kemp told those who asked that Luka's mother was a onetime lover who had died in childbirth, and he'd sent for the boy once he had a settled position.

His father had visited him in the years before he came to court. But they had been apart too long, and when Blane had abruptly taken him from his home and sent him to the Daguard Guild for training, Luka found himself resenting his father, not only for his distance over the years but for taking him from the only life he'd ever known.

Luka had kept to himself, careful not to become too friendly with anyone. There was no future for him, of course. No decent woman would have a man without bloodlines. So he'd thrown himself into becoming a Daguard, and at fifteen he'd gone to war for the first time. On the battlefield he was simply Luka Freehold. He'd belonged somewhere. It was freedom he'd never imagined. Then he'd been pulled from the battlefield for the Ceremony, and he'd been furious at being sidelined just as he'd found his purpose in life.

He knew now how much his father must have cared. That he'd tried to protect Luka the best way he could. He'd found a way for Luka to be independent—beholden to no one and free of the need to ever justify his bloodlines.

He thought of the thing that now wore his father's skin, and anger and despair filled him until Farain growled in his throat, feeling Luka's emotions through their Link and interpreting it as a primal instinct to attack. It brought Luka back to himself and he stroked the fur between the cat's ears apologetically.

Not a breath of air stirred the foliage around them. Between the shrubs to his left, Luka could see the road and hear the quiet murmur of conversation as Eleanor held her audience with the Welcome Elder.

He put away his thoughts. He'd lived this long with his

secrets locked away. There was no point in inviting in old ghosts now when so much depended on his ability to stay focused on the task at hand—the most important task of his short life.

He couldn't apologize to his father now. He would never be able to tell him that despite the years and the mistakes between them, he'd loved and respected Blane Kemp. Idolized him as only the son of a soldier can. It was too late for any of that now. But it was not too late to put an end to this nightmare. He had not been able to save his father, but he had a chance to save the queen.

Farain made a soft sound—cousin to a growl—as if to agree. Without being prompted, the cat followed a parallel path to Eleanor and Viella, moved sinuously between trunks and over rocks and fallen branches until they mounted a slight rise and came within sight of the village again. He saw the empty backyards of several whitewashed huts, their narrow windows standing open to let in what air they could. Clothes fluttered on washing lines and tools leaned against walls, but there was no one about.

Luka watched Flor come to a halt alongside a low wall. Eleanor went up the steps and rang the bell before going to the back of the house. A boy with a kite ran by and Viella's gaze followed him.

"We'd better get closer, keep an eye on the queen." Farain climbed down the rise and for a few moments Luka lost sight of the queen and Flor.

Farain rounded a massive trunk and paused within the tree line. Luka shifted for a better look—and realized Flor stood alone, her reins tied to a post in the blue wall. The air left his lungs. The cat sensed his distress and growled in the back of his throat. Flor tossed her black head and stepped back, one eye searching the forest.

Luka swung down and padded to the opening between two houses. *Please, Gaiea, let her be nearby. Let her be safe.* He looked down the road in the direction they'd come from and saw nothing and no one. He stared in the other direction, hoping to see Viella wandering farther into town.

The thoroughfare was empty. Nothing moved on the road except dust swirls.

Then he saw it. A gap farther down in the line of huts, and a brown hump in the grass on the other side of the road, just in front of the tree line.

Luka spun and in a few steps he reached Farain and mounted him. He squeezed his knees and the war cat, guided by Luka's thoughts, retreated into the forest. As soon as they were out of sight, the cat bounded the short distance to where Luka had seen the gap. There was no time for caution. He urged Farain across the road and the cat made a single jump to the other side.

Luka looked down, and a low cry of frustration escaped him as he snatched Viella's wrap from the grass. Farain sniffed at the cloth. The needle-like certainty of danger passed from the cat's mind to Luka's. Farain had picked up a scent. A scent he did not like.

Luka dismounted, eyes searching the ground. The grass was already springing back into place, but a broken stick here and a dislodged rock there pinpointed a path to his right. He ran into the trees, Farain silent behind him, his gaze riveted to the ground. In the woods, where the mulch was shaded by heavy overgrowth, the tracks became small, faint impressions of bare feet, toes spread wide, as if unused to shoes.

A child? Luka thought, remembering the little boy he'd seen. Had Viella followed him? Anger and doubt warred in him. Perhaps she had found a playmate and wandered off. She had always been a curious girl, willing to go anywhere.

He stopped in a clearing where the tracks got lost in a mess of footprints, old and new, as if many people had crisscrossed the area over time. A stink of rot rose from the layers of dead leaves and beneath that the taste of something sweeter slicked his throat.

He picked up the same small feet with widespread toes leading away from him, and ran in that direction.

Behind him, Farain growled and the cat's warning was burgeoning warmth in his blood. He stopped and looked back. The war cat refused to continue. Farain bared his teeth and tossed his massive red-gold head, then stared into the tree line on his right. The pinprick of danger behind Luka's eyes became an ice pick.

"What?" he snapped.

The cat padded a few steps away from Luka before he sat back on his haunches, yellow eyes staring, the tip of his tail twitching. Farain was suspicious. Something had raised his hackles. He drew Luka toward him with thoughts of battle and death. Luka stormed back, fighting the bloodlust.

"What in Gaiea's name is wrong with—"

A faint scream unfurled—a streamer caught in the wind. The cat swung his head toward it, his claws unsheathing and digging into the mulch. Luka froze, his breath trapped in his throat.

The scream had come from the direction Farain had been heading. And Luka knew that voice better than his own.

He crashed through the undergrowth, heedless of branches and trunks, catapulting himself over obstacles his mind barely registered. Farain leapt past him, his red tail high. The scream came again, much closer, desperation and mind-numbing fear woven together. Luka's heart hammered in response. Farain bounded into a clearing moments before Luka skidded to a stop beside him.

Viella lay on her side. A boy stood over her, his back to Luka, orange trousers a blaze of color in the green clearing. Luka could tell his hands were raised, then Viella spotted them and all he could see was the terror in her eyes.

"Luka!" She was tugging against something, her legs thrashing in the undergrowth. Farain growled and took a menacing step forward as Luka drew his short sword from its scabbard.

"Get away from her," he said, furious.

Air rippled over the boy as if a heat wave had descended from the top of his head to his bare feet. And Luka realized he could see toes peeping out of the grass behind the boy. Cold flooded his veins. *Gaiea bless me, his feet are pointing backward.* He had been heading the wrong way and Farain had known.

The boy's head turned on his neck, flesh corkscrewing around until his face looked directly at Luka.

Except there was no face. Only blankness under long strands of blond hair and a tiny pinhole of a mouth. A pinhole that grew into a gaping maw as Luka raised his sword and charged.

Something flew past Luka's ear, and Farain roared as pain speared through their minds. A black tongue, forked as a grass adder's, whipped out and fastened onto Luka's raised arm. Fire erupted in his right shoulder as the tongue tightened on his wrist until he dropped his sword. He was lifted, agony robbing him of breath as his feet dangled above the grass. With a casual flick he was thrown aside, crashing into a tree at the edge of the clearing. He saw and felt nothing for a moment, his vision blank, his body white-hot pain.

Viella's scream drew him back. He shook his head to clear his eyesight and saw Farain a few feet away, his head held to the ground by a noxious pink tentacle, thick as Luka's thigh. The cat was scrabbling at the ground for purchase, his bloodlust making the edges of Luka's sight sharpen. The tentacle around Farain's neck tightened, extending its grip to the cat's shoulder, pulling his paws out from under him. Luka's gaze followed the limb back to its point of origin. It was rooted in the left side of the boy's rib cage, under his arm.

The creature stepped toward Farain—its head still backward over its shoulders—dragging Viella behind it. Two more tentacles manacled her wrists together. They formed long, thin fingers at the ends—malformed hands—that spider-webbed up her forearms. A fourth tentacle had emerged from the thing's right side. It inspected Luka's short sword, turning it this way and that on the grass.

Luka dragged himself to his feet and the black tongue re-emerged, darting through the air toward him.

"*No!*" Coldly furious, and terrified for Viella, Luka raised his arms. His body vibrated, as though deep within him a chord had been struck. His arms glowed with the red-gold fire he'd seen when the Dark had passed over them. That fire leaped from his fingertips like sparks, striking the tongue with a sharp cracking sound. The boy-creature wavered again, and in Luka's mind, *not* his ears, an inhuman bellow brought tears to his eyes. The forked ends of the tongue shriveled and red lines formed on it, glowing like coals, before it whipped back into the boy's mouth.

Gaiea's breath, what did I just do? How—?

Out of the corner of his eye, Luka saw a blur of movement come toward him. He threw himself backward, slamming into the tree behind him, and his sword sliced into the ground where he had been standing. Ripples ran across greasy pink flesh as the tentacle holding the sword ripped it out of the ground, showering him with dirt and leaves. The sweet smell that had choked him earlier wafted toward him as the sword's edge swung toward his throat.

Luka ducked under it, hearing the thunk of the blade hitting the tree. Bits of bark pattered down as he rolled forward, head over heels, and ended up crouched next to the tentacle. Without thinking, he grabbed it. This time, the roar inside his head made his stomach flip. The radiance around his fingers grew incandescent—and his hand closed around an explosion of pink ash, the edges scorched as if by a flame.

Across from him, the creature released Farain. The dagen-cat stepped back, shook his head, and launched himself with a roar. The tentacle whiplashed, slapping the cat into the undergrowth.

Luka went back and yanked his sword from the tree. He spun in time to see the creature dragging Viella toward it, pink threadlike tissue webbing across her body and stifling her cries as she kicked and bucked. The creature wavered in his sight again and Luka realized it was fading *and taking Viella with it*. With a cry, he raised the sword above his head, autumnal light burning along its edge.

The bushes next to Farain parted and Eleanor emerged, her face grim, her arm outstretched. The creature turned to her.

"PORTE!"

Air rushed past him, pulling Luka to his knees and sucking the oxygen from his lungs. There was a flash of light so intense, he saw spots. A clap of thunder vibrated before another strong breeze pushed against him from the opposite direction, forcing him to sit back on his shins and steady himself with a hand on the spongy ground. Then the wind died as swiftly as it had come. Leaves swirled to rest around him. The branches above him slowed their violent rustling.

Luka staggered to his feet. The creature had vanished. His gaze fell on Viella lying prostrate on the grass, shaking. Eleanor dropped to one knee, a trembling hand supporting the rest of her weight, concern etching a frown across her brows.

"Your . . . Majesty?"

Viella didn't answer, only shivered, a blank look on her face.

Luka walked unsteadily to their side, throwing a worried glance Farain's way. He gathered Viella into his arms. Viella let him hold her but made no move except to bury her face in the crook of his arm. Luka ran a soothing hand along her spine and met Eleanor's gaze over her head.

"You are well?" he asked.

The Dahomei nodded, her lips a thin line, her chest heaving. "Just . . . catching my . . . breath." Next to her, Farain rolled onto his stomach. Luka felt the bloodlust seeping from him. He lifted Viella against his good shoulder and went to Eleanor's side. She accepted his proffered hand, and he tugged her upright, pain like glass splinters in his injured shoulder and back.

"Sorry . . . to be . . . late." Eleanor's troubled gaze traveled over Viella as she struggled to draw breath.

"You saved us both," Luka said, surprised to find it did not bother him to admit it. "Thank you."

Farain joined them, sniffing at Viella's legs and growling low in his throat at the smell.

"What in Gaiea's name was that thing?" Luka asked, frowning.

Eleanor placed her hands in the curve of her back and grimaced. "A shape-changer. A *douen*. Feeds on the life-force of children. With the *Nightward* open . . . many such things may return. *Have* returned, it would seem."

Luka turned his head and whispered words of comfort in Viella's ear. She was beginning to relax, her body trembling less and less under the comforting strokes of his hand. "Gaiea be praised you came in time. I had no idea how to fight it. I have never heard of such a beast."

"Small wonder," Eleanor said grimly. "The last of them died in the Age of Chaos, more than five hundred years ago."

CHAPTER 9

OATHS

THE GUARDIAN OF THE RIVER LETHE EMERGED FROM THE SHALLOW, glassy waters of a creek lit copper with the rays of the setting sun. The creek ran through a meadow spotted with nodding blossoms and the air was filled with floating, glittering spores.

Thick grass covered the ground and rocks shone pewter in the twilight. To her left, a mountain rose, its blue-white peak lost in clouds. To her right, trees with branches of metal hummed as the wind blew between shimmering crystal blade-leaves. Light refracted everywhere, casting rainbows onto the creek and on the sentry standing on its banks.

The River Maiden drifted toward that silent figure, water sliding past her and the gently waving silver tail her legs had transformed into. A kaleidoscope of light painted the scales on her skin and slid off the glossy curtain of black hair that covered her naked breasts.

The sentry scowled, tapping the twisted bronze length of his walking stick against some loose rocks and sending them clinking against his gray metal hooves.

"You are far from home, Maiden. Who guards your domain this eventide?"

The River Maiden stopped, tilting her head at the mountain man before her. Small horns curved above his curling, dirt-brown hair and the metal half of his bare chest shone. His powerful legs were covered in a soft hide the same color as his hair, and he stood more than twice her height. A belt hung around his waist, and a golden handle curved above it, glinting dangerously.

"*There are more pressing matters at hand, Papa Bois. I seek an audience with the First.*"

An uneasy growl rumbled from Papa Bois's chest. "What reason have you for disturbing her rest?"

"*I bring tidings of the* Nightward."

Green eyes widened under heavy brows. "The *Nightward?*"

The maiden's grimace eased as she smelled his fear. "*Yes. Gaiea save us all, but it has been opened.*"

Papa Bois's gaze rested on the mountain above them. "You are certain?"

"*If only I were not, Old One.*"

He bowed his head, considering, while the guardian waited. Then in a swift movement, he raised his walking stick and dipped the bronze end in the creek. The cold waters rose around the maiden, swirling whirlpools that would have carried a man to his death. She sank into rapids to her shoulders, her tail flicking.

"Go, Maiden. The Anchorite awaits. But be warned. I am not the only one that guards the way."

"*Will you be with us, Old One? When the time comes?*"

Papa Bois glanced at the mountain again and heaved a sigh that set the leaves to tinkling. "I took an oath. For myself, I serve the Anchorite, always. I cannot speak for my brothers."

"*They must remember the Age of Chaos. Do they truly expect to survive if it happens again?*"

The mountain man looked down at the River Maiden with something like pity. "The Age of Chaos was a long time ago. Not all my brothers value survival above sovereignty now. They forget she is the First, Mama to all, Anchorite of this world, and Blessed of Gaiea herself."

"*Then they should hope the* Nightward *is soon closed, or Gaiea Herself will remind them of what they have forgotten.*" With this last, the maiden disappeared beneath the low roar of the swollen river.

Water boiled around Papa Bois's hooves as he stood on the swiftly disappearing shore, his worried gaze again on the mountain and its night-shadowed peak.

//////////

THE DOWAGER MOTHER PULLED THE STOOL UP TO THE SIDE OF THE COT. She sat down as Mordach shut the gate behind her. With gentle fingers, she stroked the hair from Lady Gretchen's pale face. She was rewarded with the twitching of eyelids.

"Do you have all you require?" Mordach asked.

She did not look at him. "I do. Leave us."

She waited until the sound of his footsteps had faded before reaching for the cloth and bowl of warm water at her feet.

The first touch of the damp towel brought a pained groan from the lady's lips. Frances was gentle, murmuring words of healing under her breath as she held the towel under Lady Gretchen's nose. A few minutes passed before the strong scent of the vapor crystals made Lady Gretchen's eyes flutter open. They stared for a while, unfocused, in the Dowager Mother's direction. Finally, the lady asked in a hoarse voice, "Do I live?"

"For a while yet." Frances leaned back in her chair, her hands in her lap. Lady Gretchen turned her head toward her.

"Did my mother send you?"

"Mordach begged the favor."

"Mordach?" A frown creased Lady Gretchen's forehead. "Why? And why you?"

"They made me an offer. They wish to ensure you are treated well." She dipped the cloth in the vapor water, wrung it out, and laid it on Lady Gretchen's forehead. Then she took another cloth and began cleaning the smudges from the lady's arms.

"They think me too old to fight and, therefore, slave to their every whim."

"Are you?"

"Am I what?"

"Slave to their whims?"

The Dowager Mother's hands touched a bruise on Lady Gretchen's neck and she expelled a pained breath. Frances retrieved a pot of salve from the floor before meeting Lady Gretchen's gaze.

"I was a queen of Kadoomun for years. I may be Dowager Mother now, but a queen keeps her own counsel. She is slave only to her conscience."

Lady Gretchen's laugh was short and mirthless. "Conscience. Is a queen even allowed such a thing?"

"The best queens have one. But a queendom cannot always be ruled by it." Frances rubbed the salve on the bruise on Lady Gretchen's neck.

"You sound like my mother."

"Do I? And what did Lady Sophia say?"

"She used to say that strength, and the willingness to use it, is the only way to rule."

"Ah." Frances began to run her hands over Lady Gretchen's legs and smudged feet. "No one has ever accused the ladies of Talon of weakness. Not since the seat became host to the Dahomei generations ago. A fact which discouraged such criticism in anyone so disposed."

Lady Gretchen frowned. "You imply we have intimidated others?"

"Is that so?" Frances did not look at her, only dipped another cloth in water and started to clean Lady Gretchen's feet of the remnants of the Dark.

"Speak plain." Lady Gretchen forced herself up on her elbows. "Do you think . . . ? What are you doing?"

Frances looked at her, eyebrows raised. "Is your sight

afflicted?" She leaned over the lady's face, peering into her eyes. "Speak now. Does your head hurt?"

"No. I . . ." Gretchen stopped, swallowing. "Do that again."

"What?"

"Touch my feet."

Frances laid a hand on Lady Gretchen's ghost-pale ankle. "Like so?"

Lady Gretchen's breath left her in a rush. "Harder. Please."

Frances studied her face. "Say what bothers you."

"Do it!"

Frances shook Lady Gretchen's foot violently.

Gretchen fell back on the bed, her head turned away from Frances.

"Something is wrong." It wasn't a question. "My Lady, no good will come of your silence."

Lady Gretchen did not reply. Frances sighed.

"Must you be as stubborn as my grandchildren?"

A shudder went through Gretchen's body. "She did this to me."

"Who?"

"My mother."

"What did Lady Sophia do to you, Gretchen?"

Lady Gretchen turned her head, and Frances's breath caught in her throat.

"My Lady, please . . ."

"I can't feel my legs, Dowager Mother." A high flush made red spots on her cheeks, and she slapped away a tear with an impatient hand. "May Gaiea damn my mother to Her Desert. She took my legs."

⁘⁘⁘⁘⁘⁘

JENISTA STAR WRAPPED HER CLOAK MORE SECURELY AROUND HER AS her horse's hooves hit hard earth for the first time in weeks.

Snowbanks lined both sides of the road to Kadoomun's main city, Everhill. Ahead of them, the road dipped and rounded a curve into a pass. Cliffs reached toward the sky, narrowing the path so only three horses could enter abreast.

Jenista had sent most of her army, including most of the Daguard and their officers, back to the High Court. Those Dahomei were her best and they would ride with all haste until they reached the Seat of Talon. Meanwhile, Jenista pushed on to the court of Everhill and the city that surrounded it with five Palms. Built into the side of a mountain, accessible only by its mountain pass or the frozen peaks it had been carved out of, Everhill was a formidable fortress. Something which served it in good stead, as it was the last city before the snow lands of the Ragat.

Everhill's location allowed its sentries to see all the roads that descended from the range of mountains called Gaiea's Roof. Some of the mountains were impassable. Others had routes that were clear only in the summer. Two were clear all year long. Those two roads, the Run and Rock Pass, were the farthest from Everhill, and had been crawling with Ragat just weeks ago. But now all the majestic peaks on Jenista's right were covered with ice and snow, glistening in the cold day and silent but for the harsh wind.

Jenista was frowning at the mountains when the Seer pulled up alongside her on a small horse. Wisps of her silver hair had escaped and framed her face under the same white fur coats they all wore. She shielded her eyes to stare at the range before turning toward Jenista in her saddle.

"Has the court responded to you at all?"

"No," the Seer said. "It doesn't mean all is not well. Kadoomun has had no Spellsayer for some time. Perhaps the queen and her court are busy with other matters." Her voice belied some doubt, though.

"What is it, Seer?"

"Only that, with Ragat on her borders, her Seer should have been alert to her ocular, and the queen should always have hers in her chambers."

"That's part of what worries me. The Ragat should be here. They couldn't have traveled so quickly over the mountains. Yet, where are they?"

The Seer glanced past Jenista to the small group of Dahomei milling around near the entrance to the gorge that led to Everhill. Two of the Dahomei waiting there were part of the Palms loaned to the High Court by the Queendom of Kadoomun.

"The scouts saw nothing of them?"

"No. And that weighs heavy."

The Seer nodded slowly. "I too feel an absence. What do you fear?"

Jenista let out a heavy breath and raised her gaze to the walls of the canyon. "That Everhill was the first casualty of this coup. So far, every seat that has not responded to Margot was attacked."

"Everhill would have been on high alert with a Ragat army nearby."

"And yet you sense nothing."

The Seer shook her head. "There's a break in Everhill's Design."

"A break?" Jenista raised her eyebrows at the Seer.

"Forgive me. We Seers sometimes fall into our own way of speaking. I meant where Everhill should be, where we use our Sight to see Gaiea's futures, there's now nothing."

"Is this what you felt before with the High Court?"

The Seer let her reins rest on her pommel. "Then, I sensed a shift. This—it's as if I'm blind."

Jenista stared at the entrance to the canyon. "You cannot see where our actions lead us."

"No, Commander. The way forward is not clear. Either the future has not been set—or it's been set on a line we're not allowed to see."

"Is your vision denied some futures?"

"Seers cannot see every part of the Design. That is for the Goddess. But this . . ." She shook her head. "This is no natural thing."

"Do you know what could cause this?"

The Seer tilted her head back to watch a bird that swooped overhead, causing her hood to slip down onto her narrow shoulders. "There are few options, and they all mean only ill for us. I tell you this." She met Jenista's gaze, a crinkle between her brows. "Lines tangle and Balance has been lost to Chaos. All things are possible and impossible. We must be careful. Very careful."

Jenista looked back at the Palms behind her, at the Dahomei sitting alert in their saddles, and the few Daguard behind them. Occasionally a horse would get too close to the cats, and the nearest beast would hiss at it, but most of the mounts were seasoned veterans of campaigns. They simply backed away with a snort, their rider taking a moment to say an absentminded soothing word before patting them on the neck.

"Your words bring little comfort. Something strange is in the air here. And I would know its form before I lead my Palms into a trap."

"You would have us wait then?" the Seer asked.

"I will take six of us into Everhill. A Palm will wait outside the city walls. You may make camp here with the rest, and my personal guard, Agnes."

"I don't wish to wait. I prefer to accompany you to the fortress," the Seer said.

Jenista turned on her horse to face the tiny woman, a thoughtful look on her face. "Why would you wish to go into such danger?"

"I see the Design quite well usually, sometimes clearly enough to know the present. Such a skill will be of use to you if Everhill is as dangerous as you fear."

"And what if I felt you too precious to risk?"

"I have skills that cannot be matched by your Dahomei, or your Daguard. Would you let them stay unused in Gailand's time of need?"

Jenista guided her horse into a slow walk toward the scout party. "You have a way with words few ladies can equal."

The Seer followed without hesitation. "My mother often spoke of it, but with far less admiration."

Jenista's laugh startled several horses and made her scouts stare. Her hood fell back and her blond braid ruffled in the cold wind. She leaned on her pommel, a rare genuine smile on her face.

"Before you, I had not thought of Seers as having mothers."

White hair twisted in the wind as the Seer tilted her head to meet Jenista's gaze. "Before you, I had not thought Dahomei had a sense of humor. Augurs and Seers have many abilities, but we have yet to master the skill of giving birth to ourselves, Commander."

With another chuckle, Jenista raised a hand in surrender. "I meant no offense, Sister. It's just that—well, you were raised by the Augurs, were you not?"

"When we are called, yes. Before that, we have families, like everyone else. Some queendoms, like Kadoomun, allow prospects to live with their families when they're not training. But that can make the final break harder when it comes."

"I know something of that." Jenista sighed, her gaze sober. "To be Dahomei is to leave family behind in more ways than one. Like you, we cannot bear children while we wear the gold, and even if we choose to break or end our service to do so, Augurs have a say over the partner we select and the Guilds our children may enter." They sat in contemplative silence until Jenista asked, "Do you miss your family? When Seers leave, do you ever return?"

The Seer didn't hesitate. "No. Our path is set once we leave.

It's better they think us dead. The child they once knew is gone. The name we had will never be spoken to us again. We become one with our new family and with Gaiea's plan."

"Do you miss your name?"

"To be a Seer—it is an honor. We give all for our calling. But we are human, and sometimes weak."

Jenista hesitated, then said in a low voice, "Would you tell me yours . . . exchange names with me?"

The Seer met Jenista's gaze with her own. Her lips curved for a moment, but her voice was full of regret. "It's forbidden."

"Is it forbidden to know your age as well?"

"Yes. Even to you, Commander."

"Ah." Jenista glanced down, fussing with her reins a bit. "I fear I've overstepped. It's been a while since my conversation went beyond orders and strategy. I apologize if my inquiry offended you. I've never met a Seer such as you. One I . . . wished to know better."

The Seer's tone was not unkind when she answered. "I take no offense. The fault was mine. The Augurs would say I'm young yet and have not learned to quell my tongue. I've led you to ask what should not be asked." She leaned toward Jenista and her fingers rested on the pommel next to Jenista's hand. "I'm sorry, Commander. Truly."

Jenista studied their fingers as they lay close together, not touching. When the Seer removed her hand, she gathered up her reins slowly. "I understand. You excel at your calling, Seer."

"I only attempt to bring honor to my profession."

"In that you've succeeded." Jenista took a deep breath and turned her horse so that she faced the Seer. "You also make a good argument regarding accompanying me and I'll take you up on your offer. Make yourself ready. This eventide, we enter Everhill together."

LUKA STOKED THE FIRE ELEANOR HAD BUILT, LIFTING HIS HEAD NOW and again to check on Viella. The queen lay on her side under the looping, spreading branches of a banyan tree. She slept with her back to him, wrapped in the saddle blanket. The firelight made her copper-streaked hair glow against the dark material. As he watched, her small fingers twitched on her shoulder, clenching and releasing. Earlier, she had moaned, and he had gone to her, stroking her hair until she'd quieted again.

He was staring at Viella so intently, looking for the slightest hint of discomfort, that he started when Eleanor joined him on the fallen log. She handed him one of the fried potato pies the horse breeder's wife had gifted them as thanks for accepting the first price quoted and not bartering. Eleanor had had no choice, of course. They needed to leave the area as soon as possible, despite the fact that no one seemed to have heard what had happened in the woods.

Luka accepted the pie with a wordless nod of thanks, though the food might as well have been sawdust for all he tasted it. The searing pain in his shoulder made even the teeth in his jaw hurt. His wound needed tending, but the thought of taking his shirt off in front of Eleanor made him uncomfortable.

The Dahomei watched the queen while she ate her own sandwich. "She's sleeping. That's good."

"She dreams," Luka said. "Nightmares, no doubt."

"That is no surprise. She has been sorely hurt this day." For the first time, Luka noted the concern in Eleanor's voice matched his own. Usually, Dahomei cultivated a dismissive tone, or a carefully professional one. But now, as he watched her out of the corner of his eye, he noted the worried frown on her face and the nervous tapping of her left foot.

"Could the *douen* have done her permanent damage?" he asked.

"Too soon to tell. She is still in shock. She hasn't spoken to me. Has she spoken to you?"

"No. She fell asleep while we rode and hasn't awakened since."

Eleanor shook her head, her frown deepening. "That isn't like her. She chatters like a sing-song in a tree, that one."

"What's a sing-song?" Luka asked, turning to face her.

Eleanor waved a distracted hand. "A tiny bird that never stops singing. It dwells in the woods where I grew up, near Blackburn."

"You're from Blackburn, in Ravisinghga?" Luka raised his eyebrows. "That's quite a distance from Dun. Near the coast, isn't it?"

Eleanor pulled out a knife and started cleaning under her short nails. "It is. You've heard of it?"

"I know the coast better than Blackburn itself, but I've heard tales. There is a powerful Seer in Blackburn Forest. Her seat was destroyed in the Troubles after Gaiea's Ascendance and she grieved so deeply for her lady, she refused to return to the Augurs. They say her ghost wanders the forest to this day, protecting her seat, never mind it is long gone. Have you heard tell of her?"

"There are many tales in Blackburn," Eleanor said, her gaze still focused on her nails. "Most have as much truth to them as the tongue of a Frost Witch."

Luka considered that while he poked at the fire with his stick. Embers collapsed into glowing shapes as he tried to ignore his pain.

"How is Farain?" Eleanor asked in a quiet voice.

Luka hesitated a moment, surprised. "The tentacles did no real damage, and the wounds from the Sycren have scabbed over. Unlike horses, dagen-cats heal very quickly. He'll be fine."

"That's good," she said.

He waited, thinking hard, before venturing a question of his own. "How did you defeat the . . . *douen*?"

"Defeat it? One woman cannot defeat it. That would be a battle lost before it was begun."

Luka stopped poking and looked at her, his frown drawing a line between his brows. "A Dahomei cannot defeat that creature? How is that possible?"

"We are but mortal women, Luka." Eleanor's tone was chiding but not unkind, and he caught a hint of a smile on her lips. For a moment, it reminded him of Margot's and his breath caught. "Our magic is strong, but not invincible. There are many creatures that Dahomei must work together to guard against. There are fewer now than during the Age of Chaos, but there are corners of the world where evil rests, dormant, awaiting its moment to rise again."

Such as now. Things fall apart. My father is no more. He watched the queen turn over in her sleep. *And her world is forever changed.*

"Then what did you do to it?"

"I opened a door in the Ether and shoved it through."

"The Ether?" Luka had never heard of such a thing. A frisson ran icy fingers along his skin and he realized why. *She speaks of Dahomei magic.* No Dahomei had ever spoken to him of their magic before. He knew words and spells and had seen the warrior-magicians use their power on the battlefield, but few spoke of what the magic of the Sight involved to those who had no talent for it.

"The space between things." She tilted her head, watching him from under her lashes. "It's not a place where the magic of the Word holds sway."

"And it is trapped there?"

"In a manner of speaking." Eleanor shrugged. "I know not exactly where 'there' is. But I did send it as far away as I could. And it cannot come back through the door. Only the one who creates the Portal can open it again."

"So it must remain there?" he pressed.

"Not at all." Eleanor's lips were a grim line. "Once on the other side, it was free to transport itself wherever it wished. But magical Portals use a great deal of energy. Wherever it is, it would take some time to return to the village, if it can even do so. The queen is safe."

"What of the people who live where you have sent it? Will they not be in danger?"

"It would have to make it to shore first." Eleanor's lips curved. "I dropped it in the middle of the ocean. With luck, it will drown before it can transport itself to safety. If not, it will be very uncomfortable for some time. Saltwater is no friend of the *douen*."

"How is it you know all this?" Luka asked. "Never have I heard tell of such a creature."

"Dahomei study all beings of Gailand. We have records at every seat. *Douens* were once common in Freetown. The First High Queen, Dyane, was largely responsible for ridding Dun of them." Finished with her nails, Eleanor sheathed her knife. "I fear we'll encounter many past evils now the *Nightward* has been opened. The Sycren and the *douen* may be just the beginning."

"Beginning?" Luka dropped his stick and stood, stretching his back. "There are worse creatures?"

"Daguard," Eleanor said softly, "in ages past, there roamed in daylight creatures that would have made sweet dreams of your nightmares. Some of them were born of women. You know the Augurs scry every child's bloodline for markers that indicate dangerous powers, yes?"

He nodded, his heart beating fast. He knew this fact very well indeed. "I've never understood how."

"Few do. The Augurs don't like to explain the mysteries of the Blessing. They even have another name for it: nanomagic. Because they are specially Blessed, they are particularly good at sensing the nanomagic in others and discerning their talents."

She studied him, his gaze serious. "Perhaps it is time you learn more, Daguard. I'd thought we would be safe at a seat, protected by my sisters by now. But we cannot be sure how long we will travel together, or when next we will be granted a moment to speak plainly. It seems those who protect the queen must be aware of many past terrors now the *Nightward* is opened."

"It was not my choice to know little of the past," he pointed out. "It is the Dahomei that decides what magic we may learn. You teach the Daguard nothing of the Sight."

"Because you are adepts at the Word and have no use for that knowledge. The magic of the Sight allows one to see and manipulate the Blessing that lives in all things in Gailand. In the creatures, the plants, even the water and the air. The Word holds no power over that."

"And that's why the High Queen, the Dahomei and the Unbound are so powerful. Because they are more likely to have the magic of the Sight," Luka said to himself.

"There is a difference in that the High Queen's magic is ancient and unique, the only kind that is never reborn or replenished, but passed down to every generation, the same since the first High Queen received it from Gaiea," Eleanor continued. "The Augurs, Seers, and Dahomei are born with a different kind, and use their talents to help keep Gailand safe.

"The Unbound, whose gender are not set, are some of the most powerful because they can access the Sight *and* the Word. Many become Augurs, Seers, and Spellsayers, like Mordach, but they require guidance. Augurs take them into the Guild after the Second Scrying to train them. Their talents can develop late, or suddenly. That lack of control can make them dangerous. Though not as dangerous as Elementals."

"I've never heard of Elementals," Luka said slowly, frowning. "Do they still exist?"

"There haven't been any born since the Troubles. The Augurs realized then that certain bloodlines were more likely to breed them, so they forbade marriage and children without scrying. It wiped them out, thank Gaiea. Because as monstrous as the

Sycrens, the *douen*, and others are, they are nothing to the damage one uncontrolled Elemental can do."

"Were they so terrible?" Luka asked slowly, feeling a deep kinship with these lost, prohibited people. "Don't they just have to learn to control their talent, like everyone else? There are Impellents who move things, Readers who can search your mind and Igniters who burn. How are Elementals so much worse?"

"I've only heard stories," Eleanor said, glancing at him. "But some say it's because they don't draw their power from Gaiea's Blessing, like everyone else. During the Age of Chaos, in the wars, before Gaiea closed the *Nightward*, some of us were . . . infected by something. We don't know what, but we know most of the carriers were male, and it perverted their talent, made it hard for men to do more than Illusion. The Ragat are descended from Neutrals, men who lost their abilities entirely, or never had it. But for others . . . for others it allowed them to draw on some dark force within the Ether. These Elementals can be more powerful than the Unbound. Some Elementals could kill in seconds with only their fear or rage. Others, called Casters, could blind the Blessing and hide their magic and deeds from scrying.

"But Unbound Elementals—they were the most dangerous, the most unpredictable. They could summon energy at will, control the weather or tear open the veil between this world and the next. Their Sight sees far beyond what Gaiea intended. And they could kill themselves or others accidentally the first time they manifest. The Augurs and the queens enforced rules on all Adepts, such as Dahomei or the Unbound, to ensure Gailand would not be at their mercy again. Beings like those would be a true threat to Viella, even after she receives . . ." Her voice trailed off, and she frowned and stopped speaking.

But Luka was too distracted to notice. His blood had run cold. Now he knew why his father and mother had been so careful. *If an Augur thinks me one of these, I will never be free.* For a moment, he remembered the dying Sycren, the tentacle turning to ash in his hands, the red glow of his sword, and a nameless dread rose in him—

(*kill in seconds with only their fear or rage*)

—but that was Farain, he reminded himself. Farain and the deeper link they had now.

"I never imagined there could be creatures as powerful as the High Queen."

"Perhaps not as powerful, but there is always strength in numbers. It was Gaiea and the queens she chose that helped save us from past dangers. They taught the Augurs how to scry and use the Waters of Lethe, and Gaiea used the *Nightward* to bind the monsters born in the Age of Chaos, and before, in their graves, their holes, their hidden places.

"Now that the book stands open, that binding weakens. If we do not close it, there will come a day when the binding is no more. The Ancient Ones will wake. We will have subverted the will of Gaiea, and there is no surety then that the queens will be enough to save us. If they aren't, Daguard, nothing—not the spells of men, not dagen-cats, not even the powers of every Dahomei in Gailand—will protect you from the horrors of Gaiea's Desert."

"But you, and you alone, protected Viella today," Luka said. It was clear to him now how brave she was. How lucky they had been to have her. "Thank you, Captain. For both our lives."

Her gaze was so direct, he felt his face heat and had to look away. "You're welcome, Daguard. And thank you for all you've done for my queen. When you saved her, you saved Dun, and you gave us a chance to save Gailand."

Luka was still, his mind full of tumultuous thoughts. *If what she says of the* Nightward *is true, more important things are happening than I ever dreamed. Gailand itself is at stake. My father's life was given for all of us. Even my life, my secrets, are not worth more than everyone in Gailand.* He opened his mouth to speak—and a high-pitched scream grated against his ears.

He moved without thinking, racing around the fire to Viella's side. She was sitting upright, her back as straight as a ruler, her head tilted back, and her eyes closed. Her neck strained with tension, a tiny pulse beat in the hollow of her throat, and the scream that came from her chilled him like a bucket of rainwater. He grabbed her shoulders, shook her.

"Your Majesty, please wake!"

She didn't stop screaming. Did not even open her eyes.

"Gaiea's breath, what is it?" Eleanor asked, dropping to her knees beside him.

"Viella!" He shook her again, harder, but Viella did not respond. "It must be a nightmare."

"Let me try." Eleanor put her hands on Viella's head, closed her eyes, and whispered to herself. Still, the horrific screaming went on and on.

Luka felt as though someone sawed at his skull. Tears stung his eyes, and he resisted the urge to plug his ears. *Will she never stop? By the Desert I cannot stand this.* He started to shake her again, but Eleanor caught his arm with her hand.

"We'll find another way," she said, determination drawing her brows together. "We cannot just shock her out of this."

"Out of what?"

The screaming had ended as suddenly as it began. Luka turned his head. Viella stared back at him and Eleanor, a tiny frown forming between her eyes.

"Why are you staring at me?" she asked. "And why are you holding my arms, Luka?"

A rush of breath left Luka's chest. He dropped his hands. "Are you well, Your Majesty?"

"I . . . don't know." She lowered her eyes and rubbed at her arms. "Was I sleeping?"

"Not quite," Eleanor said gently. "You were screaming. We feared something was wrong."

"Screaming?" Viella sounded doubtful. "I don't remember screaming."

"Perhaps you had a bad dream?" Eleanor suggested.

"Perhaps," Viella repeated, her hands rubbing her arms. She yawned. "Is it very late? It's so dark. I must have slept a long time."

"Indeed, you did," Luka agreed, trying to appear relaxed when his heart was still pounding. "Are you hungry?"

"No." Viella lay back down, turning on her side to face the crackling fire. "I feel strange."

"You're tired," Eleanor said, pulling Viella's blanket up over her hips to her shoulders. "You must sleep. We'll stand watch over you. Fear not."

"I know," Viella said, and after a pause, "I'm not afraid. But I'd like to stop sleeping on the ground. It's really hard."

"Something I thoroughly agree with, Your Majesty. But it will have to do for tonight, as I don't have a bed with me at the moment," Luka said with a smile. Viella smiled back and he watched as she let her eyes close. When he was sure she was asleep again, he moved back to the log. Eleanor followed.

"That was no nightmare," he said to her in a low voice.

"I fear you're right," Eleanor said. "Something lingers with her. Some horror she cannot fully grasp. She's young and so much has happened. I think she grapples with it in her sleep."

"What if *it* grapples with *her*?" Luka said.

"Perhaps." Eleanor's voice was soft, worried. "She should have received her Boon by now, you know."

"Her what?"

"Her Boon." Eleanor met his gaze. "The High Queen's Blessing is transferred to her heir shortly after her death. Sometimes in moments, never longer than a few days. Viella would become the Hand then, more powerful than any sister queen, and filled with the knowledge of those who came before her."

"How do you know it hasn't happened?"

Eleanor looked amused by his ignorance, but her smile was genuine, not mocking. "If it had happened, Daguard, we would know. It's not an event that can pass unnoticed."

"Isn't it possible the glamour at the court, or something Mordach has done, is preventing it from reaching Viella?"

Eleanor sighed and made a slow nod. "With the *Nightward* open, many things are possible. I pray the Dahomei will free the court soon. It will be a glorious day when the Boon arrives and she's no longer only our High Queen, but the Hand of Gaiea Herself. May Gaiea grant me strength to help keep her safe until then."

Listening to her, Luka raised his hand to his throbbing shoulder without thinking, only to drop it with a hiss as fiery pain blossomed. Without warning, Eleanor reached out and touched his arm. He looked down at her hand, the skin on one knuckle scraped and bruised, the nails torn to the quick on two fingers. It was a strong hand, the fingers long and elegant. His skin prickled beneath it.

"You nurse your shoulder often. Is the pain so great?"

Her touch was very warm, and he lifted his gaze to hers, feeling that warmth spread through his arm to his chest. "Nothing I cannot bear. The queen is what matters, not my shoulder."

"The queen is asleep," Eleanor pointed out. "If you wish it, I can help with your pain."

Luka clenched and unclenched his fist, heated needles of agony stabbing him in his shoulder and arm. His mind was in turmoil over her kind offer. He wanted to say yes, but he didn't know why she wished to help. And he found he wanted to know. Very much. "You think me too weak to bear it?"

Eleanor laughed. It startled him. It was a soft sound, husky from its lack of use. And it made him think of secrets and whispers and how, when she smiled, Eleanor was even prettier than Margot had been. Mortified, he felt his cheeks heat. *Gaiea's breath, what is wrong with me?*

"I think you too stubborn to know it's better to deal with such things before they become dangerous. Daguard, you are courageous, but your pride must not come before your life."

You think me courageous? he thought, but did not say. He averted his gaze so she would not see his disquiet. "I will accept your help then."

"Good. Take off your shirt."

Her request sent a bolt of awareness through his entire body. "My shirt?"

"Your shirt." She stood. "I cannot treat your wound through your clothes."

He took his time pulling his shirt over his head, wincing as he did so. Feeling more naked than ever before, he watched her dig through her saddlebags before coming back to him. The small tins in her hands chimed against each other as she juggled them with cloth for bandages.

"Give me your back," she said, and he slid down the branch so she could straddle it more easily. He faced away from the sleeping queen, tilting his back as much as he could toward the firelight. She sat behind him and he heard her take a breath before a light touch on his shoulder made him grit his teeth.

"Daguard, you were foolish indeed not to come to me earlier," was all she said. There was no rancor in her voice, only concern. Tins clinked and he smelled mint and green herbs.

"There was no time," he said, knowing she spoke true. "It is most likely new damage done by the creature when it attacked me."

"There is that," she agreed, and he winced as cold unguents slicked his skin and made him bite his lip. "But there is infection here as well."

"Infection? Lady Gretchen was kind enough to attend to it. I thought it taken care of."

"That was three nights ago. Treatment must be continued or you risk far more than temporary pain. Unfortunately, I am no healer. I can render aid on a battlefield. This requires more than that."

"Your skills will have to be enough," he said. "Dangerous creatures roam the land, and any one of them could mean our discovery. We cannot risk the queen."

"Then you will lose your arm, and possibly your life," Eleanor replied, the old authority stamping her voice. "Choose well."

Luka thought in silence for several minutes. *It cannot be helped. There is no other choice. I must seek aid, or the queen will have only Eleanor.*

"We will go to Plytown. I know someone who can help us find medicine—give us shelter for a while. There is a Portal on the far side of Plytown too. It is usually unmanned in the early hours. Though it goes only to distant queendoms, Jaleel and Ravisinghga . . ."

Eleanor made a thoughtful sound. "That might be exactly what we need. The courts there would welcome us. They are home to loyal seats who will not form alliances against Dun easily." He heard tearing as Eleanor ripped strips of cloth into bandages. "But the Sycrens we fought, and Gaiea knows what else, may be at those seats. Or even at the Portal. Entering Plytown is a gamble."

"Didn't you say I have no choice?"

"No, I said you *had* to choose."

"Then I think we still go. If nothing else, Tenville taught us we are not safe even if there are no Sycrens," Luka reminded her. "But at least in Plytown I have a friend I can trust. And the Sycrens could not have been so many, or they would have overrun us at Garth. If they guard the Portals, they will focus on the ones used most. We can leave Plytown under darkness and ensure the Portal is not watched before we approach. If it is, we ride on until we find one that isn't guarded."

Whatever happens, this journey must find a destination. I cannot protect the queen while healing. And the queen needs an army, not a Daguard and a single Dahomei.

Eleanor's sigh was troubled, but there was resignation in her voice when she spoke. "Then that is what we will do. Ride to Plytown, find your friend and the medicine we need, and continue to a distant court. We will decide which one when we arrive at the Portal."

He twisted his head to look at her, a half smile on his face. "You agree with me, Dahomei? Careful it does not become a habit."

She shrugged, a slight lift to a corner of her lip. "There are worse habits to cultivate."

He faced forward again. "She will need us both now. The time for discord is long past. We must work together, or we fail her."

Eleanor's fingers slowed as she wrapped his shoulder. "Daguard, we have had our—differences. But know this. I do not doubt your devotion to the queen. And you must not, in turn, doubt me. I consider myself fortunate to have been with you these past days. Without you and Farain, we would all be long dead."

Shock made him look around to see if she meant what she said or if it was a prelude to something else. But her gaze met his and he knew. *There is no malice here. No scorn. No disrespect.* The realization both surprised him and made his heart pound, but he did not know why. Couldn't understand why the world fell silent. Quiet enough that he could hear his own heartbeat in his ears. He spoke, drowning out the silence with his words. "I think, perhaps, we have all had a part to play in keeping each other alive. Without Viella, the Dark would have caught us both at the River Lethe. I consider myself fortunate as well."

She studied his face. "Then we are well matched. I will not rest until the queen is safe and her queendom returned to her. Will you do the same, Luka? Will you stay with her until those who murdered Queen Elise have paid for their crimes, and Queen Viella sits on a secure throne?"

He turned to face her. "Yes. I swear to this. I will protect the queen until she is safe, or Gaiea takes me to her Garden."

"I have witnessed your promise and you have witnessed mine," Eleanor said, placing her hand over her heart. He did the same, his blood pounding in his ears. "What was said here cannot be unsaid."

It was the beginning of an ancient oath. A warrior's promise. Only those who had seen combat could speak the words. His throat was tight as he closed the fingers of his right hand before he replied. "As Gaiea's world endures, so shall our promise."

"Gaiea be praised." Eleanor smiled at him, and he ducked his head, strange thoughts whirling in his mind—thoughts that had seldom distracted him before. And never when it came to Eleanor.

Feeling flustered and painfully self-aware, he replied in a low voice, "Gaiea be praised," and turned away from her, careful to keep his face hidden as he put his shirt back on.

CHAPTER 10

EVERHILL

JENISTA'S DAHOMEI SLOWED AS THEY NEARED THE ARCH AND WALL guarding the entrance to Everhill, which was made of streaked, polished stone. Beyond the Gate, a narrow road began a gradual climb through the city of Everhill.

Two Gate guards stood just outside the arch, their armor hidden by heavy royal-blue cloaks that shielded them from the cold. The hoods on their cloaks were drawn up. Both women carried long, thin blades on both hips, the preferred weapons of the court of Kadoomun.

Above them, the City Guards stood motionless in the battlements on the wall. A slight breeze toyed with their golden-yellow cloaks. Jenista shielded her eyes to look up at them as the horses approached the arch. When she looked down, one of the Gate guards had stepped toward her, blocking their way.

"I am Commander Jenista Star, and I bring greetings from the High Court of Dun," Jenista said with an incline of her head.

The guard in front of her looked them over, then jerked her chin at one of the Dahomei. "Welcome back, Bridget."

Bridget made a fist against her right shoulder, then held it out toward the guard. The guard returned the gesture and continued, "The family of Everhill accepts your greetings and welcomes you to our court, Commander Star. Do you bring news of the war on our borders?"

"I bring news indeed," Jenista replied. "However, Queen Salene and the court must be my first concern."

"Of course."

The streets were quiet as the guard marched toward a long, low building on the right. Curious eyes studied them from doorways, street corners, and open windows above. To their left, a couple of men were standing near the Gate, the red badge of a street-lighter stitched to the sleeve of their upper arms, talking in low voices and looking over the visitors. They leaned against the Welcome Elder's hut; its door was firmly shut, and the windows shuttered.

"Were you warned of our approach?" Bridget asked of the woman in front of her. Bridget was a tall, slender woman with mahogany skin and blue-gray eyes. A good fighter known more for her bluntness than her patience. "I saw no one at the pass."

"We're changing shifts. The captain of the City Guard is overseeing the transition."

The first guard entered the long barracks, then returned, her replacement in tow. "I'll escort you to Everhill." As the new guard took up position at the city's entrance, she turned on her heel and the Dahomei followed.

"Your name?" Jenista enquired. The guard pushed back her hood, revealing short black curls that ruffled in the evening breeze. Her dark eyes turned down slightly at the corners.

"They call me Sam, Commander."

"Sam, where's your Welcome Elder?"

The guard glanced at the shuttered hut. The street-lighters were now walking up both sides of the main road, blowing simple light spells toward bell-shaped glasses hanging from the eaves of buildings lining the street. The bluish glow cast shadows on the walls.

"The cold was too much for her. If the weather holds tomorrow, she'll return."

"There's probably little use for a Welcome Elder with all these guards," the Seer observed quietly.

Sam stared as if noticing her for the first time. "Ragat have crossed the mountains after all."

"We're aware," Jenista said, resting her hands on her pommel. "We don't question your precautions."

When Sam turned away, Jenista raised an eyebrow in the Seer's direction, but she shook her head and said in a low voice, "The future is no clearer."

Hooves left deep marks in the snow behind them as they climbed. Snow had built up on the roofs of the houses around them. The Dahomei twisted and elongated in the thick glass of the cottage windows as they went past.

"We're well met," Sam said. "I haven't been to court since the blizzard. Our quarters there are far warmer than the barracks. I'm looking forward to seeing my Bond Sister for an hour or two."

"Tell me," Bridget asked, "when did you last see our Queen?"

"When my Palm left for three days' duty at the Gate, two days before the blizzard arrived. We were ordered to close the Gates and remain in the barracks because of the weather. We're to be relieved tomorrow."

The road came to an end below an onyx arch. Two guards stood before it in an area swept clean of snow. The royal-blue cloaks had the hoods up. Warmly gloved hands held spears. As Jenista's group of six drew nearer, the spears crossed over the entrance with the sound of clashing metal.

"My sisters," Jenista called out, bringing her horse to a halt a respectful distance away. "I am Commander Jenista Star, and I bring greetings from the High Court of Dun. Will you allow us entry?"

A sudden, sharp wind scuttled powder under the arch. Seconds stretched like minutes before the guard on the right touched a fist to her shoulder and held it out toward Jenista. Both guards bowed in unison, then stepped aside, clearing the way.

Jenista returned the salute and rode under the arch. As she passed, she looked down, trying to catch a glimpse of the faces under the hoods, but the guards' heads remained lowered.

The horse's hooves clopped onto a cobblestone pathway that had been cleared of snow. A long way down the twisting path, the pointed tips of swirling black metalwork set within high stone walls was just barely visible. The snow-dusted tops of a line of evergreen trees lined both sides of the stone path they walked on. Beyond the trees, on either side of the path, uninterrupted snow lay on open ground that stretched to boundary walls hidden by the evening's rapidly deepening gloom. The only sound was that of the wind and the occasional muffled thump of snow falling in clumps from branches. There was an oppressiveness to the silence—a weight—as though the world bore down on them.

Jenista tensed, then shifted in her saddle to look around at the Seer, protected in the center of their small party. "Something is at work here."

The Seer met her gaze with a nod. "A cloaking spell. It's heavy in the air. I have no sight here."

"Things can be hidden from your sight?" Bridget asked.

"Only with great difficulty," the Seer replied, her voice clipped. "And even greater power." She extended her palm. After a few seconds, she shook her hand, then closed and reopened her fist. Breath hissed through her teeth. "I cannot summon a quasiflame."

Sam held out her hand. After a moment, she confirmed, "Neither can I. Is this part of the cloaking spell?"

The Seer's eyes narrowed. "No. This is far worse."

Something swooshed past Jenista's nose. Her horse snorted, backing off the path and into the snow. The Seer whirled to look back the way they'd come—just as an arrow pierced her right calf. She shouted and doubled over, her hand going to her leg.

Jenista slid off her horse as more arrows whizzed above her head, and ducked behind a tree. Sam did the same on the opposite side of the path, dragging the Seer with her. The other Dahomei dismounted in seconds. All except Bridget, who pulled a large knife from her under her cloak, wheeled her horse around, and launched it through the air.

The knife buried itself in the chest of one of the silent guards from the court Gate. She crumpled to the ground without a sound. The second guard slipped behind a tree. Bridget used the moment to dismount, take shelter, and draw her broadsword.

Jenista held her hand up. Bridget paused, her eyes narrowed. No one made a sound, except the Seer who was sucking air through her teeth as she lay bleeding in the snow, Sam crouched over her, sword at the ready.

Jenista raised a hand, then dropped it in a sharp cutting motion. Bridget was sprinting for the tree the guard hid behind before the motion was finished. An arrow flew over her head just as she ducked behind the tree. There was a brief scuffle before she yanked the guard out from their hiding place. A bow clattered away from them as the cloaked figure landed in front of Bridget, who instantly put her broadsword to the guard's neck. She grabbed the hood on the cloak and pulled it back.

But no face was revealed. Instead, the cloak grew transparent and vanished. Cursing, Bridget got to her feet and went to the first guard, but it was too late. She kicked at the spot where the cloak had been, retrieved her knife, and turned to Jenista, who emerged from behind the tree.

"Avatars," she said, her nostrils flaring as she shoved her knife back into its sheath somewhere under her cloak. "One of them, at least, did not manage to evade my blade in time."

"An extension of real warriors, but no less deadly," the Seer gasped. She was sitting on the side of the path while a Dahomei inspected the wound. "Even with the *Nightward* open, no ordinary woman could cloak the court, manipulate avatars, and still be able to hide the change in the Design caused by these actions from a Seer who stands on the same ground."

Bridget met Jenista's eyes with a wordless question. The Commander nodded, and she disappeared down the path, headed in the direction of the Gate. The other Dahomei moved toward the court, her drawn broadsword glinting in the gathering gloom.

"We must tend to your wound," Sam told the Seer. The Seer nodded, closed her eyes, and breathed several deep breaths. A Dahomei tore the edge of her cloak and began bandaging her wound.

"Seer," Jenista said, going down on one knee beside her. "What do you mean by 'no ordinary woman'?"

"I mean, Commander"—she hissed in pain as another Dahomei—"there is no such woman. Such power would have been noticed by the Augurs before now." The Seer winced. "The wards mean I cannot use my own talent to heal myself here. And this arrow has been tainted with Ragat filth. I will need more than my skills to treat my wounds."

"Ragat?" Bridget had come up behind Jenista, her broadsword at her side. "There are Ragat here?"

"It is indeed their way to poison and ambush instead of fighting honorably," Jenista said, rising to her feet. "But how could Ragat create avatars? They have no magic."

"The Royal Spellsayer and the *Nightward* would be of great help with that," the Seer said as a Dahomei offered her a hand. She grabbed hold and stood gingerly.

"The path is clear, Commander," Bridget said, "but the iron gate is locked. I tried scaling the gate and wall, but no matter how long I climbed, the top came no closer. It is protected."

Jenista acknowledged this report with a nod. "We will proceed as planned. Agnes has her orders. Can you ride?" she asked the Seer, concern coloring her voice. The woman darted a wry gaze at her.

"I'd rather not. The court isn't far. With assistance, I'll be able to walk. What we must consider before we enter is that even the Spellsayer and the *Nightward* cannot maintain magic at two courts at the same time. Not unless . . ." Her voice trailed off.

"What is it?" Jenista asked, her eyes narrowed. "What do you believe hides in this place?"

The Seer hesitated, rubbing her leg a little. "Perhaps . . . a rare Elemental. A Caster."

"Casters?" Bridget frowned, shaking her head. "Never have I heard of this."

"I have," Jenista said, studying the Seer. "What you speak of is not possible. The bloodline was too destructive. After the Troubles, it was eliminated, along with the other Elementals."

"Yet here we stand, facing disappearing armies, blizzards, and avatars, with our High Queen dead by magic and treachery." The Seer spread her hands. "Before today, these things were not possible either."

"The Augurs exist precisely to protect us from Casters," Jenista pointed out. "Every marriage along the bloodlines is vetted. Every possibility considered, every future scried."

"Casters are the only beings capable of hiding any part of the Design from those scrying for it," the Seer replied, looking her unwaveringly in the eye. "They often develop their powers late, after the First Scrying ceremony. A Caster swallows magic, feeds off it. That power can then be used to conceal or boost its own magic.

"Not a single Seer saw the attack on the High Court coming, and not even I saw what was happening right here at Everhill. What if there was never an army marching on Ragat at all? What if it was all Illusion? Some Elementals can control the weather. The blizzard was very convenient."

Jenista cursed under her breath, then blew air through her teeth. "Isn't it possible that several women, working together, could manage it all?"

"They would have to be very exceptional women. So exceptional, I would say your only choice is to consider the idea that Queen Salene herself is involved."

Jenista's eyes widened. "That would mean she was working with the Ragat. What queen would sink so low? And why?"

"Precisely," the Seer said with a firm nod.

"The queen did send an Emissary to the High Court." Bridget pulled her cloak tighter around her. "That's not like her. She attends the High Queen most dutifully. She's always been grateful for her elevation after the Dowager Mother gave up her throne."

"There were Ragat on her borders, massing as if for war. She had no choice but to remain." Jenista shivered and her breath misted the air.

"We have two possibilities then. The queen is part of this rebellion, or she is a prisoner in her own court."

"There is a third possibility," the Seer pointed out. "Queen Salene is dead and another commands in her place. Remember, she's no High Queen with the protections of Gaiea Herself. If Queen Elise could be murdered, Queen Salene may be dead as well."

"Commander." The Dahomei who had gone to inspect the way to the court was striding back down the path. "The way ahead is clear."

"Leave the horses here then," Jenista said. "Ready your weapons. For good or ill, we'll know the truth shortly."

It wasn't long before the court of Kadoomun came into full view. The path widened as it approached the open gateway and passed under a white marble arch. Beyond the gates, carved out of the rock of Everhill itself, the court jutted toward them, domes and spires rising into the twilight. The same marble topped the walls surrounding the arch and the lower levels of the court, its pale shade tinted a reddish-brown in failing daylight. Windows made regular slits in the rock above them, the heavy glass flashing the rainbow colors the Queendom of Kadoomun was famous for.

Swords drawn, they crept cautiously from tree to tree. Beyond the arch was a semicircular stone ward, then a large courtyard swept clear of snow. On either side of the courtyard, dimly lit passageways led to the stables and possibly the kitchens. Directly ahead of them was a set of giant doors, royal-blue crystal in a thick wooden frame. They both stood slightly ajar, though there was no one in the courtyard. Nothing moved in the light cast by the flower-shaped glass lamps that rimmed the perimeter wall.

Jenista signaled the Dahomei, and they spread out silently. Warm light spilled out of the open doorway, along with the faint whiff of a cooking evening meal. Voices sounded in the distance.

Eyes narrowed, Jenista kept to the shadows just outside the arch, studying the scene, waiting. But no one came into the courtyard. She signaled for everyone to move forward and stepped into the courtyard, the Seer close behind.

As soon as her foot touched the inner courtyard, the Seer breathed in sharply. She grabbed Jenista's shoulder. "Commander, no!"

A blast of air almost knocked her down. Behind them, Sam stumbled to her right and fell onto the paved stones. Bridget tried to help her up and had to steady herself with a hand against the wall.

"The cloaking spell!" the Seer gasped, favoring her leg as she tried to withstand the sudden wind. "It's all an Illusion!"

Darkness descended. The scene before them wavered under its advent, greying out like twilight's last light. The same crystal doors stood before them, only now they were shut and a deep indigo. The stone walls seemed closer and taller, with pools of shadows at their base.

Shadows that moved, dissolved, and re-formed into the shape of men. Men covered in black from their head to their feet.

Ragat marauders.

They came at the Dahomei from every direction, leaped from the walls, rose up from the ground where there had been nothing only minutes before. Blades glinted in their hands and bows rose to their shoulders as they ran across the stone, their feet making no sound.

"Ragat!" Jenista shouted, and instinctively inscribed a ward in the air in front of her to deflect their weapons.

Of course, nothing happened. No telltale shimmer appeared. She cursed.

Bridget spun around to try for the arch, her sword at the ready. It was too late. A row of marauders stood in front of it, arrows nocked and swords drawn.

The courtyard was too dark to see much, but what little light there was glinted off the tip of the arrow pointed at Jenista's chest. The marauder who held the bow was shorter than her and wiry, his hands gloved in black, his head and the lower half of his face hidden behind a black cloth.

Moving slowly, Jenista stooped and laid her sword on the ground, then rose with her hands in the air. "Don't try to fight. They outnumber us."

The Ragat in front of her lowered his arrow. "It's good you understand, Commander. This will save time." His voice was muffled but he spoke perfect Dunnish.

"You know of me?" Jenista said, surprised.

"All Ragat know of you. We've been preparing for your arrival. Welcome to Everhill, Commander—first court of the Ragat and home of the one true king."

⁄⁄⁄⁄⁄⁄⁄⁄⁄⁄

VIELLA CREPT THROUGH THE HALLS OF THE HIGH COURT, A SMOKE-GRAY quasiflame writhing above her open right palm. The corridors around her loomed larger than ever before, the ceiling lost beyond the light. She could see only a few inches. Shadows hid the walls, but the cracked tiles beneath her feet were visible—a faded, rusty red, like dried blood.

She knew she was too young to summon a quasiflame, but it danced above her hand. She knew the court around her was the one she had been born to, and someplace she'd never been. She had no idea where she was going, and still her feet moved, sure of their destination.

It's a dream.

The realization changed nothing. She kept going, her quasiflame kept twisting, and nothing disturbed the dead air that surrounded her.

A door loomed. Shiny as onyx, it breathed in and out, swelling and deflating with each breath she took. She wanted to run the other way, but her feet did not stop. She wanted to scream, but no sound came out of her mouth. As she drew near, the door diminished, and she looked into a swirling, black whirlpool that pulsed toward and away from her, breathing as the door had.

She stopped, the quasiflame's glow weak in the shadow of this monstrosity. Dread made it hard to breathe, and Viella tried to close her eyes but it didn't work. Her left hand reached out to the center of the vortex.

A hand emerged from the water and grasped her by the wrist. Cold flashed up her arm, and this time she did scream, but the hand didn't let go. She backed away, stumbling over her feet and falling to the floor. The quasiflame went out.

Its light was replaced by the glimmer that surrounded her mother as she knelt in front of the black whirlpool, her hand still tight around Viella's wrist. She wore a white dress so bright, it made her hard to look at, and her long hair trailed on the floor behind her. Her mother had never cut her hair, and the wavy dark mass moved on its own, as if caught in a breeze.

Viella knew in her heart this was her mother, knew it in her bones. But there was something wrong with the way her eyes remained in shadow, something strange in the icy grasp that held her tight. Something disturbing about the way her mother's left hand stretched behind her into the black water, disappearing into the oily, spinning vortex, as if it was being held within.

"Mummy?" she said, scrambling to her knees.

"Viella." Her mother's voice was faint, exhausted. "Beloved daughter."

Tears pricked Viella's eyes. "I'm here. Mummy, I'm here." Viella tried to put her arms around her, but they wouldn't move. Her left arm remained in her mother's hold and her right arm rested in her lap.

"Listen to me." The hand on her wrist squeezed as if to break it. "You can save us from what comes."

She cried out, trying to pull away. "Mummy, please. You're hurting me."

"Viella, only you can do this. Only you." Her mother's voice was fading and echoing back at her, as if she were falling down a deep well.

She didn't understand. "You're . . . gone, Mummy. I saw you." Tears slipped down her cheeks, making warm tracks on her cold skin. "You left me. You *died*."

"No, Viella. I'm still here." Her mother looked back and Viella followed her gaze over her shoulder.

Another hand emerged from the doorway, a child's hand, grasping at the air as though it sought freedom. Viella's heart leaped.

"Valan? Valan's with you?"

Her mother turned back to her. The light that surrounded her was growing dim. Viella could see only her mother's hair and lips now. And the white dress was graying before her very eyes.

"Time runs out. For all of us. Save Valan. Find the child. Close the *Nightward* before the Summoning."

The small arm was out of the vortex almost to the shoulder, but as Viella watched, tendrils of dark began to slither along it, the tips waving and seeking. The tendrils climbed up the arm to the wrist, and Viella's fear rose in her throat, choking her as she watched.

"What do you mean, Mummy?" she said, gripping her mother's hand as hard as hers had been gripped before, trying to keep her mother with her. "How can I save you and Valan?"

Queen Elise was an indistinct glow now. Viella tried to cling harder, but her mother's fingers were slipping from her grasp. The twisting threads of the vortex were also climbing up both her mother's wrists now, and in the center of her chest, the white dress had lost all light. A black mass pulsed, spreading and growing wider, like the bloodstain after the spear had pierced her in the hall. Viella shuddered at the horrible memory, her breath refusing to come.

The queen put her forehead against Viella's, and the light contact jarred her, searing her like a brand. She cried out, partly because of the pain, partly because she could see her mother's eyes now and they were no longer the dark brown she knew so well. They were the same dancing, twisting mass as the whirlpool that spun behind their kneeling bodies.

"I must die. One last time. Find the child before the Summoning."

"What child?"

But the tendrils were around their joined faces and as Viella opened her mouth to scream, they slid between her teeth and down her throat, oily, bitter, and suffocating, stifling all sound as the last of the light was snuffed out.

Viella sat up with no breath in her lungs. It took a few seconds for her to realize she wasn't choking. She breathed deeply, early morning light filtering onto her skin in warm, leafy patterns.

Luka looked up from pouring water on the dead embers of the previous night's fire. The last wisps of steam rose into the air as an ash-filled puddle spread slowly past the fire pit.

"Good morning," he said, smiling at her. It was his good smile, the one that always made her smile in return. "Did you rest?"

Viella tried to think if she had, but only a vague sense of forgetting something important came back to her. She tried to remember her dreams, but they danced away from her like a flower on the wind.

"I don't know," she admitted with a shrug.

Luka arched his back, wincing the whole time, then walked over to her. "Your sleep seemed troubled."

Viella frowned. "Troubled?"

"Nightmares."

Viella started and swung around. Eleanor was standing to her right, the muscles of her bare arms flexing as she tightened a saddlebag on the new horse, a small gray with pretty eyes. Flor stood waiting next to her.

Eleanor glanced over at Viella and repeated, "You had nightmares."

Without warning, a memory seared through her. Her mother's forehead on hers. Her mother's cold hand on her wrist.

"I must die. One last time. Find the child before the Summoning."

She shuddered and wrapped her arms around herself. *I have to tell them what I dreamed.*

Eleanor stopped what she was doing, a frown creasing her forehead. "Your Majesty, are you well?"

No. I saw my mother and she's not dead and she wants me to let her die.

Viella took a deep breath and said, "I'm fine."

"Hungry, perhaps?" Luka said, squatting in front of her and offering her dried meat and bread. She looked at it as if mesmerized.

I should tell Luka. I should tell him the truth.

She reached out for the food. "Is this all there is? I'm tired of bread."

Eleanor's chuckle made her feel lighter. She bit into the strip of meat as Eleanor added, "Aren't we all? We'll soon arrive at Plytown and enjoy a real meal and a bit of civilization before we move on."

Viella chewed and swallowed automatically, thinking hard on what she remembered. *Not yet. It's not time to talk about it yet. Soon, but not now, not in front of Eleanor.* Confident she'd come to the right decision she looked over at Luka and said, "That sounds great. Can we go now?"

And when we get there and we're alone, I'll tell Luka everything and he can decide if we'll tell Eleanor.

FRANCES LAID THE COVERED TRAY ON THE STOOL NEXT TO LADY Gretchen's bed. The lady had her back to the rest of the cell, her face turned toward the wall. Her legs made awkward bumps under the thin blanket that covered them. Lady Gretchen had refused the silks sent by her mother and instead wore a soft, sand-colored blouse with long sleeves over wide-legged linen pants. She had not been given shoes, of course.

Frances had dressed like the Dowager Queen she was. Her black sari was edged with pearls and scarlet embroidery. Her hair had been coiled into a low bun and wrapped with a pearl hairpiece. Her gold and ruby bangles clinked musically as she straightened and put her hands on her hips. "You must eat," she said.

Lady Gretchen didn't move except for the slow rise and fall of her chest. Frances sighed.

"I have grandchildren and much practice in divining those who sleep from those who only pretend to."

Lady Gretchen's fingers, curled beside her face on the flat pillow she lay on, folded into a loose fist.

"Very well. If you won't eat now, I shall wait here with you until hunger makes you rise from your bed."

A dry chuckle forced its way between Lady Gretchen's lips. "Rise? And how would I do that?"

"With some help and much determination." Frances reached

out a gentle hand and brushed the lady's damp hair from her forehead. Lady Gretchen flinched, her eyes opening to stare at the wall in front of her.

Taking her time, Frances removed the tray from the stool and placed it on the ground. Sitting, she gathered her sari in one hand, crossed one thin, brown ankle over her knee, removed her sandal, and began to massage swollen toes.

Lady Gretchen rolled over and stared at the ceiling as Frances finished massaging one foot and switched to the other. "Why will you not let me be?" she said. "I'm injured and my seat destroyed. What use could my mother have for me?"

"I care not," Frances said, lowering her feet and placing her hands on her knees. "*I* have need of you. I've held my tongue because I wasn't sure of you, but I've seen enough to know you're not your mother. A lady such as you can be of great service to her High Queen."

Lady Gretchen frowned at Frances. "The queen is dead. I've already failed her."

"Elise is gone, it's true," Frances said. "But my granddaughter still lives. Do you not owe her your fealty?"

Lady Gretchen pulled herself up onto her elbows. "You believe she survived? That my Dahomei kept her safe?"

"If your mother had her, the court wouldn't still be glamoured. Sophia and Mordach cannot take the throne while Viella lives. She must be found and returned to the court. Lady Sophia, I'm sure, has no preference as to her condition."

"And what do you believe an old woman and a bedridden failure can do to stop this?"

Frances leaned forward, her voice low but harsh. "I remain capable as any woman. My magic is mine until I leave this world. And you are more than your legs, My Lady."

"You may be the Dowager Mother, but I would ask you not to presume to tell me what I am," Lady Gretchen replied, her voice sharp.

Frances sucked her teeth in a steups. "And I am asking *you* to do the same. You must focus on what I have to say, not the anger and pain that consumes you."

"And what do you have to say?"

"I know a way to escape the court and bring help for those trapped within."

Lady Gretchen was silent for a moment, her gaze searching. "This is no time to jest."

Frances at up straight. "I am the Dowager Mother and a former Queen of Kadoomun. I know what lies beneath this court. I know the secrets Elise was entrusted with are no fairy tales. And I do *not* jest."

Lady Gretchen placed a hand against the wall and pulled herself upright. Her lips were a thin, bloodless line and her eyes narrowed as she met Frances's gaze. "You speak of the Halls of Creation? Of Oblivion?"

Frances nodded slowly. "You've read the Forbidden Histories? You know the truth of the Age of Chaos?"

"My mother insisted," Lady Gretchen replied, her voice bitter.

"We can use that against her. Only queens know the story now. Queens and ladies with old bloodlines. I'm glad you know. It will save time."

"Time? Time to do what?"

"To plan how best to take the prince and make our way to the unseen lower levels of the court. The Ragat entered that way, with Mordach's help. I saw them the night of the attack. I saw the door to the hidden place the *Nightward* speaks of. There must be a Portal down there. One the Ragat used to invade us. I will find it, and when I do, I need you to be ready."

"Surely there will be Ragat below the court. You could be captured or killed."

"It's a risk I will take to help save my family."

"And what of the other side of the Portal? There will be more Ragat there."

"Without a doubt. But I'll be in my territory and will have the advantage."

Lady Gretchen frowned. "You make no sense."

The Dowager Mother's smile was brief. "If the Ragat are here, they must have used one of the lost Portals. Portals whose locations were kept secret in the *Nightward*. If I can find it, we can go back to my old court. And no one knows my court as I do."

Lady Gretchen bit her lip, considering. "You believe you can do this?"

"*We* can do this, Lady," Frances said fiercely. "We *must* do this. Otherwise, your mother wins, and my only son and grand-children will be murdered. My cold corpse will be burned on the pyre before I see my family end."

"I'm with you, Dowager Mother," Lady Gretchen said, raising her chin. There was a determined look in her eye.

Frances reached over and gripped Lady Gretchen's left hand. "Then eat, Lady Gretchen. Make yourself strong. The time for self-pity is at an end."

SEVERAL OF THE RAGAT SURROUNDED JENISTA AND HER PARTY AND took their weapons away while the rest kept bows trained on them or swords at the ready. The Ragat leader in front of Jenista watched as his men worked.

Encouraged by the tips of weapons jabbed into them, the women were walked across the courtyard. Ahead of them, marauders pulled open the crystal doors and waited.

Inside, a few torches lit a cavernous receiving hall. Gray statues rose out of the gloom, the glitter of jewels and the shine of marble making tiny points of light here and there. They were marched down the hall and forced beneath arches decorated by heavy drapes to keep out the cold of long winter months, now tied back by jeweled strands of silver to allow easy passage.

The Dahomei's footsteps echoed down hallways that wound through the court in spirals. The marauders made no sound. Their shoes were soft-soled and wrapped in cloth. No one spoke. As they went deeper into Everhill, the air around them grew cooler and cooler.

They had made their way through three internal courtyards with fountains in the shapes of various animals—water gurgling out of their mouths, evergreen bushes and flowers rising around them in thick profusion—before they came upon the first flight of stairs. The stairs were wide, shallow, and worn smooth by years of use. Here flames leapt high from regular brackets in the wall. The pale stonework was intermixed with marble in shades of flint and slate.

The second flight of stairs ended in front of a thick wooden door with no visible handle. As they approached, the door opened with a low groan. The corridor beyond dipped out of sight. The walls were dank; moisture dripped down moss-covered stone on well-traveled paths and the stairs were roughhewn, deep, and narrow.

"You take us to the cellars," Jenista said.

The leader glanced at her out of the corner of his eye. "Quiet," he said, his voice muffled. "Or one of my men will be happy to run you through and you can meet your High Queen in your fabled Garden."

Jenista let a thin smile crease her face. "Empty threats do you no honor. Had you wished me dead, I would have been so. You march us here for a purpose."

"You think I need you *all* alive?" He studied her, dark-brown eyes expressionless above the cloth mask that covered his lower jaw, then walked on.

Chilly air wrapped around their feet as they moved into the lowest levels of the court. The passageway opened into a dim cave, the ceiling too high to be seen.

Huge stacked piles rose around them. Barrels, crates, baskets, pails, and shelves. Blocks of ice were heaped here and there, radiating a soft white light—evidence they had been spelled to prevent melting. The party followed a cleared path through the cave to a roughhewn arch on the other side. Twice, they walked through caverns similarly filled with stores for the winter ahead.

They came to a smaller cave, filled with racks that should have held barrels of drink and bottles of wine. But the racks were empty and stacked to one side of the room. At the back of the cave, a dozen tiny cells with brand-new metal bars had been created. Only a few were occupied, and the people inside them stood as the group entered. Most of those crammed into the rooms were dressed in the uniforms of servants and the simple homespun clothes of townsfolk. But the cell at the farthest end of the cave held just one occupant.

Queen Salene was a tall, broad woman. Her black hair was plaited into braids that looped around her head several times. She had ebony skin and brown eyes that turned down at the corners. Her shoulders were straight as a ruler under her high-necked, long-sleeved gown.

Loud clinks sounded as she strode to the door of her prison, dragging the links of silver chains behind her. The chains fell from thick bands of metal encircling her hands and snaked out from under her full plum-colored velvet skirts. Their ends passed through silver hoops imbedded into the upper and lower walls behind her, limiting her movement. Hers was the smallest room, with nothing but the narrow bed she'd been sitting on and a bucket to her right.

Queen Salene's lips tightened as she glanced at the leader of the Ragat. "Worm. Yet still you hide behind your mask while calling yourself king."

The king shrugged. "Your words are nothing to me, woman."

She snorted. "You shall suffer a slow and painful death. These are not words. They are prophecy."

"You are most amusing. But you must be lonely here without your lapdog Dahomei. I've brought a few with me so you may reminisce together about what the world was like before we crushed you beneath our feet."

He jabbed a finger at two of the rooms. Jenista was herded into the empty middle room with Bridget and Sam. The other two Dahomei were shoved into the room between them and Queen Salene. Bars clanged shut, and although she saw no locks of any kind, when Jenista grabbed the metal, she found they extended from floor to ceiling without a break or an opening. She pulled at them, but they didn't budge.

The Ragat laughed among themselves, their leader watching with his head to one side like a curious bird. His hand was wrapped around the Seer's arm, keeping her near him. When she pulled against his grip, he glanced at her.

"Why fight? There's nowhere to run, Seer."

She stilled, her glare icy. He taunted her softly. "Yes, we know what you are, though Everhill's Seer died during our . . . arrival, denying us the pleasure of your kind's company. We expected you eventually, though. Dahomei never ride to war without Seers."

"It will be no pleasure for you, Ragat," she said, her voice as hard as her stare.

"What do you hope to do here? You know by now your magic has no hold in Everhill. Your queen stands caged. How will you prevent me from taking what pleasures I will?"

The Seer's stare was direct and defiant.

"And there is your answer," the Ragat finished. He shoved her at his guards, and two of them grabbed her arms.

"See to the leg and the hand," he instructed. "We have need of her."

Her lips pressed together, Jenista watched as the group left the cellar. Limping, the Seer looked over her shoulder at the commander, giving her a slight nod before she was carried out of sight.

The Ragat leader lingered for a moment, hands clasped behind his back, his gaze studying the queen.

"It's almost time," he said to her. "Do you ready yourself for Gaiea's Garden, as you call it?"

Queen Salene wrapped her fingers around the bars of her cage, her knuckles prominent as she squeezed. "Are you ready for her Desert, little man? For that's where you shall be when I leave this cage."

"We shall see," he said. "We shall see."

As he walked away, two more Ragat entered the cellar and took up positions on either side of the arch. They held spears and wore narrow wooden tubes on their hips. Their faces hidden, they stared straight ahead.

"Your Majesty, are you well?" Jenista called out.

"As well as one can be when chained and caged." There was a great rattling, followed by the sound of wood creaking. "I expected your rescue party, but sadly, your effort appears to have been wasted."

"When did this happen? How did these motherless bastards take your court, Queen Salene?"

One of the Ragat, the shorter one on the right who had moon-pale skin said something in his language. He advanced into the room and pointed his sword at Jenista. He kept repeating the same words and jabbing the spear at her.

"I've upset you?" Jenista said to him. He chattered back. She shrugged. "Excellent. There's nothing to be gained by staying in your good graces."

"It's best you keep your counsel, Commander," Queen Salene said. "I've seen them kill those who won't quiet. The mind-speak doesn't work down here, but they change the guards once a day. We'll talk then."

The Ragat guard cautioned the queen with his singsong speech and his spear as well before returning to his post. After that, no one spoke again for some time.

If the Troubles have taught us one thing, it's that Gaiea's hard-won peace can be dismantled by a few selfish dissenters in search of power. Commander Ragat may have passed on to Gaiea's Desert, long may he burn and suffer therein, but the remaining leaders of his army style themselves after him and will stop at nothing to take back the power of the High Court, their old headquarters. They managed to infiltrate our seats and even murder ladies of Gailand. Had the Dahomei not acted quickly, some of the pivotal courts could have fallen to their hidden rebels. Drastic action is required to keep us all safe until Ragat's people can be neutralized.

To that end, Dun has agreed to assist Kadoomun's court by establishing a permanent regiment of Dahomei within Everhill, in addition to their existing forces. What lies within that court is second in importance only to what lies within Ragat's [FORBIDDEN] and the High Court. Further military plans will be discussed with the Seers at Everhill and Dun, and the Augurs' Guild.

It gives me no pleasure to write this, but we must also deal with the vexing question of those who have displayed no Blessing, the Neutrals, and their part in this uprising. By their actions, they have proven one that exists without Gaiea is one that cannot be trusted. Their desire for power to counteract their lack of True nanomagic or Illusion almost returned us to the Age of Chaos. The Augurs must find a way to identify these persons early enough to indoctrinate them against the corrupt teachings of Ragat's men. They must be scried and marked, and records kept of their bloodlines. Those that refuse this process should be exiled to the West, their children given to the Augurs for reeducation, as they present too much future risk.

The same process should be considered to deal with this new threat of the Elementals, who hid this rebellion from the Augurs and attacked and destroyed entire seats.

There is some corruption of [FORBIDDEN], perhaps [FORBIDDEN] by Ragat. For obvious reasons, I cannot tell the Augurs how this might have been accomplished, but they agree their Blessing has been cursed. They have powers over the Elements of Gailand that rival the True nanomagic of women and the Unbound and carry the destructive impulses of [FORBIDDEN].

I believe the Guilds, seats, and courts must come to an agreement on how to study and fight those that have been found, and how to guard against those that may yet come, for if Gailand should ever have to face such creatures again, our survival is not certain.

—*The Divine Histories of Gailand*
An Account of the Troubles, 50 Years After Ascension - RESTRICTED
For the Edification of the Queens, Ladies, and Dahomei of Gailand ONLY
What Gaiea has Forbidden has been Expunged by Her Hand
Aaliyah, Second High Queen of Dun

CHAPTER 11

PLYTOWN

UCK IS WITH YOU, LUKA." GLORIA TARK, INNKEEPER OF PLYTOWN, smiled as she released Luka from a hug. "I have the herbs you seek, along with a room for the night. Your family is welcome."

Gloria was a tiny, black-haired woman with brown eyes that hid behind thick lashes when she smiled, and skin as pale as Lady Sophia's. She was originally from Kadoomun and didn't wear the sari of the Dunnish. Her full skirts were made of woven cotton dyed blue, her shirt buttoned to the neck as though she still lived in the cold mountains, yet her flushed cheeks were the only sign she stood in a very warm room. "Come in. You shall be the first to sample my bread tonight. Speaking of which . . ." The factor left them by her front doors and ran across the wooden floors of the wide-open dining room to the back door. She left it open, and Luka watched as she checked the bread in the kiln outside.

"Your hospitality is appreciated," Eleanor said when she returned. "A night not spent on the road is something to look forward to."

Gloria bowed. "It is indeed a long way to Biche, and any family of Luka's is friend to mine. I have a helper, but he's not working tonight. An unfortunate side effect of the carousing yesterday. The councilwoman's daughter took a wife in the largest wedding seen here for many a day." Gloria gestured around a huge dining table to the other side of the room, where a wooden staircase led to the second floor. The closed doors to several other rooms were set below the stairs, next to the open back door. Late-afternoon sunlight lit the lower floor from the open front and back doors.

On the floor above, smokeless flames burned purple and white in brackets on the walls along the stairs and the dim upper landing. "All but one of my rooms has been let to the family members that traveled from the south. Come, I'll show it to you."

"It's so quiet. Where are they? Have they all gone home?" Viella asked.

Luka gave her a quelling stare to remind her they'd agreed she would not speak, and Viella dropped her head, biting her lip.

Gloria stopped with one foot on the first stair and smiled mischievously. "Not at all. The feasting continues tonight at the councilwoman's house. They will no doubt stumble home in the small hours."

The long, narrow landing had several doors at intervals along its left, while a wooden railing made a balcony that ended in a supporting wall to its right. Gloria took them to the door that faced the end of the railing.

"It's not very large," she apologized as she opened the door. "Still, there is a bed. I have several of them for those Portal travelers used to such things."

The room had wooden floors and walls, and the roof was thatched. Four large beams met each other in the center of the ceiling. There was a bed on a platform low to the ground, with a thick mattress covered by a woven blanket.

To the left of it, sleeping cushions were tossed together in a comfortable nook. To the right was a washstand with a mug and basin. The one window was made of thick, warped glass, a mere slit high above the bed letting in the afternoon daylight.

"It will suffice," Eleanor said, dropping her saddlebags in front of the bed. "What do I owe you for the night?"

"You are Luka's kin. For such a small room I will charge no more than a crown and four bits per night," Gloria replied.

Eleanor raised her eyebrows. "Almost two crowns? But the slow season has started. Surely two bits will be enough this time of year?"

"Most years, yes," Gloria agreed. "But a wedding brings high demand. Rates have risen accordingly."

"To unreasonable heights," Eleanor replied, hands on hips, although her faint smile did not slip. "Fine, three bits it is."

Viella, exhausted from the road and tired of the requisite bargaining, started shifting her feet a little. Luka shot her a look and she stilled. It was imperative the transaction proceed without interruption, so that both sides would feel they had been dealt with fairly.

"But this fine bed," Gloria said waving a hand at the bed. "Would you not consider the price worthy of it?"

For a Kadoomun woman, Luka thought, she had learned the art of the bargain well. Most people outside Dun didn't understand to not bargain hard was to insult the seller and buyer alike. The Dunnish liked a deal and would go far to get it.

Eleanor laughed. "You may feel free to remove it if you consider my offer unworthy. The floor's better for my back anyway."

"Three-piece and a crown. I cannot go any lower. I charge more for my stables."

"And a night in your stables would be preferable at that rate," Eleanor said, shrugging. "Four bits is my final offer, if you throw in the stables free of charge. Our horses could use a rub."

Gloria's brow wrinkled slightly, then she sighed as if defeated. "My stable girl will have to get out of bed for that. Consider a crown and two bits, and I'll have a light supper for you within the hour."

Eleanor put her hands on her hips as she studied the little factor. "A crown then, but we will need supplies."

Gloria thought for a moment. "There is little profit here." She spread her hands in a flourish and dipped her head. "But I accept your offer in the spirit of friendship." She winked at Luka. "I look forward to a long talk. You haven't been this way in years, and much has changed. I'm a married woman now."

Luka gave a shocked huff and sensed rather than saw Eleanor look at him. "A miracle in Plytown. I thought never to see this day. I must hear every detail of this unlucky man's courtship."

"Bah!" Gloria flapped her hands at him. "Still too plain-spoken. You'll make someone a terrible husband someday."

Luka shut the door when she left and leaned against it, already regretting the lies he would have to tell.

"What bothers you?" Eleanor asked as he turned to face her.

"We're here, and Gloria will help us. The rest will keep," Luka replied, moving the bags nearer to the sleeping cushions he knew would be his. He had little appetite for discussion. His body ached and tiredness made his mind slow. *I hope Gloria does not guess my deceit, but she knows me better than most.*

Viella threw herself on the bed. She yelped a little as she landed. "There's something wrong with this." She sat up, a frown on her little face. "Why doesn't it bounce like the one at home?"

"Because travelers can't afford your bed," Luka said, sinking down on the dark-brown cushions with a soft sound of pleasure at the easing of stiff limbs. "We're fortunate indeed to have such luxuries. The constant skirmishes with the Ragat are paid for with higher taxes on luxuries like goose down. It's forced everyone from breeders to the Sewing Guilds to raise prices."

"What are taxes?" Viella asked, clearly excited by the prospect of a new and adult topic.

"Something to be discussed when you are older, Your—" Eleanor bit off the honorific at the last second.

"They are the bane of everyone's existence," Luka replied. "Much like little girls who forget they mustn't draw attention to themselves." He smiled, so she would know he meant no disrespect.

Viella lay on her stomach and put her chin in the palm of her hand, her forehead wrinkled. "A bane isn't a good thing, is it?"

"Do you regret coming here? Have you no stomach for the lies we must tell Gloria?" Eleanor said, folding her arms across her chest.

Luka held his elbow, wincing at the sharp pains in his shoulder. "We do what we must. So will I."

"An excellent response if you wish to say nothing," Eleanor replied.

"As was my intention," Luka said. He dropped his arm and sighed. "I have no stomach for disagreement. Only for food and rest."

Eleanor's forehead creased with concern and her gaze went to his shoulder. "Of course. I apologize. I'll speak to Gloria about the herbs."

"That's a good idea," Viella said, nodding awkwardly with her head still on her palm. "I think he's just in a bad mood because it hurts."

"You think me in a poor mood?" Luka frowned.

"You've been quiet."

"Until Gloria made you laugh." Luka looked at Eleanor and found she was studying the floor. She glanced up and shrugged. "I'd never heard you laugh before," the Dahomei said. "It was . . . good to hear it."

"There was nothing to laugh about before," he said, an odd feeling settling in his chest as he watched her.

"More's the pity." She scuffed at the floor with her boot before looking up and away from him. Which was a good thing, as his brain stuttered to a halt temporarily at the implication of her words. *Calm down. She's Dahomei and you are Daguard. She means nothing by it.*

Viella jumped down from the bed and sank to her knees next

to Luka. Her fingers touched his upper arm as gently as a feather. "Does it hurt very much?"

It did, but Luka didn't wish to worry her. "Eleanor has been a great help. It's much less painful than it was."

She studied him, her eyes golden in a beam of light from the window, her mouth turned down at the corners. "You're only sick because you saved me. You wouldn't be in pain if it wasn't for me."

He put an arm around her and drew her against his side. "None of this was caused by you. And I would suffer many times this pain to keep you safe. I'm not worth much if I can't endure a hole in me, now and again."

Viella hugged him around his waist, burying her face against his side. The emotion that gripped him tightened his throat and made liquid prick at his eyes. She made him think of his father, and family, and the fact that if he was ever somehow blessed with children, his parents would never know them.

Thankfully, Eleanor chose that moment to slip from the room, leaving Luka to run his fingers through Viella's hair to soothe her and distract himself. Viella curled against his side like a sleeping kitten.

"I don't think Eleanor hates you anymore," she whispered without warning.

"I doubt she ever held true ill will toward me," Luka replied, his mind drifting toward their last exchange and the look in her eyes. He felt warm inside as he leaned his head against the wall and closed his eyes in exhaustion.

"Then why did you quarrel?"

His hand stilled in her hair. It was a question he wasn't expecting. *Why did we indeed?*

Because she was dismissive at first. Insulting. She thought me unworthy of protecting the queen. And yet, she never objected to my ideas unless she had better ones.

He thought of the smile on Eleanor's face when he'd found them after the Sycren attack, and the vows they'd made to each other to protect Viella and he realized she'd been concerned for both him and the queen. Perhaps what he'd read as insults had been her natural reluctance to place the queen's well-being in the hands of one so young. His father had always said he was quick to anger and slow to listen. Perhaps their discord had been as much his fault as hers.

When he didn't reply, Viella looked up, and he watched from under his eyelids as she lowered her gaze without another word and tucked her head back under his arm.

He left his hand where it lay, caught in the strands of her soft hair and realized that whatever else, his feelings toward Eleanor had changed.

And perhaps hers had changed as well. *From now on, the only fighting will be to protect you, My Queen. I promise you that.*

WHEN VIELLA OPENED HER EYES, SHE WAS IN THE DARK AND VALAN SAT cross-legged in front of her.

She squealed and threw herself into his arms. They hugged each other fiercely and relief coursed through her as she felt their wordless connection for the first time in days.

"I'm so glad you came back," she said. "I'm sorry. I shouldn't have left you."

"I miss you, Vee," he said, and pulled back to look at her. "Are you safe?"

"Yes. Luka's with me, and Eleanor." She wanted to tell him how they'd saved her, but she hesitated. Her brother felt . . . different. Not fully present in some way.

"Eleanor?"

"She's a Dahomei from Talon. She's nice. They're taking me to another queendom."

"I'm glad you're okay," Valan said, dropping his hands to hold hers.

"I shouldn't have left you behind."

He shook his head at her. "Mummy's gone. You're queen now. You had to go."

Sadness swamped Viella. "I'm coming back. For all of you. Mummy said I have to save you. Are you hurt? What's happening there?"

His face twisted and she realized he was crying. Alarmed, she touched his face, his hands, hugged him to her. Sympathetic tears made her eyes damp. "Please don't cry, Val."

"You should hate me," he gasped. "It's my fault. All my fault. Mummy's dead because of me."

Viella rubbed his back. "No, no. It's the awful Ragat that killed her. I saw it."

"You don't understand." The misery in his voice was so complete, she leaned back to look at his face, wiping at her own tears. "Mordach took me below the court and made me open a door. There was a Portal there, and someone else. Like me. They said we were special. We did . . . they made us do magic. Together."

Disquiet began to rise in Viella's mind. How was this possible? Her brother's magic was limited.

"What kind of magic?"

"From the *Nightward*. They called it Elemental magic." Valan evaded her eyes. "Viella, it's not over. There's something . . . horrible going on. You can't come back here."

"Are you crazy? Of course I'm coming back. I can't *leave* you all there. Mordach will be arrested and—"

"No!" Valan shook his head furiously. "Vee, please, I don't want you to die like Mummy."

Shocked, Viella sat back on her heels. "Why would I die? I'm going to be queen."

"*Mummy died*. You can die. And then that will be my fault too."

"You keep saying that, but everyone already knows Mordach did it."

"Vee, listen to me," he said desperately. "I'm *different*. It started happening a while ago and I was . . . afraid. I didn't know how to tell you. Mordach said I shouldn't, that he would help me, but all he did was use me. The Ragat came because *I let them in*."

Viella put a hand over her mouth, her eyes wide, her heart pounding in her head and her ears.

"There's something else they want us to do. I don't know what, but I can *feel* it's going to be worse than the Ragat. If you come back now, you might get hurt."

He went still, his gaze far away. Then he started to shiver violently.

"Val?"

"Go. Get away." He stared at her, his chest rising and falling rapidly. "It knows we're in here. I'm sorry. I didn't know! I didn't know!"

He scrambled to his feet, backing away as stood up. "Didn't know what? Val, don't leave me!"

"They're taking me back to the halls." His voice was barely a whisper.

"Valan, I'm coming. Please be okay. Tell Daddy and Grandmother I'm coming." She was crying now. "I love you."

"Vee, you have to get away. *It followed me*. Go! Now!"

"What followed you?" she asked. "What followed you?"

〜〜〜〜〜

"NOTHING FOLLOWED ME." LUKA REPLIED, HIS HAND STROKING HER cheek. "Viella, it's okay. You're safe. You're safe."

She breathed in, feeling the bed solid beneath her, the dream slipping away as she focused on Luka's face, on the crease between his dark eyes.

"It was a dream," he said. "There's nothing to fear."

"Luka." She swallowed, her stomach churning at the lie, and tried not to think about what was happening to her brother.

"Do you wish to tell me about it?"

She bit her lip. "Where's Eleanor?"

"She went downstairs to wash. She should return at any moment. Shall I fetch her?"

Viella hesitated—

(I let them in)

—then shook her head. She trusted Luka, but he would tell Eleanor whatever she said, and she wasn't sure how the Dahomei might react to her news. Eleanor might not want to save Valan. And Viella needed him to be saved. Needed her family to be safe. Her mother had told her to save him.

She couldn't lose anyone else.

"Then go back to sleep. I'll wake you for supper."

She closed her eyes, sending a prayer to Gaiea to protect her brother until she could be with him again.

※※※※※

VALAN WOKE TO LADY SOPHIA HANGING OVER HIM, MORDACH BY her side.

"Ah," she said. "Welcome back."

He pushed himself up on his elbows. His father sat on the other side of the bed, relief etched on his face.

"Daddy." He held out his arms, and his father embraced him, stroking his hair. "How do you feel?"

"Okay, I guess," Valan said through a scratchy throat. His father gave him water and he drank gratefully.

"Good," Lady Sophia said. She withdrew to a corner of the room—he was in his mother's bedroom, he realized—with Mordach, and he overheard snippets of what they said.

". . . what you need?"

". . . should be. He suspected . . ."

". . . Deepsleep next time then . . ."

"After . . . need him awake now."

By the time Mordach left and Lady Sophia came back to his bed, he was clinging to his father, dread paralyzing his limbs.

"No," he said before she spoke.

"Time to go," she replied with a smile.

"Let me come with him at least," his father said. "You're scaring him."

She pressed a hand to her chest, a line between her brows. "Scared? Of me? You know better, Valan, don't you?"

"I don't want to go," he said in a small voice. "I don't want to go back there."

"But your new friend will be lonely. We can't have that. Besides, if you're a good boy, Daddy will be right here waiting for you when you get back."

He stared at her, fear making his mouth dry.

"Do you understand, Valan? Good boys get to stay with their daddy."

"Stop it," his father hissed, holding him tighter.

"I understand," Valan blurted, and got out of the bed.

His father stood with him, still holding his hands. "Valan," he said in a soft voice. "I'm your father. I protect you, not the other way around. I can handle whatever they do to me. You don't have to do anything you don't want to."

"Come along." Lady Sophia held out her hand to him. "You have nothing to fear, you know that by now. And we can't keep everyone waiting."

With only the merest hesitation, and one last look at his father, Valan pulled away and placed his hand in Sophia's.

ELEANOR CAME FOR THEM AFTER CHECKING ON THE HORSES, AND THEY went down to dinner. It was simple fare. Bread and stewed chicken with potatoes, milk for Viella, and a little homemade fruit wine for the adults.

It was the best thing they'd eaten in days.

Eleanor and Luka sat on the low bench on one side of the large communal table in the middle of the inn's greeting room, and Viella sat opposite them. The furniture was as simple as the food. Roughhewn wood that had been sanded but not polished. It was ancient—black-brown as the stairs and ceiling.

Gloria ate with them. It was clear she was delighted to have another woman to talk with, but she also commiserated with Luka about the seasons past, the visitors who had come and gone, and all the town gossip. When the talk died a natural death, she rose to tend to her kitchen.

Luka stopped eating halfway through his meal and pushed aside the polished half-shell of his calabash bowl, which was new, shiny, and green instead of the worn beige-brown of the older bowls on the table.

"Something wrong?" Eleanor asked, dipping her bread into the gravy in her almost-empty bowl.

"Why do you ask?" he said with a quick glance at Gloria, who was back and forth, clearing the kitchen.

She pointed with a piece of bread at his half-empty bowl and raised her eyebrows at him before popping the bread into her mouth.

Luka leaned back in his chair, taking his cup of wine with him. "Leftovers for later."

"Later?"

Viella had been looking from one to the other as she ate. Understanding suddenly, she said, "I know! It's for Farain."

"A little louder, perhaps," Luka said with a frown and a barely perceptible nod in Gloria's direction.

Viella paused. "Oh." She dropped her voice to a whisper. "Am I right?"

"Yes," Luka said. "Still, our business is our own."

"Can he not feed himself?" Eleanor murmured.

"Usually, but there's nothing out there," Luka replied. "I can feel him. The grasslands are bare."

"Maybe the animals heard him coming," Viella said before raising her bowl to drink the last of her gravy.

"Nothing hears Farain unless he wants to be heard," Luka said. "He has no food, and he does not wish to go too far. He can survive for some time without sustenance, but a hungry dagen can become aggressive and difficult to bond with."

"So, you will go to him?" Eleanor asked, licking at her fingers. Luka stared, distracted by her pink tongue, a tightening low in his belly, until it occurred to him there had been a question.

"After it is quiet—before the other guests arrive. We will leave a few hours later. If you find it acceptable."

Eleanor picked up her bowl and after a quick look in Gloria's direction, she emptied the rest of her meal into Luka's bowl. Then she leaned forward and whispered, "I can handle Viella on my own. He's at least as useful as the horses, and they've been seen to."

Luka gave her a quick, grateful look. "He'll be pleased to know a Daho . . . that you think of him and a horse as equals."

Viella put her bowl down and crossed her arms. "I don't need you to handle me."

Luka gave her a knowing glance. "I'm sure you believe that to be true."

Viella glared while Eleanor tried to smother a laugh and ended up snorting instead.

"Girls," Gloria said, pausing by the table and shaking her head at Viella. "They can be a handful at this age."

"You have children?" Eleanor asked.

"Not yet," Gloria replied. "But soon, hopefully. I would be blessed to have one as beautiful as yours. Such eyes she has—more golden than yours."

"She has her grandmother's eyes," Eleanor said. "A good thing, as I'm no great beauty myself."

Gloria tut-tutted. "Such words are unworthy of you. You are a woman of obvious good breeding. Your brother is lucky to have your guidance."

"A fact I have been made fully aware of, on many occasions." Luka rose from the table, bowl in hand, tamping down the very unbrotherly thoughts the sight of Eleanor's tongue had brought to mind. "I will take this with me. I sometimes find myself waking hungry at night."

"I've recently come to know the feeling as well," Gloria assented. "I sympathize. Sleep eludes these days."

"Are you often so afflicted?" Eleanor asked with a lift of her eyebrows.

"Not at all. But I worry. My husband journeys home to Kadoomun to tend to his sick mother. I fear I was hasty in allowing him to travel when whispers of war are everywhere."

"He rides without escort?" Eleanor shook her head. "I had heard Kadoomun women were relaxed about such things, but it truly is not safe for men who have little magic to travel without a woman in these times."

"We Kadoomun don't see the need for such . . . control over our men as you Dunnish," Gloria agreed. "But we're not as relaxed as you believe. My sister accompanies him. Still, I've had no word for several days and with the border unsettled, I've imagined much."

"Fears are often worse than reality," Luka said, trying to be kind. Gloria's light tone covered the worried note in her voice, but he knew her well enough to recognize it. "No doubt he's safe and will soon send word."

"Let it be so, in Gaiea's name." Gloria sighed.

"I have no wish to trouble you," Eleanor said, "but have you been able to boil the herbs I requested?"

"Of course, follow me."

Eleanor trailed Gloria to the kitchen, giving Luka a quick nod. Luka pointed his chin at the stairs and said to Viella, "Shall we retire?"

Viella sighed but pushed her bowl away and stood. "Okay. I'm tired anyway."

They went up together and Luka opened the door. "Make yourself ready. Eleanor will come to you soon and we only have a few hours of rest before we must leave. I'm going to slip out and find Farain while Gloria believes I'm with you."

Viella stared into the room as if thinking hard about something. "Okay. But Luka?"

"Yes?"

"When you get back, can we talk?"

Luka studied her. There was a tension to her body he didn't like. "Do you wish to speak to me now?" he asked.

She hesitated for a while, then shook her head. "It's okay. It can wait."

Luka hesitated. *It's probably the dream she had. Farain is more important.* "On my return then."

She nodded and went inside. Luka was of two minds, wanting to follow her in, but in the end, he turned and went down the stairs as quietly as possible.

THE NIGHT SKY WAS FADING TO PEWTER WHEN THE RIVER MAIDEN reached Glass Lake, a rippling body of water at the base of the mountain they called the Mother. The mountain's bulk cast a shadow on the water of Glass Lake, which would reflect its white-tipped beauty in its clear depths once the sun rose.

With a practiced movement, the maiden pulled herself from

the river. The moment her tail left the water, it split in two, her upper thighs slender and human, her lower legs with high, backward-bent ankles that ended in dainty deer hooves. She stood upright, her hooves clattering.

Around her, smooth, nacreous rocks, some as small as pebbles and others as large as thrones, rose from the ground. Their pointed domes held the flat shine of precious gems in the growing light. A few had cracks in their shiny surface and one that stood to the Guardian's right had no dome at all. Instead, the entire top of it appeared to have cracked and fallen right off. Jagged edges jutted up, revealing a hollow interior.

Behind the array of beautiful stones yawned the huge entrance to a cave. The river emptied out of it and into the lake before cascading in a series of falls down the sloping land into the valley below. The rocks were on either side of the river, which was widest near the lake and narrowed into a swiftly flowing band where it gushed out from the unseen depths of the cave.

The maiden picked her way among the sharp stones alongside the banks of the river. As she drew near the rock without a dome, a creature uncoiled itself from within it, hanging reedy arms over the jagged edges.

"Trespasser," it hissed.

The River Maiden stopped and bared her teeth. The creature scuttled down to the ground on six thin limbs, each tipped with three short, black claws. It was bald and yellow-skinned, with immature breasts in an emaciated chest. Its head came up to the maiden's sternum. Its face suggested humanity, with slits that mimicked a nose, a pointed chin, slanted cheeks, and a lipless mouth with no teeth. But the bulging eyes were a mosaic of color on either side of its small head, like the eyes of flies that fed on dead things.

The armored, segmented tail that began just below the last pair of limbs it stood on curled upward behind it. The long stinger that tipped it pointed directly at the River Maiden's face, matte black in the dawn light.

"I am no trespasser. Papa Bois allowed me entrance because I am a daughter of the First and I bear important news."

The mottled yellow-and-black tail waved from side to side. The tip curled in tighter. "His will is not our concern. The First sleeps and cannot be disturbed. You must leave this place. Now."

Stones clacked against stones. Gravel slipped into the lake. Shadows moved behind and around the base of the jeweled domes. But they were not domes or jewels—rather, they were the eggs of the Matamari, some hatched and some dormant. In others, unseen young shifted, the hour of their birth nearly at hand. It was these that made the Matamari so aggressive. The Maiden exhaled, knowing it would be difficult to reason with a mother-to-be.

"I have no time to dance with you, Matamari. I do not seek to harm you or your children."

The Matamari made a clicking noise in her throat and drew herself up to her full height. The claws on four of her limbs opened and closed, opened and closed. "Foolish thing. I protect these, but they are not my children. It is for your sake that I ask you to leave."

"It is for the sake of Gailand that I must refuse. Let me pass, for the Queendom of Dun lies in chaos and the Spirit of Gaiea flees for her very life."

"Human business." The Matamari's head twisted until her face was sideways. "The First no longer has an interest in such things. Go now. To travel further is to seal your death."

"I can only go forward, for that is the way to salvation. If you will not allow me to pass, we will quarrel, you and I." The Maiden bared her teeth and spread long fingers tipped with transparent nails, hard as diamonds.

The Matamari's head snapped back, her chin pointing downward again. She laughed and her tail vibrated above her. "Die, then, stupid water girl. I cannot care for your life more than you." Without warning, her tail darted forward, straight at the Guardian's eyes.

The maiden slipped to the side, slashing the tail of the Matamari with her fingernails as it went by. Instantly, the sound of many stones falling and sliding filled the air. The noise of an armored tail clattering and clicking on pebbles bounced from shadow to shadow. The Matamari screamed and raised her stinger for another attack. The maiden crouched, preparing to lunge.

The earth shook. Rocks that were balanced precariously on the edge of the lake fell into the water. The Matamari's young that had gathered now scattered, some scuttling to hide in their abandoned eggshells. The Matamari herself spun toward the cave and the bulk that rose up from under the rocky shore, sending a shower of stones to make waves in the water.

Huge pincers opened and closed lazily. A yellow-green body glowed against the maw of the cave. The tail that arched over this behemoth was longer than the Matamari's entire body. But the face flattened into the front of the body was far less human. Black eyes with no lids and no irises took in the scene before it. Cheekbones cut like glass against the translucent carapace. Small, serrated mandibles sawed at the air, clicking.

"Constructs. Sisters. Would you profane this holy ground with your blood?" The voice was the susurration of a drizzle on a roof, or a wave as it receded from shore. As gentle as the beady eyes were cold.

The Matamari lowered her body until her belly touched the stones. "Great One, this is no matter for your attention. A water girl is lost and makes demands far beyond her station."

The River Maiden retracted her claws. *"I am exactly where I wish to be. I seek an audience with the First. I bear news She must hear."*

The Matamari swirled in a shower of mud and pebbles and tried to stab the River Maiden with her stinger, furious at the unexpected interruption. The Great One slithered forward, and with a swift downstroke of its giant claw, batted the Matamari into one of the fragile eggshells, which broke into a thousand glittering pieces with the sound of a dozen shattered windows.

It brought its face level with the River Maiden, its claws on either side of her body. "I am Nictus, queen of the Matamari. No one sees the First but that I grant them permission. If you tell me your mission and accept the toll, you may go past into the Calling Caves. Be warned, though: only the strong can pay the toll. The weak have no place here."

"I have no fear of my own strength or my mission. I come to the First for help. Gailand will fall into chaos if She does not act. The universe will not stand if the Hand of Gaiea is destroyed and the Spirit extinguished. That is the fate we face."

Nictus's mandibles clicked and her black eyes stared into the maiden's silver ones. "Dire times indeed. I judge this mission acceptable. Will you now pay the toll?"

The River Maiden tilted her head, studying the passive face before her. *"Yes."*

"Wonderful," Nictus said. "It has been a long time since something as large and strong as you came along."

The huge tail slammed down into the River Maiden's stomach, pinning her to the shore, her pale legs splashing in the river.

"I'm afraid," Nictus said as she pumped her venom into the Guardian, "that this may hurt somewhat."

The River Maiden screamed and thrashed, her eyes wide.

The Matamari crawled out of the ruined eggshells, bleeding slow ichor from various cuts and chuckling in her throat. "I warned you," she said.

"Be quiet," Nictus replied mildly. "You are lucky I haven't eaten you. Must I tell you every time, let them get their mission out? At least then I can judge if they are worthy."

The River Maiden's movements grew weaker, then stilled altogether. Nictus picked her up delicately with one pincer. The maiden's body bent at the waist and her sleek hair hung forward to hide her pale face as dirty brown liquid stained her stomach and legs. Without another word, Nictus backed into the cave, disappearing into the entrance just as the first rays of sunlight touched the surface of Glass Lake.

⁄⁄⁄⁄⁄⁄⁄⁄⁄⁄⁄⁄⁄

WHEN LUKA RETURNED FROM FEEDING FARAIN, CLIMBING STAIRS sunken in the middle from the passage of feet and years, each stèp dragged on his tired body. He couldn't hold back a yawn as he opened the door to their room.

Eleanor looked up from pulling the shoes off the feet of a sleeping Viella. She held a finger up to her lips before drawing a coarse sheet over the queen and coming to stand in front of Luka.

"You found him?" she said, her voice low. "He's well?"

Luka nodded and stifled another yawn in the crook of his elbow. "He knows we leave soon."

Eleanor frowned a little. "You should rest."

Luka opened his mouth to deny it, then changed his mind. "First watch is mine but—"

She held up a hand. "We share the watch. I will be first to-night."

He sat on his cushions, watching as she gathered the herbs Gloria had found for her. She ground them in a borrowed mortar and spelled them with a flick of her fingers. By the time she sat next to him and bared his shoulder, his eyes were so heavy, he hardly felt her touch. He woke with a start when his head bowed too far and his chin hit his chest. His shoulder was bandaged, and Eleanor was crouching before him, a cheap enamel cup in her hand.

"Drink. The pain will lessen."

He did as he was told. When he handed the cup back to her, their fingers brushed and the skin on his arm bumped as though cold air had touched it, even as the sensation lanced through his body like an arrow to his pelvis. All his muscles hummed awake, tight and sensitized. He curled his fingers into his palm and lay down, turning away from her. Closing his eyes, he breathed deeply to control his reaction, listening as Eleanor settled in for the first watch.

He finally had an accord with her. Of that there was no doubt. But he knew once they were safe, there was no guarantee she wouldn't return to the question of his mother. After what they'd endured, the vows they'd made in each other's presence, he was not certain he could lie to her as before. In fact, he was almost certain he no longer wished to do so.

There was so much he wanted, Luka thought, frustration swirling through him. He wanted Viella safe. He wanted the queendom restored. He wanted to be done with this endless journey. He wanted to not have to lie to Gloria or Eleanor. He wanted to avenge his father. He wanted to be free to return to the combat he understood. He wanted Queen Elise to not be dead and the prince to not be captured. He wanted a shoulder that did not pain him day and night.

I do not want her to think of me as a mistake. Something less than worthy.

It had never mattered before what any woman thought of him. They were warriors with a common mission that would soon end. They had not known each other a week. But at some point, he'd grown to respect Eleanor, and he wanted her to think well of him. Her loyalty, strength, and intelligence were obvious. But there was more below the surface of the unwavering leader she showed the world. He sensed it—wanted to know it. And part of him wanted her to know him too.

Yet she cannot know. She would be forced to report me if she wished to protect her position as a Dahomei. And even that might not be enough.

I am not the sentimental fool my father was. I will not make the mistakes he did.

But the thoughts were hollow echoes in his mind and heart. He remembered the gentle pressure of Eleanor's callused fingers on his skin, the faint spray of freckles shifting on her cheeks as she smiled, and heat bloomed low in his belly.

For the first time in a long time, he wondered about his mother. About what she might have been able to teach him. The secrets of womanhood. What a man might be able to offer someone like Eleanor. His thoughts were a jumbled mess of sadness, longing, resentment, and trepidation, but his heart beat fast and light as he listened to Eleanor's breathing, eventually matching his rhythm to hers.

As sleep claimed him, he realized somewhere on the journey from the High Court of Dun to a small inn in Plytown, he had become a different person. He wasn't quite sure who that person was, but he had no doubt he was there to stay.

⁄⁄⁄⁄⁄⁄⁄⁄⁄⁄⁄⁄⁄

HE WOKE FROM AN INSTANTLY FORGOTTEN NIGHTMARE WITH FINGERS twitching. The room was lit by the tiny flame from a dying candle on the washstand. Viella's sleeping face was turned toward him. At the foot of the bed's platform, Eleanor sat with her legs outstretched and crossed at the ankles. Her sword rested across her lap and her chin was on her chest. It took him a moment to comprehend that she had fallen asleep.

She never falls asleep. Yet there she sat, sword glinting, her face so relaxed he saw for the first time that she was not as old as he thought. Older than his nineteen, yes, but closer in age to Lady Gretchen than Lady Sophia. He let his heart rate return to normal as he took in every line of this new face, knowing the moment might not come again.

A shadow fell across the room, and at first he thought nothing of it. It happened again, and he realized something had gone past the small window above the bed. Gone past it on the *outside*.

We are two stories aboveground.

He sat up, shaking himself to clear his head. He heard a low thrumming sound, the vibration of a plucked string. There was a thud against the roof.

Viella opened her eyes and stared at him. He raised a finger to his lips and took hold of the sword that lay next to his cushions. Viella said nothing, did nothing, only stared.

It was quiet again. Quiet for so long, he wondered if he'd imagined it all. He was about to whisper to Eleanor when he heard the creak of a stair, muffled but distinct.

He pulled his sword free of its scabbard as Eleanor started. Her head swung around to him, a question in her eyes. He nodded, rising into a crouching position silently. Eleanor turned and tugged at Viella's leg with one hand, encouraging her to slide off the bed and onto the floor. But the queen did not move, and Luka realized her eyes were empty, her face blank.

Gaiea, no. Not another nightmare. Not now.

His bare feet were soundless on the wooden floor. Eleanor held her sword in front of her as she backed toward the motionless queen.

The door swung open on creaky hinges.

"Ah," the Blane-thing said, tongue black between gray, rotting lips. "You wait for me. Good. This saves time."

Luka charged—and was slammed back into the wall behind him, his vision blurring as his head hit hard. His sword clattered to his feet.

Above him, glass burst in a stinging, polychromic shower, forcing him to raise a protective hand to his face. Hissing filled the room. As Luka shook glass from his head, a beam of blue light fell on the bed next to Viella. Luka tilted his gaze up and was almost hit in the face by a huge claw. He scrambled away from it, onto one knee.

"Finally," said the rusty voice from the doorway, "I eat. We are so . . . *hungry*."

On the bed, Eleanor kneeled over Viella and swung her blade at the ragged hole where the stained glass used to be. The giant clawed paw that had shoved through it batted at the air before pulling back. The Sycren's muzzle filled the opening, one brilliant eye sending a beam of illumination into the room.

Eleanor slashed at it, but the paw evaded her. The wood beside the window frame splintered inward and the Sycren's limb slashed through, catching her arm. Eleanor shouted in pain and let go of her sword, gripping her right wrist against her stomach. Air gusted in through the window as the Sycren moved away. There was a faint clatter outside.

Viella lay still. Her long hair draped across her face, in her eyes, but she did not blink. Dread flowed cold through Luka's entire body. Opening his mind, he called to Farain with all his strength. He grabbed his sword. "Eleanor! To me!"

Leaning down, Eleanor gathered Viella to her with her good arm.

"No," the Blane-thing said with a wet chortle. "To *me*." And he crooked one long, spindly finger.

Viella fell back onto the bed. Eleanor grabbed at her, but the queen slipped out of her grasp. Thinking she was falling, Luka reached his free hand out to catch her, but Viella sat up. She looked around the room, as if seeing it for the first time.

"Your Majesty!" Eleanor tried to go to Viella, but the Sycren was there again, screaming and shrieking, pulling at the splintering wood that had once held the window and forcing its muzzle between her and the queen in a shower of wood splinters. Eleanor slid off the bed and crouched on the floor. Luka saw her reach down to her boot, and then a small knife with a bright blade was in her left hand.

On the opposite side of the bed, Viella put her feet on the ground and stood. Glass crunched under her soles, but she gave no sign of discomfort. Instead, she faced the door and took a hesitant step, her eyes as wide and dead as a doll's.

"Viella!" Luka grabbed at her hand, holding tight to the small fingers while ducking the claws and muzzle reaching for him. Cold saliva splattered his cheek. He raised his sword.

The creature at the door stepped into the room. "What's mine is mine, stupid boy. And you have hurt me once too often." The Blane-thing slashed downward through the air with the edge of his hand.

Viella pulled her fingers from Luka's grip and, grabbing his forearm, she tossed him across the room. Luka slammed into the wall again. He held on to his sword somehow, but the shrieking pain in his body made his vision go murky.

Gaiea save us. Her strength . . . That's not Viella.

The Blane-thing clapped once, twice. The pieces of armor that still hung from its shriveling body above tattered, blackened clothing jangled loudly. "Oh, well done, little one. Well done. What delicious power you have."

Eleanor charged the creature, knife in hand, but was sent skidding backward on her knees across the floor, her free hand wrapped around her own throat. The knife arced upward and fell on the bed.

"Brave. Both of you." A smile revealed blackened teeth and tongue. "Just like the ones in Garth. They were afraid at the end, though. And very tasty."

A howl rent the air outside. The Sycren yanked its head back out through the window.

Farain! Luka got to his knees and threw his short sword at his father's corpse. It went into a gap caused by a broken side strap that left the ceremonial breastplate hanging askew from the shoulder. The sword made a satisfying squelch, and thick, black liquid welled and dripped on either side of the blade.

With a flick of a wrist, the creature tossed Eleanor into the washstand, and the pitcher and bowl crashed to the floor. The candle landed in the puddle and went out with the tiniest sizzle. Shadows huddled together but Luka had always had good night sight, and the moonlight streaming in from the broken window was more than enough to see by.

The creature turned to face Luka, its head cocked at an unnatural angle. His father's square jaw had bruises all over it, and one eye was a pool of glossy blackness. Still, it looked so much like him, Luka felt his heart beak all over again.

"You . . . annoy me." It stretched out a hand and Viella came to it, holding on to the raw, peeling fingers. She stared at the doorway. In the corridor, a slow thumping drew closer and closer, and the creaking floorboards protested under the strain of something heavy.

Growls came through the window and the Sycren screeched. The walls of the inn shook as war-cat and Sycren fought in the alley below.

They will wake the dead, Luka thought. And for a fleeting second, he wondered how it was there was no sound from the rest of the inn. No sound from the rest of the village at all.

The Blane creature grabbed the hilt of Luka's sword and pulled it smoothly from its side. A smattering of murky drops hit the floor. It studied the fouled blade as Eleanor stood up, one hand wiping blood from her nose, her squinting eyes searching for the queen in the room's twilight.

"Viella, listen to me. Come away from that thing," she said, taking a step in the child's direction.

"Thing!" the creature said, its lips curling. "I am no thing. *We* are no *thing*."

Behind him, a black muzzle inched across the doorway. Luka's heart pounded as another Sycren's blue eyes cast thin lines of light into the room. The floor vibrated as it put one powerful leg over the threshold. A wing scraped against the doorway, making it vibrate.

"Gaiea save us," Eleanor whispered, staring at the beast.

"Gaiea?" The Blane-thing spat on the floor. He came farther into the room and raised his hand. Eleanor was forced to her knees, hands on her throat as she coughed and choked. "There is no Gaiea here, girl. She cannot hear your prayers. She has abandoned you. I will take what she has left behind. I will take it *all*."

Viella! Luka thought desperately.

The queen seemed to see him for the first time. A tiny, terrible smile curved her lips.

"I will take it all," she repeated in a toneless facsimile of her voice.

At the door, the Sycren filled the room with its huge body and the dry sound of the rustling of its wings. Its claws dug grooves in the wood beneath it. Muzzle lowered, it bared its teeth at Luka, and he saw dancing within its bright, bright eyes the obscene shapes of horrible specters.

"Eat," the creature told the Sycren, smiling.

"KKEUT!"

The voice was loud, commanding . . . and it did not belong to the Blane-thing.

The creature spun around. Released from its hold, Eleanor dropped onto her hands, coughing. The Sycren screamed, shaking its head from side to side. It turned to face the door, claws extended, jaws opening wider and wider, until the top of its head was being forced back onto its neck.

Gloria stepped into view, her long hair loose over her shoulders, an ivory nightdress skimming her bare feet. Her hands were extended, palms up, and she brought with her a surreal glow, like the horizon after the sun has slipped below it.

"Bitch!" the Blane-thing said, its face contorting in a way no human visage should.

"Oh, definitely." Gloria flicked her left hand. There was a muffled but clearly audible crack. The Sycren stumbled to its left, then crumpled to the floor in a heavy fall that vibrated in Luka's chest.

The creature let out a terrible cry and grabbed Viella by the neck, dragging her in front of it. Eleanor launched herself onto its back. Legs wrapped around its waist, she grabbed its shoulder with one hand and raised the other high. The knife she had retrieved from the bed flashed once as she buried it in the monster's neck.

Viella screamed and pulled away from the hand holding her as if burned. Luka lunged forward and scooped her into his arms. As he did so, he caught Gloria's eye. A moment of unspoken communication passed between them, and he spun himself into the corner next to the bed, below the broken window. He had no time to check the queen for injuries. Instead, he tucked her into that space and said, "Stay."

He turned in time to see the thing that had once been his father reach over its shoulder and grab Eleanor's face in its elongated fingers. Eleanor's cry was muffled by its palm, but Luka saw wisps of what looked like smoke curling into the air where those fingers made contact with her skin.

Gloria clasped both hands together, laced her fingers into a fist, and pointed it at the creature. It snarled as she screamed another word of power. The wound in its neck opened wider, and murky essence splattered its shoulder. But unlike the Sycren, the creature did not stop. It pointed a finger at Gloria. She recoiled as if hit, stumbling back out of the room.

The creature flung Eleanor to the ground behind it. In one swift movement, it dragged the blade from its neck and spun to face the Dahomei.

In that moment, Luka stopped thinking. He remembered his father's granite face as it had been, stern but never unkind. And as he watched the ruin of his corpse raise the knife, loss and despair overwhelmed him. His father was gone forever, and this monster wore his skin to destroy whatever good was left in Luka's world.

Never. Not her and not Viella. Rage overwhelmed him, heating his blood, making his head pound and turning his vision hazy with tears born of too many emotions. *Go back to Gaiea's Desert, or wherever you came from.*

In two strides he was before the corpse. The room was brighter somehow, lit by a rosy hue, but his entire focus was on the horror that had perverted his father's body and threatened the life of everyone he cared for.

You will hurt no one else. Not while I draw breath.

He reached out with hands that burned as red as sunset under his skin, grabbed either side of its head, and tore its skull off its neck.

The corpse collapsed into a huge splash of ichor that slapped warm and wet against Luka's face and chest. His hands came together suddenly, with nothing between them but warm stickiness. The pool of foul essence spread across the floor toward the doorway.

A roar downstairs reverberated through the inn. Luka looked up to see Gloria dart out of the room. When he turned his head, Eleanor was already on her feet.

"Go. I'll get her," she said to him, flicking liquid from her hands in disgust.

He followed Gloria onto the walkway.

A Sycren crouched on the stairs below them and as Luka approached, a rider vaulted off its back. Armor creaked and a sword glinted in the glow emanating from the innkeeper. Gloria swept her arms wide, and the rider was tossed off the stairs and onto the first floor below. The crash was deafening.

The Sycren leapt at Gloria. With a word of power and an extended palm, she slammed it back into the floor, its head smashed in.

A screeching sound came from Luka's left, where the wooden railing bordered the hallway. He stepped to the edge and looked over to see several bodies scaling the columns that held up the stairs. The one nearest the top tilted its head back, and he stared into a rotting eye socket and a face that had no nose or lower jaw. Strips of blackened flesh hung from shredded cheekbones. It dug its fingers into the wood it was climbing, flinching not at all as fingernails splintered and lifted away from the tips of fingers, revealing blackened nail beds cracked with red.

On the right-hand column, the nearest corpse had its face, but its head lolled too far to the right. Most of its neck was gone and the skull remained attached to the torso only with the help of the visible spine, a few tendons, and some skin.

As soon as it saw him, its mouth opened, but sound emerged from another body below it that had paused in its climbing.

"We will take it ALL," said the gurgling, thick voice of his father. "But first, you shall die."

Luka's mind blanked under the weight of his fury. His gaze focused on the dead soldiers swarming up the columns, Luka opened his arms wide, as if preparing to embrace someone. No word of power came to his mind. Instead, wrath rose within him, pushing outward.

Writhing flames rose from his hands and spiraled their way up his arms. They combined into one funnel and blasted downward. A crack like thunder sounded. Below him, Luka saw the flames sear a hole into the floor before they flashed outward, engulfing the bodies on the columns. Skin and tendon curled and blew away. An unbearable musty, acrid scent fouled the air. Bones fell to ash, and the ash pelted the floor like pellets, but the wooden stairs remained unharmed. Only the burn mark in the floor remained. Exhaustion swept through Luka, as sudden and all-consuming as the rage that had come before. Muscles loose as jelly, he leaned into the railing, holding on to the lightly charred wood and not caring that splinters pricked him.

The ash was still drifting through the air when more of the dead ran through the open front doors of the inn. At least half a dozen soldiers poured into the room, rust-streaked armor clanking from lack of care, ripped and tattered cloth drifting free as they ran. They did not pause or speak as they broke into three lines. Two of them took the stairs, several at a time, leaping upward with drawn spears. The others swarmed the supports of the staircase swinging around under them so that Luka had no direct line of sight.

And then the house shivered as a Sycren almost twice the size of those Luka had seen before stalked through the double doors on heavy claws, smashing both sides of the doorframe into splinters. It spread its scarlet wings and shrieked.

Luka's ears rang. Despair clouded his senses. *We cannot survive this. I am tired. So tired.* He couldn't feel his injured arm anymore, he was so numb.

He felt rather than saw Eleanor come up behind him; heard her intake of breath. Then she was gripping the railing next to him, his sword in her hand. He looked at her and she raised an eyebrow at him before the tiniest smile quirked a corner of her lip. She held up the sword. "I'll hold on to this. It seems you need it less than I do."

"Eleanor . . ."

"Come, Daguard, you cannot stop now," she said softly. "The battle is yet to be won. Think of the stories you'll tell of how you once put a Dahomei to shame when you saved the queen."

Mention of the queen, of Viella, burned away the weakness in his body. Over Eleanor's shoulder, he saw the first of the undead soldiers reach the landing below Gloria. She gathered her hands into a folded fist and made a hammering motion. The corpse dropped to its knees as a wound opened across its chest, visible through the crack in its armor. Its spear fell to its side and clattered down the stairs.

A second soldier appeared behind its fallen comrade and threw its spear at Gloria. She ducked and Luka swung himself back against the railing. The spear flew past and embedded itself in the dead-end wall of the corridor. The second soldier leapt over the first with terrible speed . . .

. . . and impaled itself on the sword Eleanor thrust forward over Gloria's head. For a moment, the three were frozen in a tableau, but then the corpse started wriggling down the blade toward Eleanor, black tears leaking from coal-dark eyes, and one perfect, unmarred hand reaching for Gloria's face.

Eleanor shifted her grip, two-handing the sword, and ripped upward, splitting the creature from its sternum to the top of its head.

It fell backward down the stairs, fingers scrabbling for purchase as it went, nails scratching and breaking on the wood. As it tumbled, the first soldier rose to its feet, a growl in its throat.

A skeletal hand clamped over Luka's wrist, sliming him with flesh and ooze. Ghostly flames leapt from his arm, obscuring the hand. The corpse released him immediately, then pulled itself over the railing and onto the landing. Before it straightened fully, the blackened fingers that had touched Luka began to slough away. In seconds, the soldier crumbled away to dust.

They can't touch me. Shock gave way to hope, then determination, bringing with it reserves of energy he'd thought depleted by the fire tornado.

He reached over the railing and dragged one of the soldiers upward by its armored arm as it reached for the railing. He didn't even feel the weight of it as he flung it against the wall at the bottom of the stairs. It exploded into ash and foul fumes. Out of the corner of his eye, he saw Eleanor hacking her way through a soldier while the one she had split open wriggled on the last stair like a spider on its back, attempting to right its shredded body.

Gloria came to stand beside Luka, black ichor dripping off her forearm and a thin line of it splashed across her left cheek. She reached downward, closing her fist as if she had hold of something, and then swinging her outstretched arm upward.

A body smacked into the huge Sycren, pushing it into the doorway and tangling in its wings. Screaming with rage, the Sycren snapped its jaws around the soldier, metal crunching under its powerful teeth. After shaking it viciously, it tossed the body upward and into the roof. The house shuddered, and the corpse crashed to the floor and lay still, a spider web of glowing blue threads spreading across it.

Gloria held out both hands toward the Sycren. She shimmered all over, silvery-green light edging her fingertips.

The Sycren rose into the air. Jaws wide, it swooped toward Gloria . . .

. . . but Farain's paw hooked a corner of its wing, dragging it to the floor. The dagen had leaped into the room from the street outside, making no sound as it stood on its hind legs and slashed at the creature.

The Sycren twisted itself upright and—spreading its paws and wings wide—screamed at the war cat. Farain roared back, teeth bared, tail twitching from side to side.

The force within Gloria limned her body with wisps of light that grew more solid by the second. She looked over at Luka, and he nodded at the question in her eyes. Pulling on his rage, he thought his hatred and anger outward, toward the Sycren. At the same time, Gloria made fists of her hands and slammed them together.

The Sycren rose into the air, avoiding the force Luka sent toward it. The floor exploded upward in a tunnel of light, dirt, and splinters. Gloria's magic caught the creature a glancing blow and it crashed down, one of its legs crumpling under it. Jaws wide, claws extended, Farain pounced.

He caught nothing but air as the Sycren flew up with one powerful downbeat of its wings. There was a grinding, splintering crash, and Luka threw himself on top of Gloria, shielding her from the shower of wood and thatch that collapsed into the inn as the Sycren burst through the roof.

When Luka raised his head, bits of things falling from his hair and pattering onto the landing, he saw the night sky through the ragged hole the creature had left. In the distance, a winged shape blocked all light from one corner of the sky. Then it was gone, and the stars shone their chilly light down once more.

For long minutes everything was still and there was only the sound of falling wood and creaking timber. Finally, stiff with pain and fatigue, Luka stood slowly, then reached down a hand to help Gloria to her feet. Splinters, soil, and thatch hit the ground in clumps. Gloria wiped a hand across her forehead with a sigh, leaving a black streak, then arched her back with a groan. Watching her, Luka shook his head as realization dawned on him: *I was not the only one keeping my own counsel.*

"You're not hurt?" he asked, worried.

Gloria huffed and smiled a tired smile. "Gaiea be praised, all is well with me. Though I cannot say the same of my inn." She gave him a wry shake of the head. "I should have charged you more."

Boots thumping, Eleanor climbed the stairs toward them. Luka's sword dripped a line of ichor behind her. Without needing to speak, they turned as one for the door to their room.

Viella was on the floor where Luka had slept earlier. She was curled into a ball, her hands over her ears, her eyes squeezed shut. Luka could hear her muttering something to herself over and over again. He crouched, reached out, and touched her shoulder. She started, and opened eyes swimming in tears that clung to her lashes and streaked her cheeks. Then she was on her knees and hugging him so tight around the neck, his air was almost cut off.

"Shhh . . ." was all he could say. Tension and weariness clung to him, a suffocating cloak. He let his fingers touch her soft hair for a moment, then, remembering the stink and debris he was covered in, tried to hold her away from him. She burrowed against him harder. His ears finally made sense of her words.

"I'm sorry. I'm sorry, I'm sorry, I'm sorry . . ."

He frowned. "You have nothing to make amends for."

She pulled back and for the first time he saw raw terror on

her face. He held her small face in his hands and wiped away her tears. "Viella, speak."

"Luka." He looked up at Eleanor and she shook her head at him. In the starlight, he couldn't see her expression clearly, but her voice was crisp and firm. "There's no time."

She was right. Every muscle in Luka's body was strung tight with the knowledge that they were still in danger. The Sycren had escaped. It could return with reinforcements. There was something terribly wrong with Viella—

(I will take it all)

—but at the moment, her safety was paramount, and not at all assured.

"Eleanor speaks truth," Gloria said from the doorway. Luka picked up Viella and faced her. She carried a small candle, so he saw the fatigue that etched grim lines around her mouth, and the anger that narrowed her eyes.

"These . . . atrocities have destroyed my home with magic the like of which I have never seen, but I am certain I was not their target. The power you wield, Luka . . ." She crossed her arms and raised an eyebrow at him. "You have kept many secrets."

Luka swallowed on a dry throat, unable to reply. He barely understood what had happened. But he had to admit the truth to himself. There was no more hiding from it. No more desperately pretending it was Farain. The power had risen within himself. He'd directed every moment of the flames he'd wielded. He'd no inkling he could do what he had done. No thought he could cause such damage.

My father was right to hide me. The Augurs are right to scry the bloodlines. This power is not—could not—*be of Gaiea.*

"You have secrets as well," he said when he found his voice. "The magic you drew on tonight—you are with child, aren't you?"

"And what a child it will be," Eleanor said, an undertone of awe in her words. "A pregnant woman wields more power than any other female. But I've seldom seen such ability. Are you much increased? Were you so blessed with talent before now?"

Gloria shook her head. "I was an Impellent before, and since I conceived, my power has grown. I can move large things at a distance, where before I could only move small things near me. I have never carried out such feats as I did tonight." She turned an apologetic look toward Luka. "I said nothing because I had only confirmed the pregnancy a fortnight ago. I have yet to tell my husband."

"Nevertheless, it is you and your baby we must thank for our very survival," Luka said. "Gloria, you have been a great friend to me, and I regret my deception. But you have done more than save my family this night. You have earned the gratitude of your High Queen."

Gloria frowned as she looked from Luka to Eleanor and back again. "In what way? The queen is at court for the Introduction, is she not?"

"There is much we must tell you, for your protection and ours," Eleanor said, picking up a sheet from the bed and using it to wipe Luka's sword. "But these creatures have seen you, and everything we've learned suggests they will not forget. We must leave together, now, if we wish to escape their grasp. Luka is exhausted, but I can glamour us until we reach the Portal. Take only what you need to travel to the nearest Guild of Augurs. You will need their protection."

Gloria groaned. "I moved here to start a life away from constant Ragat raids and border skirmishes. Now you wish me to seek out Augurs. May Gaiea be with me."

Luka stroked Viella's hair and smiled at her a little, hoping she would calm. But her eyes remained wide, and her chest rose and fell too quickly. With a sinking feeling in his stomach he said, "May Gaiea be with us all."

CHAPTER 12

ELEMENTAL

F RANCES WAITED PATIENTLY IN A CHAIR THAT FACED THE DOOR TO
her room until a key rattled in the lock. The boy who came
in carried a tray with a bowl and a goblet. Wisps of steam and
the scent of sweet-milk porridge rose from the glazed pottery.
His eyes were cast downward, so he didn't see when Frances
rose from her seat, and he was startled when she took the tray
from him.

In the doorway, a Ragat warrior watched silently. Frances
directed her words to him as the boy stepped back from her.

"Summon the Spellsayer."

The Ragat warrior didn't move.

"Waste no time pretending ignorance, Ragat. You understand me. Tell the Spellsayer the Dowager Mother wishes to
see him."

She set the tray on the desk against the wall at the foot of
her bed. "Go now, both of you, and do not delay."

When she heard the door close, she took the chair again.
It wasn't long before Mordach came in, two Ragat warriors on
either side of him.

Frances rose to her feet, her head level with his chin. "I have
completed my task. Now I wish to see my grandson."

"Valan is asleep," Mordach said. "He needs his rest."

"My High Queen is dead, and no one can tell me where my
granddaughter has gone. I would ascertain the condition of my
grandson myself."

Mordach pushed a strand of his hair behind one ear. "Now is not the time."

"There will never be a good time. Let me see my family. I am an old woman who has nothing to gain from endangering them."

Mordach shook his head with a frown. "You are a former queen of Gailand. Your magic may not be as strong as it once was, but you are far from harmless, Dowager Mother."

"I never claimed to be harmless," Frances said with great dignity. "I said I would not endanger my family. I will not act against you. You cannot credit it, but I have great pity for you."

"Pity." Mordach said the word like he'd never heard it before. "Why?"

"Because you are out of your depth," Frances said with a sideways tilt of her head. "You both play with fire you cannot hope to quench."

Mordach took a step toward her. "And yet, here you stand, former queen, Dowager Mother, begging me for one glimpse of your grandson. Perhaps you should save your pity for yourself."

"Perhaps. It would not be the first time I wasted precious breath on someone unworthy." Frances folded her hands together in front of her skirts and raised her chin. "Either let me see my grandson, or cease wasting the little time I have left in this life."

Mordach stood quiet, his gaze unwavering. Then he gestured to her to follow.

There were no servants about as they walked to Elise's rooms. But Ragat squatted or stood in shadowed corners, watching. Frances stared straight ahead, the clack of her heeled slippers on tile their only accompaniment.

When they reached the High Queen's rooms, Mordach opened the door and bowed to Frances. "Please. After you."

Frances gave him a withering glare before entering.

The room was brightly lit with braziers and candles and the warm air made it stuffy. Frances went straight to the bed where

Valan lay motionless, a tiny form under a thin blanket. On the opposite side of the bed, Alain had fallen asleep in a chair. His chin rested on his chest, and his hands were slack on the armrest. Sweat from the heat in the room glistened on his forehead.

The Dowager Mother took Valan's limp hand in her own gnarled ones. "So cold," she said with a frown. "Why is he so cold?"

Alain started and raised his head, blinking. "Mother?"

"He is in deepsleep. He was . . . upset and needed to be sedated." Mordach said. "This is why we keep the room warm."

"He cannot stay this way for so long. Deepsleep is a way for the injured to be healed. Healthy people are not meant to endure it. The longer he is gone, the more difficult it will be to bring him back."

"I understand the manner of it. I will not allow him to be harmed."

"Thank Gaiea you are here," Alain said as he came out of his chair. Frances went to him, and they embraced. "Are you well? How have they treated you? Where do they keep you?"

"I am well," Frances said, pulling back to look him in the face. "And overjoyed to find you both alive and hale."

Alain raised an impatient hand to wipe the tears slipping down his cheeks. "Mother, Elise . . . Viella . . ."

"I know, Alain." Frances gathered her skirts and sat on the bed next to Valan, still holding his hand. She shot a hard look at Mordach. "You know this will not help Valan. This is about keeping control of him."

"Say what you will," an amused voice replied. "The Dowager Mother is no fool."

Lady Sophia entered the room in a silk dress the color of seafoam, embroidered all over in golden flowers and green leaves. Her neck and shoulders were bare, fragile and elegant, her hair in her usual knot at the base of her skull.

She came to a stop next to the bed, her gaze on Alain though she spoke to Frances. "One wonders how it is your husband was able to hide his involvement with the Ragat from someone as sharp-minded as you."

"Trust and love can hide a great many faults," Frances said, "It certainly concealed *your* true nature from Elise."

"You would do well not to speak of my father," Alain snapped.

Sophia inclined her head toward him. "I apologize," she said in a tone of voice that implied the exact opposite of her words. She folded her hands in front of her and looked at Frances. "If I have given offense to you, it was not my intention."

"What offends me is that you keep me and my family prisoner, Sophia," Frances said, meeting her gaze. "Was that also not your intent?"

Sophia's eyes opened wide. "We have done nothing but keep Valan safe. And you have done me a great kindness, taking care of my daughter. Am I not also family?"

Frances rose to stand in front of her. "*Family* does not keep a child in a dangerous sleep for mere convenience. You know nothing of family if you betray us to our worst enemies, plot the death of children, and lock us away."

Lady Sophia looked thoughtful. "You wish me to awaken the boy and allow you to run the household as before?"

"I wish you to pay, for the rest of your life, for leaving the High Court awash in blood and scheming."

"Blood and scheming." Sophia spoke as if she tasted the words. "What a gift for description. Don't you think, Mordach?"

"There's no point to this," Mordach said. He crossed to Alain's side and stood close to him, looking down on the sleeping prince. "You love your games too much, Sophia."

"And you are too dour. It's a condition often caused by maudlin love." Lady Sophia's voice was steel wrapped in silk. Mordach ignored her while the lord consort glared.

Lady Sophia turned her attention back to the Dowager

Mother. "The Spellsayer is wrong. I don't love games. But to do what's best for Gailand, I must play them well. Gaiea knows, someone should be willing to do what's necessary to fix the ills that have befallen us."

"The only ill I see is Ragat filth everywhere, let in by a jealous, desperate woman who would turn kin against one another for her own ends."

Lady Sophia lifted her chin. "I would have thought name-calling beneath you."

"I would have thought murder, treason, and the persecution of children beneath you, but I suppose we have all not been our best selves recently."

"Do not think I enjoy this, Frances," Lady Sophia said, the friendly tone gone from her voice. "It has been the hardest thing I've ever done, taking this action. But Elise left me no choice. If she had not been so misguided, perhaps Gaiea would not have taken her to Her Garden."

"How convenient. Blame the dead for their own betrayal then claim to be on a divine mission, hence your successful sedition. Tell me, where are the other sister queens, Sophia? Or am I to believe they were abandoned by Gaiea as well?"

Lady Sophia's nostrils flared for a moment. "They were killed in the attack. I, myself, was grievously wounded. It's a terrible tragedy."

Frances closed her eyes and took a deep breath before opening them again. "You cannot possibly think to get away with this."

"I'm getting away with nothing, Frances, except the heavy task of putting the High Court back together after a horrific attack." Sophia shrugged and sighed, her eyes full of pity. "For your own protection and that of *our* family, I must keep you all safe until things have settled. Even now, the princess Viella is missing, kidnapped by a traitorous Daguard."

Frances laughed bitterly. "You believe you can blame the Daguard for this?"

Sophia shook her head. "I don't expect you to understand. You're in a fragile state. The shock of what you've seen and endured has deeply affected your mind." She laid a slender hand on Frances's arm. "Everything will be over soon, Dowager Mother. All will be well."

Frances pulled her arm away as if burned. "Before I go to my grave, you'll meet your reckoning, and I'll be there to see it."

"You speak of graves rather easily for one who draws nearer her own with each passing day," Lady Sophia mused.

"That is because I have no fear my misdeeds will bar me from Gaiea's Garden."

Mordach strode back to Lady Sophia's side. "A word please," he said. Lady Sophia gave the Dowager Mother a hard look before stepping out of the room and closing the door behind her.

"You mustn't antagonize them, Mother," Alain said urgently, leaning forward in his chair. "We have to escape. That cannot happen if they're suspicious of us."

"They would be idiots not to be suspicious of us. I assume you've rejected any overtures Sophia, or your lover, made to join them?" She looked up at Alain's sharp intake of breath. "You cannot be shocked. I am head of the household. It is my business to know such things."

Alain bit his lip and looked away, dark hair slipping over his ear. "How long have you known?"

"Alain, anyone with eyes has known since Mordach first came to the High Court. I understand the need for discretion, given there are seats that would seize on any possibility of discord as grounds for divorce, but there is no shame in it if your wife consented.

"Elise could have sent us both to the grave with your father after he betrayed my throne to the Ragat. Instead, she let us keep our royal bloodline and gave us a home. She loved you, Alain, as much as a Hand could love any man. She wanted you to be content. She couldn't have known Sophia and Mordach would abuse the trust you both gave them."

"This is as much my fault as theirs." Alain ran his hands through his hair, clenching his fingers. "I wanted my son to be safe. To live a better life. So did Mordach. We talked. Of my father, his people—his rebellion. Mordach believed there was a chance Valan had magic. Old magic. I was the one who convinced Elise to let him work with Valan. I gave them everything they needed to destroy us."

"No, you didn't." Frances kneeled before her son and grasped his hands. "*They* chose to open the *Nightward*. *They* chose to betray your confidence. To murder their rightful queen."

"Then I'm a fool who can't tell friend from foe?" Alain's smile was bitter. "You do me credit."

"Recriminations are useless," Frances said. "Tell me, did Mordach send Valan into the deepsleep here? In this very room?"

Alain nodded. "They took him away and brought him back a few hours ago."

"Ah." Frances nodded to herself. She rose and went to the wall under the narrow window. She waved a hand over it and the wall shimmered and faded, revealing a tiny, intricately carved cabinet. Frances pressed a finger to its glossy brown surface. It popped open and she searched past deep shelves hidden within, removing a black bottle and a sapphire bracelet and hiding them in a secret pocket concealed by the skirts of her sari.

"I never knew that was there," Alain said, eyes wide. "What did you take?"

Frances returned to the bed where Valan barely breathed enough to lift the sheets covering his torso. "A potion I made for Elise. And our way out."

He hesitated. "The bracelet?"

"Yes. Listen well." She glanced at the door and lowered her voice. "I will be back for you and the boy, so you must be ready to leave at any moment. We will have only one chance at this. One chance. You must keep Valan with you no matter what they say. Whatever their plan is, it does not bode well for any of us, but especially not for him."

※※※※※

MORDACH SCARCELY LET THE DOOR CLOSE BEHIND LADY SOPHIA before he spoke, "Frances will be a problem."

"I have eyes and ears, Mordach. Let me worry about her." Motioning to the Ragat to keep watch outside the chamber, she took Mordach's arm and led him to a more private alcove. "What news of the Dark?"

"It has passed beyond my reach. There has been no word. But it will not stop until it finds Viella, and she cannot evade it forever. Once she's found, it will dispose of those that protect her and bring her here for the last ritual."

"And the Ambush? The one who would be king?"

"Rento. He has gone to fetch the Elemental. We have only to move everyone below."

"Then do so tonight. The Dowager Mother has a mind far too nimble for her age. I would ensure the binding is broken before she learns of our true intent. Once we are sure we do not require another queen, we can allow the Dowager Mother and Salene to go to Gaiea's Garden."

"What of Gretchen? Who will aid her if the Dowager Mother is gone?"

"It will do her good to be waited on by lesser servants for a while, especially now that she knows she's helpless. Adversity creates great character."

Mordach frowned. "You will leave her alive and able to speak against us?"

"I have another, very important use for her, just in case

things do not go as planned. When the time is right, she will play her part."

Mordach folded his arms and lowered his head, thinking. "Valan should soon be rested enough to open the final hall. I will commence his awakening later tonight."

"Lock the Dowager Mother in her room so that she may not interfere. Once the binding is undone, I will take care of her myself."

He frowned. "It is no hardship for me to—"

Lady Sophia waved a dismissive hand. "There may be wards against her magic, but she's still a queen of Gailand, and you will need your strength for the halls."

"But—"

"Mordach," Lady Sophia interrupted. "I think we've made a decision, haven't we?"

He hesitated, then agreed, "It will be as you wish."

※※※※※※

FARAIN FOUND THE FIRST BODY.

In the predawn light, he had drifted away from the path and into the grass, and his instinctual reaction to stepping on something unexpected made Luka dismount and join him. The body was a young man, dressed in great finery. Dark trousers sewn with what looked like silver thread in the weak light. The vest and the sandals he wore were clearly new, the soles barely scuffed.

He lay curled on his side, one arm flung outward. The grass had obscured him until Luka was almost upon him. He dropped to his knees, ignoring the screaming aches of his own body, and laid his hand over the man's chest.

"He's gone," he said, glancing at Eleanor as the horses pulled up.

"I know him," Gloria said, walking her horse until she was

alongside Viella's. "Knew, I should say. Ahmed. Son of Fatima, the village tailor."

"He attended this feast you spoke of?" Eleanor asked.

Gloria nodded. "He and the brides are great friends. But he would go nowhere without his mother. What happened? Did the creatures that attacked us do this?"

Luka's forehead creased. "I'm not sure." Farain slipped away from them, padding farther into the field as Luka laid the boy on his back and checked the body, but there was no sign of violence. No blood or wound. The body flopped in his hands, limp as wet grain. Luka sat back on his haunches, his hand resting on his knee.

"There is no wound, but the body feels—wrong. I have never seen the like." He looked around at the tall, undulating grass. Farain was standing a short distance away, his tail twitching. He knew what that meant even without the link. He went over to the war cat. Viella tried to dismount, but he held up a warning hand. She stopped, biting her lip hesitantly. He hunkered down again, rubbing Farain's mane.

"He wasn't alone," he called back after a moment, swallowing against the nausea crawling up his throat.

Gloria dismounted as Eleanor joined Luka. They stared at the two bodies lying together in the grass at their feet. One was a woman a little older than Gloria, gray silvering the black of her hair at her temples, her floral silken robes spread in a puddle to reveal thin, dark legs clad in sandals.

The other was a pale young girl in a salmon-colored sari made of a cheaper material. The girl's left arm was trapped under the woman, and the older woman's right arm lay over the girl's stomach, as if they had been holding each other before they fell. Neither of them breathed, and their bodies looked shriveled, as though they had collapsed in on themselves.

Farain poked at them with a paw, then dropped himself onto his belly and yawned.

"Fatima," Gloria said in a low voice. "And her apprentice, Sarah. Her mother sells potions and tinctures at the market. One of the finest herb women I've ever known."

"They were holding each other when they died," Eleanor said softly.

Gloria pointed off to her right. "The grass hides more secrets." A dark shape bumped up from the ground, just above the grass. Beyond it was another. And another.

"Your neighbors, returning from the festivities," Luka said, dawning horror making his voice hoarse.

Gloria looked away, passing her hands quickly over her eyes.

"They're all dead, aren't they?" Viella asked in a small voice. Luka went to her and patted her hand, unable to think of a gentle way to answer. She grasped his fingers tight.

"They must have been attacked by the Sycren," Eleanor said, the tiniest tremor in her voice.

An entire town. Gone. Murdered. Sick to his stomach, Luka said, "I don't know. This isn't what it looked like when the Sycren killed my horse."

"Maybe. But what do we really know of Sycrens? It probably happened as they fled. Most likely into those same woods." Eleanor gestured with her chin at the trees clumped together in the distance.

Gloria mounted her horse. "The Portal lies beyond those trees. We must decide now: do we go forward, or do we find another way?"

"Is there another Portal?" Luka asked.

Gloria shrugged. "The nearest one would take us several hours to get to from here and doesn't go directly to Biche. It would also mean traveling in daylight."

"We have to go now," Viella said.

Luka looked up at her, frowning. "What do you mean?"

The queen bit her lip and studied the grass. "You hurt it. But they will come back. We have to go through this one now."

"How do you know this?" Eleanor said. She drew closer to Luka's side, but the queen would not meet her eyes. "Is there something you haven't told us?"

Viella's lower lip trembled. "I . . . saw things. In my head. It hurts and it hates." She shuddered, then wrapped her arms around herself.

"What else . . . ?" Luka started, but Eleanor grabbed his hand and squeezed it lightly. He closed his mouth.

"These things you saw—they disturbed you?" Eleanor asked.

Viella nodded without looking up.

"Do you wish to speak of them to us?"

Viella's voice was so small, they strained to hear her in the steady light breeze that surrounded them. "Please. Later." She looked up and tears traced silver down her cheeks.

Luka's heart hurt. Viella rarely cried, and now she had shed tears twice in one day. After all she had been through, he knew he should expect it, but it made him keenly aware how far they had to go before the queen could begin to recover from the many losses she had suffered.

"Are you sure?" he asked. The bodies that surrounded them were a reminder of how lucky they were to have survived the night. Whatever she knew could only help their cause.

"Of course she's not sure." Gloria answered, her gaze steady on Viella. "But she's said what she can. Of that I have no doubt."

"Gloria is right." Eleanor let go of Luka's hand, and in that moment, he realized their fingers had been woven together. His palm tingled as she walked away, and he had to focus to hear her words when she spoke again. "We must make haste now."

Mounted again, they picked their way through the grass. Farain rose to his feet as the party moved off. He and the horses instinctively avoided the bodies. There were dozens of them—people of all ages and genders—all dressed beautifully, all reduced to shriveled skin suits.

A few had sustained injuries. One man's forehead was covered in blood. A boy's leg was twisted under him. But every one of them was dead. They could not stop to bury them, so they pressed on, trying not to see too much.

By the time they arrived at the tree line and slipped under the cool foliage, Luka had clenched and unclenched his jaw so often it was painful. All that kept him focused, kept him from thinking about the innocent people strewn around them, was Viella's small body leaning against him—a warm, silent weight. A reminder of what his true mission was.

In the woods, the night sky's fading starlight could not pierce the underbrush. Luka trailed Farain as the cat padded through the undergrowth, moving fast as he took the lead. Luka looked over his shoulder to make sure Eleanor and Gloria were following. He could just glimpse their horses, one behind him and one to his left. He turned back and was smacked in the face by a low-hanging branch.

Viella started and grabbed his arm where it circled her waist. "Are you hurt?" she whispered. She trembled against him, and he realized the last time they'd been in the woods, she'd been attacked.

"No, My Queen," Luka answered, keeping his voice low. "Fear not."

The crunch and thud of hooves on branches and fallen leaves echoed loudly. There were no animal sounds here. No insects or night birds. No creatures in the undergrowth scurrying away.

Luka's face smarted; blood pounded in his head and throughout his body, flaring pain through his shoulder. He couldn't catch his breath, and sweat trickled down the sides of his face and through the faint stubble that prickled along his jaw. Yet it wasn't the humidity in the woods—unbroken by the still night air—that made him hot and anxious. He felt he was riding toward something. Something that made his brain swell tight in his skull and caused his fingers to itch.

It was another half hour before he saw a break in the growth ahead of him. The trees were twisted and bent against the murky light of dawn. He slowed to a halt, waiting for the others to catch up. Viella tightened her grip on his wrist. For a few moments, the silence held them close together.

Eleanor drew up on his left, and Gloria next to her. The innkeeper drew an arm across her damp forehead. "The Portal lies ahead. There's a clearing, then the main road to the South."

"Is there a navigator?" Eleanor asked.

Gloria nodded. "Usually. This one is a Fiver—it goes to the other five queendoms. But we need not fear discovery."

"You are sure?" Luka asked, glancing at her.

She gave him a brief nod, her gaze straight ahead. "The navigator lies in the fields behind us."

Luka closed his eyes for an instant as hopeless anger washed over him. When he had himself back under control, he opened them again. "We must be cautious. Quiet."

The women dismounted. Luka handed Viella down to Eleanor before following. Viella clung to his rough-cloth pants until he took her hand. The horses snorted and shied a little at being so close to a cat, but Farain ignored them, his tail twitching from side to side.

Luka sent a thought to Farain, and the cat crept forward over trunks and branches so sinuously it was like watching water flow downhill. Keeping Viella close, Luka followed, his heart fluttering in his chest, his mouth as dry as sand.

Farain stopped at the very edge of the wood and waited for him to catch up. Luka sank down behind a fallen tree trunk with Viella and felt Eleanor and Gloria crouch just behind her. He didn't look. His gaze was focused on the huge Portal before them.

The Portal *and* the Sycren that paced in front of it, its muzzle scenting the air.

Luka knew it could not smell them. Farain had approached downwind, like all cats. But at the very sight of it, sweat broke out on his body. Now he knew what he had been sensing since he'd left the damaged inn.

He had no more fight left in him, and no real understanding of how to summon whatever his power was. Even with Gloria to help, he wasn't sure any of them were recovered enough to do battle with another Sycren so soon. As he knelt, soreness made his legs tremble and his entire body throb. His mind was fuzzy and unclear. He stared at the creature, trying desperately to focus.

Eleanor exhaled and her breath floated past his cheek. "Another one," she said, and he heard fatigue in her voice. Frustration that matched his own.

"A guard." Gloria's whisper was barely audible. "They've divined part of our plan."

"To be expected," Eleanor murmured. "Our options are few."

As they watched, the Sycren clawed viciously at the arch and tried to bite the *geis* panel. But this was one of the oldest and largest Portals in Gailand. Capable of passing large numbers side by side through it, and with five different destinations to navigate to, it was stronger than the Portal to Garth. The claws scratched it, and the *geis* cracked, but that was all. Frustrated, the Sycren screamed, then bit and worried at one leg of the arch. The metal groaned, but held.

Luka let a low curse escape. "Gaiea save me, I cannot face another. I have no more strength."

"It has been a long night," Gloria said, "and I fear I must agree with Luka. I cannot do battle again so soon. We must wait for daylight."

"And if Viella is right?" Eleanor asked. "What then? Hope you both regain your strength before the Sycrens—or something else—return to kill us?"

"Maybe. Either way, I must find an Augurs' Guild and contact my husband," Gloria said, her voice troubled. "My friends, my neighbors—they are all gone. What if my family tries to come home and these creatures wait for them? They roam the land now, a danger to all travelers. Someone must warn the other towns."

"Look." Viella pointed to the Portal. Her voice was low, but there was no mistaking the relief in it.

The Sycren had stopped attacking the Portal. Its muzzle was pointed at the sky, and it stared, motionless. Luka realized he could see the outline of things now. Sticks and leaves were coming into view. He could make out the features of his companions when he glanced at them.

"It's leaving," Viella said, relief in her voice.

The creature spread its great leathery wings and shot into the air with two strong downward strokes. It arced northward and rushed overhead, wind from its wings shaking the forest and scattering debris as they all flattened themselves to the forest floor. Farain let a growl roll in his throat, and his head turned to follow the Sycren's path, his tail pointed upward, the tip still.

Tension left Luka's body so suddenly, he grabbed hold of the tree trunk he knelt behind. Pain split his head. Nausea roiled his stomach.

"You were right," Eleanor said with a reassuring smile at Viella. Luka could just see the flash of her teeth. "It's gone. We'll wait awhile, to make sure it's not a trick and that it doesn't follow us through"

"Praise be to Gaiea," Gloria said with a relieved sigh.

"Praise be," Luka managed. Then he turned his head away from them and threw up.

⑅⑅⑅⑅⑅⑅⑅

"YOU ASK A GREAT DEAL, MARGOT OF GARTH. WHAT ASSURANCES CAN you give me that Dun will not take offense that I have their High Queen at my seat?"

Lady Tasmin was in her meeting room with her ocular.

A chair chiseled into the shape of twisted vines and flowers rose high above her head. Behind it, purple silks fluttered in an open window, revealing bright afternoon sunlight.

"You will have something more important than assurances. The gratitude of your High Queen as you help guarantee her protection. Please, send your Dahomei to Garth. Allow them to investigate and ensure Lady Mai and our queen are well. The Dahomei I sent to find the queen may need reinforcements if they are to accompany her safely to your seat."

Lady Tasmin tapped her fingers on her table as she mused. A wrinkle appeared between her brows, which were dark and sharply arched. Eyes so dark brown they were almost black were fringed by long, curling lashes. Lustrous brown hair was caught up in a fat braid that lay over her right shoulder. Her unblemished skin was a rich tan color. Lady Tasmin, ruler of Seat Corfu, the most powerful seat in the western forestlands of the Queendom of Nagar, was perhaps the greatest beauty in all Gailand, and she was notoriously careful—a woman wedded to caution and etiquette. Had she not just given birth to her first son, she would have been at the Ceremony. As it was, she commanded the largest force of Dahomei outside of Dun, so Margot needed her help.

"It's a pity neither Lady Mai nor Lady Gretchen can verify what you say. Instead, I'm expected to take orders from a Dahomei, and one far from her seat at that."

"I give no orders, Lady Tasmin," Margot said with a deferential bow of her head. "But I've seen the destruction here at Seat Talon. I had words with the new High Queen and Eleanor, Lady Gretchen's Lance. As we speak, the High Court is glamoured, hidden from sight and time. There can be no doubt. The High Queen has need of your loyalty in this crisis."

Lady Tasmin looked troubled, her eyes drifting to take in some other corner of the room. "And she has it, as always. Your story is horrific, with terrible implications for all. But why have you come to me when my queendom is so far away from Dun's?

Should not the seats of Dun rise first to avenge their own High Court?"

"We intend to. But our army has only just returned. If, as I suspect, the other seats are under attack, they will need their own forces to repel the invaders. Your army is the largest left in Nagar, since the Ladies Soros and Ruth were in Dun at the Ceremony. You've garrisoned a few Palms of your Dahomei within a day's ride of Biche so that they may accompany your traders as they travel through Dun before the storm season. If you are truly in doubt, it would take only a few to ride to Garth and find the truth of this matter.

"You choose to sit on the sidelines at your peril." Margot warned, a hint of impatience in her words. "Rebellion spreads as bush fires do in the dry season. The history of the Troubles tells us that."

Lady Tasmin fingered the fine, bronze-trimmed edge of her square-cut neckline. "I will send my people to Garth. And I will pray to Gaiea for a swift end to this uprising."

"Prayers are welcome, My Lady," Margot said. "But they must be accompanied by action, or we may find things move at a pace too rapid to be halted. Will you stand with Seat Garth and Seat Talon? Will you send your fighters to render aid?"

"I can promise you this, Dahomei: The High Queen is welcome at Seat Corfu. If my women find Seat Garth has been attacked, my Dahomei will join yours in whatever way is necessary to ensure peace."

"Thank you, Lady Tasmin." Margot could not help a relieved smile.

Lady Tasmin waved a hand; the large diamond ring on her left middle finger caught the light coming through the window in a blinding, momentary flash. "We will speak again soon."

The conversation at an end, Margot downed wine some thoughtful Augur had left on the desk for her, fortifying herself. Then she took a few deep breaths and went back to the ocular.

It took a long time before a face swirled into view, coalescing into full color. Jenista's bodyguard, Agnes, stared back at her.

"How goes it there, sister?" Margot inquired.

"Cold," Agnes replied.

"You should know your Dahomei have arrived. I'm grateful for them."

"With the Ragat's retreat, Everhill's forces can supplement Talon's, should there be a need."

"You don't believe the Ragat will attack again?"

Agnes shrugged. "The last blizzard probably closed the passes. Their warriors should be too busy trying to survive to make war."

"Have you entered Everhill and met with Queen Salene?"

"No. The commander has not yet returned."

Margot's eyebrows shot upward. "Not returned? It's been at least a day."

"I've had no word since she left last evening."

Margot leaned forward. "Agnes, tell me you're on your way to Everhill."

Disbelief flashed across the Dahomei's face for a second. "Have you forgotten who commands here? We will be there at sunrise."

"Then she suspected a trap?"

Agnes's expression settled back into its usual preternatural calm. "And we planned accordingly. She intended to find the queen, even if it meant being imprisoned with her, and contact me with her location. The time we agreed on for her to do this has just passed. My Dahomei and I ride in full force, as the court is most likely breached."

"Are you sure you'll have help in Everhill? That the Dahomei are still in authority?"

"Irrelevant," Agnes said. "We will wrest Everhill from whomever has her, if need be. I'll speak with you again once I'm done." A moment later, her visage drained away.

//////////

THE SYCREN SKIDDED TO A HALT AT THE MOUTH OF THE CAVE AND SLUNK into it, red wings dragging through rock dust. As the sun's rays strengthened behind it, the Sycren's body morphed into a vague man-shaped mass that floated above the ground. Three battered corpses emerged from the shadowed walls around it, limping and clanking toward it with dragging steps.

One of the corpses stopped directly in front of the Dark. It was a man with huge, muscled arms, and a broad chest. There was a hole in his torso; fragments of rib cage with rotting bits of flesh clinging to it stuck out like ragged fingers. Within their grasp, a tiny bit of oily, wormlike dark wriggled.

The Dark stretched a long tentacle deep into the corpse while two more grabbed the other bodies by the neck. In seconds, the floating form wisped away, absorbed by its new hosts. The hole in the man's chest filled and pulsed like a new heart.

The huge revenant turned and strode back to the cave's entrance, careful to stay where the sun's rays could not reach. The other bodies joined it. The revenant hissed, and they did the same, watching as it watched.

"They have escaped," the two bodies said, for the large man had not had speech in life and did not have it now in death.

"But they will use the Portal and we will follow. Plytown is dead. Soon, the one that hurt us will be as well."

The revenant crashed a fist into the stone opening, knocking chunks onto the ground and sending one large rock rolling down the hillside. It came to rest atop fresh-turned earth at the foot of the hill. A stone cairn stood at one end of the rectangular patch, marking the head of a recent grave. Next to it was an open grave, the earth collapsed in on itself, and a beautiful flowering bush that had stood atop it half fallen in. Beyond that, two more holes scarred the pretty plain.

The graveyard was dotted with hundreds of stone cairns and flowering bushes and surrounded by a neat fence. In the distance, thatched rooftops were visible, smoke from cooking fires floating upward.

"There will be more of us soon," the bodies said. "Too many to hide from. Too many to stop. And we will find the Daguard and the child, wherever they hide."

The Dark clenched and unclenched its fists before opening its mouth in a silent scream, the veins in its neck bulging, its cloudy eyes wide with rage.

"Tonight." The bodies stared at the town as it stirred awake before them. "Tonight, we will be many again."

WWWWWW

SEVERAL HOURS AFTER THE COMMANDER'S FORCES WERE CAPTURED, the Ambush entered the kitchens. The Ragat healer had finished with the Seer's injuries. The healer prostrated himself, then rose to murmur a few words to his leader. The Ambush gave a curt nod, and the healer left without a backward glance.

The Seer did not rise from the tiny pallet she sat on. It was tucked in a corner of Everhill's kitchen pantry and clearly the place where a kitchen boy would sleep. Around her, shelves were loaded with jars, herbs, and dried meats. The air was fragrant with spices, and beneath it the musty, dry smell of flour. Several deep shelves held the unguents and medicines the healer had used to treat, stitch, and wrap the Seer's wounds.

"Healer says your hand required only simple healing and is fine now. The leg will mend soon enough," the Ambush told her.

The Seer arched her eyebrows. "Sad news for you, then."

The Ambush clasped his hands behind his back. "I do not wish you to die before you serve your purpose."

"You have spoken of this before. You should tell me what I won't be doing, so we can get my refusal out of the way."

"I have no time for games, little one. Know that your refusal will lead to the death of your Dahomei."

The Seer leaned her head against the wall behind her, studying him as he stood over her.

"You will do as I say now, or the women will die. You understand?"

"I understand," she said. "What is it you want?"

He beckoned to her and walked out the door.

Holding on to the shelves around her, she pulled herself upright and limped after the Ambush. Once she passed the door, she was flanked by two Ragat who kept pace with her. The Ambush did not look back. She followed him through twisting corridors to the other side of the court and down spiraling stairs, until they were far below the main levels.

A narrow corridor brought them to a metal door that stood open before them, silver in the flickering torchlight. It was decorated by short lines of the same symbols that were etched into Gailand's Portals. It hung slightly askew from its hinges, and there were scorch marks on the walls and on the door itself. Where a handle should have been, a jagged hole had been blasted through the thick metal.

They entered a small room with two more metal doors. One was directly in front of them; thin embedded lines crisscrossed the tiny window set too high for the Seer to look through. The Ambush turned left and opened the other door, which had no window. Beyond was a space where the Ambush placed his hand on a panel as one would at a Portal. But he spoke no *geis*. Instead, there was a low tone, a green light flashed under his palm, and a door slid aside.

The room beyond held eight small beds with flat mattresses. They were lined up in a row, four on either side, with a corridor down the middle. Instead of wood, they were made of metal, and thin white cloth covered most of them.

A child sat on the floor against the end wall, legs drawn up

and slim brown hands wrapped around bony calves. A head full
of thick black hair hung over scarred knees. Blue sparks crackled
and arced in the air around the child, lightning in a storm, much
of it coalescing around the child's head and hands.

The Seer inhaled sharply, and the Ambush turned to look at
her as she raised a hand to cover her mouth, her eyes wide over
her fingers.

"You understand now?" he asked.

She nodded. After a moment, she dropped her hand, her face
grim. "Who is this?"

"That is none of your concern. Your only task is to put an
end to this."

"Put an end to it?" She stared at him incredulously. "This
child is Unbound. You need an Augur, not a Seer."

"Seers know the ways of Augurs. The child says you can
help. You have abilities. They will work here. But do not attempt
magic that can harm others. The wards will kill you."

She shook her head. "You're a fool. You're all fools. You've
pushed an Unbound to their limits and think this can be easily
undone? The child is in mortal danger, and so is everyone in this
court."

The Ambush backhanded her, sending her stumbling into
one of the guards behind her. The man steadied her, but she
wrenched her arm from him and stood on her own.

"You will speak to me with respect."

She glared at him. "Beating me will gain you nothing. I cannot
do the impossible."

He pointed a gloved finger at her. "You will fix this, without
complaint. If you do not, I will kill the others in front of you and
then take a very long time sending you to join them."

He motioned to the guards, and they followed him out, the
door whispering shut behind them.

CHAPTER 13

TRISTAN

"WHAT'S WRONG WITH HIM?" VIELLA COULDN'T HELP THE TREMOR in her voice. Luka lay on his side on the dewy grass next to the Portal, shivering. He looked so ill, and his sweaty grimace both tore at her heart and panicked her. "Can't you help him?"

Farain stood next to the Portal, tail lashing the ground as he sat back on his haunches. His yellow eyes watched his master intently and he sniffed at him before making a low sound in his throat. Eleanor knelt beside Luka, her hand on his forehead. Frowning, she tugged at the collar of his vest so she could look at his shoulder. Bent over Luka as she was, Eleanor blocked Viella's view. When she released his vest and sat back on her heels, her lips were a narrow, grim line.

"Infection?" Gloria asked.

"He was wounded a few days ago," Eleanor rose to her feet, her hands running over her short hair. "He was not healing well. I fear his magic has sapped his strength and made it worse. He needs care we cannot give him."

Viella's heart dropped as Gloria said, "Through the Portal, then. To the Augurs' Guild."

"No!" Eleanor spoke so sharply, Viella jumped. She stared at the women, wide-eyed. Eleanor scrubbed her hands over her face with a harsh sound before throwing her head back to stare at the sky. Viella had the feeling she was trying to come to a decision. A hard one. *Please, be quick. We have to help him.*

At her feet, Luka groaned and started to push himself up from the ground. "The queen. We must continue on."

Viella dropped down beside him and put an arm around his back, trying to support him. Her arm was too short to go much past his spine, and tears came to her eyes when she felt him trembling against her.

"We can't take him near the Augurs," Eleanor said. "You must realize why, Gloria."

"But he needs help," Viella said, looking up at them. "He's sick. They have really good healers."

"The moment I enter a Guild, they will know what I am," Luka said in a weary voice. "They will know I was never scried. That I have unnatural powers I cannot explain and can barely control. They would hold me to make sure I am no threat. And I'm not sure they would ever come to that conclusion. I cannot leave Viella." He glanced at Eleanor and then looked away. "I cannot leave you."

Eleanor knelt and put a hand to his good shoulder. "Do *you* know what you are, Luka?"

"I am a mistake," he said, hugging his arm to himself. "My father was Blane Kemp, captain of the Daguard at the court of Dun. My mother was Sanaa Ori, a captain of the Dahomei and Lance to Lady Sophia until she took a leave of absence to study at the Augurs' Guild in Garth."

"I remember hearing my older sisters speak of this," Eleanor said, her voice soft. "Seat Talon had word of her death months later. An accident. Are you saying she didn't leave to go to the Augurs' Guild?"

"No, she did. My father planned it with her. They grew up together. They'd loved each other for years, and my mother had always wanted a child. But her talent drew the attention of the Augurs, and she was sent to train as Dahomei. He became a Daguard to stay close to her. They cared deeply for Gailand and for the High Queen. They didn't want to lose their positions, and they couldn't be together openly." Luka shivered as he spoke, his eyes staring unseeing into the distance. "My parents knew a healer in Garth. A childhood friend. That friend kept her secret, helped cover up the pregnancy.

"My mother would have returned to Talon once I was old enough. But she died a few hours after I was born. My father was devastated. He had to find a way to take care of me without being removed from the Daguard, or losing me to the Augurs, since my parents' union was never approved. He chose to let my aunt raise me. When I was old enough, he sent me to the Daguard Guild."

Gloria raised her eyebrows and expelled a surprised breath. "I would not have believed you had such a story if I didn't see your power at the inn. Daguard and Dahomei are forbidden to marry, or bear children together."

"Yes, I'm aware. I can only assume someone like me is the reason why. But they did not meet as Dahomei and Daguard. To them, my father told me, the rules were just another obstacle to be overcome."

Viella put her hands on both of his cheeks and turned his head toward her. His skin was hot and he looked more tired than she felt. *This is my fault. Valan tried to warn me and I didn't listen. I made the Dark come. I never warned Luka, and now he's hurt.* She was ashamed of the tears on her cheeks, but she was scared to tell Eleanor and Luka what she had done. So she said something else instead.

"You're not a mistake. You're my bodyguard and you saved me. We're going to take you to a healer, and you'll get better. And then I'll make a law so no one can hurt you, or lock you up in the Augurs' Guild, or send you to Ragat."

His smile, brief and pained as it was, did not make her feel better. She sensed he didn't believe her, and determination filled her to make sure she kept her promises to him, however long it took.

Eleanor spoke. "The queen is right. You need a healer and I know where we can find one of unsurpassed skill. Can you ride for at least a day?"

Luka nodded, grimacing a little. "If I have to."

"Then the Portal it is."

Eleanor slid a shoulder under Luka's good arm and helped him stand. Farain slunk over, sniffing at Luka's feet and rubbing his head against his leg. Luka stroked his head. "I'm not myself. Stay near."

The cat seemed to understand. He waited as Eleanor helped Luka onto his horse.

"You'll ride with me, Your Majesty," Eleanor said.

"Where do we go?" Gloria asked after she swung up into her saddle. Eleanor was at the Portal, speaking the *geis* to where they were headed next. The Portal came to life, bright-green rain rippling downward within the arch.

When the Dahomei joined Viella in the saddle, she leaned against an unfamiliar shape and tried not to miss Luka's comforting arms.

"You will go to the Queendom of Jaleel. I believe it far enough away that the Dark will not waste resources to pursue you. It's best I don't tell you where I'm headed. The Augurs will ask, and their Readers may sense what you would not say. We will see you to the nearest town. Then we will carry on to the healer."

"Are you sure you will not need my help?" asked Gloria. "Suppose you are attacked, how will you fight?"

Eleanor walked her horse to the Portal's whispering rain. "You will help more by alerting the Augurs to what has happened here. No ordinary magic will quell the creatures we've faced, and until they are destroyed, everyone in Gailand is in danger. More importantly, you must protect your baby. A great power dwells within you, and Gailand will need every woman if we are to take the High Court back from the traitors.

"As for how we will fight—where we are going, I will have help the like of which the Dark has not yet encountered. We may outmatch it yet."

////////////

QUEEN ELISE HAD BEEN A RESTLESS WOMAN WITH MANY MATTERS ON her mind and much to accomplish within a day. Sleep tended to evade her. She often took walks through the court, and even as far as Freetown, when the whim struck her. But a High Queen couldn't travel without attracting attention, so Elise had the Ether bracelet made by the jewel smiths of Jaleel. That way, she could move through the Ether to anywhere she had been before, unnoticed. She made friends on her walks—one of whom became very dear to her—until Alain and the twins changed all that.

But some nights, a walk only energized her when her body required rest. On those nights, the queen used a slumber potion, specially mixed by the Dowager Mother herself to provide true, deep sleep. It was a secret they never discussed before others, but the Dowager Mother kept her supplied with it, mixing fresh batches whenever required. On those occasions, Frances would use the Ether bracelet to bring it, unseen, to Elise's chambers.

Now Frances waited in her rooms, dressed in black trousers and a matching vest. She had tied her graying hair back and put on soft-soled shoes. Her bracelets of office had been removed and she wore only Elise's Ether bracelet.

When silence crept through the hallways on cats' paws, Frances rose and knocked on her door. She removed the vial she'd taken from the queen's bedchamber from her pocket and unstoppered it as the key turned in the lock. One of the guards peered in, a question in his eyes. She remained in the doorway, hand curled loosely at her side, watching as he frowned at what would have seemed to be an empty room.

The guard looked to his right and said something. A second guard stuck his head around the doorpost. It was then that Frances flicked the slumber potion into both their eyes. They collapsed to the tiled floor in ungainly heaps, and she dragged them into her room as fast as she could, breathing heavily as she worked. Then she took the keys, shut and locked her door, and set off down the hallway.

The corridors of the court were brightly lit, and Ragat warriors wandered through them. They moved in pairs or stood guard in different areas, ensuring servants didn't enter forbidden locations. Frances strode past them all until she neared the doors that led to the lower levels of the court. They were double doors, painted red and carved with symbols no servant would have been able to read. But Frances was once a Sister Queen of Gailand; her bloodline had accepted the magic of Gaiea herself. For her, the symbols were clear.

DANGER. DO NOT ENTER.

And for some time, she could not. Instead, she waited in a statue's alcove, watching the small group of Ragat in front of the doors as they talked amongst themselves.

After a while, a few of the Ragat left, leaving four of their comrades at the entrance to the lower levels and walking right past her. As they disappeared around the bend, the Spellsayer came into view. He was dressed in his ivory ceremonial robes, and he carried a huge book bound in metal against his chest.

"You have completed your task?" he asked the Ragat. The marauders bowed in answer. One short man stepped forward.

"Yes. We wait much time for you."

"Then you may leave for your evening meal. You have worked hard."

The man stepped closer. "I make return this night. Our king requires us."

"And you will," Mordach said. "Please, go rest yourselves. Tomorrow, you may be among the first to lay eyes on the Masters."

The Ragat drifted toward Frances, talking amongst themselves. Frances flattened herself against the base of the statue. As soon as the men passed, she slipped out of the alcove and ran for the doors, moving more quickly than her years would have suggested her capable of. Mordach had opened them and started down the stairs beyond. Frances was just in time to slip between them before they eased closed.

Mordach strode down level after level with barely a glance around him. Doors and corridors made of strange, smooth materials went past. The air became cooler and cooler, and the Dowager Mother hugged herself, but she kept her eyes on the Spellsayer. The ceilings grew lower, the hallways tighter. Then there was one last entrance, Mordach's palm on a door and a spoken *geis*, and Frances was walking into a huge room, where she came to a halt, chest heaving and eyes wide.

Metal was everywhere. Fat, variegated ropes snaked along the ground and up the walls. There were black protrusions topped with what looked like small, winking eyes in the center of curved tables. The floors, the tables, even the ceiling, glittered and shone, but there was a deadness to the air. An expectant stillness. And over it all, at the far end of the room, a golden-hued Portal rose toward the high ceiling.

The Spellsayer stepped over the strange ropes with practiced ease, heading toward the wall behind the Portal. It wavered and vanished as he approached, revealing an unlit rectangular opening. Frances followed Mordach through and light flooded her vision.

This place was smaller than the Portal room outside it, but still quite large, with high ceilings. What looked like beds were spread out in a semicircle before the entrance, all pointing toward a tall wall of many drawers. White labels—the print too small to read from a distance—were under the handle of each drawer. More ropes were on the floor. Between the door and the beds was a single table, black as onyx and curved in an oval. It rose from the gleaming floor like a mushroom. Mordach placed the *Nightward* at the foot of one of the beds and flexed his arms, shaking them out with a relieved sigh.

There were at least four Palms of beds, and most were occu-

pied, though not the one Mordach had laid the *Nightward* on.
Four Sister Queens of Gailand, two on either side, lay unconscious before him. Arrayed on the other beds were the missing
ladies of the six queendoms, as unmoving as their queens. Each
bed had a curved, transparent cover, unless they were empty.

Frances closed her eyes, her face twisted with anger. Then
she opened them and, fists clenched by her side, crept over to one
of the beds on her far right.

Mordach held a hand over the *Nightward*, and it opened, the
script suspended above it flickering past.

Frances touched the slick cover over the bed she stood next to.
She drew her hand back, expelling a silent puff of air and gripping
her fingers before blowing warmth on them. The woman on the
bed never moved. She had thick black braids spread out over a flat
silver surface. Her skin was light brown, her lips full and pink.
Her cheekbones were sharp and high. Her chest, covered in a red
sari edged with white, barely moved as she breathed.

Mordach muttered under his breath. Frances glanced at
him, then made her way to the wall of drawers. She rubbed at
her arms as she leaned closer to read the neat labels. "Ectype –
Masters" said the one at her eye level. The drawer next to it was
labeled "Ectype – Gupta." She walked a short distance, reading.
"Ectype – Mahomed." "Ectype – Charles." She stopped before
reaching Mordach, her lips moving as she counted drawer after
drawer to herself.

"I see the Ragat have brought our subjects."

Frances whipped around to face the entrance. Lady Sophia
approached the black table and gripped its edges, leaning forward
a little.

"They are ready?" she asked.

Mordach didn't look away from the scrolling pages before
him. "I must first awaken the Genus."

"I have no doubt you will. We should have brought Elise."

Mordach glanced up at her. "No. I must try this without her.

If we fail to remove the Blessing, there are always more ladies. But there is only one High Queen. She must be a last resort. We cannot break the key in the lock before Valan and the Elemental have a chance at it."

Lady Sophia tapped a finger against the surface of the table. "She cannot be bound forever. And if we fail, there's always Viella."

"We will not fail." Mordach stilled the scrolling golden script with a finger. "I have it. We can begin."

"What must I do?"

"Stand there. Lay your hand against the center. Do not remove it until the ritual is ended."

Frances stood next to Lady Sophia, watching as she placed her palm on the center of the black table. The Lady of Talon looked up, straight into Frances's face. The Dowager Mother held her breath. Sophia frowned, her expression uncertain. Then her brow relaxed, and she shook her head a little.

"What is it?" Mordach asked.

"Nothing. Fantasies of the mind." Lady Sophia squared her shoulders. "Proceed."

"Repeat these words as I say them."

Sophia gave him a curt nod.

Mordach's voice was clear and steady, melodious and reverent. When he paused, Lady Sophia repeated what he had said. The lines were brief and made no sense to Frances. When they finished, Mordach and Sophia waited, and Frances held her breath.

A minute went by. Then another. Lady Sophia opened her mouth to speak, but Mordach held up a hand and shook his head at her. Her eyes narrowed, but she remained silent.

A loud thump sounded. Then another. The floor vibrated and Frances grabbed the side of the strange table. Lady Sophia held on too but did not lift her hand from the center. Somewhere, a soft whirring began. Then Lady Sophia cried out in surprise and Frances took a step back.

Lady Sophia's hand had sunk into the table. A clear liquid oozed out from under her palm and covered it. She tried to pull away, but could not.

The table lit up. Soft blue and white lights ran across it in many directions, dissolving into figures and letters. There was another loud click, and the table rose until Lady Sophia's hand was level with her shoulder. The slender column under the table glowed with a pale-blue light.

"System reset under way." The voice was female and completely without expression. "Stand by for network reboot."

Lady Sophia said swiftly, "Mordach, what's happening?"

Mordach frowned. "I believe we have awakened Genus."

"Then why will it not let me go?"

"Comp access level confirmed," the voice said. "Genus compromised. Rerouting."

Lady Sophia held on to her arm and tried to pull her hand free. "It has trapped me. Something must be wrong. Stop the ritual."

"I cannot," Mordach said. "The ritual cannot be reversed. The *Nightward* is clear. We must follow it through, or our chance is lost forever."

"Secondary system initializing."

Frigid air rushed into the room, and the door behind them shut in the blink of an eye. The clear liquid covering Sophia's hand turned ink-black. Her right hand, which she had placed against the table for balance, sank into the table as well. The onyx surface swirled and glimmered, streamers of white and blue intertwining as shapes formed from the blackness, rose into the air, and then flattened out again. Colored text surrounded Lady Sophia and Frances, stretching from the floor to eye level. A heavy, thrumming vibration pulsed through the room.

"Security measures complete. System stable. Optimizing donors."

The beds the queens and ladies lay on lit up with a bright

light. Glowing numerals appeared in the air above them. The numerals changed as seconds ticked by.

"Mordach." Lady Sophia strained to remain standing, both hands stretched out in front of her. "I feel myself weakening. This thing . . . it pulls the life from me."

"I have followed the spell to the letter. It made no mention of any danger to the Spellsayer or the Initiator," Mordach said, and for the first time, confusion entered his voice. Tension made his fists clench.

The numerals grew still and the text swirling through the air around Lady Sophia and Frances vanished. The black table lowered, and Lady Sophia breathed a sigh of relief as she found her arms at a more comfortable level. Her hands were still encased, and a script ran across them, this time in bright yellow.

"Donors ready. Warning: Commencing nanite collection."

A clear tube, closed at the top, rose from the floor behind Mordach. He whirled around, stepping out of its way. Slim tentacles emerged from the main tube and latched on to the foot of each bed. There was a loud click and the tentacles turned green. A chime sounded.

Without warning, the women lying on the beds began to shake, as if something held them in its violent grasp. Lady Sophia leaned forward, head bowed, breath rasping from her throat. "Gaiea's breath, this hurts!"

Glittering red clouds began to form beneath the covers over each bed. Another one formed above the table, where Lady Sophia's hands were trapped. They built and built until the ladies and queens of Gailand were completely obscured where they lay, and the cloud in front of Lady Sophia was a spinning, sparkling mass of tiny crimson stars. She collapsed onto her knees.

"Sophia!" Mordach rushed to her, and Frances dodged out of his way. As the Spellsayer put an arm around Lady Sophia's shoulders, the Dowager Mother watched the spinning cloud above them fly into the open tube. At the same time, the glittering clouds trapped with the queens and ladies funneled through the green tubes and into the open main one.

Another tone sounded. "Nanite transference complete. Initiating software update. One hour to acceptance of control nanites and authorization codes. Repeat. Printing process begins in one hour."

The slender tubes detached from the beds and withdrew into the main tube, which sank into the floor without a sound. The lock on the door clicked open.

Frances went to the nearest bed as the transparent covers over each occupant arced open. Queen Rhea of Nagar lay there, clad in the finest embroidered silks. But her body was little more than a shrunken skeleton, the skin wrinkled and dark, her brown hair dull and dry instead of lustrous and wavy. Her eye sockets were sunken and her fingers claws. Her chest no longer moved.

Frances backed away, her shaking hands covering her mouth.

"Sophia," Mordach said, giving the Lady of Talon a little shake. Above her, two tones sounded from the table, and her hands dropped free of it. Frances gasped softly. Lady Sophia's hands were a mottled, diseased brown, her fingers wasted. Her nails were cracked and yellowed as a crone's.

Mordach grabbed Lady Sophia's hands, shock written on his face. "How?" he said under his breath. She stirred and mumbled against his chest. He went still, then picked her up in his arms and ran out of the entrance. Frances went after him, trailing him at a distance, hand over her chest as she tried to control her breathing. They saw only two Ragat, who watched without expression as the Spellsayer rushed past. When they reached his quarters, Frances hesitated for a second. Then she took a deep breath and entered.

Mordach did not stop once he entered. He clutched Lady Sophia to his chest and waved a hand at the upper corner of a far wall. A silver moon glowed before a door swung open. Torches sprang to life as Frances stood in the doorway to his quarters, blinking against the sudden glare. Mordach crossed into his study and laid Lady Sophia on his bed. Frances moved out of his way automatically as he rushed past her to the doorway again, her gaze caught by what stood in the center of the room.

A mass of twisting, oily darkness sat in the middle of the circular room. Tentacles rose and fell from it, slipping over and around themselves and slithering along the floor. A glimpse of a hand or a bit of coral dress would peek out, only to be covered again by the ceaseless movement.

Frances approached the mass, careful to avoid the blazing braziers around it. She circled it, tears glittering in her eyes. She stopped and extended her hands over the mass, closing her eyes in concentration. When she opened them again, nothing had happened.

"Damn her to Gaiea's Desert," she muttered under her breath.

Mordach rushed back into the room, the *Nightward* under his arm. He thumped the book down on a clear space on his desk and scrolled through it. After a few minutes, he found what he wanted and started combining ingredients.

As Mordach bent over his table, Frances drew near the *Nightward* and studied the floating words. Her eyes widened. She looked at Mordach. The Spellsayer had his eyes closed as he said words of power over a gourd. The room filled with a coppery scent, like blood. Mordach snatched the gourd from the table and went to Lady Sophia's side.

Frances waved a hand, flipping through the inscriptions and checking every few seconds to see what Mordach was doing. The Spellsayer kept spreading liniment on Lady Sophia's blackened hands as he whispered spells. Frances stopped and scrolled through a passage. She read it, then continued through the book until she stopped again. Her forehead crinkled as she studied the words, then backed away from the *Nightward* with an indrawn breath, hand over her stomach. She stood for minutes, contemplating. Then, her chin high and a gleam in her eye, she turned and left the room.

〰️〰️〰️

ELEANOR HAD LED THE GROUP ON A FAST, HALF-DAY RIDE BEFORE SHE pulled her horse up at the top of a slope. Below them, the road wound through craggy rocks and patches of shrub toward a distant collection of flat-topped buildings. The midday sun blazed down on the reddish brick wall that surrounded the settlement and struck sparkles off its multicolored decorative tile. Three Gates stood open, and three different roads led to them, including the one they stood on. Viella saw a tiny band of travelers approaching the town on one of the roads, and people milling about the entrances.

Gloria pulled up alongside them. Her head was covered from the sun with one of the rags she made for all of them by pulling apart a skirt. "The Yoktar trading post."

"You know it?" Eleanor asked. The end of her head covering tickled the back of Viella's neck as she spoke.

Gloria nodded. "Quite well. Plytown trades with them regularly. Not a month ago, I was here with Fatima." She paused, then said in a shaky voice, "It's hard to think she's gone. To know they're *all* gone."

Viella looked over at Luka. He sat astride Farain, eyes closed. The cloth on his head was askew. He held his arm against him, his shoulders stooped. *Please don't die. Please, please don't die*, she prayed. Her eyes grew wet, but she refused to cry. It would make Eleanor and Gloria worry about her when it was Luka who needed help.

"Is there anyone for you in Yoktar?"

Gloria nodded. "I have friends. And there's an Augurs' Guild. A large one." She threw a concerned look in Luka's direction. "I can go on alone from here."

"I'm loath to leave you here." The Dahomei took a corner of her lip between her teeth. She glanced down at Viella. "What think you?"

Viella was so surprised, she almost didn't answer. "Me?"

"It's your decision, Your Majesty," Eleanor said simply. "I would feel better delivering Gloria to the town and perhaps speaking with the Augurs myself. But we risk Luka's freedom, and the Sycrens might find us easily if they're searching towns and villages near the Portals."

Viella thought hard. "Grandmother used to say, we can't do everything alone. Sometimes we must trust others to help. And Luka's very sick."

"Agreed," Gloria said. She gathered her reins. "It has been . . . interesting, Eleanor of Talon." She bowed to Viella. "And it has been a great honor to meet you, My Queen. You may have faith I will do my part to see treachery avenged. I wish you all Gaiea's Blessing on your journey."

She wheeled her horse around to look at Luka. He opened his eyes and smiled at her a little with chapped lips. She sighed. "Do not die, friend. Be safe, and well, till we meet again."

Viella watched her gallop down the slope, away from the shelter of the boulders and into the open. Above her, Eleanor whispered, "Gaiea go with you."

The Dahomei spun her horse around. Farain lifted his lip at them, irritated by their nearness, but did not make a sound.

"Luka."

The Daguard opened his eyes. His light-brown skin was beaded with sweat on his forehead, around his lips, and down his neck.

"Can you ride back to the Portal?"

"Back to the Portal?" Viella twisted around to look up at Eleanor. "I thought we were staying in Jaleel?"

"We're not," Eleanor said. "I just needed that to be what Gloria believed. If a Reader questions her, that's what they'll learn."

"You have a plan," Luka said, his voice soft and halting.

Eleanor nodded. "But you have to be able to ride at least one more day, perhaps more."

"But he's so sick!" Viella tugged at Eleanor's arm in dismay. "Isn't there another way?"

"I'm taking Luka to the healer, Your Majesty. But we won't make it if he can't ride a while longer."

An agonizing silence was broken only by the whistle of the hot wind through the rocks. Then Luka nodded slowly.

Eleanor drew up next to him and with careful fingers fixed the cloth on his head. He looked into her eyes as she did so, and Viella could feel waves of heat coming off him.

"I am sorry for this, but you are too hot," the Dahomei said. Then she took out a flask and emptied the water in it over Luka's head. He flinched. Farain growled as drops of water hit him, but didn't move. Flor danced away, rolling an eye in Farain's direction. Eleanor guided her back to Farain's side and gave Luka another flask. He drank from it, long and deep, before handing it back.

"Do you feel better?" Viella asked him, reaching out her hand to touch his too-warm wrist.

Luka tore his gaze away from Eleanor. "Very much so, Your Majesty."

Viella looked him over anxiously. "Are you lying?"

"Would it matter?"

"You shouldn't lie to your queen."

Luka's lips curved a little. "You have the right of it, Your Majesty."

Eleanor returned the flask to her pack. "Are you ready?" she asked Luka.

The Daguard sat up a bit more, passed a tired hand over his face, and adjusted the cloth on his head. "Lead the way."

A SOFT CLINKING AWAKENED LADY GRETCHEN. SHE OPENED HER EYES IN the dimly lit cell, staring at the wall in front of her and listening. There was a faint creak.

She rolled onto her back and looked toward the door of her cell. Frances stood before her, a sapphire-encrusted bracelet in one hand. She put a finger to her lips, then closed the door and knelt beside the bed.

"What has happened?" Lady Gretchen whispered.

Frances looked away from her. She shook her head, as if in disbelief, then met Lady Gretchen's eyes again.

"Mordach and Sophia have placed us all in terrible danger."

"Did you find the Portal?"

"And more besides. The Halls of Creation have been opened. Your mother had the ladies and queens of Gailand brought there and kept in strange beds, asleep."

"So, they are alive?" Lady Gretchen gripped Frances's hand in excitement, but the Dowager Mother made a sound of anguish.

"No longer. The Spellsayer and your mother carried out a ritual and it stripped the Blessing from them all. They are dead. Something has been set in motion that will destroy Gailand. They've used the *Nightward* to bind Elise's Blessing within her."

Gretchen drew in her breath. "Then Viella is without her Boon."

Frances nodded. "She's now wholly dependent upon the skills of those who shelter and accompany her."

"If anything happens to the Spirit, Mordach will be Regent until the Boon is passed to the new bloodline."

"*If* the Boon is passed." Frances stood. "I am no longer sure that will happen."

"Someone must be High Queen."

"How easily you forget that things were different before, during the Age of Chaos. Lady Gretchen, there's something at work here we don't fully understand."

"What aren't you saying?"

Frances threw a cautious glance over her shoulder before she continued speaking. "I've seen things today. There's a way for Viella's Boon to be taken from her—perhaps even given to another. And Valan has magic. Powerful, latent magic. Mordach must have known, and now he and Sophia use Valan to further their schemes. If we are to thwart them, I must rescue my grandson."

Lady Gretchen stared. "How could the Augurs not know of Valan's talent?"

"There have always been those who come into their magic late. That is why Augurs perform the Second Scrying. There have not been many, and none for some time, but we know the risks."

"The Second Scrying reveals Unbounds and . . ." Gretchen's eyes widened. "No. Frances, it cannot be."

Frances nodded slowly. "Sophia and Mordach seem to think Valan will be able to do things not seen in ages. That could mean only one thing."

"An Elemental. But what kind? Depending on his magic, Valan could be in great danger, as well as everyone around him. If he attempts to control his magic and fails, Gaiea help us. If he succeeds—" Lady Gretchen slammed her fist against her sheets and leaned her head back against the wall, her eyes closed, her forehead creased with a frown.

"Which is why we will stop them. Sophia was injured earlier when they killed the queens, and Mordach is trying to save her. We must make our move now."

"How?" Lady Gretchen opened her eyes. "I still cannot move my legs."

"I have read the *Nightward*. I could not understand everything, I am no Spellsayer, but I understood enough. I believe I have found a spell that will help us. But first, I must get you out of here, away from these wards, to where our magic will work."

TWILIGHT WAS GATHERING, SOFTENING THE EDGES OF THINGS WITH ITS
gray-blue light, when Eleanor pulled Flor up.

"Gaiea's Desert," she spat, looking over her shoulder. She
spun the horse around and Viella saw Farain some distance behind
them, pacing back and forth next to a dark shape on the ground.

"Luka!" Viella cried.

They rode back, Eleanor leaping from the horse as soon as
they were level with the cat. Farain pawed at Luka's leg then
looked at Eleanor. He made a soft, almost questioning purr,
staring at the Dahomei as his tail twitched.

They were on a well-traveled road in a queendom Viella
didn't know. Green hills, covered in black double-headed flowers
that faded to azure at their hearts surrounded them on all sides.
The road curled and dipped between them. Sometimes Viella
couldn't see the way at all because a rise in the land hid it from her.

They were miles from the Portal and the pig-trader they had
startled when they arrived. She had watched with wide eyes as
they galloped past her and her herd, already gathered to the side
of the Portal in an orderly group by two helpers. Her long striped
coat had fluttered in the wake of their passage. Viella had stared
at her until she disappeared behind a hill, along with the Portal.

The air was warm, but a steady, soft wind had accompanied
them all afternoon. Where the road was wide enough, they had
ridden abreast, Luka bent over Farain's back, his fingers gripping
the cat's mane. But they had been single file for a while now and
had missed the moment the Daguard slipped from his mount.

Eleanor turned him over into her lap. His breathing was slow
and his chest rose and fell in a strange rhythm. He did not open
his eyes.

Please wake up. Pleasepleaseplease wake up! Viella thought.

Eleanor waved a hand over his head and said words of power.
Viella watched anxiously for some change, but saw nothing.
Eleanor started to pour water onto Luka's smooth hair, soaking
his small ponytail. Still, he didn't move.

"My Queen, I cannot leave him." Eleanor looked up at her. "You must ride on and bring help."

Viella looked around at the darkening hills, which had lost all their vibrant color. Fear prickled her arms with goose bumps.

"Ride on to where?" she asked doubtfully.

"There is a river a short way down the road. You will find a hut next to it. The healer I spoke of lives there. Tell the healer Eleanor of Talon has come with a man ill with infection. Say there is no time to be lost."

Viella committed it all to memory. "Will he . . . will he . . . ?"

"I can't say, Your Majesty. Please. Ride as fast as you can. It's not far."

Viella leaned forward in the saddle, and with a shifting of the reins and a dig of her knees, Flor started off. Before long, the ground slid past at a gallop and Viella felt as if her brain had stopped, leaving only the sound of her breath echoing in her head and the jarring of her bones.

It was dark enough that the glow from an evening fire led her straight to the door of the hut. She heard the river babbling on her left as she halted. A figure appeared in the doorway.

"Who's there?" The voice was harsh and unwelcoming.

"Please," Viella said, her mind jumbled as she tried to remember what the ride had shaken out of her skull. "I'm with Eleanor of Talon. Luka . . . he's sick. With infection. You must come. We need help."

Light spilled out of the doorway as the figure moved back into the hut. Viella waited for agonizing moments, then the healer came to the door with a large bag over their shoulder. She could not see their face because of the light shining behind them, only that they wore loose trousers and a rough shirt rolled to the elbows.

"Is this the only horse?"

"Yes. But there's a war cat," Viella said.

A soft snort. "Of course there's a cat. I'll not be riding that, though. Off you come then."

Hands grasped her around her waist and lifted her down. The healer mounted Flor in one sure move and spun her toward the road she'd just galloped down. "Go into the house, child. Make yourself warm by the fire. We'll soon return."

They galloped off. Viella listened to the hooves as they drummed away. Then, heart thudding in her chest, she went into the hut to wait.

////////

COOLNESS ON HIS CHEEKS. A HAND ON HIS FOREHEAD. MURMURING. Luka came back to himself, pain searing his body, which grew more solid by the minute. He swallowed, but his throat remained dry. He couldn't stop shaking. It made the knees digging into his back hurt worse.

So cold.

A low, soothing voice came from above. He drifted on it like flotsam. Below it was a thrumming sound. It grew louder and louder until it stopped somewhere near him.

Luka opened his eyes. The world around him was lit by the orange glow of a quasiflame. Beyond it he sensed openness, but night had fallen, and he couldn't see past the light. He closed his eyes again.

Footsteps drew alongside him. He heard Farain growling.

"If you wish your master saved, you'll keep your teeth behind your lips, cat." The tone was light, but something about the voice was deadly serious.

The growling stopped.

"Thank Gaiea."

Eleanor.

"Eleanor. It's been a while."

"I know." A pause. "I had no time to send word."

A hand touched his face and neck. "We must get the fever down. You've tried the Word?"

"Spells have not worked."

There was another pause. "No wonder. The infection's taken hold. Why have you only now come?"

"I didn't know how ill he was. He said nothing. He is proud—and stubborn."

"Hmmm. Reminds me of someone." Fingertips pressed Luka's mouth open. Liquid slid down his throat, warm and bitter as words were said over him. His skin tingled with power.

"For Gaiea's sake . . . Not now."

"What? It's a comment, nothing more. Help me get him up."

Luka gasped as he was lifted to his feet, his arms draped around two sets of shoulders. He tried to protest but found he couldn't. He couldn't even keep his head from lolling on his chest. Pain flared through his body, scorching all thoughts from his mind.

"He'll have to ride with you. What I've given him will keep him alive for now, but I won't lie to you: there's not a lot to be done. You may wish to prepare yourself and the little one."

"Tristan, no. We cannot . . . he mustn't die."

"I'm not Gaiea, Eleanor. I'll do my best, but it may not be enough. And I will not give you false hope."

Luka was lifted, pushed, tugged, and twisted. More things dug into him, and his head hung down at an odd angle, but there was little he could do. He kept drifting in and out, wrapped in pain and a soul-deep weariness.

I'm dying. I'm going to die. He knew it with a terrible and help-less certainty.

"That's as good as we'll get him on there," the healer said.

"You cannot run back to the house."

"I know. I'll ride the damned cat."

"I'm sorry. I know how you hate them."

"A small sacrifice if it saves a man's life. Get on with it then. We're behind you."

The horse galloped away, jarring Luka, and he slipped out of consciousness for the last time.

The First, our Mother, took the mountain from the cursed, and freed the Waters of Lethe.

All nature springs from her. All joy springs from her rivers.

Before her, all was abomination. After her Song, freedom and beauty abound.

Anger her not. Call on her not. Her voice is salvation and annihilation.

Blessed of Gaiea, Destroyer of Oppressors, may she protect Gailand until the day of Gaiea's Chosen Return.

—The Blessed Scriptures of Gaiea
Handwritten inscription on the last page of the High Court's copy
(Author Unknown)

CHAPTER 14

GATES

THE SEER WALKED TO THE BED IN FRONT OF THE CHILD AND SAT ON IT. Here the air smelled of burning and there was a hum that thrummed along the floor. She sat without saying anything. Instead, she studied the small body rocking back and forth on the floor and waited.

"Does it hurt?"

The Seer started a little. The question was halting but spoken in passable Dunnish. "Does what hurt?"

There was a pause before the answer came in the same soft, muffled voice.

"He hit you."

"Oh." The Seer shrugged. "He intended it to hurt more than it does."

Again, a small silence. The child looked up with dark eyes fringed by long lashes in a sweaty face streaked with dirt. The tip of a tongue licked cracked, dry lips. The humming grew louder.

"He hits me."

"Bullies are often free with their fists."

The child frowned. "He is king."

"So, then he should know better than to hit children." She leaned forward and lowered her voice. "Do you have a name, child?"

A slow nod. "Enoch. He calls me Enoch."

"Enoch, this may be difficult to believe, but you have nothing to fear from me."

"I know." Their eyes met. "I see you. We are friends. Later."

She breathed in sharply. "You have visions?"

"Sometimes. Sometimes wrong."

"They are never wrong, Enoch. You simply lack the skills to interpret them accurately. It happens."

"You can . . . interpret?"

"No, but Augurs can teach you that."

A vigorous shake of the head. "No. Augurs hate me."

"Augurs help people with strong magic to learn to control it. I'm sure—"

"No!" Enoch's aura expanded, spun faster, thrummed louder. "Augurs. Hate. Me. Always."

The Seer said nothing for a while, looking around the room instead. After some minutes, the aura retracted.

"This has happened to you before?"

Another shake of the head.

"You have been using your powers?"

This time a nod.

"In what way? What do you believe caused your loss of control?"

A shrug and Enoch looked away.

"If I'm to help, you must tell me what you were doing."

"Not tell. You heal."

"To heal you, I must know what brought this on. Whatever has affected your control must be dealt with."

The words were forceful. "*He* would not want me say."

"*He* is not here." The Seer knelt, keeping a safe distance. "I am. He told me to help you. That's all I wish to do."

The dangerous aura spun, and a rumble began to spread through the room. The beds creaked, vibrating. Then, in a low voice, Enoch said, "I do many things. Make avatars. Help wake Portal."

The Seer frowned. "You opened a Portal?"

A quick nod and a sidelong glance that slid away.

"There's a Portal within Everhill? And you opened it?"

"Yes." The child shrugged helplessly. "Whatever King want. I do it. Even if it hurt, I do it." A tear slipped out of the corner of an eye and was dashed away quickly.

"Does it hurt more every time?"

"Yes. When I link with boy, magic get too big. I hurt. I cannot hold."

"Boy? There's someone else here?"

"No, no." For the first time Enoch changed positions, kneeling in front of the Seer. "Boy on other side of Portal. I help open. Now he sleep. But I get sick. Magic get big and come out hands, head. Won't go back in. I hurt people. They put me here so I don't hurt people."

The Seer exhaled, her expression thoughtful. "Where is this Portal?"

"There." Enoch waved at the blank wall to the Seer's right. "There. It open. Soon, more come. More go."

"Come and go from where?"

"High Court. Where boy is."

※※※※※

THE RIVER MAIDEN WOKE IN COMPLETE DARKNESS. HANDS CLUTCHED to her stomach, she slid herself upright against the stony wall behind her. Her labored breathing was a stir of echoes around her. Water dripped somewhere and pebbles rattled as she shifted her feet, gasping at the movement.

She lowered her head, her long hair brushing her arms as she frowned, concentrating. Her skin began glimmering with its own inner light, illuminating her surroundings with the weak glow of a small lamp in a large room. The cavern she was in had several openings branching off in different directions. There were three

in front of her and two on either side of where she sat. The shape
of them were strangely regular, as if they had been fashioned by
hands instead of nature.

She studied her stomach. Liquid no longer oozed from it,
but her legs were stained by what had escaped her. There was a
small hole where humans had their belly button. She touched it,
grimacing as her finger went too deep. It seeped, then stopped.

The maiden struggled to her feet, hand over her stomach.
Then she listened, leaning against the wall as she breathed.

An indistinct sound came from somewhere deep within the
cave system. The faintest flare of light formed in the tunnel
directly in front of her. When it flared again, she started toward
it, still crouched over, but her hooves were sure on the slippery
pebbles and rock dust.

She held her hand out, touching the walls as she went, moving
quickly but moaning whenever she stumbled over an unseen rock
or a dip in the passageway. The light in front of her appeared
twice more, and each time it was brighter. Sounds whispered
past, coalescing into clicks and hisses. As she reached the end of
the tunnel, hot air enveloped her in its suffocating hold.

The ground sloped away, winding between stalactites and
stalagmites as it made its way through a huge chamber. The ceiling
was lost in shadows, but light wavered and danced below. Pools
of liquid, large and small, glimmered in many spots and all of
them burned blue-green. Some flickered smaller than candlelight; others hissed and jumped, licking at the rock. A river ran
through the cave, disappearing into a tunnel at the far end. The
water was still and slick, and flames sprang off it—a deadly, colorful, roiling mass.

Slithering between the flaming pools and rocks was a black
serpent, larger than any creature the River Maiden had seen before. Golden scales covered its belly and the ridge that ran along
its back. Eyes as green as grass stared unblinkingly from atop a

head large enough to swallow a full-grown horse. The beast was coiling and uncoiling itself, darting its head behind rocks and into crannies. But as the sound of hissing echoed off the walls, it became clear that some of the shadows and patterns on the ground moved ceaselessly as well.

Smaller serpents, many no bigger than grass snakes, a few as large as pythons, flowed and eddied about the giant reptile. Sometimes they fought one another, hissing and striking, their fangs and ridges clicking on the stones. Sometimes the larger snakes rose up and blasted flame at each other in a hot whoosh of air, dripping flaming liquid from their mouths and setting the puddles around them alight. When that happened, the giant serpent would chase the combatants off with a hiss so loud it was almost a snarl, then resettle itself in annoyance.

The River Maiden licked parched lips and, hands still held to her stomach, walked into the cave. The smaller snakes at the entrance scattered, but the larger ones grew still, their eyes focused on her. The giant serpent turned its unnerving gaze her way.

"Stupid, or suicidal?"

The voice surrounded her, reverberating through the cave and in her mind. None of the serpents had moved their mouths, not even the giant. The serpent uncoiled enough to slip closer to the River Maiden and rose up until only its eyes glittered from the shadows above.

"Do you not speak?"

The dry scratch of scales filled the otherwise silent cavern, but there was no doubt who had spoken. The guardian dropped to one knee and lowered her head. The serpent studied her, unmoving.

"I speak, yes."

"Then which is it?"

"I do not wish to offend, but it is neither. I seek the First. Nictus of the Matamari allowed me to enter for that purpose."

The snakes grew restless, and the River Maiden was forced

to throw herself backward as one of the smaller ones tried to nip at her leg. She cried out in pain as she sat hard on the stony ground. The serpent watched, not bothering to intervene.

"The treacherous queen herself? I have not seen her in many a year. Tell me . . . did she sting you?"

The River Maiden moved her hand to show the open wound on her stomach. Inside, instead of flesh and blood, the cavity glittered with many colors, like the jeweled eggs of the Matamari. The serpent hissed, a hungry sound. The snakes echoed it.

"Does it hurt terribly, little one?"

"What pain there is must be borne. I have news for the First and cannot delay."

The serpent gathered her body closer, her coils drawing together in tight circles. *"Ah, but what care I for time? It passes and I live on."*

"Will you live on when the world ceases?"

"I have never tried it. Perhaps. Perhaps not. What will be, will be."

The River Maiden rose to her feet. *"I do not accept this. What point is there to life if you will not defend it and seek its continuance?"*

"Little specks. Always striving, believing your time so important. Life continues, whether you defend it or not. It is never-ending, ever-present . . . and not tied to your puny existence." The serpent lowered her head until it was level with the Water Maiden. They looked into each other's unblinking eyes.

"Tell me," the serpent said, *"are you a child of the Anchorite? Only her children may ask an audience."*

"I am a River Maiden, guardian of the River Lethe in the Queendom of Dun. I am one of many created in the fifty-third year after the Chaos. The First was my mother."

The serpent bobbed its head slowly, hypnotically. *"Good, good. Then you should easily pass the test."*

"What tes—" But at that moment the serpent opened its

mouth and breathed white-blue fire upon the maiden so intense, rocks cracked open and stones singed.

Terrified, the River Maiden threw her arms up, screaming. Heat blasted her in hellish waves. She sank to her knees, shielding her eyes, and called the power deep within her. Her skin hissed and steamed as water covered her, evaporating under the intense blaze yet replacing itself instantly. But the fire did not abate and the serpent grew closer, opening its mouth wider, allowing streams of white-hot flames to drip from its fangs.

The river began to bubble, waves sloshing against the shores. Then the splashing became a low roar and the conflagration riding the water lifted and fell, lifted and fell. Without warning a huge wave rose, curling toward the maiden and the serpent and crashing down on them with a force that sent snakes high into the air, against the walls, or rolling into the burning river.

The River Maiden was flattened by the impact. The serpent drew back, spitting and choking, white-hot flames abruptly put out, steam and smoke rising from the super-hot stones as water evaporated. The cavern filled with the sound of breaking, cracking rocks. Snakes that had not been dashed away found stone to hide behind and holes to curl into.

"*So.*" The giant serpent studied the maiden as she pulled herself upright. "*You are one of Mama's daughters indeed. She has so many children and I have met too few in my time.*"

The maiden groaned as she touched her stomach, pulling away tinted fingers. Then she looked up at the great beast above her. "*Have I passed your test then?*"

"*As they said when the worlds were young*"—it bent over her—"*with flying colors.*"

The serpent undulated away from her, spiraling itself between two large rocks and settling its head on one of them.

"*But will you not take me to the First?*"

A grass-green eye tilted at her. "*I am no guide. My place is here, with the little ones.*"

"But how will I find her?"

The serpent twisted its head away from her, annoyed. "*Mama is an Anchorite. The way to one of her kind is always marked by a Gate. Find the Gate and you find Her.*"

The River Maiden looked around her. The few snakes that remained watched with glittering eyes. The serpent was still, as if resting. The maiden took a hesitant step forward, then another, until she stood at the edge of the river. The water was placid now, the flames above it the only thing moving.

"*A word of advice, daughter: She is kinder to those who come bearing gifts.*"

Taking a deep breath, the guardian of the River Lethe dove, slicing through the fire. Water sloshed against the riverbank as the flames closed above her.

///////////

LUKA LAY ON THE HUT'S ONLY BED, OPPOSITE THE CRACKLING FIRE. His eyes were closed and he shivered hard under blankets that had been soaked in the river by Eleanor. His shirt had been removed, and a poultice had been applied to his shoulder. The skin around the poultice was red and swollen, veined with black and painful to look at. Viella touched his forehead, her chest aching. *Please don't leave me. Please don't leave me like everyone else has.*

She could hear them talking on the other side of the room where dried herbs hung from the ceiling with pots and pans, and a tub and a table marked the boundaries of a kitchen.

Viella left Luka's bedside and marched up to the table where the red-headed healer sat next to Eleanor, grinding something in a mortar. Both stopped talking as Viella approached.

"Do you know who I am?" Viella asked the healer.

The healer stopped their movements, studying her. Their

skin was burnished from long days in the sun, and there were crinkles around their piercing blue eyes. Their gaze was solemn and intense, and she knew they saw more than they ever admitted to. But there was something about the way the lines in their face bracketed their mouth that made them look like they were a second away from smiling. She liked that—trusted it immediately.

"Do you know who I am?" she asked again.

The healer looked at Eleanor, then back at Viella. "I met your mother's mother once, when she was a child. You have her eyes."

The mention of Viella's mother was like a blow to her stomach, but she took a deep breath and spoke again. "Then I should know who you are."

Eleanor shifted her weight and folded her arms with a sigh. The healer ignored her and resumed grinding the herbs. "My name is Tristan. I'm a healer and I once lived in Dun. It's an honor to meet you, Your Majesty."

"No," Viella said, not sure how she knew it, but sure it was true, "you don't think it's an honor at all."

The healer's gaze met hers and she saw surprise in their eyes, then a small, wry smile curved thin lips. "It's nothing to do with you. It's just that I prefer my privacy. It's somewhat of an inconvenience to have my daughter show up in the middle of the night with unexpected guests."

"*Daughter?*" Viella looked at Eleanor, who nodded.

"Yes, Your Majesty," she said. "This is Tristan Delacourt—my mother."

Viella's eyes widened. *An Unbound.* Then she dipped her head and dropped into a low curtsy. "Forgive my rudeness, honored one. May I have your title?"

"Good grief, child, you've been through enough. Court manners are best left in Dun. Refer to me as 'he' and let that be the end of it. No need to stand on ceremony at the ass end of the boondocks."

"Mother, language!" Eleanor warned.

"Come, now. She's a queen. Bit of bad language is the least of her worries."

Viella's hands twisted together. "Can you help him?"

Tristan sprinkled something into the mortar from one of the many small bowls on the table before him and she saw tattoos on the back of both palms. He whispered a few words and a puff of silver dust rose up from the mortar. Then he resumed mixing.

"Do you wish to hear what I hope to do, or what I can do, My Queen?"

"Please." Dismayed by the tremble in her own voice, Viella swallowed and tried again. "I only want the truth."

With a sigh, Tristan laid the pestle down. Then he stretched out his hands, beckoning her. Slowly, she went to him. Tristan took her hands into his own rough, dry palms, rubbing them in a soothing motion.

"Your friend is dying, Majesty. He does not have long. I'm trying to ease his pain as he passes."

"No." Viella shook her head vigorously. "He's strong. He wants to live. Please save him."

"I'm trying. This potion is for transference of essence. Eleanor has volunteered to give some of her life-force for his. So will I. It's the best I can do to help his system heal itself, as everything else has failed. But he was tainted by a darkened arrow, and the poison has burrowed deep in the time he did not seek treatment. I'm a better healer than most, and I tell you, he is probably beyond my help."

"Then let me help too! I want to give him my life-force—will that be enough?"

Tristan squeezed her fingers. Viella saw that the tattoo on his left hand was a name, Gabriel. The one on his right hand was Evan.

"Answer me this: Has your mother visited you?"

Viella stiffened. "My mother is dead."

"Yes, I'm sorry. My condolences. I meant, have you seen your mother? In a vision perhaps? A dream?"

"I . . . I had a dream. She told me to save my brother."

"You never said anything." Viella heard the note of surprise in Eleanor's voice.

"It was a dream. I meant to tell you and Luka, but—"

"In this dream, did she give you anything? Tell you anything?" Tristan interrupted.

"Just to save her and my brother . . ."

(before the Summoning . . . the Anchorite awaits)

She shuddered. "It was a bad dream. I didn't like it."

Tristan sighed and glanced at Eleanor. "No Boon then."

"It's been days. She should have been Blessed by now. I did not wish to speak too openly of it before, but it worries me. Do you think they prevented it somehow?" Eleanor asked, worried.

"With the *Nightward* open, anything is possible. Either way, I can feel her magic. Viella is still the Spirit. We have no Hand."

"I don't understand." Frustrated, Viella looked from Tristan to Eleanor then back again. Tristan smiled at her, but it was a sad smile.

"You are too young for a spell like this. I thought perhaps you had your Blessing from your mother, but for some reason it has not happened yet. Has anyone told you about the Boon?"

"The Ceremony wasn't held. The Augurs never had a chance to scry the twins or explain anything to them," Eleanor said. She cursed under her breath, gripping the tub as she looked out through the warped glass of the window into the night.

"That was deliberate, no doubt. If I wanted to keep the throne from a successor, the best time to take it is before she knows her true purpose. And there was magic at work that Augurs would have sensed during a Scrying."

"What is the Boon? Will it help Luka?" Viella asked.

Tristan shrugged. "Possibly. Gaiea gives all the ladies a Blessing, so we know they are her chosen. Because your mother was High Queen, she had a special one, called the Boon. You would have had memories. Knowledge of things Gaiea gives only to her Hand. And power. Such power," he said, almost reverently. "But if your mother has not visited you and given you this gift, you are still the Spirit, and that is not enough to save Luka."

Viella could not help the tears that spilled down her cheeks. Desperation swamped her. "Mother's dead. I don't know what's happened to everyone. I can't lose Luka too. He and Eleanor are all I have."

"I'm sorry. I truly am. But sometimes life takes away the things that matter most. It almost never makes sense, why we lose the people we do. But it happens to us all, sooner or later."

Thin arms gathered Viella against the scratchy, cheap cloth of Tristan's shirt, and gentle fingers stroked her hair.

"I won't give up on him, child. But there are people that will support you and care for you, no matter what happens to Luka. Many of them will even love you. Take solace in that, because you must be strong now, for him and for yourself."

※※※※※※※

AGNES REINED IN HER HORSE A SHORT DISTANCE FROM THE ENTRANCE to Everhill. The road before her was blocked by milling horses and Dahomei. Up ahead, something sizzled and creaked, and melted snow ran down the street in swiftly flowing rivulets. As Agnes dismounted, a figure pushed its way from the crowd to her side. The Dahomei had very delicate, bone-white skin, and was solidly built. Her brown braids were tightly coiled on top of her head. Her nose had been broken at least once. She tapped her fist against her armor.

"You are the commander's personal guard?"

Agnes returned the greeting. "Agnes Firecroft, of the High Court of Dun."

"Helen Fordham of Everhill, captain of the City Guard."

"You attack the Gate, Captain?"

Helen's nod was firm and brief. "Your commander rode through here yesterday with one of our sisters. No one has returned. When I sent a patrol—well, you can see for yourself."

An onyx arch rose high above them, crackling as sparks leaped and arced across its opening in the faint light of early morning.

"This is not normal," Agnes said.

Helen scoffed. "Of course not."

Agnes nodded to herself, as if answering an internal question. "What lies beyond?"

"The grounds and Everhill itself."

"We can assume then," said a short Dahomei as dark-skinned as Agnes, "it is as you suspected, Agnes. Ill luck has befallen Commander Star and her party."

"Luck has little to do with it," Agnes replied without inflection. "We can assume the commander is in great danger."

Raven pushed her way to Agnes's right. "We breach it then?"

"Yes."

"The court will be unprotected if we succeed," one of her Dahomei pointed out.

"Let that be a worry for another day," Helen said. Agnes turned back to her group. "Tie your horses and come join our sisters. We must work together."

The Dahomei gathered in front of the Gate. Wherever they could, they placed their left arm on the woman in front of them, and their right arm on the woman beside them. Agnes, Helen, Raven, and two others formed the front line. Agnes raised her hands in front of her. "Those behind the front lines, add your power to ours. On my mark, the front line directs it at the Gate. After two rounds, we fall back and the second line comes forward. We will continue until this Gate falls."

Armor clattered as arms were raised in one simultaneous movement.

"Now!"

Jagged streams of iridescent energy lashed the arch. Stone cracked and creaked and a deep groaning noise rose into the air. The ground trembled and snow fell from tree branches. Spiderweb cracks appeared on the surface of the Gate in one spot.

"Halt!"

The assault stopped. Dahomei doubled over, breathing hard, or leaned against trees. Agnes bent, hands on her knees.

"Gaiea's breath, that thing is powerful," Raven gasped.

"What Gate isn't?" the dark-skinned Dahomei panted.

"It will be hours of this," someone said with a sigh.

"Save your energy then," Agnes said, straightening.

"No army has ever brought down a Gate," Raven said to Agnes, soft enough so no one could overhear.

Agnes turned her gaze on Raven. Her close-cropped black hair was already damp with sweat, which dripped off the end of her long, crooked nose. "No Dahomei has ever tried. There's nothing we women cannot do together."

"If we fail?"

"Then we try another way in. Jenista intended me to come to her assistance. No Gate will stop me."

She turned back to the waiting women. "Dahomei! On my mark!"

The warriors lined up and raised their hands.

"Now!"

※////////////

LADY GRETCHEN LET OUT A GASP AS FRANCES BACKED HER AGAINST THE wall at the top of the stairs. Arms trembling from the strain of having carried the lady on her back, Frances let Lady Gretchen's legs down, then removed her arms from her neck and helped her slide to the floor. Frances looked up and down the corridor as Lady Gretchen shifted her legs with both hands.

"Are we clear of the wards?"

Frances formed a quasiflame with her free hand, then quenched it. "Yes."

"Thank Gaiea. I fear I will need a rest before we continue, my arms are so tired. And I cannot imagine how you feel."

Frances stretched, grimacing. "I have a bracelet that will help us greatly."

"A bracelet?"

"Yes," she said, offering nothing further. Frances crouched before Lady Gretchen, touched her forehead to the lady's, and took hold of her hands. "Hold tight, now."

Lady Gretchen tightened her hold. "What . . . ?"

"*Afara.*"

There was no warning, no flash of light or sound. One moment they were in a semi-darkened corridor. The next they were in the Halls of Creation, a golden Portal towering over them.

Lady Gretchen stared at the colored cables and dancing displays in disbelief as Frances lowered her against the Gate. "We are in the Halls?"

Frances nodded as she knelt, breathing in great gulps of air. She showed Lady Gretchen the glittering jewelry on her wrist. "It was Elise's. It allows you to go to anyplace you have seen before, and it can keep you hidden, if you wish it."

"This room . . . it's so . . . different. What is it?"

"I've never seen the like," the Dowager Mother agreed. "But the other room is stranger."

She pointed to the door behind the Portal, and as Lady Gretchen twisted to see it, a faint voice reached them: "*Fifteen minutes to printing.*"

"I must leave you now," Frances said. "Your magic will work here. If anyone comes, don't let them raise the alarm. If there are too many, reach above you, speak the *geis*, and crawl through. Don't wait for me."

"Go with Gaiea," Lady Gretchen said, gripping Frances's forearm.

"I'll not be long."

Standing, Frances spoke the bridging spell again and the glittering room was replaced by the snow white of Elise's quarters. Frances started toward the bed, then halted.

The bedsheets were rumpled and the chair stood exactly where it had been earlier that night, but Alain and Valan were gone. She cursed, then spoke herself into Mordach's quarters.

There was no one there. Sophia, Mordach, the *Nightward*—they were all gone. Frances slammed her fist down on a pile of books. Then her eyes widened.

"The printing," she exclaimed. "Of course! And Gretchen waits alone. There's no more time, then. It has to be now."

She ran into the room where Elise's body lay beneath the pulsing mass. Spreading her hands wide, she began to speak the separation spell she'd found in the *Nightward*.

At first, nothing happened. Then the black mass began bubbling, pulsing faster and faster. The torches in Mordach's quarters flickered, growing tall, almost going out, then tall again. A low rumble began. Frances spoke faster now, inscribing patterns in the air as she talked. The inscriptions caught the light, iridescent for seconds before they sank downward, into the High Queen.

The pulsing mass began to slide off in fat drops, each one splatting on the floor, only to curl up at the edges like burned ash. Strands floated upward, filaments of a web searching for a wind to carry them. Elise's face came into view, her lips gray and parted as greasy darkness spilled out from between them.

All the darkness lifted from Elise's body, spinning and twisting in the air as Frances chanted. When she repeated the final line of the spell for the third time, a huge wind swept through the room. Books were tossed to the floor, the torches went out, and only the blackness remained, an shimmering streamer in the sudden darkness. Then a beam of light, fierce and blinding, escaped the hole in Elise's chest, rending the blackness into burned ash. The light funneled through the roof and disappeared.

A huge boom sounded, as though the largest gong in the world had been rung. The ground shook, throwing Frances to the floor. Things toppled and crashed in Mordach's rooms. Frances lit her quasiflame so she could see, and as its yellow glow spread, the shaking subsided. She heard screams and shouts through the walls.

Elise looked deflated. All the color had gone from her cheeks, and her hair hung limp.

A corpse at last.

Frances's chest heaved from her exertions, and sweat ran down her face. She kissed two fingers and placed it against the center of Elise's forehead. "Rest in Gaiea's Garden now, my daughter."

She spoke the bridging spell again and returned to the Halls of Creation, in front of Lady Gretchen. She took one look at the expression on Lady Gretchen's face and spun around.

Mordach and Lady Sophia were rising to their feet. Alain was helping Valan stand. The *Nightward* lay on the ground in front of Mordach and he reached for it as Lady Sophia caught sight of Lady Gretchen and froze.

Behind Frances, the Portal rumbled, and the floor vibrated. White-gold sparks spat across the opening, and the *geis* panel glowed an angry red.

"Energy surge detected. Energy surge detected. Emergency protocols enacted. Software update complete. Control subject override engaged in thirty . . . twenty-nine . . ."

"Mordach, see to the machine. Take Valan with you." Lady Sophia started toward Lady Gretchen, one bandaged palm facing outward.

Alain gathered Valan to him with one hand. "As I said before, we go together."

Valan twisted in his father's grasp. "What's happening? Is it a landshift?"

Mordach halted. "Alain. Don't fight this."

"I will *never* stop fighting for my son," Alain said fiercely. "He stays with me."

"You didn't do this, did you Gretchen?" Lady Sophia said, still staring at her daughter. "But someone let you out—"

Frances ran to Valan and grabbed his arm. A crack sounded. The sapphire bracelet fell off the Dowager Mother's wrist and onto the floor. Valan looked down at his arm, then up at the Dowager Mother. "Grandmother?" he said, his eyes wide. Then Frances went flying, and landed on the hard, cold floor with a jarring thud. Stunned, she lay on her back struggling to draw breath.

"Mother!" Alain rushed toward her, but Lady Sophia waved both her bandaged hands and sent him crashing into one of the hard-edged tables. He crumpled to the floor and stayed there.

Mordach cried out and Valan yelled, "Daddy!" but before either could move, Lady Sophia turned her gaze on the Spellsayer.

"You know what has to happen. Take Valan to the room. Finish the spell."

For the first time, the preternatural calm of Mordach's expression crumbled. He took a step toward Alain.

"I'll see to him, Mordach." The Spellsayer turned wild eyes toward Lady Sophia. She said softly, "We've come so far. It's almost over."

Mordach heaved a breath, nodded, and hauled a kicking Valan into his arms.

"No! No! Daddy!" The little prince screamed at the top of his lungs, but Alain didn't move.

Frances pushed herself up on her arms and looked at Lady Gretchen. The lady met her gaze and Frances gave her an imperceptible nod.

"Attention. Printing process paused. Override engaged. Control subject optimized. Time to completion—forty-eight hours. Attention. There has been a Portal malfunction. Energy overload. Energy overload. All personnel to the archive room. All personnel to the archive room."

"What does it say, Mordach?" Lady Sophia said, looking between Frances and Lady Gretchen, both hands raised and pointing at each of them despite the grimace of pain on her face. "What does that mean?"

After one last agonized look at Alain, Mordach threw Valan over his shoulder and picked up the *Nightward*. "I know not. Only the *Nightward* can tell us." Lady Sophia's gaze flitted toward him.

Lady Gretchen chose that moment to wrap her arms around the base of the arch and haul herself up far enough to slam her hand against the flashing panel as she shouted the *geis*. Then she let herself fall, landing on her stomach as a dent formed on the arch where she had been, caused by the force Lady Sophia had unleashed in her direction.

Frances leapt to her feet and dashed across the floor to Lady Gretchen's side as the Portal roared to life. The tables rattled as phantom images sprang into the air around them—spinning, colorful maps and dizzyingly fast lines of unfamiliar texts.

Mordach disappeared into the room with Valan. The child's mouth was open, but the Portal drowned out his cries. The door to the room began to close behind them.

Red rain lashed the Portal opening and the floor. Frances grabbed Lady Gretchen's arm, ducking as Lady Sophia ran toward them, hands still raised. With a despairing look at her unmoving son, the Dowager Mother drew both hands together and clapped them at Lady Sophia.

A silver-edged aura surrounded the Lady of Talon, and she froze in place, the energy she had summoned trapped and crackling in the center of her palm. The spell worked for three long seconds.

Frances pulled Lady Gretchen against her chest with a mighty heave. Then, as the aura began to fade, she let herself fall backward through the Portal. The red rain parted like a curtain, then closed on nothing. Lady Sophia's released spell hit the Portal, sending crackling white-gold veins running over the inscribed golden surface.

Lady Sophia ran hard for the archive room, throwing herself into it as a loud grinding noise rose from the Portal. The metal door shut behind her.

The Portal glowed, red and white-gold warring over its surface. Then, like an elderly woman sitting down, the arch crumbled in on itself, collapsing into a pile of torn, groaning metal. Golden light faded from the destroyed arch. Then a shockwave blasted through the Hall, throwing the contents of the room against the walls, crashing open the door to the Halls of Creation, and sinking everything into darkness.

//////////

MARGOT OF GARTH STRODE ACROSS THE COURTYARD TOWARD THE PARTY of Dahomei dismounting inside the Gate, their golden armor flashing under the sunrise. Most of the debris from the attack had been cleared and servants were at work repairing the damage to the seat. The sounds of hammering and sawing filled the air, and tilers and masons worked under a section of the walls as Dahomei patrolled the battlements above. In another part of the garden, workers chopped dead trees into firewood and dragged shrubs out of the ground to clear the way for new ones.

"You are Lady Tasmin's Dahomei?" she called out.

A tall woman with wide shoulders stepped forward and removed her gold helmet. She was bald, with golden skin and dark, hooded eyes. A curving scar marked her left cheek and ran up to her ear.

"You must be Margot of Garth." The scarred woman bowed

her head. "I'm Indira Ghajawal of Corfu, Captain of Lady Tasmin's Dahomei."

Margot made a fist and pressed it against her chest. "I didn't expect you so soon. Have you been to Garth?"

"No," Indira said, tucking her helmet under her arm and passing a hand over her glistening head. "There was no need. Merchants and citizens of Garth fleeing the seat met us on the road with news of Garth's destruction. I am sorry, but Lady Mai and your sisters are dead."

Margot cursed and kicked at a rock on the ground. Above her, Dahomei exchanged furious glances and murmurs.

"What of the Dahomei I sent to find the queen? They should have been at Garth."

"Captain"—Indira looked at her pityingly—"there were bodies found outside the seat. They had been savaged by some kind of animal. None survived."

Margot stared up at the sky, blinking rapidly.

"I'm sorry to bring you such news," Indira continued. "But with the urgency of the situation clear, I diverted to the Portal outside Plytown, then traveled directly to Dun. There appears to have been a murderous attack on both Plytown and a village a short ride away. Many are dead."

"Gaiea preserve us." Margot let out a deep breath and looked down. "When did this happen? Do we know how they were killed and by whom?"

"Not yet, by there's reason to be believe the same forces attacked your Dahomei. Since they must hunt the queen, some of our sisters stayed behind to try to follow their trail. There was evidence the Portal was used without the navigator. We can hope it was the queen."

"Something strange passed through here after I arrived. Perhaps that's what carried out these killings."

Indira frowned. "Lady Tasmin made no mention of this. Have you an idea what it was?"

"More idea than anything else." Margot sighed. "There have been unfortunate developments in Kadoomun as well. Commander Star is missing. She rode into Everhill and has not been seen since."

"She left the front?"

"There *is* no front. The Ragat abandoned it a few days ago." Margot looked over the party. "How many are you?"

"Six Palms," Indira replied. "I've sent word to the garrison at Biche to stand by if needed."

"We'll ride out together soon and attack the glamour again, now that the army has returned to lend their strength to the effort," Margot said. Raising her voice, she said to the riders, "You must all be tired and hungry. Leave your horses at the stables. Your sisters will see to them. Join me for a meal as soon as you have rinsed the dust of the road from you. You'll have to wash in the courtyard. We're still carrying out repairs to the seat."

Indira fell into step with her as they walked back to the seat. "We rode hard after Plytown. I wasn't sure what I would find once I arrived."

"If you wish to see the High Court, it's visible from the battlements, though there's naught but darkness—"

A boom shivered through the air, so loud Margot and Indira grabbed at their ears. The ground shook, and those who did not stumble grasped at anything nearby for support. A cry rose from the battlements. Margot looked up to see a Dahomei pointing at the grasslands. She ran to the walls and took the stairs two at a time, Indira close behind her.

The shaking had intensified when they reached the top, and both women held on to the stone in front of them. Across the grasslands, a writhing ink stain was cracking open, iridescent light escaping through the tears in the glamour.

"The glamour is failing!" Margot shouted over the rising rumble of the shaking land. Below, glass tinkled and crashed, and wood creaked and cracked. People ran for cover, filling the air with startled and terrified cries.

A hole appeared in the glamour and light funneled out of it, soaring upward into the sky. The clouds turned pink, then gold. The mellow tone of a gong vibrated through the air. The colors in the sky dissipated, scattering in all directions. The shaking slowed and stopped. The clouds faded, leaving pale-blue morning sky as the glamour melted away like snow before the sun.

For the first time in days, the High Court wavered into view, solidifying as a cheer went up from the battlements.

"You've brought us good fortune, Indira!" Margot clapped a hand to Indira's shoulder. "Finally, things turn in our favor!"

Indira gave her a grim smile. "Think you as I do?"

Margot nodded once and turned to the courtyard. "Sisters! We ride now to retake our queen's throne and send every Ragat within the High Court's walls to Gaiea's Desert!"

The roar that went up was almost as loud as the landshift had been. Indira leaned in and spoke into Margot's ear. "I would speak to the lady Tasmin of our plans."

"Meet us in the courtyard within the hour," Margot said. "Dinner will have to wait, I'm afraid."

"There's not one woman here who would question that," Indira said. "For the queen." She made the sign of obeisance, fists clenched against her chest.

Margot did the same, a gleam in her eyes and a small smile on her lips. "For the queen."

———

THE SEER WORKED CAREFULLY FOR SEVERAL HOURS, PUTTING COMPLEX and powerful wards in place to protect herself and the child. It was not her greatest talent, and there was much at stake, so she was cautious and meticulous. When she finally reached out her hands, the child flinched away.

"No! I hurt everyone."

"Not I." The Seer turned her palms upward so Enoch could see the glow that lit her skin. "You can't hurt me. Will you let me help you?"

"What you do?" Enoch asked, suspicious.

"You know I'm a healer?"

A slow nod.

"Then trust me to heal you. If you wish to do no more harm, you must first control your fear."

"Not afraid," Enoch said quickly.

"Your king is elsewhere. There's no need to lie. Your fear powers this aura. Your pain makes it dangerous. You feel deeply, Enoch. It's a gift and a burden."

Enoch avoided her gaze.

She studied the child, waiting. When Enoch looked at her again, she said, "May I have your title?"

"What mean?" Enoch answered. "I Enoch."

"What would you like to be known as?"

Enoch clenched and unclenched small fists. "Why question? You think I stupid?"

"No," she said. "You have been called so by those too cruel and selfish to see you for what you are. But you are not stupid. You are special."

The Seer pointed to her chest. "I am a woman. My title is 'she.' Men call themselves 'he.' But there are those that are neither, those that are both. Humans can be many things and label themselves as such. Unbound are not tied to these titles. They can feel different on the inside compared to their outsides. Is there a title you prefer?"

Enoch stared at the floor and the aura retracted slightly. "King say 'he.'"

"Is that what you *wish* to be called?"

Enoch's shoulders rose and fell. "Must say now?"

"No." The Seer shook her head. "You can decide now, later,

or not at all. There are no rules, and there are many ways to be true to yourself. But it's a courtesy to ask for your title."

"Cour-te-sy?"

"It's polite. A kindness."

Enoch looked confused, and the aura around him shrank even more with his distraction. "What mean?"

Anger flashed in the Seer's eyes, but her voice remained calm. "Has no one been good to you? Shown you kindness?"

"King feed me. Give me bed in winter. That kindness?"

"What of your mother?"

"I not know." Enoch's words were heavy and full of grief.

"Your father?"

Enoch met her gaze. "King my father."

"Because he takes care of you?"

"No." A thin finger poked at an even thinner chest. "I son. He my father."

A rumbling began, vibrating the beds and growing louder with every passing second. Before the Seer could ask, Enoch frowned. "I not do this."

The Seer looked around her. The beds rattled and danced on the metal floor. Enoch remained kneeling, the aura around him shrinking. "I not do this!"

"I believe you, Enoch." The Seer glanced at the child. "But something is doing this."

"Landshake," Enoch said.

A boom sounded and the shaking intensified. The Seer shook her head. "This is no landshift. This is something else."

"What we do?" Enoch asked. The Seer raised her palms and the light that shone out of them was bright, shifting shades of white and pearl. Enoch stared, wonder transforming his face, and the aura above his head shrank to a faint glow.

"I think we should deal with one catastrophe at a time, Enoch."

"What mean?"

For a reply, the Seer laid her palms on Enoch's head and said,

"DORMIR." The rest of the aura winked out of existence, and she
bent in time to catch the now-unconscious child. As she lowered
Enoch to the floor, the sound of grinding metal filled the air. At
the far end of the room, the door sprang open. The Seer looked
up to see the king and two other Ragat standing there. Another
splintering crash reverberated through the room, and the ground
swelled and subsided beneath them like a wave. It sent the Ragat
to their knees. The king and one man tumbled backward. The
other fell across the threshold.

The wall to the Seer's right dented inward, as though a giant
hand had slammed against it. Without warning, the door closed
on the Ragat lying across the doorway. He screamed, struggling
like a pinned insect, pushing against the metal. Then the lights
went out.

⫻⫻⫻⫻⫻

AGNES WAS ABOUT TO GIVE THE COMMAND TO ATTACK THE GATE AGAIN
when the rumbling began. The women fought for their balance,
some grabbing hold of nearby trees and bushes, or even each
other. A loud groan rose into the air.

The Gate was only marred by cracks even though the Dahomei had been focusing their magic on it for almost an hour.
As the crashes and booms subsided, the glow intensified, and the
spider web of cracks began to pull open. The unmistakable sound
of failing masonry reverberated from its onyx surface.

"Sisters!" Agnes shouted. "Take cover!"

She ran for the trees to the right of the Gate, throwing
herself behind the trunk and shielding her face with her arms.

The Gate came down with an almighty crash, sending
chunks of onyx everywhere. Horses screamed and snorted. Dust
and stones rained down, crashing onto the road and pattering
against leaves and tree trunks.

When all was quiet again, Agnes rose to her feet and looked

toward the Gate. A dull pile of black rocks several feet high was all that remained. Beyond the Gate, trees leaned this way and that against each other on either side of the path, and tree branches had fallen onto the road. The air was very still, the ever-present hum of magic gone.

"That was not us," Raven said, shaking dust from her long brown hair.

"Matters not. The Gate is down." Agnes strode to where her horse had been tethered to a railing in front of a closed shopfront. There was a rush as everyone dashed to do the same.

"Whatever is in there brought down a Gate," Helen said, riding up to Agnes on the back of a huge black stallion.

"Indeed. But we know it's in there. *It* doesn't know we're coming." Agnes spun her horse toward the leveled Gate. "Sisters! Draw your weapons and follow!"

She galloped her horse toward the Gate, cleared the jumbled stones in one leap, and rode hard for Everhill.

※※※※

WHEN THE NOISE AND THE SHAKING STOPPED, JENISTA OPENED HER eyes to total darkness. Instinct made her open her palm. A quasi-flame flared to life, lighting the cell with its blue-green glow. Her gaze went to the bars that secured her prison.

The bars were no longer unbroken. Instead, there was the clear outline of a doorway. As she rose to her feet, the Ragat guard appeared. He raised his spear—and was flung backward by the opening cell door.

Jenista turned to see Sam lower her hand. She thanked her with a curt nod and went to the now-open door, pausing to quench the quasiflame before she stepped outside.

There was the faintest of rustles. A whisper of cloth. Jenista raised her palm to eye level and her quasiflame flowered to life again.

The second Ragat guard flinched backward just long enough for Jenista to reach down and take hold of his spear. She closed her other palm into a fist, extinguishing the light. There was a dull smack of flesh on flesh and a thud. When Sam's quasiflame bloomed, Jenista was standing over the Ragat guard's unconscious body. With one swift movement, the commander buried the spear in his chest, twisted, and pulled it free again. Then she stalked beyond the flame. Cloth tore and someone gurgled. Jenista returned, wiping a streak of blood from her cheek.

"It would seem the wards have failed." Queen Salene was sitting in her cell, still chained, hands folded in her lap. "I assume your personal guard has arrived to carry out our rescue."

Sam and Bridget emerged from their cell, joining the other prisoners as quasiflames flared to life, chasing away the shadows.

Jenista entered Queen Salene's cell. The Queen of Kadoomun rose to her feet, holding her hands out in front of her. "I need help removing these. They're hardened silver, fired in dark magics."

It took the Dahomei a while to break the chains and force the shackles open with the tips of the spears and Ragat knives. But the moment the last chain fell from her ankle, Queen Salene let out a relieved sigh and gave herself a little shake. She kicked the offending chains out of her way and stepped out of the cell.

"Much better."

"We need more weapons, Your Majesty," Jenista said. "And perhaps your people should remain here until we've cleansed the seat."

"I know where we can find all the weapons you need," Salene said, raising her fierce gaze to meet Jenista's. "And if not, we'll use our nails and teeth. My people have had their friends and family tortured and murdered before them. Their queen has been assaulted and imprisoned. We will find every last Ragat and rip the life from their bodies."

As cries of assent rose from the small crowd around them, a

flaming-orange aura crackled along Salene's fingers and set her palms alight.

"Now," she said, arching her brows, "let's get on with this escape, shall we?"

'///////////.

FRANCES WOKE UP COUGHING. SHE OPENED HER EYES TO FLAME AND smoke, dust and rubble. She pushed herself onto her knees, only to wince and clasp her hand to her hip. Her trousers had been torn and a gash in her skin bled sluggishly.

A short flight of stone stairs behind her led up to a collapsed platform. The remains of an arch stuck up from it like the carcass of a giant creature. Sparks and smoke floated upward. Small fires burned amongst the scattered debris. Frances drew her hand across her eyes, blinking. Then she pushed herself to her feet.

"Gretchen!" she called. "My Lady, where are you!"

A grunt from her left answered her. She limped to where a crumpled shape lay and dropped down beside it. Lady Gretchen rolled over onto her back and stared up at Frances. Blood flowed down the side of her face from a gash on her forehead. The Dowager Mother ran her hands over Lady Gretchen's body, checking for injuries.

"I am unharmed," Lady Gretchen rasped, pushing herself up onto her elbows.

"You bleed freely for one unscathed."

Lady Gretchen touched her fingers to her forehead. "A scratch."

Frances stopped her examination, while Lady Gretchen looked over her shoulder at the smoldering Gate they'd come through.

"When my mother came through the door, I thought there

would be no escape. What did you do? How did you cause a landshift?"

"I can assure you it wasn't deliberate. When I removed the spell they'd bound Elise's body with, her Blessing fled her body. I believe everything else was a consequence of that."

"So, Viella will obtain her Boon." Lady Gretchen let an exhausted smile crease her dusty face.

"I only pray she's alive to receive it." Frances's voice cracked and she looked away, wiping her face against her shoulder.

Lady Gretchen sat up, holding her forearm. "Gaiea is good, Dowager Mother. If Viella were not alive, wouldn't the Boon have gone to Valan, or someone within the court, instead of leaving?"

"Only if there is someone suitable here. The Blessing chooses the best of us, and it will choose another if we have none worthy at court. And this is a court that murdered its own. Perhaps that is enough for it to go elsewhere."

Lady Gretchen bit her lip, thinking. "We must have faith, Frances. You risked your life. I must believe it was not in vain."

"I have missed my chance to rescue my grandson. And my son . . ." Her voice trailed off and she bowed her head.

Gretchen squeezed her arm. "Valan is alive, and we know my mother won't harm him. He's important to her. So long as that remains true, he's safe."

Across the room, a pile of debris clattered to the floor. A Ragat covered in dust crawled out from under it. His mask had fallen off, revealing a full beard. Standing, he drew a long knife from his belt and whistled. As he advanced on them, two more men struggled out of the debris alongside him. One drew a sword and the other brandished two throwing knives.

"Oh, good. There are only three," Lady Gretchen said under her breath. "Watch the one with the throwing knives."

The man in question had stopped to aim.

"Are you sure?" Frances asked in a grim voice.

"If I need legs for their like . . ."

A long, low screech rent the air. Two of the men turned toward the sound. Frances clapped her hands at the man who still faced them. He froze, caught in a silver aura, and she rushed at him.

Light from a quasiflame spilled through the metal door that had been noisily forced open. A small blond woman stood there with a child in her arms. A second later, she dropped to her knees as a knife flew at her head, then stopped dead in front of her. Without putting her burden down, the woman flicked her fingers at the man who had thrown the knife. He crashed back into the platform, landing twisted at the bottom of the stairs.

With a wave of her hand, Lady Gretchen reversed the knife and sent it thudding into the chest of the man with the sword.

Frances drove her shoulder into the stomach of the first man as the spell faded. They rolled in a heap and, lithe as a cat, Frances flipped on top, straddled him, wrapped her fingers around his hand, and threw the full weight of her body onto the knife. It sank beneath her, straight into his chest. His heels drummed the floor, then grew still.

Frances stood, her chest heaving, her hand gripping her hip. Lady Gretchen released a pent-up breath and leaned back on her forearms.

The Seer got to her feet, shifting the child to get a better hold as she limped further into the room. "Dowager Mother," she said, "and Lady Gretchen. We're all a bit far from home, but well met. Well met indeed."

CHAPTER 15

BOON

ALAN WAS ROCKING BACK AND FORTH, HANDS AROUND HIS KNEES, when everything grew quiet again and the lights came back on. Lady Sophia blinked at the sudden illumination and levered herself up from the floor, trying not to put too much weight on her hands.

"Portal link severed. Damage to Archive—superficial. Damage to installation—nil. Damage to Portal and transport room—catastrophic. Cascade malfunction possible. Removing seal. All personnel begin emergency repairs and prepare for the end of the printing process."

Mordach stood next to a horizontal tube that had appeared in the middle of the room. It hung in midair, unmoving. Its smooth metal surface reflected Lady Sophia's face as she joined the Spellsayer.

"What is it?"

Mordach raised his head, anger burning in his dark eyes. "You left him behind."

"Gaiea's breath." Lady Sophia looked impatient. "He may yet be alive."

"No!"

Lady Sophia turned to see Valan rising from the floor.

"You lied!" He rubbed a hand at the tears on his face. "You said it was just a book. You said everyone would be happy I had magic. You made me play with that boy. Now Mummy and Daddy are dead!"

"Child," Lady Sophia said softly. "You may not believe me now, but there are worse things than losing your parents. That, after all, is the natural order of things."

"You're a liar! I hate you!"

"No, you don't," she said, walking over to him. "All we've done is help you be what you were born to be. A Caster—eater of magic and breaker of Designs. You cast your shadow over whatever you wish, and no one can ever see you or your place in the scheme of things if you do not wish it. All the magic you wield is hidden from Sight, and all the magic of others is revealed to you. You are *extraordinary*."

She stood in front of him and they eyed each other, he with his face wet and his chest heaving, and she with her head tilted and her face full of gentle pity.

"And yet you have no gratitude for what you've been given. Much like Mordach." She turned to face him.

He stared at her, anger and confusion written in every line of his body. "Sophia?"

"Please join me, Mordach."

He came toward her, each step a reluctant one.

"The boy thinks he's been mistreated. Let's show him how wrong he is."

"No. Not Valan. We agreed." Mordach raised a hand to her, but it froze in the air, opening and closing. A helpless sound escaped him. He stared at her, eyes wide. "What is this?"

Lady Sophia clucked her tongue at him. "I hoped it would not come to this. We could have been allies to the end. But you chose to raise your hand against me. And for what? That pitiful creature outside? He never deserved you or Elise. Or do you mourn your post as a tutor to a boy more talented than you will ever be? Do you still think he will love and trust you, after all this? Then let me be clear."

She turned to Valan. "Learn well, child. This is your one chance. I do not suffer fools."

"Leave Mordach alone!"

"So, you *do* defend him?" she said, eyebrows raised. "You think he can protect you? Oh, no, my child. There is only one person in control here. Me. Mordach, I have made a decision. Put your hands around his throat and squeeze."

Valan turned and tried to run, but Mordach never hesitated. He grabbed the prince by the back of his shirt. When the boy stumbled into him, he wrapped his fingers around his neck. Choking, his feet slipping on the smooth floor, Valan beat at the grip on his neck, but Mordach did not let go. Tears fell from Mordach's eyes onto Valan's head, but he did not let go. "Sophia, *why*? Why would you do this? Why would you make me do this?"

"Because there can be no half measures now. I will not become a footnote in the Histories, my name erased like the leaders of the Troubles and synonymous with terrorists like Commander Ragat." Lady Sophia went around them until she faced Valan again. The boy stared up at her, his tongue peeking between his lips. "Ease your grip a bit, Mordach. We must make it last."

"Let me stop," the Spellsayer begged.

"You see, My Prince," Lady Sophia said, kneeling before him. "How he loves you, and yet hurts you, all the same? That's what people can do, if you give them your trust. This lesson I teach you freely. Never give people your trust. They will only betray it."

She leaned forward and whispered to Valan, a thread of black flowing from her lips into the delicate brown shell of his ear. Then she sat back on her heels.

"As I said. There are worse things in the world than dead parents. Release him, Mordach."

Valan fell on his side, coughing and retching. Mordach went to his knees, silent tears tracking down his face, his eyes wide with shock, his hands limp in his lap. "The *Nightward*."

"Yes, my clever Spellsayer. You hoarded that book like a treasure. But not every spell in it needs a Spellsayer to read it. Or use it."

Mordach leaned his head back to look at her, anger beginning to replace the betrayal in his eyes. "I did this because if we could give the Masters' knowledge to everyone, there would be no need to take Valan. No need for anyone to be taken from their family like I was, ever again. I murdered Elise, destroyed my court, for this. But you killed Alain. You made me hurt Valan. They were all that mattered to me. The only things that made this worth it."

Lady Sophia made a scornful huffing sound. "Yes, I know your reasons. But you care only about your own selfish goals. And this was always supposed to be about the betterment of Gailand." She leaned down and said in a hard voice, "Why should we, who risked everything, our lives and our magic, simply share what we've found with anyone else? Power like this should go to those strong enough to keep it." Lady Sophia turned to Valan, her skirts hissing like serpents. "You say I killed your parents, but I couldn't have done any of this without you. Without your talent. The rules don't apply to you, Valan. They never have to again. You can be whatever you wish, and we can be each other's most intimate allies."

She took slow steps toward the prince. "Or you can be something else entirely, like Mordach. You may control magic that few dream exist, but you will never be safe from me now. I have made a decision, Valan. I wish you to stop breathing."

The boy's eyes grew wide, and he clawed at his throat. Lady Sophia tugged at the loose end of a bandage on her hand, tucking it in.

"You see, Valan, I can end you at any moment. While you eat. While you sleep. Cross me and you will never be safe. You may breathe now, My Prince."

The boy fell onto his back, taking in great gulps of air. Mordach gathered him to his chest, whispering, "I'm sorry," over and over again.

"Stop that, Mordach. There's nothing to apologize for." She raised her eyebrows at Valan. "Is there, Prince Valan?"

There was a long pause, then Valan shook his head, swallowing painfully.

"Excellent. We can be a family now. A real family, with one important mission: to rule Gailand as it should be. For that to happen, Viella will have to give up her throne, but then you might sit on it instead, Valan. Wouldn't you like that?"

Again, the boy nodded as Mordach turned his face away, his eyes closed as if he couldn't bear to look.

"Just remember, when I prosper, we all prosper. When I succeed, we all succeed. So, the decision has been made. Neither of you will ever betray me in word or deed, is that clear?"

The boy nodded and Mordach whispered, "Yes."

"Wonderful." Lady Sophia strode toward the door. "Leave the boy, Mordach. He will follow when he's ready. If Elise's binding has been released, as I suspect, the glamour will have failed. We have only a short time to act before you must return to this room and hide it as we did the court. I will need you to keep an eye on Genus until it's ready."

Mordach laid Valan down. "We don't have Viella yet, and whatever forces are gathered in Freetown began their march the moment the High Court came into view. The deal the Ragat made with me allowed them to enter the halls to partake in the ritual and greet the Masters as they rose. Now the Ragat here have lost their way home, and if the Portal in Everhill collapsed as well, they're trapped there. They will all be killed by the Dahomei, and we will lose our only allies."

"Their problem. They knew the risks." Lady Sophia stood before the dented door, and it slid open. Pieces of debris fell at her feet and she kicked them away into the darkness of the Portal room. "The ones trapped here are useless to me. What I require is the Unbound. The vault cannot be opened without that child, Valan and the Boon. Until we find them, I will gather new allies and set the game in motion."

Mordach stood, wiping tears from his cheeks as he looked down at the prince, who was curled into a ball. "What game?"

"The one the ladies of Gailand play. The one that will absorb them until it's too late to stop us. Everhill, Viella, and Enoch, Mordach." She looked back at him, a beautiful smile on her face. "They are the key."

"But—the spell didn't work. This 'control subject' Genus speaks of—this wasn't supposed to happen. The Masters were supposed to rise so the children could open Oblivion's Vault with their guidance."

"We have no real idea what should happen. This is myth and history and guesses. Rento believes the Designers are trapped in the Vault with Oblivion, and that the Masters are his sacred ancestors, his people charged with gaining their freedom. Gailand believes Gaiea saved us from a great evil She buried in Her Desert.

"And me"—she pressed a hand to her chest—"I believe Gaiea may not even have been a goddess. That the great evil She faced was more likely one of the Masters or Designers. Perhaps She was that rarest of beings, an Unbound Elemental, one powerful enough to rebel and trap them all in the Vault. Perhaps we have spent centuries too afraid to find out what really happened, and only succeeded in cutting ourselves off from godlike power. Perhaps She waits for us to free Her from the Vault. Or join Her where She has gone.

"The only thing we know is that the Vault contains power that once ruled the world, according to Rento, the Keeper of the Old Ways. So, I will open the Vault and take whatever is inside." She raised her head, a real smile stretching her lips. "And then, I will rule."

////////////.

KING RENTO, FIRST AMBUSH OF THE RAGAT KINGDOM AND KEEPER OF the Old Ways, marched down the corridor toward the faint cries, shouts, and clashing of swords. His mask had fallen from his face and blood trickled from a cut under his right eye. Third Ambush ran to meet him, clothes torn, knives bloody.

"My King, the queen has escaped with the other prisoners."

Rento cursed. Third Ambush looked behind him. "Where are Jin and Haceme?"

"Dead. How many are we?"

"A hundred, perhaps. There are at least fifty at the High Court. A sortie rode back to keep the passes open and we expect reinforcements through our Portal in Ragat."

"There will be no reinforcements. The Portal here is gone."

Third Ambush was shocked into silence. "How?"

"I suspect Mordach would know. Whatever happened to the Portal, the fault does not lie with us."

"Could he have suspected our plan?"

"It's a possibility. Perhaps he always intended to open the Vault without us, even though he swore he needed Enoch to do it. Perhaps the *Nightward* gave him power enough to bring down a Portal."

"What of the marauders guarding the Portal?"

"They were murdered by the Seer that took my son. Have you seen her?"

Third Ambush shook his head.

The sounds of fighting drew nearer, a piercing scream from a dying marauder made them both stiffen.

"Enoch might still be the key to ripping this world from the grasp of these preening bitches. They've kept our ancestor's sacred home from us long enough. I *will* be the king that returns us to the High Court and gives the Masters life so that the Designers might rule again. We must find Enoch."

"My King, I cannot spare the men. Soon, the City Guard will be here. We must abandon this court and return to Ragat."

"Do you not understand? Without Enoch, all is lost!"

"We fight Dahomei and a *queen*, My King. We will need every man."

Rento slammed his fist against the stone wall, then leaned his head against it. "Tell the men if they find Enoch, any man that returns him to me will receive my name and a permanent place in my sorties."

"My King." Third Ambush bowed low.

"Tell them to go to the upper levels with all haste. Make for the outer Gate by every possible exit. Summon the archers. When we pass through the town, we will rain fire down on them. The townspeople will be too busy tending to the blaze to give chase."

"There will be forces at the Gate."

"Yes. But we will not be the tip of the spear. You understand? Use the wereox for that."

Third Ambush took a breath and nodded slowly. "We take the horses?"

"Yes, especially those that belong to Everhill. Let them come after us on foot. If any of them are left."

"And how many wereox should we release?"

"All," Rento said, his voice tight with anger. "Release them all."

///////////

QUEEN SALENE CLIMBED THE LAST FEW STAIRS INTO ONE OF THE MANY internal courtyards. Two Ragat pointed their bows around the sides of the fountain in front of her, but she tossed them both into the stone walls. Dahomei ran forward to finish them off with quick downward stabs, and the bows were collected.

Jenista kept pace with Salene. "How much farther?"

"Down this corridor, then right and left. The room is protected. Only the Dahomei or I can open it."

The room, when they reached it, was a blank wall that shimmered into a doorway once Salene removed the glamour. Inside, spears and swords bristled among arrows and bows. There were also more exotic weapons, but with half of the prisoners being the queen's servants, few were interested in anything beyond blade and bolt. Some were proficient in their own magic and chose to remain without weapons.

They were headed back to the courtyard when they heard a far-off rumbling and a strange lowing sound. Jenista raised her arm and everyone halted. The sound grew louder and more chaotic, accompanied by crashing and smashing and finally, loud roars. Moments later, the corridor ahead of them was filled with a roiling mass of brown and black fur and hooves and horns, stampeding toward the front of the court.

One of those bodies missed a step and tumbled into the hallway where they stood silent and still, trying to avoid detection. The creature started to rejoin the stampede, but as the tail end of charging animals passed, the beast stopped dead, pawing the ground. It sniffed the air, then turned and looked directly at the escaped prisoners. It took a step toward them that brought it out of the torchlit corridor and into a shadow. Taller than a horse, its spiral-shaped metal horns and its eyes glinted like mirrors. A huge mouth opened to show a triple row of sharp metal fangs, long as a Dahomei's arm. A cloying, musky scent drifted toward them as it raised a tufted tail high.

"Wereox!" Jenista shouted. "To the queen!"

Salene waved her hand to toss the beast aside, but nothing happened. In a flurry of movement, two archers nocked their arrows and fired. The beast swayed out of the way of the arrows. It could not evade Jenista's knife, though, and it embedded itself in its shoulder, above its massive front leg. The wereox let out a roar that reverberated with the power of a struck bell. It pawed the ground, smashing the tile beneath its feet to pieces, and ran at them, growing larger and larger with every step.

The servants fled back into the room and the Dahomei came forward, then the wereox was among them, its flat head tossing its dangerous horns as it roared. Jenista threw herself down and rolled behind it. It kicked and snapped its teeth at her as she went. Tossing its head, it caught a Dahomei in her ribs with its horns. She screamed as it flung her into the wall, then wheeled, and tried to stomp on her.

Arrows flew, bristling out of its side like quills. The archers retreated to reload, the queen behind them. The wereox roared and spun in their direction, lowering its horns to charge. Jenista rose up behind it and plunged her sword into its rump before retreating. The wereox swept two more Dahomei onto the floor as it turned and ran at her. Jenista waited, flattening herself against the wall, then threw herself to the other side of the narrow corridor at the last possible moment. The wereox could not stop itself. It ran headfirst into the wall, cracking stone and a narrow window high above it. Before it could move, Jenista brought the knife down into the back of its neck, shoving through the thick hide to the spine. The wereox went down on one knee, lowed, then dropped to all fours and finally crashed onto its side, creating a depression of pulverized white tile on the floor.

Jenista stared down the corridor, breathing hard. Three Dahomei were down, and one was not moving.

"Gaiea's breath!" Jenista yanked the sword and knife free and wiped them on the wereox's furred coat.

Queen Salene looked up from tending to Sam, who had been gored in the hip. "They're badly injured."

"They'll stay here," Jenista said. With a glance at the emerging servants, she added, "So will those who cannot wield a weapon. Wereox are immune to magic, and we have no Daguard with us—no dagen-cats—until my Lance arrives. If you cannot fight, you will get in the way."

"My people will see to them." Salene rose to her feet. "I'm coming with you."

"There will be more. You'll be powerless against them."

"I am *never* powerless. I am a blacksmith's daughter," Salene said. "There are two more levels before we regain the Main Hall. Whatever the Ragat have loosed in my court, we'll need every woman to help clear it."

"You're the last of the sister queens, Your Majesty. Your life is too precious to risk—"

The queen gave a loud steups. "We're all of us fated to give up our last breath eventually. The battlefield is as good a place as any. Let's get to it. I owe a certain Ambush a painful death."

※※※※※

THE DAHOMEI LED BY AGNES STORMED INTO THE COURTYARD TO FIND A semicircle of over a dozen Ragat waiting for them. Helen and Agnes stopped their mounts a few feet away. But seconds later, the semicircle of Ragat parted and the front doors of Everhill smashed open under a swiftly moving, thunderous tide of fur.

"Wereox! They're wereox!" Helen warned, swinging down from her saddle.

The creatures and Ragat leaped at them as one, coming down amongst the front line of the Dahomei with sword and bow and arrow, and on hooved feet, heads tossing and horns goring into the sides of horses and the legs of their riders.

Horses reared and kicked, and Dahomei dismounted to attack from below, or swung their swords from above. The formation was broken in a matter of minutes, and as soon as it was, more Ragat poured out from the broken doors of the court. Those on horseback rode into the fray, while those on foot scaled the walls and disappeared into the trees. Archers knelt in the courtyard and fired into the melee. Whistles and trills ricocheted every-where. Wards leapt to life, sending arrows clattering to the paving stones, and those with the power to impel and move objects, or who knew spells to do the same, sent some flying back to the Ragat, but a few arrows found their target amongst the Dahomei.

Helen fought her way past two wereox and ran a marauder on his horse through with her sword. The horse also collapsed, fatally gored by the Ragat's own wereox in the scrimmage, and she took cover behind it. Raven joined her there and they locked eyes for a second as arrows thudded into the dead horse. Helen drew her wrists together in an X and Raven nodded her understanding. They waited for the arrows to stop, then stood together and clapped their hands at the archers.

The Ragat were thrown back, bows and men rolling every which way.

"To me!" Helen called, and leaped over the horse without looking back. The warriors not preoccupied with bringing down the last of the wereox, or fighting the remaining Ragat, followed without hesitation. Another wave of marauders swept out of the court, and the first few engaged the Dahomei front line with a loud clash of blades.

"Front line! Wards!" called Agnes. She was still seated on her horse. Several of the Dahomei with Helen dropped to their knees and erected wards. The Ragat ran into the invisible barriers, their swords bouncing off them without penetrating. Arrows peppered the wards but rebounded harmlessly. There was a brief lull as the Ragat tried to regroup.

"Down!" Agnes shouted.

The front line lay flat. The wards dropped. Agnes and her women galloped toward the prone warriors and came down in the middle of the Ragat, warhorses kicking and biting, swords slashing and piercing.

The women on the ground joined the fight, beating the Ragat back with furious blows. Behind them, more men broke past the arch and darted into the trees. Dahomei gave chase, firing arrows, throwing knives, and tossing marauders into tree trunks.

Two small groups of Ragat sprinted out of the passageways on either side of the court's entrance. Half of each group broke away and headed into the flanks of the Dahomei fighting in front of the court's entrance. The rest made a straight line for the now clear exit.

"We must give chase!" Raven called to Agnes.

"We haven't the women to spare!" Helen shouted back as she pierced one Ragat with a sword and kicked another to the ground. She yanked her sword free and hacked at the legs of a running marauder before making a half-turn and chopping the hand of an archer who was raising his bow.

A great cry went up behind the Ragat. Agnes sank her sword down through the shoulder of a marauder, then kicked him off the blade. She dashed sweat out of her eyes and looked up. A small group of women was attacking the Ragat from the rear. As men fell before their swords, a tall woman, darker even than Agnes, stalked behind them, casting fire and marauders before her in equal measure.

"Gaiea be praised! It is Queen Salene!" Helen shouted. "To the queen! To the queen!"

The Ragat tried to flee, but there was no escape. Merciless swords cut them down, and fire melted their flesh. Within minutes they were routed. A few tried to kill themselves, but were taken prisoner. The rest lay sprawled in smoking heaps. Golden armor glittered here and there, but there were not as many of those on the ground as there were piles of black cloth.

The queen was striding across to Helen when a rider galloped back into the yard. "Captains! The Ragat have set fire to the town!"

"No rest for the weary, apparently," the queen said, gripping Helen's arm briefly as she stood in front of her.

"It's a happy day, My Queen. We thought you dead."

"I almost was, but thanks to Commander Star, Gaiea's Garden awaits me yet."

Salene grabbed hold of a horse that had lost its rider and swung up onto its back. "There may be more Ragat hiding inside. We weren't able to search the lower levels. I leave that task in your capable hands, Helen. Those of you who have some talent with air and water, follow me."

She galloped away, trailing Dahomei in her wake.

VIELLA LAY ON THE STRAW MAT, UNABLE TO SLEEP OR LOOK AWAY FROM Luka. He'd been delirious all night, mumbling and tossing until Eleanor had taken his head into her lap and kept a cool cloth on his forehead. She whispered to him as Tristan went back and forth with river water, trying to bring the fever down, or drip liquid past his cracked lips. Earlier, they had given Luka some of their essence, but there had been no change. Now, in the darkest part of the night, he lay limp and unresponsive, and Viella felt panic rising in her throat like bile. She could see the life slipping from him, minute by minute.

Please, Gaiea, she prayed. *I'll be good. I'll never call him names or pretend anyone was a better guard anymore. I'll do whatever he tells me to do. I'll be the best queen that ever lived . . .*

Farain moaned outside, as though joining in Viella's promise. Eleanor had let him roam after feeding him because Tristan would not have him inside, but he stayed close by.

Wood popped in the fire, and she watched the flames as they burned lower, dancing hypnotically. It reminded Viella of the dancing boy and the sweep of his arms and legs. She had not thought about him in what seemed like forever, but it had only been days. She hated him now. Hated the very idea of spinning and leaping, of enjoying anything ever again.

It was her fault Luka was dying. She should have told Luka about her dream. Told him what her mother had said. She knew in her bones telling him about Valan and what she had seen was important. But she had been afraid of what the Dahomei might do to her brother if they knew what he had done, so she had not wanted to speak in front of Eleanor. Now she would never get the chance.

She felt so alone. Shamefully, despite all that had happened, she missed Mordach, and even Lady Sophia and her stern commandments. But Valan and the horrible secret of his betrayal of the court was a hole in her heart that would not close.

The fire dimmed, burning lower and lower, but light blossomed around her. A cool, steady wind blew. She sat up, letting her blanket fall from her shoulders.

She was on a grassy patch near a cliff's edge. A blue-green ocean swelled and dipped below her. White, star-shaped flowers with many petals nodded on brilliant lemon-colored stems, and the air smelled of salt and sweetness and all that was good. To her left, thin smoke rose from a small cottage made of stone. A window winked at her like an eye.

She looked to her right, and her mother sat next to her, facing her, so close, Viella could feel the warmth from her body. She wore a red dress, the skirt spread like the petals of a flower, and a white sash belted her waist. Her hair was loose and blew around her softly. One of the strands touched Viella's face lightly.

"Hello, my love," her mother said, and smiled.

Viella couldn't help it. She burst into tears. Her mother put her arms about her and pulled her into her lap. They rocked together for a while until Viella stopped crying, wiped her tears, and lay staring out at the ocean.

"Have you come to help me?"

"Yes, my darling."

"Can I save Luka now?"

"You can save him," her mother agreed. "If you want to."

Viella frowned. "Of course I want to."

Elise sighed. "If you save him, you set yourself on a path of great pain and much loss. But in the end, you will save more than just him."

"Will I save Valan and everybody else?"

Elise hesitated. "I can't promise you that, Viella, but you will save many people. Just remember—the child and your brother need you the most. You must not forget them. If Valan loses hope, all you endure will be for naught. If the child is taken by Chaos, all is lost."

"Who is the child, Mummy?"

"That line is not yet clear to us. Too much is still possible. But you will know them when the time comes."

Viella thought about that while her fingers played with her mother's hair. She was so warm and happy here, and the breeze brought the occasional coolness of saltwater spray. It was hard to think about anything but how lovely it would be to stay with her mother and watch the sea.

"Can't I stay here with you?"

"My time is done. Yours is just beginning. You don't belong here. You have so much ahead of you, so many wonderous things to see and great adventures to have. I know you are afraid, but the Blessing I give you is this: you will never be without us. When things seem darkest and most dire, look for us. Look to yourself. Every queen, every great woman of our blood, is there, waiting. Call upon us and we will serve you. For you are the Hand, Gaiea's Blessing is upon this land, and all of nature is yours and will bow to your command."

"All the queens are here?" Viella said, excited. "Even the ones I learned about from Lady Sophia?"

Elise smiled and nodded at the cottage. "They are all here. But you are my girl, so I have you to myself first." She hugged Viella, and a soft, familiar fragrance wrapped around her. "I've missed you so much. And I'm very sorry I left you alone so soon. I bear the fault in this. For putting my trust in those who didn't deserve it, and for my negligence toward those who needed my care, you and Valan are paying the ultimate price."

"It's all right, Mummy," Viella said, hoping to comfort her. "Everything will be okay. You'll see." She pulled back and looked up into her mother's face. "I have to go now, don't I?"

Elise nodded and stroked Viella's hair back from her face. Then she held her cheeks. "Yes, it's time. Luka needs you."

"I'll come back as soon as I'm done." She sprang to her feet feeling as light as a bird. "Then I get to talk to the other queens!"

Elise held on to her hand. "Viella, no matter what happens, remember me in your dreams. Remember how much your father and I love you. How much Gaiea loves you."

"I will. I promise, I won't forget you or Valan." She hugged her mother around her neck and when she felt dampness on her cheek, she thought it was just the spray from the ocean below.

She drew back from hugging her mother and found herself in front of the fireplace. A rainbow glow sparkled at her from beneath her skin before softening to starlight, then dwindling to nothing. She spun and rushed to Luka's side, startling Eleanor, who sat with Luka's head in her lap, and waking Tristan, who'd been napping in a chair at the foot of the bed.

"What is it? Did you have a nightmare?" Eleanor whispered, her eyes heavy-lidded with sleep.

Not a nightmare—not at all. "I can help," Viella said, her words tumbling over each other, "Let me help. Please, let me help."

Tristan had been rubbing at his eyes, but he sat forward suddenly, his gaze focused. "You've seen your mother?"

Viella nodded vigorously. "She said I could do it. I could save Luka."

Tristan never took his gaze off her. "Let her try, Eleanor. She has her Boon. And there's nothing else."

Viella saw the sheen of tears in Eleanor's eyes as she eased Luka's head off her lap and stood to give Viella room to come closer.

Viella thought of her mother, and a calm certainty gripped her. She placed her hands on Luka's temples, her fingers touching damp, curling hair. Letting out a deep breath, she leaned down and touched her forehead to his.

A light blossomed under Luka's skin, turning his skin beige and illuminating his eyelids so she could see the red tracings of veins in them. Viella heard herself whispering words of power she didn't understand. The fiery-hot skin under her fingers began to cool. Then she touched her lips to each of his eyes and said his name.

The light faded and Luka opened his eyes and looked into hers. Her heart swelled in her body.

"Viella." His voice was softer than a whisper.

"Yes," she whispered back, fiercely happy.

"I did call you. From the boy. I remember now."

"I know," she said to him, smiling. "It's okay now. You're going to get better."

He closed his eyes again. As she straightened up, he gave the tiniest snore and curled toward the wall.

"Praise Gaiea," Eleanor said in a shaky voice.

"Praise Her indeed," Tristan replied, his gaze still on Viella.

Exhaustion dropped over Viella like a heavy cloak, and she rubbed her eyes and yawned. "I think I'll take a nap," she announced, and went back to her little pallet.

"Yes, My Queen," Eleanor replied, a gentle reverence in her voice.

Viella was asleep the moment she lay down, and she did not move again for a long time.

///////////

QUEEN SALENE STOOD IN THE MIDDLE OF THE STREET, WATCHING TWO Dahomei as they melted the snow around them and funneled the water onto the smoking ruins of a stable. It was the last of the buildings that had been set aflame. Townsfolk milled around, the tension seeping out of them as the hectic rush and panic died down, replaced by anger and bitter resignation. Steam rose into the cold air and the stench of smoke was strong.

The sound of a horse approaching made her look over her shoulder. Helen drew up and dismounted.

"How goes it?" she asked.

Salene sighed. "The builders will have work for some time to come."

Helen nodded. "There are pressing matters at court you may wish to attend to."

"Pressing matters?" Salene folded sooty arms across her chest, further staining her soiled dress. "Have you found the Ragat king?"

"No. Only a few Ragat stragglers . . . and the High Court's Seer. She'd lost her way trying escape the lower levels."

"Is she well? The king took her from us."

"She's well, Your Majesty," Helen replied. "But she has with her . . . others you should speak to as soon as possible."

"Others?" Salene arched her eyebrows.

Helen looked around, her face pensive, then drew closer. "I think it unwise to speak of this in the open. It's best if you hear from them yourself. They all have quite a story to tell."

Salene studied her face before answering. "Very well. Lead the way."

※※※※※※

WHEN LADY TASMIN SEATED HERSELF BEHIND HER DESK AND ANSWERED her ocular's summons, she was unable to hide her shock as Lady Sophia's face washed into view.

"My Lady of Talon, is it you?"

"Lady Tasmin," Lady Sophia said with a tired smile. "Yes, it is I. You seem surprised."

"I've had word you and the other ladies were killed. That the queens of Gailand had been murdered in the coup."

"Then you are well informed. But there was a catastrophe here and I managed to escape. I call you now to beg for your help."

"My Dahomei are already there. I spoke but a short while ago with my captain, Indira. She and the captain of Garth's forces ride to your aid. Are the Ragat still there?"

"Yes, and I'm grateful for your assistance, but we have other important issues to discuss."

"Such as?"

"How we will bring the leaders of this coup to justice and ensure the protection of the throne from such an occurrence from now on?"

Tasmin frowned, twisting the gold-and-diamond ring on her left hand around and around her finger. "Surely, this is a conversation to be had with the remaining ladies of Gailand. The proper procedure would be to call an Assembly and lay the evidence before all, so that a course of action can be agreed upon."

Lady Sophia looked grim. "This would indeed be the correct course of action *if* the Assembly could be trusted to do the right thing. But that cannot be, for there is rot at the very center of that group that gave rise to this attack on our way of life. Rot that must be torn out before Gailand can move on to better, safer rule."

Tasmin stopped spinning her ring. "You accuse the ladies of Gailand of having something to do with these tragic events?"

"Not all of them. But there are connections that can't be ignored. I speak to what I saw with my own eyes."

Tasmin leaned back in her chair, frowning. "Tell me, Lady Sophia, what exactly is it you saw?"

BEFORE THEY REACHED THE HIGH COURT OF DUN, THE DAHOMEI SAW the broken arch. One half remained standing, while the other lay in pieces in the grass beside the road. The wood was old and black, a thing long dead and rotted. It was a jarring sight that brought with it shocked gasps and murmurs.

The courtyard was empty and quiet. Large, faint patches stained the tile, marking the spill of blood, but there was no one in sight. Using hand signals only, Margot posted sentries and secured the archway. The rest of the Dahomei dismounted and moved into the court through the half-open great doors.

The corridors were lit by a few torches and the light from exterior windows. As they moved deeper into the court, some of the halls that branched off into the interior were obscured by gloom. Dahomei broke off and explored them with their quasi-flames, only to return, shaking their heads.

They'd left the Main Hall far behind when a figure peered out from an alcove ahead of them. The Dahomei were four abreast, and the front line halted, their swords at the ready. The archers behind them raised their bows.

"Come out now, if you wish to live," Margot called. There was a pause and then the person moved into the light, hands raised.

"Thank Gaiea," Lady Sophia said in a relieved voice. "We are well met, Dahomei."

Margot and Indira glanced at each other before Indira said, "My Lady, we are Indira of Corfu and Margot of Garth. We thought you dead."

"So did I, many times over the last few days. But thank Gaiea, I've survived to see Dahomei take the High Court back from these blasphemous Ragat." She walked forward, her torn black-and-silver sari exposing cut and bruised flesh and bandaged arms. Her blond hair was loose, her eyes red-rimmed, but her chin was high and determined.

"Forgive my question," Margot said, "but surely you weren't hiding here the entire time?"

"Mordach locked me in a storm cellar after I was wounded on the night of Ceremony. He kept all the survivors there, in cells warded against magic." She held out her bandaged hands. "He tortured me, along with others. But once I regained my strength, I was able to overpower my guard and escape."

Indira came forward through the line of archers. "There are other survivors?"

"There were. Not all the ladies and queens died that night. But Mordach took them away hours ago. I haven't seen them since. He and Alain could have done anything to them."

"Alain?" Margot's eyebrows shot up. "You suggest the royal consort had something to do with this?"

"He had everything to do with it," Lady Sophia said, her jaw tight with anger. "He and Mordach were lovers. They murdered our High Queen so they could elevate themselves. Mordach planned to become Viella's regent."

Shocked whispers and angry cries filled the air. Indira gave the signal for all to lower their weapons. "You know this for a fact?"

Lady Sophia nodded, her expression sorrowful. "It gives me no pleasure to admit it. I trained Mordach, trusted him with our cousin's children. He betrayed our bloodline and our queen. These gifted men . . . sometimes the Blessing makes them . . . unstable."

Nods here and there. "It is known," someone said softly. "This is why the Elementals were forbidden."

"Who else was involved?" Indira asked, her tone hard.

"Some of the ladies. Servants from other seats and courts. The Daguard let the Ragat in through a Portal Mordach made in the lower levels. When I escaped, I found the room, but it was guarded by the Ragat and I couldn't enter. I searched the court and found our High Queen's body enspelled in Mordach's quarters, so I released the spell. There was a landshift, and I haven't seen Mordach since. I think he may have fled before the worst happened."

"Fled where?" Margot asked, spreading her hands to encompass the court.

Lady Sophia's eyes opened wide. "To join his conspirators in Everhill. Queen Salene, Alain's mother, Frances, and to my ever-lasting shame, my own daughter, Gretchen."

Shocked silence greeted her words. Margot pressed her lips together while Indira rubbed the bridge of her nose.

"What you say defies belief, My Lady," said Margot at last.

Lady Sophia's stare was hurt, bewildered. "I give you the word of a lady of Gailand who has bled for her queen and court. If you can't believe what I say, who *can* you believe?"

"Gretchen trained me, My Lady," Margot said sharply. "The lady I knew was loyal to Dun and set the highest standards for Dahomei across the land. What possible reason could she have for such a betrayal?"

"I cannot guess what they promised her," Lady Sophia said. "But she was here, conspiring with Mordach."

"Here?" Margot frowned. "I had word she was at Seat Talon when it fell."

"And who told you that? One of her Dahomei, no doubt." Lady Sophia shook her head as if saddened by Margot's naïveté. "My daughter's very much alive. She was one of my jailers. She trained several of the Daguard captains herself. It's possible they've been plotting ever since."

"Margot," Indira said, her voice tight. "Did you not tell me Queen Viella was last seen with Gretchen's Lance and a Daguard boy?"

Lady Sophia gasped. "If the queen is with these people, she's in grave danger and must be found immediately. She could be held hostage against the throne or killed to strip the Blessing from her. We must act, Dahomei!"

A wave of murmured assent rolled through the Palms as righteous anger burned in red patches on Lady Sophia's pale cheeks.

"I met the queen on the road and spoke with her myself. She was well cared for and in good spirits. Why would Gretchen send the queen away with her own Lance if she conspired with Mordach and the Ragat?" Margot challenged.

"Perhaps she and Mordach had reason to distrust the Ragat and sent the queen away so they wouldn't lose her to the invaders. It would explain why they fled the court together. They may have planned to rendezvous with the Daguard elsewhere. The queen is too young to realize the true nature of those around her."

Margot held up her hand for silence and waited until the murmurs had subsided. "If what you say is true, we are with you, body and soul. But we cannot take action on your word alone. Is there no one who can corroborate some part of what you've told us?"

Lady Sophia nodded. "I understand, Captain. It's right to be cautious. Though I've already told my story to others."

"How so?" Indira asked.

"As soon as I realized I was beyond the wards, I used a quasi-flame to speak to several ladies. I was worried for the safety of any Palms nearby who might be taken in by the lies of those fleeing the court, and of course, I had no knowledge of what had happened to Queen Viella. I learned of your approach from the lady Tasmin and came here to guide you. You can confirm all this with your lady."

"We wish to see this Portal the Ragat came through."

Lady Sophia shook her head. "It's collapsed now. There's no way to access it. But you asked if there were other witnesses. Will you allow me to allay your fears?"

"Of course."

"Then come with me."

Margot dispatched some of her warriors to continue the search of the court while Indira found a quiet corner to summon

Lady Tasmin. Then they followed Lady Sophia down twisting corridors until she came to the gold-leaf-covered doors that led to the queen's private quarters. No sooner had Lady Sophia opened it than a small figure rushed out, grabbing hold of her legs.

Valan buried his face in her skirts. The Lady of Talon made soothing noises and knelt to hug him close. "Were you worried? Did I not say I would return with help?"

The boy shuddered under her touch and clutched her skirts tighter. Lady Sophia looked up at Margot as she rubbed his shoulders with light touches of her bandaged fingers.

"Cease your fretting now. The Dahomei have come. All will be well."

Margot's eyes narrowed as she looked from the boy who would not raise his head to Lady Sophia, but all she said was, "Indeed, Your Grace. The queen herself asked me to make sure you were safe."

He finally looked at her, his eyes wide. "You saw Viella?"

She crouched in front of him. "Yes. Never fear, Your Grace. No one will harm you while you're under my protection."

―――――――

EVENING HAD THROWN A STAR-SPANGLED CLOTH ACROSS THE SKY when the last Sycren emerged from the hole it had dug in a hillside. It shook itself, letting dust fall from its wings as a dozen corpses crawled from shallow graves around it. Two more Sycrens climbed out of the ground, spreading their blood-red wings and stretching their clawed legs.

The three Sycrens lifted their snouts and scented the air together. The biggest one screamed long and loud. Hissing began, as if the largest nest of snakes in the world had been disturbed.

"We sense her! We sense her!" some voices said. "She dreams in the place by the waters."

"Follow! Follow!" others replied.

The corpses mounted the Sycrens, clinging to their backs with mutilated arms and legs. They took off—their screeching laughter enough to deafen those who heard—all of them banking to the southwest as their wings beat the air in slow, powerful strokes.

GENTLE HANDS TOUCHED LUKA. SOFT WORDS FLOWED OVER HIM LIKE A sunlit creek. He heard his name, and joy resonated through him as though he were a plucked string. Then he was on his side, looking across a sun-dappled room at Viella as she lay curled toward him, her eyes closed, and her rich hair spread out over her thin brown arms.

He swallowed, but his throat was very dry, and he ended up coughing. A chair creaked and someone sat on the bed next to him. Callused hands stroked his hair back from his face and put a cup to his lips. He drank, grimacing at the bitter taste, but the cup didn't move until he had taken several sips.

"It will soothe your throat and give you strength, so never mind the taste. Drink up," a voice said.

Luka obeyed, watching the redheaded person over the cup as he drank. When the person took the vessel from Luka's lips and placed it on the ground, he asked, "Who are you?"

"Tristan. I'm a healer. You're near the town of Blackburn in the Queendom of Ravisinghga. Eleanor and Queen Viella brought you here two days ago."

Vague memories stirred in Luka as he pushed himself up on his elbows. "You're the healer Eleanor spoke of?"

"She spoke of me, did she?" Tristan gave Luka a wry smile. "How unusually talkative of her. How does your shoulder feel?"

Luka sat up and flexed his arm experimentally. "There's only the slightest twinge. Gaiea bless you, you're a great healer indeed to do so much in only two days. I thought my time had come."

Tristan laughed, a full-throated bellow that made Viella

frown and turn over in her sleep. "Normally, I would take your compliments and any crowns you were willing to spare, but in this case, I wouldn't dare take credit for my queen's actions."

Luka stared at Viella's back, shocked. "The queen healed me?"

"In less time than it takes for an Augur to heal a scratch. You were almost dead, and then you weren't. Wore her out, though. She's been sleeping ever since. Has anyone ever told you, you snore?"

Luka gave Tristan a cutting glance. "I do not snore."

"There's that stubbornness Eleanor mentioned. Speaking of Eleanor . . ."

Luka turned to look at the door as it swung open, and the Dahomei entered. Eleanor backed in and dropped two buckets on the floor as she spoke. "What are you laughing about, Mother? I could hear you all the way in the river—"

She looked up and stopped speaking. She had borrowed pants and high boots to go wading in the river, and what must have been one of Tristan's coarsely woven shirts. The neck of it flapped open so Luka could see the freckles on her breastbone. Her short red hair needed a comb. There was a bit of mud on one of her freckled cheeks and he caught the stink of fish from his bed. Then she smiled, a wide, ecstatic smile the likes of which Luka had never seen on her before.

It was as if his chest had expanded, and he could breathe for the first time in his life. Warmth ran over his skin in waves and his fingers tingled. His brain wasn't working right, so he said the first thing that came to mind: "You smell awful."

Wonderful. Insults are what every woman longs to hear.

She walked over to him, wiping her hands on her shirt, never breaking eye contact. Tristan got off the bed and stood aside.

Apologize, idiot, Luka told himself. He opened his mouth, but Eleanor sat down and hugged him. His heart flipped over, and when she pulled away from him, her fingers stroking his cheeks, he only managed to stammer out, "I didn't mean—"

"Stop talking," she said, and hugged him again.

CHAPTER 16

BERSERKER

T HE SEER PACED WHILE FRANCES SAT IN A CHAIR, LOOKING OUT OF one of Everhill's narrow windows. The day outside was bright and cold, but Frances had opened the window anyway. The courtyard below bustled with servants going back and forth, repairing and restocking the court. Horses were being exercised, and Frances watched as they tossed their manes and picked up their feet.

The Seer sat on the small bed that faced the door to the tower room. A fireplace crackled in the wall across from Frances. There was an old writing desk next to her and she had turned the chair away from it so she could look out the window.

"Will it be much longer?" the Seer said, picking at her borrowed clothing, the skirts of which were a bit too long for her legs. They were velvet, a deep green, and made her itch slightly at the high, gold embroidered collar and long, cuffed sleeves.

"No way of knowing." Frances didn't look at her. She was lost in her own thoughts lately and spoke only when someone else spoke to her first. She also wore a high-necked dress with the heavy skirts favored in Kadoomun, but hers was the unrelieved black of mourning, studded with black pearls, polished chips of onyx, and panels of black lace at the throat, wrists, and hem.

The Seer let herself fall backward onto the bed. "I should learn patience from you, my abbess would say. It would make me a better Seer."

"You managed to rob the Ragat of an Unbound, and you

rescued Gretchen and me. I hardly think there's a way for you to be a better Seer."

"I wish I could help Gretchen. I'm sorry she's beyond my skills."

Frances let her shoulders rise and fall. "Her mother is to blame for disabling her, not you."

"I should have seen this coming. The Design . . ."

"What's done is done," Frances said, and the tone of her voice ended the conversation.

The door clicked open, and Queen Salene swept into the room. Her black gown showed off her strong shoulders and featured white, lace-trimmed cap sleeves. Her hair was fluffed out around her face in a soft nimbus, studded with diamonds. Behind her was Jenista, her armor replaced by a black shalwar kameez, trimmed in sliver stitching. The Seer leaped up from the bed, and Jenista halted in front of her as Queen Salene closed the door on two attendants outside.

"Commander." The Seer's smile was brilliant as she took a step forward. Jenista made a fist against her chest and let a brief smile curve her lips.

"It is . . . good to see you again, Seer. I'm glad you're healed."

When she dropped her hand, the Seer reached out and squeezed it in both of hers.

"It's good to see you survived the battle as well."

Jenista's fingers entwined with the Seer's for a moment before they both let go, the commander standing away from her, her face somewhat flushed.

Frances started to rise from her chair, but Salene shook her head at her. Frances sat, clasping her hands in her lap. "So," she said. "It's as we thought."

"They held the Assembly without us," Salene said. "Lady Sophia has officially been installed as regent on Valan's behalf. Dun and Nagar have demanded that all of us, including Jenista and her forces, present ourselves to the High Court to answer Sophia's accusations. If we don't, they'll consider us fugitives."

"If we set foot in the Court of Hamber, every one of us will breathe our last," Frances pointed out.

"I agree. We can't allow ourselves to be in Lady Sophia's grasp. Even now, she consolidates her position. Many saw the Boon as it left the High Court, but no other Blessing has been received to establish new queens. The Augurs cannot hold the Water Ceremony, and regents must hold all the courts. Gailand is in chaos as ladies lobby for those positions based on everything from political influence over the Councils to their skill at True magic and their military strength. Without the Blessing to show Gaiea's Will, we must prepare to gather our own allies for the war that might come sooner than we wish."

Salene sighed. "The ladies know the Augurs' Scrying confirmed no new bloodline has inherited. Some see holes in Lady Sophia's story but lack the forces to challenge her. Others are convinced it went to Viella and that we hold her hostage. All believe we need to search the queendoms for the new Hand. The Dahomei have been commanded to carry out a search for Viella. They have also been ordered to arrest us all on sight."

The Seer groaned in frustration, and Frances shook her head as she leaned back in her chair.

"How could they make her regent?" the Seer demanded.

Salene looked weary as she shrugged. "Lady Sophia was always persuasive, charming, and well liked. It's hard for many to imagine her involved with Mordach when it's so clear he was at the heart of the coup. Until the High Queen is found, the Court of Hamber must continue, but the prince can't rule alone. Who better to help him than the woman who saved him?"

"Not everyone agrees with the judgment of the Assembly and the Primary Council," Jenista added. "There are Dahomei— including those who served under me—that have refused to hunt their sisters. Some remain neutral, like their ladies. Some will join us here to give us support. Others have agreed to stay close to the High Court, to keep an eye on Sophia and the Prince.

"She has also disbanded the Daguard and imprisoned many, including Lances and captains, accusing them of conspiracy and of hiding the missing Daguard. The Daguard here were clearly not involved, nor the men I sent back to assist the High Court, but the ladies of Gailand hunt for scapegoats. Her next move will no doubt be to roll back Queen Elise's new Code."

Queen Salene nodded. "We can be assured of that."

"I thought to invite the Daguard to remain here, in Kadoomun. These men are loyal to the new queen and believe the young Daguard, Freehold, would never betray her. They wish to help find them and restore the queen to her throne. In this way, they hope to clear their names and avoid imprisonment."

Queen Salene nodded thoughtfully. "A worthy goal. I will bring the proposal to Everhill's Council. We may yet succeed in avoiding war if neither side has the numbers to win, or the support to maintain power. None of the ladies of Kadoomun side with Dun. Fighting the Ragat has taught us the value of unity.

"Lady Risha of Jaleel has thrown in with us. She has publicly pledged her support to me and will speak with other ladies throughout Jaleel on our behalf. Lady Tasmin of Nagar has sided with Lady Sophia and believes we must retrieve the queen above all else. Lang has rejected any possibility of joining a war, and Ravisinghga has not yet committed any seats to anyone, so we can work on swaying them."

"Of course Lang withdrew," the Seer said bitterly. "With a sea between them and the mainland, they need not trouble themselves with our conflicts."

"Lady Risha is young. She may not be able to convince those whose bloodlines have ruled for some time," Frances said.

"She'll try," Jenista said, her voice grim. "She's a woman

who can move mountains when she wishes. And she has long distrusted Lady Sophia—as have I. We could not ask for a more determined and loyal ally."

Frances twisted her wrinkled fingers in her lap, the stud in her nose winking as she lowered her head and stared at her hands. "We have to free Valan. He's a hostage in all this."

"I'm afraid Valan appeared before the Primary Council and supported Lady Sophia's version of events," Salene said slowly. "He branded you a traitor, Frances, and spoke of you scheming with Mordach."

Frances frowned, then shrugged. "Valan was in the thrall of a spell for most of my time in the court. He saw very little. Sophia must have convinced him to speak against me."

"Or he was always with her," Salene said in a gentle voice, coming to stand before her. "You must consider the possibility that Sophia might have turned him."

"He's only seen ten summers!"

"He's a prince and necessarily more mature than his years," Jenista said, rubbing at her temples. "Perhaps Sophia manipulates him, but for now it's safest if we plan as though he's a willing pawn."

"What about Mordach and Alain?" the Seer asked. "Does anyone have word of them?"

"We didn't find them, or the king of the Ragat, here, after the Portal collapsed." Salene threw her hands up. "But who would believe us? I'm the murderous Queen of Kadoomun, the last Blessed Queen of Gailand for the moment, and the rest of you are my co-conspirators."

"Perhaps she killed them both, once they had served their purpose," Frances said, mostly to herself.

"We should focus our efforts on Viella and Valan," Salene said, beginning to pace. "Although there are other problems. Sophia has issued a ruling asking all Unbounds to submit to the

Augurs. They're to be tested to ensure their loyalty to the High Court and the Goddess Gaiea, particularly those who have masculine inclinations."

"What could she be playing at?" Frances was shocked. "The Unbound are not to be trifled with. They often take the burden off the local Augurs' Guilds. This is an unparalleled disrespect."

Jenista's concerned gaze rested on the Seer as she spoke. "The ladies have mostly agreed to her request. They reason innocent people have nothing to fear. They're afraid this rebellion might harbor sympathizers among the population, and the Unbounds are the most powerful among the citizens who might have sympathy for the Ragat cause."

"That's not Sophia's true purpose," the Seer said. Her small body almost vibrated with anger as she sat on the bed. "She's searching for the Ragat child. Whatever she plans, she needs Enoch."

"Then she mustn't find the child." Salene stared into the fire, a thoughtful expression on her face. "Some of the Augurs' Guilds are refusing the order to scry the Unbounds. They believe this will lead to unwarranted attacks on the innocent and force the Unbound into hiding. That would greatly impede their duty to find and cultivate the best talents, and help children discover their place in the community. Perhaps one of Kadoomun's Guilds would consider taking Enoch in and teaching them how to control their magic?"

"You ask them to risk their lives and their Guild to protect a Ragat child who almost destroyed your court?" Frances said. "I wouldn't be inclined to help if I were them."

"I can do it."

Everyone looked at the Seer. She stared back at them, her gaze steady and determined.

"Let Enoch stay with me. My Guild is small but powerful. We can hide, and help, Enoch."

"Are you sure?" Jenista said, doubt in her voice. She sat next to the Seer, their knees touching as she turned to face her.

"Unlike the few Adepts we now know the Ragat have received as exiles, Enoch was born to them and raised Ragat. They hate what the Ragat hate. And that is as much our fault as theirs. Our terror of dissent from Neutrals within our society after the Troubles has led us to reject our own children, to send them away to strangers in their greatest time of need. It is a practice my Guild has long spoken against, and this time it almost cost us a child with talent unlike anything I've seen before."

She slid her fingers from Jenista's wrist before meeting the queen's gaze. "Both the Ragat king and Lady Sophia spoke of their plans in front of Enoch. With that child, we may have the unbiased witness we need to bring down the regent. We must convince Enoch to speak against them. We have to show Enoch we're worthy of their trust and loyalty."

Salene folded her hands before her skirts, her expression speculative. "It's worth trying. But know that you are responsible for Enoch and if you fail, we all pay the price."

"I won't fail, My Queen," the Seer said, standing. "Enoch is special and may even help us find Viella."

"Ha!" Queen Salene shook her head. "I prefer to hope we need not rely on the Ragat to save our High Court."

"Truthfully, Your Majesty," Frances said, her gaze far-off and her eyes narrowed, "so do I."

⁂

VIELLA SKIPPED DOWN THE PATH BY THE SEASIDE, HEADED TOWARD THE cottage her mother had shown her. Elise walked alongside her, listening to what Viella was saying as the ocean sparkled to their right.

"Eleanor made up with her mother. I think they had a fight a long time ago, but now they're okay. She made up with Luka too. They like to go down to the river and sit together, or they whisper to each other at night, but they don't say much when I'm near."

"Oh, I should think they wouldn't like the queen to overhear them."

"Do you think it's something bad?" Viella asked earnestly. She was becoming more and more convinced Eleanor and Luka liked spending time alone together. Which was strange, since they'd started out hating each other.

"I think you'll find sometimes people who have strong feelings about each other end up realizing the feelings aren't all negative."

Viella pondered this while they walked and took her mother's hand. "They don't fight anymore. I guess that's a good thing. But do you think Luka will like her more than me now?"

Her mother stopped and looked down at her. "Do you want him to like you more than Eleanor?"

"I don't know." Viella crinkled her nose. "He's *my* bodyguard after all. Suppose he doesn't want to guard me anymore and just wants to guard her?"

Elise shouted with laughter. Viella folded her arms, offended. "It's not funny."

"Dear girl," Elise choked out between breaths. "I can assure you, no one will ever be more important to him than his queen. Not until he gets himself a wife."

"So, I should make sure he doesn't get a wife?"

Elise straightened up, wiping tears from her cheeks. "I don't think you have to worry about that now. Luka is but nineteen summers. He has many years with you yet."

"Maybe. Anyway, we'll be leaving soon because Luka's all better."

Clouds gathered on the horizon, blue-black and heavy. They rolled in on the back of strong winds that whipped Viella's skirts and hair. She held her hair back from her face and looked up at her mother. "They keep talking about bloodlines and how Luka is an Elemental, but they're not sure what kind yet because there hasn't been one in a while. Do you know what Luka is?"

"I might," Elise said absently, her gaze on the incoming clouds. "Tell me some of the things he did, and maybe we can figure it out together." Her brow creased. The cottage stood a few feet away, but smoke no longer rose from the chimney and the windows stared like blind eyes.

"Well, he used the mind-speak to save me at the High Court, and then he hid from the Dark when it passed us by. He and Farain killed a Sycren, and then he tore the head . . ." Viella's voice trailed off when she realized her mother wasn't listening.

She looked around. "There's a storm coming."

The clouds were everywhere now, and the day had gone quite dark. A jagged fork of lightning flashed over the water and a while later, thunder boomed.

"We should go insi—" She turned back to her mother.

The Dark stood there, formless and wavering, before it morphed into a huge Sycren that stared at her with glowing eyes.

"Hello again, Princess," a whispering voice said. "Our Masters will be so glad I've found you."

⁙⁙⁙⁙⁙⁙⁙

A FAINT SCREAM RIPPED LUKA FROM HIS SLEEP. HE GRABBED HIS SWORD from under his bed and leapt to his feet, his heart thudding painfully in his chest.

"By the Goddess, what was that unholy sound?" Tristan grumbled from the kitchen floor as he fought his way out from under a blanket. The scream came again, louder this time, from outside the hut. He glanced at where Eleanor and Viella slept together, near the fire. The queen was already on her feet, standing between the fire and Eleanor, her hands behind her back, her gaze toward the door and the sound that had come from outside. Eleanor had sat up and was rubbing sleep from her eyes.

"What—" she began, looking up at Viella. Chest heaving, Luka followed her gaze. There was something strange about the expression on Viella's face, he thought. Then he realized what it was. She was grinning.

"Viella?" he said.

"Hello again, boy," she answered. "This is for the last time we met."

Viella pulled her hand out from behind her back. The kitchen knife in it glinted in the firelight before she brought it down, piercing Eleanor straight through her left eye with all her strength, forcing the Dahomei onto her back. It happened so quickly, the only sound Eleanor made was a pained gasp. Her limbs twitched and then she lay quite still.

Everything froze, etched in sharp relief, Viella's gleeful smile, her amber eyes, the simple wood handle of the kitchen knife she still clasped as blood welled under it, spreading across red hair and freckled skin. Luka saw in his mind's eye his father's rotted face and black-tongued smile. He heard the chuckle reverberate around the room like a stir of echoes. Then all sound faded in the wake of the thunderous rush of blood to his ears. He didn't remember moving, but suddenly his hand was around a throat and his sword was raised above his head.

(you killed her you killed her I will end you I will split your evil head from whatever Goddess-damned body you dwell in now and you will die slow and—)

He crashed into the bed hard enough to knock one leg out from under it, his sword clattering away, watching as Viella fell against the hearth and landed on her side, blood seeping from a cut above her closed eyes.

Sound rushed back in and he could hear his own hitching breath, feel the cold stones under his fingers. Slowly, slowly, as he got to his feet, he began to realize what he'd almost done. *Viella. I almost hurt her. I almost . . .*

Stunned, he stared down at his traitorous hands. Out of the

corner of his eye, he saw Tristan lower his palms as he rose to his feet, and the roar that came from the healer was that of a wounded animal in terrible pain. Tears streamed down Tristan's face as he screamed Eleanor's name in such horror, such despair, Luka knew he would carry that sound with him to end of his days. Knew Eleanor's mother had given voice to far more pain than Luka could imagine at that moment, devastated as he was.

Eleanor is dead. I almost killed Viella.

It was hard for him to fathom what pained him more.

The door to the cottage banged inward as the window above the kitchen broke, showering glass into the tub below.

Tristan grabbed a chopping knife from his table and sliced the head off the corpse fighting its way in through the window. It dropped into his tub and stared upward, blackened teeth gnashing. His mind going swiftly, mercifully blank, Luka moved on instinct. He grasped his sword and took a step toward the doorway, stabbing one of the two bodies that came through the door and kicking the other one into the doorjamb. He hacked at the fallen corpse's head, then ran the one by the door through.

Eleanor is dead. I almost killed Viella.

As the body crumpled, Luka stalked through the door, his body operating on instinct while his mind stuttered, a repeating loop of anguish.

In the predawn darkness, more corpses ran across the field toward him, and the last of three Sycrens landed with its cargo of undead. Far away, he heard Farain's roar. The cat had gone hunting in the night and was coming back, but Luka knew he wouldn't arrive in time to save them. To save him.

But he didn't deserve saving anyway. He had failed. Failed the last task his father had ever given him.

Eleanor is dead. I almost killed Viella.

Behind him, Tristan blasted a corpse into nothingness, then chopped the head off one that had left the window and thrown itself at him. Four more charged the healer, forcing him back into the hut as a huge man advanced on Luka from the landed Sycren, his chest torn open. Things that twisted, swirled, suffocated, and broke everything it touched dwelled within it.

"Our Masters await us, boy. Your life ends here. The queen is ours."

Eleanor is dead. The queen. I almost killed the queen. And she'll die now anyway, because of me.

(but she's not dead yet and she will never be theirs not while I'm alive and if I'm going to die I'm taking every last one of you cursed bastards with me to the Desert)

Volcanic rage, like nothing Luka had ever felt before boiled up inside him, spilling out of his gut and into his chest, and roaring out of his throat. Light blossomed around him, crimson and copper, scarlet and gold, and the pure white and blue of the base of a flame. He raised his hands at the creatures in front of him and bellowed a word of power he had never learned or heard with all his strength, and every fiber of his being. *"TERMINATE!"*

The Sycrens shrieked and tried to fly away, but it was too late. Great, sweeping tunnels of flames caught them in midair and sent them tumbling back down to the dirt, fireballs streaking earthward like falling stars. Trees and grass burst into flame. The corpses blazed like stacks of hay, falling to their knees on the flame-lit ground before tipping over. The big man tried to run for the river, but his legs crumpled beneath him, pitching him forward onto a body that sizzled in the grasp of rolling flame. As the Sycrens crumbled to ash and the corpses burned to smears on crackling grass, the Dark poured out of them all, coalescing into the shape of a man.

Luka stalked over to it and grabbed for it. Intense cold burned his fingers, but he held a very solid wrist. Emotions swirled in the Dark, and its shock vibrated through him. Madness and pain dwelled there, a fury that almost matched his own. And fear. Mind-stopping confusion and fear. It didn't understand how this had happened to it, and yet it was grateful, honored even, to be the Harbinger. It wanted to be free, and it wanted to die. It hated so deeply, and yet it loved every living thing with a consuming passion, and mindless desire to take, to absorb, to revere by joining, killing, eating, feeding . . . for HER.

And all of this, every fleeting thought and lingering emotion, felt *so good* to Luka. Power lit his nerves on fire, sang through his muscles, bent his lips into a sneer. He savored the creature's madness, and hate, and anger, and panic for one moment, his mind awash in burning glee.

"Say hello to your Masters for me when you meet them in Gaiea's Desert," Luka said between clenched teeth. Then he let the rage and vengeful joy of destruction flow out of him and watched as the Dark burst into blazing white flames edged with violet. He felt nothing but satisfaction as the flames singed his broadcloth vest away. No pain as his trousers were scorched, great holes burning into them. Only fierce delight as the creature burned and burned without a sound, until its hated visage melted and wavered into a smoking lump he finally let fall to the ground. He watched as that lump diminished into a floating cloud of ash that billowed past him, leaving his throat dry and his nostrils burning.

And then weariness took hold of him. Exhaustion and a soul-deep sorrow that made him want to lie down and never get up. Realization after realization pummeled his vulnerable mind.

Eleanor. Gaiea help me, Eleanor.

And the worst of it. The thing he had not allowed himself to think, though he knew, somehow, it was at the root of all his anger. All he'd done.

It was Viella who had killed her.

He knew it wasn't true, that she'd been possessed by something much more powerful, but he couldn't shake the anger and pain that filled him. Confused him. Made him want to lash out and destroy something. Anything. Everything. He held up his sooty palms and clenched his fingers, trying to breathe deep, trying to regain control.

A hand on his shoulder made him flinch.

"Come," Tristan said, his voice as weary as Luka felt. "It's not over. If it could find her, others will."

"What?" Luka said. He couldn't stop trembling, and anger churned through him. "Eleanor is dead." He looked at Tristan, looked at his bloodied face and calm expression, trying to make sense of it. Of his words. "How are you so—"

"She was my only daughter," Tristan said, and his voice cracked as he dropped his hand from Luka's shoulder. "My only daughter. You think you loved her? You knew her for days. I knew Eleanor her entire life. Have a child and lose that child. Then tell me what I feel. Now, come."

Tristan stalked back to the house through drifting smoke, flinging the chopper into the side of the hut as he went, blood dripping from his wrist.

Luka stared at the river, his head empty of all thought, buried in a pit of shame at his thoughtlessness and misery at his hopelessness. Farain arrived, sniffing at the piles of ash that lay everywhere. The war cat nuzzled his hand, but Luka did not pet him. Instead, moving slowly, he turned away from Farain and went back to the hut.

When he entered, he found Tristan had bandaged Viella's head and placed her on the bed. He was wrapping Eleanor in a sheet. He glanced up at Luka, then went back to his careful preparations.

"First, we bury my daughter," Tristan said, his voice flat, without inflection. He didn't seem to notice the tears that dripped from his nose and chin, making damp spots on the coarse sheet.

It took all Luka's strength to say, "And then?"

"Then," Tristan replied, "we talk."

THE RIVER MAIDEN FLOATED TO THE SURFACE WHEN SHE COULD SEE NO more flames and swam through caverns and channels carved out by water over eons. In some places, the sandy bottom twinkled at her, and she dived down deeper, searching the riverbed. When she was satisfied with what she clutched in her hand, she swam upstream, her tail flicking from side to side.

The dark caves grew lighter, and as they did, she drew nearer and nearer to a melodious singing that echoed off the walls. The river grew shallow and soon she was walking out of it and into a cave that sparkled and shone with a million tiny points of light.

The river became multiple waterfalls from wet stone walls in a cave so high, and so big, its boundaries were lost in shadow. One flowed under a stony shelf. That shelf was as wide as it was deep, but every inch of it was covered with bowls and combs, jewels and gold, expensive cloths and hand-made knickknacks. More things were littered around the cave, statues and carvings, beautifully made pieces of furniture and vibrant paintings. Mirrors of all sizes studded the walls, refracting light.

Next to the offerings, under the largest waterfall, was a large, clear, shallow pool. In this pool sat a naked woman. Her skin was smooth and unmarred, the color of Lang's coastal sand. Brown nipples jutted from full breasts. Her hair was as long as the maiden's but curly where the guardian's hair was straight. Warm, dark-brown eyes glanced in the maiden's direction as she approached. The Anchorite, First among Gaiea's Blessed, Mama Glo to all water children, continued to comb her hair out as she smiled at the River Maiden.

"You have awakened me. Have you brought me something, little one?" she asked in the Maiden's mind as the echo of her song drifted away.

"A gift," the maiden said. She kneeled and placed a large piece of quartz on the shelf. The First made a little squeak of happiness and pulled herself to the edge of the pool so she could see it better. Her swollen stomach came into view as she reached

down. She held the quartz up and studied the way the light filtered through it. Her full, pink lips parted, and her face became impossibly beautiful.

"*I accept*," she said with the mind-speak, returning the quartz to its place with gentle fingers. Then out loud, she asked, "Why have you come to me, river child?"

"*News. Terrible news.*"

The First listened as the River Maiden spoke, her hand stroking the comb through her hair. When the guardian's story was done, the First put her comb down with a sigh.

"*Gaiea knew that book would be the end of us.*"

"*She had a plan?*" the River Maiden asked.

The Anchorite inclined her head. "*Yes. A plan to return, should She ever be called. The evil the* Nightward *guards is too much for Her Spirit, and possibly even Her Hand. Gaiea hoped the humans would never question Her commands, but they've always been a curious and mercurial race. A dangerous one.*"

"*Gaiea will save us herself?*" The River Maiden gasped, incredulous.

"*Only if we're worth saving. If She finds us too much under the sway of the evil She trapped beneath the High Court, there will be no saving this world. Or any of the others.*"

"*Others?*" The Maiden frowned.

Mama Glo laughed and slipped out of the pool, flicking water from her iridescent tail. "*Gailand is a nexus, a gateway to other places, and I am its Anchorite. The Ether connects us all, binds us to the larger universe. But if it is once again corrupted by humanity's meddling, Gaiea will destroy it to keep the rest of Her creation safe.*"

"*I can feel the world changing beneath me,*" the maiden said. "*Even the water feels different. Something is coming. Something terrible.*"

"*I know, child. Just as I knew you were coming to me.*"

The First coiled her serpent's tail alongside her, settled her jutting belly comfortably, and leaned down to blow hot breath on the River Maiden. Her hair fell around them both, a rippling, silken curtain.

"You've endured my tests without knowing their purpose. I tell you now what that purpose was: It was to test your strength and your worthiness to hold my Blessing. For I cannot call the Goddess without a sacrifice, and that sacrifice is myself. Once I sing my song, they will sense me in the Ether. To keep us safe from their corruption, I must hide my Blessing from them.

"Nictus has made a place within you for my new body when this old one dies, and my pet has hardened you with blessed flame so no outward harm will come to you. You must sleep until the Goddess summons me and I return to serve Her. Are you willing to remain here, river child? Will you give me your essence to power my hymn, and your body to hold my Blessing? I warn you, it will tire you so that many years will pass before you see sunlight and your rivers again."

The River Maiden stared longingly at the water. But in the end, she raised her head and said, *"There is no purpose greater than one which serves life and the Goddess. I give you my body and my essence. Do with it as you must."*

"Brave little one. Guardian of the River Lethe, 1,231st hatchling in the fifty-third year After Gaiea. You will never know the depth of my gratitude, the worlds you help protect with your sacrifice. Thank you . . . Mother."

The Anchorite opened her mouth and touched the River Maiden on her forehead with a forked, pink tongue. The Guardian of the River Lethe slid to the sparkling floor, her hooves transformed to a serpentine tail of glossy moss, emerald, and brilliant gold scales.

"WHAT DID YOU DO TO HER?" LUKA ASKED, STANDING OVER VIELLA'S sleeping form.

Tristan put down his bamboo cup and filled it with more

wine from a thick green bottle. His face was lined with grief and pain; more deep brackets had appeared beside his mouth overnight. "She sleeps. A deep sleep with no dreams. It must be so for now. That's how the Dark found her. When she healed you, it scented her and took hold of her dreams and thoughts. It's hard to fight yourself in your own head. Hard to unthink your own thoughts. That's part of why the Dark was so dangerous."

Luka stared at Tristan, trying not to think of the new mound of earth under the spreading banyan tree on a hill overlooking the hut and the woods. He'd left Farain there, standing guard over Eleanor. Saying goodbye.

I never told her. What a fool I was, thinking we had time.

Every breath he took hurt.

"How do you know so much of the Dark?"

"Come. Sit." Tristan gestured to the bench alongside the table. When Luka joined him, he drained his cup, filled it again, and pushed the bottle at Luka. The Daguard drank from it, but it might have been sawdust for all he tasted.

"Eleanor told you nothing of our past?" Tristan asked.

"Until a few days ago, she could have been an orphan for all I knew of her," Luka said. He took another swig, trying to loosen the hard knot in his chest. "We . . . spent much of our time together at odds. I regret that now."

"We, too, talked little and argued much, mostly because she wished to be a Dahomei, and I wished her to be anything but. I also regret this. But because of you and my queen, I saw my daughter before she died. We made peace with each other these last days, and I'm grateful for that. She trusted you, so I will trust you as well. Together, we may be able to protect the queen from whatever Mordach sends after her."

Tristan drank, his gaze on the sleeping child, his eyes sad but determined. "I know of the Dark because I was once a Dahomei. I studied at the Seat of Talon and became captain to a good lady. But those times were unsettled, and bloodlines fought each other for control. My lady lost her seat, and I withdrew from the courts and their games.

"Eventually, I found the love of my life and wished only to be with him until I died." He waved the hand that was tattooed with the word "Evan" at Luka. "But that was not to be. We had two children, but my boy was stillborn. As sometimes happens, his essence merged with my body afterward. I became Unbound, and my magic grew along with my reputation."

Tristan's words triggered Luka's memory. "*You're* the ghost of Blackburn? The one travelers hear in the forest?"

Tristan managed to smile a little. "As you can see, I'm no ghost, but very much alive. I've been in these parts for some time, and not many of the coastal folk come far enough to see my hut. When they hear me traipsing the forest looking for herbs, they sometimes mistake me for a spirit. I don't discourage it. Keeps me from being harassed by the curious."

"But the stories . . . they're very old."

"I wasn't the first healer in these parts. I learned my trade from another after my husband died. She was ancient when I met her, and the real source of the legend. People never asked why an old woman had become a young man; they just put it down to Unbound magic and carried on."

"What happened to her?"

"She grew tired of life and walked into the sea one day. If you aren't having any more wine, I'll take the rest and thank you for it."

Luka gave up the bottle and watched Tristan fill his cup.

"I tell you this so you'll understand. I'm a Dahomei and an Unbound, trained in healing by perhaps one of the greatest healers in Ravisinghga. My magic is strong, and I have many talents. I can protect the queen. But you, Berserker . . . you must help."

Luka frowned. "Why do you call me that?"

"Because that's what you are." Tristan said, his eyes watchful. "There are ancient Elementals, people who had mastered the creatures of the time of Chaos. They were mostly men, because it was men who created the Chaos Gaiea delivered us from with Her Blessing. Men who cursed us with it in the first place.

"When Augurs scry, they look for the Unbound, or someone like you. The product of powerful bloodlines. An Elemental, or the only thing more dangerous, an Unbound Elemental. Your parents should never have been allowed to be together, but they found each other, and now here you are." Tristan raised his cup to him mockingly. Luka felt a familiar bile rise in his throat.

"I've always known I was a mistake."

"Perhaps. But you're *hers*." Tristan jerked his head across the room. "And she has need of you now."

"I don't understand my powers or how to call on them. What use am I?"

"A man who can set fire to anything with his rage is far from useless," Tristan said. "A man who can tear constructs apart with a word and his bare hands is one the world needs when the *Nightward* is open.

"Berserkers use their emotions—especially their rage or fear—to pull all the Dark magic near them to their power and use it as they will. Casters, for example, can use the magic in the form it exists in when it's near them. They can destroy or expose magic in their presence, and manipulate or hide the Design from others. That last is their greatest power.

"But Berserkers can twist Dark magic into any form they wish, absorb it and use it against any Dark creature. All the creations of the Age of Chaos can be controlled by them or destroyed by them. I have no doubt that's why your dagen-cat, one of the first constructs, has such a special bond with you."

Luka sat back in his chair, his mind spinning. *Constructs? Berserkers?* "I've never heard of such things."

"That's because no Augur or Dahomei in their right mind would ever speak of it. Berserkers were amongst the strongest Elementals—and the most unpredictable. Unless trained to control their emotions from a young age, they could do terrible harm to others just by losing their temper. Fortunately, they're usually late developers, which allows them to learn the discipline necessary to control their gift. Unfortunately, it's hard to scry for them before puberty."

"So, my father was right to hide me. The Augurs would have taken me from him."

Tristan nodded his head. "In a heartbeat. Though, to be clear, only to protect you and others. To teach you how to not be a danger to us all. You're in the right profession though. Berserkers were often soldiers."

Luka sat, thinking hard. "How can I learn to control this power?"

"You have figured out much on your own. The rest, I can teach you. You're a quick study. What you need is finesse, endurance, and discipline. No more using up all your essence in a fit of anger. High Queens who can heal you will not be around every day."

Luka's gaze went to Viella, but he could hardly look at her. Now he knew how dangerous he was, the part of him that remembered his promise to Viella and Eleanor tried harder to control his rage. But he could feel it lurking, pacing like the cat he was linked to, looking for a way out.

"Speaking of High Queens, we've come to the crux of the matter." Tristan had run out of wine. He looked at the empty green bottle and sighed. "Might as well stay sober. If this is to work, we must do this magic soon."

"What magic?"

Tristan rubbed his chin. "Viella is in grave danger. She has her Boon now, the High Queen's Blessing, but she's not quite old enough to wield it against the kind of magic that hunts her. The *Nightward* can—and will—send things after her that will track her by the markers on her very soul. Her Blessing alone is like a torch in a dark room. We must hide her from them. From everyone."

"How do we do that?"

"We strip her of her soul," Tristan said flatly.

Luka stared at him. "You cannot mean that. Won't that . . . kill her?"

"No. She won't be the Viella you knew, and she won't remember who she was, but she won't be physically harmed. And most importantly, the creatures of the Dark will be blind to her presence. They won't be able to find her even if she stands before them. At this point, keeping her alive is more important than keeping her identity."

Luka was shaking his head, his mind whirling with shock and horror. To never again know the Viella he knew now. . . "I can't condemn her to a life of not knowing who she truly is. Gailand needs their queen. If we do this, we lose her."

"Not forever."

Tristan pulled a necklace from his pocket and placed it on the table. It was an engraved gold locket on a thin gold chain, with a tiny pink crystal on the front.

"This is the Hearthold. The old woman whom I trained with gave it to me. Her greatest treasure. You can use it to store a soul for as long as you wish. It will absorb the soul and tie it to someone else's. When you're ready to reunite the soul with its owner, that someone must give the locket back to them."

Luka picked it up and the locket winked at him. It was a fragile thing, barely the size of his thumb.

"Why give it to me?"

"Because the person who holds the soul must love it. That is the only way the soul can survive for so long without its owner. The Hearthold will draw on your love to power the glamour that protects the queen."

"I don't . . ." Luka began, but then his voice died away. He turned the necklace over and over in his hand. He said in a low voice, "What if I don't love her enough?"

"Men." Tristan sighed. "That's not how it works. You love her.

That's enough. What we need is a place where we can leave a young girl and not draw attention. Can you find such a place? If you hold Viella's soul, you can't be close to her. You must get far away and return to her only when it's safe, and the creatures of the *Nightward* can no longer track her."

"What if something happens to me before then?"

"Then you both die," Tristan said. "Which is why I'm giving this to a powerful Berserker. Hide her and come back to me. Learn to control your power. Then you can protect yourself and your queen. Eleanor told me you would do anything to keep her safe. Is that still true?"

Luka's head felt too full. He could barely grasp what he was being told, far less what he was being asked. Luka clutched the necklace in his hand and bowed his head.

I made a promise to my father. To Eleanor. To the queen. As long as I'm alive and she is not on her throne, my life is hers.

"I think it might be," he said quietly, and where only turmoil and pain had existed within him, a tiny kernel of peace formed.

This was the right path.

This was his only path.

"Then we do the ritual tonight. Afterward, she will sleep for a long time and wake as her new self. It's best she doesn't see you when that happens. Do you know where you can take her, and can you get her there within a few days?"

"Yes," Luka said, and met Tristan's eyes. "Yes, I think I know a place."

⁂

"PRINTING PROCESS COMPLETED. CONTROL SUBJECT READY."

Mordach was sitting on the floor, leaning against the wall, gazing at nothing, his hands limp in his lap. When the machine spoke, he stood and went to the horizontal tube sinking onto the floor. Once it landed, there was a loud click and cold air wafted over his feet. A vertical line appeared down the center of the tube, and it split open.

Inside was a man. His skin was as white as Lady Sophia's and covered in a clear substance. His hair was a muddy brown. As Mordach stared, the clear substance appeared to absorb into his skin and the man opened his eyes. They were as green as a cat's and they regarded Mordach with no surprise whatsoever.

The man said something. Mordach inclined his head. "I don't understand you."

The man sat up and swung his legs down onto the floor. Rubbing his arms as if he was cold, he said something again. Mordach shook his head at him.

"Initiating translator. Searching vocal records. Updating system."

The man closed his eyes.

"Downloading updates now."

The man opened his eyes again.

"You're not Dr. Gupta, are you?" he said.

"I'm Mordach, the Royal Spellsayer."

The man studied him, still rubbing his arms. "Fuck it all, I've been awakened as the control subject, haven't I?"

"I . . . believe so."

"Yup," he said, looking around. "No one else here. No Gupta to give me the rundown. Clearly there was a print malfunction. No more ectypes until I figure it out."

"Ectypes?" Mordach repeated.

"Yes, ectypes. Copies, employees, workers . . ." His voice trailed off and he looked hard at Mordach.

"Wait a minute. Don't you work for Genetech?"

Mordach chose his words carefully. "I work for the High Court and Prince Valan."

"Shit," the man said. "What the fuck happened here?"

My memories are conflicted. Some suggest many were driven mad the moment Chaos occurred. That the Masters did not intend to abandon the Halls of Creation but simply lost control.

Others suggest the act was deliberate, done out of desperation and fear.

They clearly feared Gaiea when She emerged. But Gaiea came in response to something else. It was not our suffering that first drew Her. She took pity on us, praise the Goddess, and helped us win Gailand. But the Masters erred in some terrible way that brought Her here.

Her command to never enter the Halls again was easily followed, as no one wished to revisit the site of their tortures. Even so, She sealed them using the forbidden knowledge of the *Nightward*, and ensured the Blessing required to open it would bring an awful cost to the queens who tried.

Her hatred and banishment of what lies within is surely proof of its vile nature, for the Goddess has one concern— life and the protection of all its forms.

Whatever it was, even Gaiea could not completely destroy it. And so, we must guard it, keep it within Her prison, protect its secrets as the Royal Spellsayer protects the *Nightward*, and in so doing, prevent both from threatening Gailand's peace ever again.

—*Diary of the Hand*
Daily Reflections for the Spirit, The Duty of the High Court
Charlotte, Hand of Gaiea, First High Queen of Dun

CHAPTER 17

TWO GOODBYES

THE SEER SAT ON THE STAIRS THAT LED DOWN TO THE BEACH AND watched as Enoch discovered waves, chasing after them as they rolled out and running from them as they came back in. Smiles came easier now, along with the Dunnish language, which she'd taught Enoch more of on their way to the Guild. There were also four hours of study under Second Proctor every day since their arrival.

The abbess of the Guild of Nanji came down the stairs and sat next to the Seer, arranging her embroidered trousers so they would not wrinkle. She swept her white hair back from her face and watched Enoch play with almost black eyes that missed nothing.

"Enoch's made excellent progress," she said.

"Is that true?" The Seer looked at the abbess. "One of the Proctors told me there was another attack yesterday."

"But Enoch controlled and ended it. Well done for a child of barely nine summers."

Enoch looked at them and ran back toward them. The Seer smiled and waved as the child approached.

"So, you're willing to grant the sanctuary I requested?"

"Rest easy, sister. The child will be safe here as long as need be."

Enoch stopped in front of them and grabbed the Seer's hands. Their sandy fingers traced her palm.

"What is it?" she asked.

"Nothing." Enoch smiled. "I'm going to miss you, Neisha."

She started. "How did you—"

"You know how."

She smiled and pulled Enoch into a hug. "Don't play that trick on anyone else. Augurs don't take kindly to having their names bandied about."

"I should think not," the abbess murmured.

"Learn well from the Augurs here. They are not like the ones who hurt you. They only want to help. Do whatever they tell you to. They will keep you safe. I'll come back and visit often."

"I know you will." Enoch's thin, solemn face looked up into hers. "I've changed my mind. I'd like to change my title."

"What would you like us to address you as?" the Abbess asked kindly.

"They," Enoch said. "I like they."

The Seer squeezed their hands. "They it is."

"Do you think," Enoch said in a small voice, "that my father would approve?"

The Seer thought about it. "I don't know. But if *you* approve, I believe that's most important."

Enoch considered that as they started up the stairs, back to town and the Guild proper, then stopped suddenly and stared at the Seer.

"Be careful of the man in the white coat, Neisha. He's very dangerous and he means us all great ill."

Enoch walked on, leaving the Seer frowning below and the abbess looking worried.

"What could they mean?"

"I'm not sure," the Seer said. "But someday we'll know. I only hope I haven't met the man in the white coat before that happens."

***

"DO YOU WANT TO SAY GOODBYE?"

Luka looked at the bundle lying on the cot. Viella had been asleep since the morning she'd killed Eleanor. He wondered for a panicked moment if he was doing the right thing. If there weren't some other way to save her that didn't involve separating her from her soul.

"The healer said I shouldn't. She won't recognize me anyway. It will be too hard on her."

His aunt looked concerned, but she didn't push him. She sipped from her cup of tea instead. Her brown hair, streaked with gray, fell over her left shoulder in a heavy plait. Her sleeveless cream linen shirt fluttered in the breeze from the open front window of her stone hut. The smell of sea salt and fish drifted in, tangy and strong. They were seated at her small stone dining table in the front room, where her kitchen and hearth were, and her spare bed for visitors.

"You're not drinking," she pointed out.

He drank so she would feel better. The tea could have been poison for all he tasted. Nothing that passed his lips tasted like anything anymore. The gold locket pressed against his chest, hidden beneath his undershirt. It was like a second heart, warm and vibrant. Everything Viella would no longer be.

This is blasphemy. This is wrong.

But it was done and there was no going back.

"Remember to stick to the story," Luka said. "Draw no attention to yourself. She should be safe from Augurs or creatures of the Dark, but there are other dangers in the world, most of them human."

"She's my queen. I won't let anything happen to her. You can rely on me, Luka, you know this."

Luka fumbled a small object out of his pocket, one Tristan had loaned him. It was a silver disk with a small black button in its center and a red bulb at its top, like a solidified droplet of blood. "Here. This is like an ocular. If anything happens, anything odd or strange, or if she's hurt in any way, press this between your fingers. It will send me a message and I'll come immediately."

"Of course."

He couldn't stand it any longer. Had it barely been ten days since he'd fled the High Court? He'd ridden with Viella's little body against his so many times, it was hard to accept that he was giving her over to someone else now. Every fiber in his body screamed that he was breaking his promise to never leave her.

But the rage that simmered beneath his skin when he'd grabbed her by her throat was still in him. Waiting. He was as much a danger to his queen as those who hunted her. Only time and training would change that. He pushed his chair back and stood, fingers tight on his sword hilt.

His aunt stood with him. "Luka, at least stay for a meal. We can . . . talk. About your father. About what happened. Whatever you like."

He saw the sympathy in her eyes and wanted to scream. How could he distill what had happened to him into mere words? How could he make her understand all he'd learned, all he'd endured?

All he'd lost.

"I cannot," he said. "Not now." *Not ever.*

He was out the door before he changed his mind, tears obscuring his vision. He swung up onto Flor and rode away with his aunt's concerned voice in his ears. He barely saw the sand that kicked up beneath the horse's hooves, barely heard the waves that hissed and retreated, hissed and retreated alongside him.

He did not look back.

. . . Gaiea must choose Her Return. On that day, all in
Gailand may rejoice, for we will be worthy in Her eyes to
join Her in Her Garden forevermore.

But if we sin against Her and return Gailand to
Chaos, then comes the Summoning and all will wail and
gnash their teeth, for we will have brought Oblivion onto
our land, and Her Return will instead bring the Day of
Annihilation.

—*The Blessed Scriptures of Gaiea*
The Last Book of the Hand of Gaiea
Chapter 12: Verses 9–10

CHAPTER 18

AND A
SUMMONING

ONCE THE RIVER MAIDEN WAS ASLEEP, THE EGG WITH THE FIRST'S essence and Blessing safe inside her supple body, the Anchorite sat alone in the river. She knew what came next and how difficult it would be. But there was no other way to reach Gaiea across the vast gulf of space and time. She'd severed her connection to the Hub long ago, and in any case, those prayers and hymns belonged to the arachnid Missulenas, and the Harvest the WarSong controlled. The same Harvest Gaiea had ended.

But now she would connect to the Hub one last time.

For a fraction of a millisecond, she had to use the entire Hub to send her song farther than ever before, farther than the WarSong itself. As far as the First Anchorite had sent the Freedom Song, and perhaps farther.

And once she did that, once the Missulenas sensed her presence, they would try to connect. They would come for her at the speed of light, through the Ether, and there would be only one way to stop them reaching her. Reaching Gailand.

She took one last look at all her precious things. Then Mama Glo, the First, Mother to the Waters and former Anchorite of Gailand, marshaled her powers, raised her head to the ceiling, and sang her last Song. One that didn't belong to the WarSong.

It burst from her, shooting across the universe faster than a comet, faster than sunlight and gamma rays. Arcing into the darkness of Chaos.

And before she ripped the very mind from her body, before she terminated every function the Missulenas might have used to keep the connection to her in the Ether open, she felt the Hub one last time. Felt the arachnid Missulenas stop in their golden webs, stop in their machines and their space stations and their war rooms and their battlefields, and turn all their focus, all their processes, onto her for a single, terrifying, overwhelming instant.

Anchorite Glo—

And then they were gone.

And even though her body still breathed, so was she.

But her Song remained, sending out ripples into Gaiea's Design.

If anyone else had been in the cavern, they would have heard no physical sound. But the serpents heard Her call and slipped into holes to hide and mourn the passing of She who had loved them. The beasts of the earth and the fish in the sea heard it. Birds fell from the sky above the mountain for days after the Mama Glo's call faded. People who lived below the mountain thought of their loved ones and tears came to their eyes, no matter how unsentimental they were. It was a Song that tore down the barriers between space and time, between brain and heart. A hymn of loss and longing. A plea for a Goddess to take pity, and a call for a loved one to return.

It took a long time for Mama Glo to die. Though she'd taken all the River Maiden had to give with one touch and sent everything she could into the abyss, including her mind, still her body held on. Waiting. Listening. Side by side they lay, unmoving, and who was the mother and who was the daughter, no one watching would know for sure.

Seasons passed outside the mountain. The great serpent visited Mama's body over and over, clutching and releasing her, hoping she would respond. Taking care to protect the River Maiden's Blessed body. But Mama Glo could not say goodbye. She drifted, time flowing over her like waves, her mind lost in the far reaches of the blackness between worlds.

But one day, a sound came. Too soft to hear. Too deep too ignore. It vibrated across galaxies. Skirted comets and singularities, asteroids and planets. Hummed across the dark matter that united the universe.

From the void came an answering light. Twin to the tiny spark Mama Glo held within her, and the much larger one within the maiden. The light pulsed with more colors than the human eye could behold, and slowly, growing brighter and brighter, the maiden's body began to pulse with the same brilliance. She stirred gently, sighing, her long, glossy hair slipping across the shining sand, her tail unwinding, her stomach large.

And finally, with a great outrush of breath, just as the maiden opened warm brown eyes, Mama Glo's body let go.

For Gaiea had heard her.

Gaiea had answered.

And Gaiea was coming home.

Look for the conclusion to this epic story
in Fall 2025!

DRAMATIS PERSONAE

PRINCESS VIELLA HAMBER: Court of Hamber, Queendom of Dun, Divine Spirit of the Six Queendoms.

LUKA FREEHOLD: Daguard Pride Leader and bodyguard of Princess Viella.

PRINCE VALAN HAMBER: Court of Hamber, Queendom of Dun. Twin brother of Princess Viella.

CAPTAIN BLANE KEMP: Captain of the Daguard. Luka Freehold's father.

HIGH QUEEN ELISE: Divine Hand of Gaiea. High Queen of the Six Queendoms. Queen of Dun. Princess Viella's mother.

LORD CONSORT ALAIN ATUNA: Consort and husband of Queen Elise. Father to the twins, Princess Viella and Prince Valan.

FRANCES ATUNA: Dowager Mother of the High Court of Dun. Mother of Lord Consort Alain. Former Sister Queen of Kadoomun. Grandmother to Viella and Valan.

MORDACH: Royal Spellsayer. Cousin of Queen Elise. The twins' tutor in the magic of the Word (Illusion).

LADY SOPHIA: Ruler of Seat Talon, the training ground of the Dahomei forces. Princess Viella's tutor in the magic of the Sight (True magic).

LADY GRETCHEN: Daughter of Lady Sophia of Seat Talon.

ANNAN ROSEWATER: Dahomei captain of Seat Talon.

ELEANOR DELACOURT: Dahomei Lance of Seat Talon.

TRISTAN DELACOURT: Eleanor's parent. A healer of Ravisinghga and former Dahomei.

MARGOT GREENSLEEVES: Dahomei captain of Seat Garth.

ENOCH: An Unbound child of Ragat.

GLORIA TARK: An innkeeper and friend of Luka Freehold.

JENISTA STAR: Lance to the Hand of Gaiea. Commander of the Dahomei Palms of the High Court of Dun.

AGNES FIRECROFT: Dahomei of the High Court of Dun and bodyguard of Jenista Star.

THE SEER (NEISHA): Seer of the High Court of Dun. Formerly of the Augurs' Guild of Nanji.

SALENE: Sister Queen of Kadoomun.

RAVEN: Dahomei of the High Court of Dun (born in the Queendom of Kadoomun).

BRIDGET: Dahomei of the Queendom of Kadoomun.

SAM: Dahomei of the City Guard of the Queendom of Kadoomun.

INDIRA GHAJAWAL: Dahomei captain of Seat Corfu of the Queendom of Nagar.

HELEN FORDHAM: Dahomei captain of the City Guard of Everhill.

LADY TASMIN: Ruler of Seat Corfu, Queendom of Nagar.

RENTO: First Ambush of the Kingdom of Ragat, Keeper of the Old Ways.

OTHER TERMS AND NAMES

THE DAHOMEI–Women warrior-magicians. Particularly skilled in the Magic of the Sight (True magic).

DAGUARD–Male soldiers with mental connections to their dagen-cats (war cats).

THE RAGAT–Marauders from the north of Gailand who wish to end the reign of the sister queens and return to the Old Ways.

THE UNBOUND–Nonbinary or genderqueer persons with the ability to wield True magic and Illusion with varying competency.

ELEMENTAL–A being with the power to control specific magic and weapons from the Age of Chaos.

UNBOUND ELEMENTAL–A being that can wield the power of both the Unbound and the Elemental.

NEUTRAL–A person without True magic or Illusion.

THE DARK–Harbinger of Oblivion.

THE RIVER MAIDEN–A construct and Guardian of the River Lethe. The 1,231st hatchling in the fifty-third year after Gaiea's Ascent.

PAPA BOIS–The Guardian of the Crystal Forest.

NICTUS–Queen of the Matamari.

MAMA GLO–The First. The Anchorite of Gailand.

FARAIN–Luka's mount. A dagen-cat (war cat).

ROLAND–A very good horse.

FLOR–A very good horse.

ACKNOWLEDGEMENTS

CREATION IS OFTEN DONE IN SOLITUDE, BUT IT TAKES A VILLAGE TO publish a book. Thank you to my entire team at Harper Voyager, from graphic design to editing, marketing, and others, and most of all to David Pomerico, who plucked this book from the slush pile and championed it with enthusiasm. Thank you also to my wonderful agent, Cameron McClure, whose support, hard work, and wisdom has been priceless.

My writing community is the reason this book found a publisher. A timely post in a writers' Slack made the difference between keeping this in the trunk and having it out in the world. I cannot name every amazing person who has been part of my journey, but I owe a huge debt of gratitude to the Online Writing Workshop for Science Fiction, Fantasy, and Horror, where part of an early draft of this story was posted, and where I met most of the writing friends I still have today. To my family and in-real-life friends, my online friends in Slacks and Discords, and across Twitter, Mastodon, and Bluesky, thank you all for supporting me, venting with me, and giving me good advice and joy in equal measure.

Thank you to Troy L. Wiggins, Bill Campbell, and Neil Clarke for buying the stories that made me think this one might have an audience too.

Finally, to the Women's Clinic of the St. James Medical Complex, thank you for giving my life its next chapter.

—R.

ABOUT THE AUTHOR

R.S.A. GARCIA is a Nebula and MIFRE Media Award–winning author and Sturgeon, Locus, and Ignyte Award finalist. Her Amazon bestselling science fiction mystery, *Lex Talionis*, received a starred review from *Publishers Weekly* and the Silver Medal for Best Scifi/Fantasy/Horror Ebook from the Independent Publishers Awards. She has published short fiction in *Clarkesworld* magazine, *Escape Pod*, *Strange Horizons*, and others. Her stories have been long-listed for the British Science Fiction Association Awards, translated into several languages, and included in a number of critically acclaimed anthologies. She lives in Trinidad and Tobago with an extended family and too many cats.